My
Inconvenient
Duke

By Loretta Chase

LORETTA CHASE

My Inconvenient Duke

A
DIFFICULT DUKES
NOVEL

AVON

An Imprint of HarperCollinsPublishers

MY INCONVENIENT DUKE. Copyright © 2025 by Loretta Chekani. All rights reserved. Printed in the United States of America. No part of this book may be used or reproduced in any manner whatsoever without written permission except in the case of brief quotations embodied in critical articles and reviews. For information, address HarperCollins Publishers, 195 Broadway, New York, NY 10007.

First Avon Books mass market printing: January 2025
First Avon Books hardcover printing: January 2025

Print Edition ISBN: 978-0-06-309455-0
Digital Edition ISBN: 978-0-06-309452-9

Avon, Avon & logo, and Avon Books & logo are registered trademarks of HarperCollins Publishers in the United States of America and other countries.

HarperCollins is a registered trademark of HarperCollins Publishers in the United States of America and other countries.

FIRST EDITION

24 25 26 27 28 LBC 5 4 3 2 1

In memory of Jeannine Hubbard

Acknowledgments

Thanks to:

My readers, first of all, who not only hand over actual money for my books but also send me their warm, kind, witty messages and interesting questions; who make the writing job even more fun than it usually is; and who make the not-fun parts less ghastly;

May Chen, my editor, whose patience and encouragement go far above and beyond the call of editorial duty;

Nancy Yost, my agent and cheerleader, who has supported me unfailingly through all the highs and lows;

Jessica Fox, my assistant who not only wrangles social media for me, but also provides expert advice regarding horses and horsemanship, and makes everything more fun;

Janea Whitacre, Mistress Milliner and Mantua-maker, the Department of Historic Trades and Skills, Colonial Williamsburg Foundation, Colonial Williamsburg, who continues to answer my tedious questions and has so generously shared her work, wisdom, and insights, to help me dress my ladies properly;

Mark Hutter, Master Tailor, the Department of Historic Trades and Skills, and Neal Hurst, Associate Curator of Costume and

Textiles, both of the Colonial Williamsburg Foundation, Colonial Williamsburg, who also unfailingly and patiently answer my sometimes unintelligible queries, and spark fresh outlooks and ideas, all in the cause of clothing my gentlemen;

Susan Holloway Scott, my dear friend and partner in Nerdy History Girl-ness, with whom I can speak of nerdy writing, fashion, and historical matters as well as countless other topics; as if this didn't suffice, she also supplies me with pictures and information that make my books better;

Author Caroline Linden and Meena Jain, Library Director at the Ashland Public Library, who've made it possible for Romance readers and authors to gather in person once again and thereby provided so many joyous and inspiring experiences in recent years;

The Regency Fiction Writers, who've stimulated and educated me with many an obscure detail of early nineteenth-century life;

Cynthia, Vivian, and Kathy, my sisters—with bonus thanks to Cynthia and Kathy, who are always ready to bolster my spirits, and happy to join me for plot development, beach stays, and shopping;

Walter, prince among spouses, who has endured years of writer's despair and endless brainstorming sessions, yet never falters in his belief and support, and takes me away from it all when necessary.

Kindly give credit for errors and general blockheadedness to me. Everybody else did the best they could.

My Inconvenient Duke

Chapter 1

*R*aucous laughter. Drunken shouting.

"Devil take them." Lady Alice Ancaster opened her eyes and stared up at the tester. "What time is it?"

She sat up in not quite complete darkness. She pulled the edge of the bed curtain to one side. The window curtains remained closed, meaning her maid hadn't yet risen—though the drunken louts would soon rouse Aunt Julia's household.

Dawn had cracked, it seemed, but only just.

It was remarkable how much noise three inebriated men could make. She'd last seen them departing for the fishing house for a night of carousing. They couldn't have stayed there? They must come here, directly under her window?

"I have to kill them," she said.

She flung back the bedclothes and said bad words. She pushed the bed curtains fully open and said worse words. She stumbled getting out of bed, but found her slippers. As her eyes adjusted to the heavy grey light of a damp morning, she discerned her dressing gown neatly laid out at the foot of the bed. She pulled it on and started for the window.

More shouting and laughter. Then the crack of a pistol.

She leapt to the window in time to see her brother fall to the ground. "Hugh!"

She ran from the room.

"Is HE DEAD? He'd better not be dead." Alice tried to pull free of the Duke of Blackwood's grasp. "Let me see."

He wouldn't loosen his hold. She jammed an elbow into his ribs, not gently, and struck her heel against his shin. He made a small noise, barely an "oof," but his grip eased enough so that she could pull free.

She fell to her knees beside her brother. Black powder streaked Ripley's face. Blood, too. He seemed so still.

She put her hand on his chest. Through layers of coat, waistcoat, linen, she felt warmth and the unmistakable rise and fall. Breathing. Still alive.

She swallowed panic and made her voice clear and sharp. "Don't stand there like the worthless pieces of lumber you are. Send for a doctor. *Now*. Call for a litter. Make haste! He can't be let to lie here."

"Stunned, y'know, thash all," the Duke of Ashmont said. "Pistol. Went off in Ripley's face, dinnit?" He turned his bleary blue gaze to Blackwood.

Blackwood blinked, one dark eye opening more slowly than the other. He nodded. "Went off in his face."

"Get help!" she said.

Ashmont dragged a hand through his blond curls. He shook his head, as though he had a hope of clearing it that way. Then he started away, stumbled, and fell over. And lay there.

"Juno, give me strength," she said.

She became aware of the Duke of Blackwood crouching beside her. "Not . . . dead," he said. He swayed, and she put out a hand to push him away. That was all she needed, one of these great oafs falling on her.

"He might have been killed," she said. "What is wrong with you? Drunk, shooting off pistols, so close to the house—and this house, of all places. Do you three think of anybody else, ever? And *you*—the one I believed had a functioning brain. *You* let this happen."

She bent over her brother. "Oh, Hugh."

She brushed his black hair from his face. His eyes opened. Green like hers. Also bloodshot, unlike hers. She took one of his hands. The glove was burnt in places.

"I reckon it mish-mif-misfired," Blackwood said.

A corner of Hugh's mouth turned up. "You . . . reckon?" He laughed, then winced, then started coughing.

Blackwood pulled her back and dragged her to her feet, an instant before the Duke of Ripley rolled over and cast up his accounts.

"He's all right," Blackwood said. "Stunned, thash all."

"He's burnt!"

"Yes. Go back to bed now. Cold out here. Damp. You'll catch your death." He waved a hand up and down, indicating her attire. "Not enough clothes."

He was swaying, blinking, his words slurring together.

She grasped his lapels and shook him, an impossible feat had he been sober. This was because the Duke of Blackwood, like his two friends, was over six feet tall and solid muscle (including his head) and could not be moved when he chose not to be moved.

"*Wake up*," she said. "Get my brother out of the wet and into the house. I don't care how you do it, but you'd better not upset Aunt Julia."

Their selfishness passed all bounds. To behave so, at a house to which death had brought such acute grief. If Ripley had been killed . . .

An image flashed into her mind of a smirking face and a short, unpleasant conversation.

But her brother wasn't dead. Yet.

She nodded toward Ashmont, who remained on the ground, smiling up at the cloud-thickened sky. "And while you're at it, drag Luscious Lucius over there to a trough or pump and get him back in his senses—to the extent that is possible. Do you understand?"

Blackwood's gaze slid from her face down to her hands, still clutching his lapels. "Best let go, then, don't you think?"

She jerked her hands free, and he staggered back a pace.

"I hate you," she said. "I shall never forgive you."

She wanted to cry. She wanted desperately to cry. She was so tired of this. And it was never going to get better. She knew that. She'd known it for a good while.

They were hopeless.

Their Dis-Graces. That was what the world called the three dukes, and the world wasn't wrong.

But she would not cry in front of them.

Ripley was alive—for now—and there was nothing she could do for or about him.

Time to face facts. These were the men they'd become. They were not going to turn into better men. They'd only grow worse, and it was mad to hope otherwise.

She would have to make a plan.

GILES BOUVERIE LYON, eighth Duke of Blackwood, Marquess of Rossmore, Earl of Redwick, etc., etc., became suddenly and unhappily sober.

He watched Alice march away, dressing gown floating about her in the morning mist, and revealing a great deal more of her tall, shapely body than her usual attire did. No stiff petticoats concealed her hips. No gigantic sleeves turned her arms into balloons. Her nightcap had fallen askew, her braid was loosening, and long, waving locks of black hair trailed over her shoulders.

The stuff that dreams are made on.

A dream, no more. He'd made his choice years ago, an easy choice at seventeen.

His friends or the girl.

He'd made the choice here, at Camberley Place, during the annual late summer gathering of cousins and friends. He, Ripley, and Ashmont had gone down to the fishing house, as they usually did, but Ripley was watching him in an odd way. Then, when Ashmont settled down to serious fishing, Ripley drew Blackwood aside.

"Don't look at Alice that way," he said.

And Blackwood, heart pounding with guilt, instantly took offense: "What way?"

"You know what I mean. You're getting ideas and you'll give her ideas, and it won't do."

Too late, he could have told his friend. He'd got the ideas. He understood the warning all too well, though. Alice was fifteen. She was a gently bred maiden, a lady. He, Ashmont, and Ripley were wild and rebellious and ill-behaved. They broke any number of rules. But innocent girls were sacrosanct. Also dangerous and complicated and far too much trouble for too little fun.

Best to pretend they didn't exist.

"If you want Alice, you've got to take the respectable road," Ripley said. "My sister deserves Sir Bloody Galahad. And that's not us. Not me, not you, not Ashmont, by a long stretch. If you're with us, you can't be with her. I won't have her trifled with. I won't have her hurt. She bore enough of that with my father."

"I would never hurt Alice."

"Then make up your mind. Us or her."

Not the hardest choice at seventeen: a life of excitement—adventures, pranks, fights, parties, not-so-innocent girls, and general rule-breaking with the two fellows who'd stick with you through thick and thin—or a life of following rules.

At seventeen he'd had more than enough of following rules.

He'd chosen the friends.

Easy enough at first. Easy enough when he and she were miles and miles apart. But when Alice was nearby, inches away . . .

He'd lost his head once and hurt her. He'd stuffed the memory into a deep mental cavern, but it escaped from time and time to haunt him.

It was all too easy for a man like Blackwood to hurt her, to cause damage unthinkingly. Had Ripley been killed this morning . . .

But he hadn't, and the best way for Blackwood to atone was to clean up the mess he and his friends had created.

He made himself look away from Alice's retreating figure and attend to the business at hand.

He gazed down at Ashmont, who still lay on the ground, smiling up at the dark clouds massing overhead.

"This always happens when you're about," Blackwood said. "Can't take you anywhere."

The pistol. Ashmont's idea. An ancient pistol they'd found . . . where? He couldn't remember.

Had they been so lost to reason as to let Ashmont load it? Or had Ripley done that?

Or did I do it?

Blackwood's stomach knotted. He knew, better than anybody, the correct way to clean and load a pistol.

He turned back to Ripley.

Black in the face, with streaks of red, and . . . well, not pretty, in short.

All things considered, not so bad.

Still.

"Done puking?" Blackwood said.

Ripley sat up fully. "Daresay."

"Want a doctor?"

"Hell, no."

One of the servants burst through the door of the south front and ran to them. "Her ladyship said there was an accident."

"Don't fuss," Ripley said. "Send Snow to me."

"Not only Snow," Blackwood said. "All three of our manservants. And have the carriage readied."

"Carriage?" Ripley said. "We got here only the day before yesterday. My aunt—"

"Lady Charles has seen enough of you. You've never been beautiful, but at present you'll frighten small children and dogs. You most certainly will upset her. We'd do well to make our exit, and quickly."

Lord and Lady Charles Ancaster had always made Blackwood feel as welcome as their nephew. Their home had been a refuge from the time he, Ripley, and Ashmont had first become schoolmates and friends.

Lady Charles had lost her husband two years ago. She missed him very much. They all did.

They three had behaved badly. True, they always did, and true, she was used to them and forgave a great deal. All the same, they ought to have confined their games and dares to the fishing house down by the river, well away from the main house. As to shooting the old pistol: unforgivably careless.

He put out a hand. Ripley grabbed it and winced as he hauled himself upright.

"M'sister frightened you, that it?" Ripley said.

"Yes."

"Me, too, sometimes. Not sure how she does it, but mustn't let her catch on. Can't let her forget who's head of the family." He looked over at Ashmont. "What about him?"

"We'll throw him over a horse and take him to one of the inns at Guildford," Blackwood said. "The servants can follow. I want to be gone. Now."

Most of all, he wanted not to be ashamed.

But there were cures for that and for many other maladies.

THE DUKES WISELY vacated the premises. Since out of sight did not equal out of mind, after breakfast Alice walked down to the fishing house. There she knew she'd find the solitude she needed. She brought a book with her.

The small stone building was a square one-room structure. It held a fireplace, an ancient marble table, and three chairs. When the dukes visited, the servants brought down camp beds, linens, and other furnishings as well as food. Not luxurious by any means, but luxury wasn't what one came here for.

The servants had tidied the place promptly after the dukes' departure.

All Alice had to do was rebuild the fire before she settled at the table to read. From time to time she looked up at one of the diamond leaded windows.

> *. . . man, from the remotest antiquity, found it convenient to exert his strength to subjugate his companion, and his invention to show that she ought to have her neck bent under the yoke; because she as well as the brute creation, was created to do his pleasure.*

Mary Wollstonecraft's *A Vindication of the Rights of Woman* was not precisely Alice's bible, but close enough.

"Forty years," she said. "Forty years since you wrote this, Mrs. Wollstonecraft, and nothing has changed."

She set down the book and rose. She walked to the door, opened it, and looked out at the river.

More than two years had passed since her Uncle Charles's funeral. A fog of grief blanketed those days. One incident, though, remained starkly clear.

After the will had been read and everybody else had apparently left the library, Alice had returned to search for the book about the Knights of the Round Table.

A number of fine ancient items lived in the room. There was a chest once belonging to King James I. One of King Charles II's writing desks had been another perquisite of some ancestor's position at Court. The curio cabinets held scores of treasures. But the *Recueil des Romans des Chevaliers de la Table Ronde* was most beautiful and precious to her, on more counts than one. It had captured her imagination shortly before her tenth birthday, after her own knights in shining armor, Uncle Charles and Aunt Julia, had rescued her from the Tollstone Academy for Girls.

This day she found her unpleasant cousin Lord Worbury lurking in the library. He was bent over the book, which lay on the royal writing desk.

He gave her an assessing look, up and down, his light brown eyes mocking.

She responded with a coolly polite smile. She'd humiliated him years ago. He'd got what he deserved, though he'd never see it that way.

"Congratulations," he said. "Ripley gets everything."

Uncle Charles's will hadn't mentioned Worbury because Uncle Charles knew he was a poisonous black mold on the Ancaster escutcheon.

"It was mainly Ripley's to start with," she said. "Camberley Place was our father's and his father's, and so on, as you know."

Uncle Charles had taken it over when she was a child, when her father had begun neglecting his properties. *Economizing*, Papa called it.

"And Ripley's heir will inherit everything," Worbury said. "Not you. Not Lady Charles. None of her daughters."

"How kind of you to be concerned on the ladies' account," she said. "But as you must have heard a short time ago, my uncle left his wife amply provided for. His daughters have married well. Certainly Ripley will make sure that no member of his family wants for anything."

"I daresay he will. Ripley's a generous fellow. And if—heaven forfend—he leaves us, John Ancaster will carry on in the same manner. All will be well."

He smirked and stroked the book cover, and it wanted every iota of her self-control to keep from bashing his head on the desk.

How dare he touch it? How dare he pollute this house with his presence? But he was a vulture, and somebody had died, and he was bound to hope he could pick at the carcass. Nobody had wanted to chase him away, because he was all too likely to make a scene and cause Aunt Julia further distress. They'd treated him to cold courtesy instead. He pretended not to notice, but of course he'd nurse a grudge.

"Quite so," she said. She started to turn away, to put distance between them before her temper got the better of her.

"Let's hope they both live long, then, eh?" he said. "Or sire sons before they go. Because after them, it's . . ." A long pause ensued while he pretended to think. "Oh, dear. The next in line for the dukedom seems to be me." He shook his head. "And then, I suspect, it will not be quite the same."

Alice came back to the present, her gaze still upon the river, sparkling in the capricious sunlight.

"No, nothing will be the same," she said softly.

Only a simpleton would believe the day would never arrive when Worbury inherited, when all this and more would be his. The morning's events had made that as clear and sharp as a slap in the face.

She remained at the fishing house, looking into the future. Eventually rage and anxiety settled to a bearable level. Late that afternoon, she felt composed enough to consult her aunts Julia and Florentia.

The conversation was long and painful.

When she wrote to her best friend, Alice kept matters to essentials.

My dearest Cassandra,

It seems I cannot go on being content with my life as it is. My brother and his two friends show no signs of moderating their behavior. To ask for maturity is asking for the moon. With John Ancaster's recent death, my not-distant-enough cousin Worbury becomes my brother's heir. Since Ripley's behavior promises an untimely demise, I need not explain the consequences for the dukedom and all those dependent upon it. I am only one of many, but one of the few able to do anything about it.

I'll soon be five and twenty, and as the aunts pointed out, my situation is not secure. Unlike you, I haven't seven more or less loving brothers or open-minded grandparents. Ergo, I must undertake the perilous quest of finding a husband. This involves two dragons: Society in general and Men specifically. The ton isn't wrong to disapprove of and fear my brother and his friends. These same people don't know me very well, which means I shall have to establish my Perfectly Unexceptionable Wife credentials. As to the Male of the Species: You know what my father was like. My mother had no inkling when she wed him, and she was helpless to stop him from sending me away to that so-called school. Marriage is a gamble, and one isn't wrong to worry about choosing badly. Still, you and I have taken all the precautions we can. We're not helpless women.

In sum, I cannot rejoin you in Florence, and you are not to think of returning to England for the present. The aunts say it will want six months to a year for the scandal to die down and for your father to "achieve a calmer frame of mind," as Aunt Julia puts it. She, meanwhile, is writing a letter to Ripley, warning him to stay away from London until I have completed my quest.

This is a horrid short letter on so grave and disruptive a subject, I know. However, it is as much as I trust myself to say intelligibly at present. By the time we return to London, I hope to have achieved a calmer frame of mind myself.

I love you dearly and miss you dreadfully,
Your most affectionate,
Alice

THE DUKE OF Ripley was late joining his two friends at Ashmont House. They gathered in Ashmont's capacious dressing room, as they often did before an evening's entertainment.

"Change of plans," he said. "Can't stay in London."

He flung himself into one of the three chairs set before the fire and tossed a letter onto the small table there.

Blackwood took up the letter. He recognized the handwriting. "From Lady Charles."

"I'll save Ashmont the trouble of reading it, rather than risk injuring the delicate workings of his brain," Ripley said. "Aunt Julia says Alice is going on the Marriage Mart, and I'm to keep well away, so as not to cast a shadow over the proceedings and frighten away her lovers."

Blackwood froze, his startled gaze on his friend and his mind going black for an instant, as though Ripley had thrown him against a wall.

He was aware of Ashmont speaking, but the voice seemed to come from a great distance.

"Marriage Mart?" Ashmont said. "Alice? But she never bothered about it before."

"She's bothering about it now," Ripley said.

"That's a facer," Ashmont said. He rubbed a knuckle against his perfect nose. "Alice getting married. Already. What a funny thing. I had an idea she'd marry me one of these days, you know, after I was ready to be reformed and everything."

"Alice is too intelligent to marry you, even if I'd allow it, which I wouldn't."

"To tell the truth, I wouldn't allow it, either, if I were you," Ashmont said. "If I had a sister, I wouldn't let her marry any of us."

Of course not, Blackwood thought. Out of the question. Alice deserved Sir Bloody Galahad, not a drunken troublemaker of a degenerate who let his friends fire defective pistols.

All the same, it was . . . hard to take in.

He found his voice at last. "This is a surprise. She said nothing of such plans. The opposite. She and Lady Kempton planned to return to the Continent."

"Read it for yourself," Ripley said. "The point is, I've promised my aunt I'll be a good boy and go away, as she commands. It was bound to happen sooner or later. Past time Alice thought of marrying. I ought to be glad she doesn't mean to try her luck with foreigners. Titles over there don't mean much, and half these so-called noblemen haven't a pot to piss in."

Blackwood unfolded and smoothed out the letter his friend had wrinkled. He began reading, but the words blurred as his mind retreated to the past.

The first time he'd seen Alice, she was ten years old. He'd watched, heart in mouth, while she climbed out of a second-floor window of Camberley Place and descended via the ivy-encrusted bricks.

Alice was escaping durance vile, her brother had explained.

"She had a bad time of it early in the year," he said. "A grim sort of school my father sent her to. Don't know exactly what happened there, but it didn't agree with her. Now she and my Aunt Julia's niece Cassandra Pomfret are practicing to be warriors or knights or some such. Maybe both. All things considered, it's best to let Alice go her way, because she will, whether we like it or not, and then things get complicated. So the rule is, we keep out of it, unless, you know, there's murder or that sort of thing."

Other memories crowded in. Alice that day, jumping to the ground and throwing a triumphant grin his way as she ran by the two boys. Alice teasing Blackwood when he failed to decipher the girls' secret code. Alice squinting as she aimed a pistol while his hand guided her arm to the correct position. Alice, her head tipped back, looking up at him and laughing, her green eyes sparkling with mischief.

Alice, in his arms, once.

All in the past and the past was done, he told himself. He'd
made his choice, and it was a decade too late to un-choose.

He let the curtain fall, shutting out the scenes.

He refilled his wineglass and read the letter through.

He set it aside. "We'd better start packing," he said.

Chapter 2

FASHIONABLE ARRIVALS

Lady Kempton and Lady Alice Ancaster, on Wednesday afternoon, at Sussex Place, the Regent's Park.

—Foxe's Morning Spectacle
Thursday 5 April 1832

Since the return to London of a high-ranking peer's beautiful and charming sister, floral tributes fill the rooms of a fashionable Regent's Park abode, and a steady parade of callers may be seen on days when the ladies are at home.

—Foxe's Morning Spectacle
Wednesday 11 April 1832

Hatchard's Bookshop, Piccadilly
Wednesday 11 April 1832

She came. She saw. She conquered.

The Duke of Doveridge didn't know he was conquered. Men rarely do, until it's too late.

Others in the vicinity could have enlightened him. One of these was Lord Frederick Beckingham, uncle and erstwhile guardian to the Duke of Ashmont, and very possibly the most perceptive gentleman in London—to a point.

Although Doveridge had appointed to meet him here, His Grace, caught up in a discussion with the senior clerk, failed to notice Lord Frederick's arrival.

Doveridge noticed the one shortly afterward, however.

Still busy with the clerk, he felt the air stir about him. A glance at the entrance showed him two ladies.

He broke off mid-sentence, his grey gaze fixed on Lady Kempton's tall, dark-haired companion.

She was not pretty, any more than a goddess is pretty.

Her features were firmly sculpted: a straight, decided nose, splendid cheekbones and jaw. As to her mouth . . . oh, not a pretty mouth at all, but one that put mad ideas into a man's head, though he was no puppy or green schoolboy, but a hardened bachelor of two and forty years.

It was the mouth, some wise observers said, that reduced a man to a blithering idiot.

It was unfashionably wide, full, and inviting and at present offered a faint, dangerous hint of a smile, the kind that seemed to hold a universe of possibilities.

None of these distinctive features offered a clue to what she was thinking.

I know her, he thought. *I'm sure I know her.*

He ought to. He knew everybody.

He was a duke, a preposterously rich and influential one. He'd been one of the previous King's favorites and continued in that not always enviable position in the present Court.

Forgetting whatever it was he'd come for or had been talking about, he walked away from the clerk and toward the goddess.

He did recognize her chaperon, Lady Kempton, a handsome, middle-aged widow. He greeted her with his usual grace and charm, but it wanted all his sense of dignity not to let his gaze fix on the young lady with her. He was aware of his heart beat-

ing in an immoderate manner while he tried frantically to remember something, anything to do with this stunning creature.
Had he not read something, very recently? No use. His mind
refused to function properly.

"Ah, Duke, we had not looked to see you back in London
quite yet," said Lady Kempton. "But you are fully well, fully
recovered, I see."

He was too old a hand to flush at the reminder of his recent
infirmity: a bout with sciatica that had nearly crippled him,
and common enough in men and women of any age. All the
same, he'd prefer not to be reminded when a shockingly attractive young woman was present. Perhaps he winced a little on
the inside.

"A mild indisposition, no more," he said. "Along with a dis-
position to breathe cleaner air and get away from the noise of
politics for a time."

Then *she* spoke. "I know that look," she said. "Duke, you are
trying to put a name to my face."

Lady Kempton threw her a reproving glance, which she ignored.

"I am asking myself how I could forget," he said.

"Easily. We were introduced during my first Season. You were
so gallant as to dance with me. Pray don't trouble your mind
trying to remember. I've been abroad a great deal, and I was not
memorable that evening. It was my brother and his friends who
attracted all the attention."

"I fail to see how you could fail to attract attention," he said,
"if an elephant irrupted into the room, chased by six lionesses."

"It wasn't an elephant but a goat," she said. "Almack's. The
creature was introduced to the company. You will remember
her, a peaceable being who took no notice of the fuss. She was
last seen being led out, the calm eye in the midst of the storm. A
silk rose from a lady's dress dangled from her mouth."

The scene appeared in his mind instantly: the women shriek-
ing, running about, feathers flying, turbans toppling. Three

young men under the orchestra stand, laughing themselves sick. He had laughed, too.

He laughed now, and heads turned their way. "Good heavens, how could one forget?"

"That was my brother's doing," she said. "Ripley and his friends. I'm the wretch's sister—and now, I see, the light dawns."

He was enchanted. "Lady Alice. Of course."

She bowed her head a very little, and the artistic furbelows of her hat danced with the movement. She was dressed in exquisite taste, in a redingote of deep onyx. His own taste being exquisite, he did not fail to notice details indicating the forefront of Parisian fashion.

He didn't remember the young lady he'd danced with. He was one of London's best dancers, and the patronesses could always count on him to lead out his share of debutantes. Whatever Lady Alice had been like on that night some half-dozen years ago, she was altogether different now. This sophisticated young woman would be impossible to forget, goats or no goats—or elephants, for that matter.

"We've come for the latest sensation," Lady Alice said. "Mrs. Trollope's book about the Americans. We're behindhand, it seems, having been abroad for so long."

"Not so far behindhand as the Americans, according to the author," the duke said. "Be warned. The book is not for the squeamish."

Lady Alice's green eyes sparkled with mischief. She smiled, clearly amused, and the smile made him dizzy.

At that point, Lord Frederick Beckingham joined them, and the duke, aware that he was in danger of making a fool of himself, gently took his leave. He left the shop, with no recollection of his appointment. He had other things on his mind.

He did not see Lord Frederick's faint smile as he watched him go.

One of Society's most admired young ladies has caught the eye of London's most dedicated bachelor. Where so many other fair have failed to win the gentleman's hand, will this exotic succeed?

—*Foxe's Morning Spectacle*
Monday 23 April 1832

Newmarket
Wednesday 25 April 1832

THE LONDON NEWSPAPERS of days earlier lay scattered about the coffee room of the Rutland Arms. Few gentlemen had given them more than a glance. Rumor, opinion, counter-opinion, and the occasional fact regarding the Reform Bill filled most of the columns. Hardly soul-stirring. And the columns titled "Sporting Intelligence" could offer only old news to those on the spot at the Newmarket Craven race meeting.

It had rained yesterday. It rained harder today. Nonetheless, the Dukes of Ashmont and Ripley had gone out to the racecourse, and were very possibly draped over railings or lying on their faces in the mud at present, having enjoyed an eventful evening.

Though he had no plans to lie on his face in the mud, the Duke of Blackwood intended to join them at some point. He'd laid out a sum on the Oatlands Stakes. Afterward, win or lose, one could look forward to festive dinners. Depending on the host, one might encounter attractive women of less-than-strict morals. Most certainly one could expect gambling. Probably fights. No, since Ashmont was about, fights were not *probably* but *definitely*.

At the moment, however, Blackwood was studying *Foxe's Morning Spectacle*, seeking confirmation of news he'd heard this day.

A crease formed between his black eyebrows.

He frowned and tore out the offending page. He stared at it

for a moment, then crumpled it. Not his affair what Alice did or with whom. He'd made his choice.

He was about to hurl it into the fire when Ripley flung his great carcass into the room. "Where the devil'd he go?" he said.

Blackwood stuffed the scrap of newsprint into his coat pocket. His valet would go into spasms, but what were pockets for, if not to put things in?

"Ashmont, you mean?" Blackwood said.

"Who else? He was there. Then he was gone." Ripley threw up his hands. "Went off with a girl, I'll wager anything—the one I had my eye on, most likely—but he might have dropped a hint. I looked about, you know, and up and down, because you can't tell with him. Up on a roof. Down in a ditch."

"Half drowned in a horse trough," Blackwood said. "Hanging off the back of a haycart."

"Almost got himself trampled yesterday."

"Yes. I was there."

"After this and the First Spring Meeting, we'll go on to Castle Ancaster," Ripley said. "Give him a rest cure."

Ripley's ancestral pile occupied a sizable expanse of Yorkshire's West Riding. He'd spent thousands restoring this and his other properties.

It was a beautiful place. Quiet. Even with Ashmont there.

London was not quiet.

A fierce inner struggle ensued. It was none of Blackwood's affair what she did. He wasn't Sir Bloody Galahad.

His mouth opened, and the wrong words came out: "You'll have to go on without me. Tell Ashmont I've business in London that won't wait."

Ripley gave him a long, hard look. He'd healed well enough from the pistol explosion. Since his had never been the prettiest countenance, being rough-hewn rather than classically beautiful like Ashmont's, or otherworldly like Alice's, the small burn scars were hardly noticeable.

You let this happen . . . I hate you. I shall never forgive you.

Alice's choked voice.

The tender way she'd brushed Ripley's hair from his damaged face.

Watching her walk away into the mist.

"Business," Ripley said. "In London. Must be deuced important."

Blackwood took out the torn piece of paper and gave it to Ripley, saying, "You promised your aunt you'd keep away."

"Mustn't frighten off Alice's lovers. What do you reckon? They'll forget I exist? Out of sight, out of mind? But Aunt knows best." He glanced over the scrap. His green gaze grew puzzled.

"I must agree with your aunt. The husband-hunting will go more smoothly if you're not looming over the proceedings."

"Wasn't intending to loom. What the devil do I want with their mealymouthed Good Society? Hour after hour of propriety until a fellow wants to stick a fork in his eye."

Blackwood didn't want it, either. He'd had too many years of freedom to relish the idea of reentering the suffocating world Alice had entered.

"Wasn't intending to interfere," Ripley went on. "Her beau—whoever he turns out to be—will have to come to me in any event for all the legal matters. If I don't like him, I'll pitch him out. Simple enough. But these women fuss over every little thing, and one must do as Aunt Julia says."

"There's a bit of a problem. Rumors I heard today." Blackwood waved a hand over the heaps of newspapers. "Nothing there. But it turns out your cousin Worbury's in London, after all. He slunk back quietly. No mention of him under Fashionable Arrivals."

Ripley stared at him. "Back, is he, by gad? Everybody said he was in Calais or Calcutta or some such, hiding from his creditors."

Pryce Ancaster, Ripley's great-great-uncle Edward's son and the first Viscount Worbury, had been a military hero who'd fully earned his title. Pendric Ancaster had inherited the title but none of his late father's stellar qualities.

"It seems he had a run of luck at cards," Blackwood said. "So he claims."

"A run of luck at fraud, more likely. Or he did away with his French landlady for her life savings."

"However he contrived it, he's in London."

"I don't like it," Ripley said. "You remember the time at Camberley Place, when Cassandra Pomfret and Alice gave him a drubbing and left him sobbing in the river."

"Because he tried to drown a kitten."

"Two little girls. Twelve years old to his sixteen."

"I remember."

"They march off, bruised, filthy, and wet, leaving us with the problem of what to do with him."

He and Ripley had been fourteen, their fathers still alive. In those days, Blackwood held the courtesy title Marquess of Rossmore. Ripley was Earl of Kilham.

Blackwood saw the scene, as clearly as if it played on a stage before him.

Worbury cries for help as he struggles to get out of the river.
Rossmore and Kilham look at each other.

Kilham: Not likely to drown. Water here's shallow.

Rossmore: The stones, though. Slippery. Weeds, too. The swine could get tangled and fall and break his skull.

Kilham: The world will be a better place, then.

Rossmore: I agree. On the other hand, there's bound to be unpleasantness, and I should like not to have my visit cut short.

Kilham: You think this fits the Murder or That Sort of Thing category?

Rossmore: Very possibly.

Sighs and swearing ensue. They climb down the riverbank to assist the battered bully to solid ground. They offer Wormy, as he was known at Eton and elsewhere, a few parting words of wisdom.

Kilham: My advice to you, cousin, is to hold your tongue about this little contretemps. On account you might not come out so well in the telling.

Rossmore: And on account you might have a painful accident if you blab.

Kilham: One more piece of advice. Don't annoy Alice. That sort of thing never ends well.

A silence ensued while the two men reflected upon Alice.

Then Blackwood said, "Your aunt said Alice's situation was delicate."

"Because of me. Us. Yes, yes, I know. My sister needs to prove she's respectable. She doesn't need her public menace of a brother about, striking terror in her beaux' hearts."

"Do you imagine Worbury won't try to undermine her? You know he never forgives or forgets. You know he's a liar and a sneak."

"A swine. Yes, I know." Ripley scowled. "This isn't good news. But we're not good for her, either. We're supposed to play least in sight."

Out of sight, out of mind. That was best. On the other hand . . .

"I realize this is Alice we're talking about," Blackwood said. "She isn't the typical wide-eyed innocent. She wasn't that during her first Season."

"Alice can take care of herself. Alice *wants* to take care of herself."

"The trouble is, she's lived abroad. She doesn't know London as we do. She doesn't know the men as we do. Somebody ought to be on the spot. Somebody needs to keep an eye on the men, not only Worbury but the fortune hunters and other bad characters. Discreetly, of course."

Ripley was taking it in, thinking. "And it's Alice," he said. "Which means somebody needs to be on watch for Murder or That Sort of Thing. If my sister needs to right a wrong, there's no saying what might happen. Didn't she have to leave Barcelona or one of those places because of a fuss with a donkey seller? Hit him with the stick he'd beat the donkey with and set off a to-do." He sighed. "Alice."

"I don't doubt she'll do her best not to make a spectacle of herself or put herself in danger," Blackwood said.

"As long as there isn't Injustice with a capital *I*. Then all bets are off."

"You understand, then. Somebody needs to be there, discreetly. You promised to keep away. Ashmont is—"

"Out of the question. Discretion is a foreign country to him. On Mars."

"That leaves me," Blackwood said.

Chapter 3

Sussex Place
Friday 27th April

My dearest Cassandra,

Please forgive my delay in answering your last. The round of social events is not entirely to blame for leaving me with hardly a moment to think, let alone write. But all goes as smoothly as one could hope. Further acquaintance with the Duke of Doveridge has only made me admire him the more. He is one of the most diligent members of the House of Lords, as I'm sure your father will agree. The duke is well-read, intelligent, witty, but above all, a kind and generous man. He is a staunch supporter of Madame Girard, and with her I find a cause after my own heart.

I daresay your grandmother will know who she is, if you have not heard of her already. The lady is Haitian born, but grew up in Paris, where she wed. Upon M. Girard's death, she inherited an enormous fortune. She moved from Paris not long after her bereavement and settled in London, where she founded the Minerva Society as a vehicle for her philanthropy. Among other worthy schemes, it was her idea to revive the sixth Baron Digby's practice of arranging, twice yearly, the release of some of the most *wretched of the Marshalsea debtors. We did this on Easter Sunday, then treated them to dinner at the nearby George Inn, as he used to do.*

I needn't describe to you prison conditions and the state of the debtors. You know what they are like, and this represents only one aspect of her charitable efforts. Of special interest to me is the Minerva Society's recent decision to begin the work of founding schools for pauper children.

Oh, Cassandra! You know better than anybody how I feel about the subject. I spent only three months at the Tollstone Academy for Girls, and every minute of the experience is branded in my memory. Of course we both understand that it was by no means the worst of places to send unwanted or unruly children. I was unruly, certainly, not the most manageable little girl. But to send a nine-year-old to such a place, ten miles from home and mother—no great distance, but an infinity to a child who sees no hope of ever going home again . . .

Ah, well. You know all about it. Uncle Charles and Aunt Julia rescued me. Now the Minerva Society presents an opportunity to rescue other children in vastly worse circumstances. And what do you think? Doveridge is one of our most generous benefactors. He reminds me of Uncle Charles, and that, as you well know, is high praise indeed.

Still, I cannot put all my eggs in one basket. Doveridge is handsome and charming, and a prize catch, but he has eluded the parson's mousetrap for years. There is also the Earl of Lynforde, a widower nearer to my brother's age. Handsome and charming, but he, too, is in no haste to wed, from all I've heard. Several other gentlemen have paid me attention. This is gratifying for a girl who doesn't quite fit in. All the same I do find the Husband Quest trying. You and I have spent so little time here that we are not used to London Society—nor, may I add, is it used to us. We were never truly part of Parisian or Florentine or

*any other Society, either—and honestly, I had rather be
elsewhere, on less humiliating business. But thanks to my
brother and his friends, I have no choice. Without a husband, I shall not be able to help myself, let alone anybody
else. I made up my mind to do this, and I shall.*

Your most devoted and loving,
Alice

Crockford's Club, London
Early evening of Saturday 28 April 1832

Damned waste is what it is," said one of the gentlemen loung-
ing by the drawing room window. "The raven-black hair. The
evergreen eyes. The goddess-like figure. Lady Alice Ancaster
might have any fellow in England. Crook her little finger and
he's hers. And she picks *him*? Forty if he's a day."

This window, like its counterpart in the dining room, looked
out onto St. James's Street. Lord Consett having failed to glance
that way at the crucial moment, it was now too late.

"Two and forty, to be precise," Lord Worbury said. "In the
Duke of Doveridge the lady acquires a valuable antique as well
as the bright prospect of early widowhood. As I calculate, the
assets include seventy thousand a year at the very least, some
dozen or more immense properties, including extensive portions
of London, a collection of jewels surpassing the royal trinkets in
the Tower, any number of—"

"If I may interrupt," came a low voice from the doorway.

A silence fell. Or crashed, rather.

"My hearing must be faulty," the voice went on. "I had the
oddest notion that the name of a lady of my acquaintance was
being casually bandied about the rooms of a gaming establishment. Perhaps I was mistaken."

All the color drained from Lord Consett's countenance and he
froze, mouth open.

He was not the only one of the room's occupants to grow pale. Several gentlemen, despite having nothing to do with the conversation at issue, surveyed the room for alternate departure routes.

Worbury arranged his own mouth into a bland smile and set his brain to work at great speed. He could not count on his friend. The Earl of Bartham's eldest son did not own mental faculties of the highest quality.

One might say a great deal about the second Viscount Worbury, and undoubtedly will. However, what one could not possibly say was, "He wishes to die young and make a pretty corpse." The Duke of Ripley's heir presumptive did not wish to make a corpse of any kind at any time, unless, that is, he made it of somebody else.

"I spoke in a general sense, Duke," Worbury said. "Merely enumerating the gentleman's advantages. These are by no means contemptible, as all the world acknowledge."

The gentleman in the doorway bent his dark gaze upon the paralyzed-with-fright friend.

"J-joke," Consett said. "M-mean to say, not a j-joke but the f-fellows . . . That is to say, all jealous, you know. Of any f-fellow the lady would smile on. I was—erm—trying to cheer 'em up. Ghastly choice of words, though. Not what I meant at all. Beg your pardon, Duke. Meant no disrespect. Furthest thing from my mind. Only got carried away. For a moment."

"Better hope you aren't carried away permanently, on a litter," somebody murmured from behind a newspaper in another corner of the room.

The recent arrival stepped into the drawing room. "My memory, sadly, is imperfect," he said. "Do you know, it's altogether possible for me to forget a few indiscreet remarks, should the perpetrators pass quickly out of my sight."

Worbury's color rose, and an unfriendly spark flashed in his light brown eyes. But while ruthless in many circumstances, he was, as mentioned, not eager to end his life quite yet.

He turned to his friend. "As it happens, we could do with a breath of fresh air."

Chances of their obtaining that article in London on this damp, fog- and coal smoke–shrouded evening were small. Since present company refrained from mentioning the fact, Worbury contrived to leave the room with his usual swagger, his acolyte following close on his heels.

The Duke of Blackwood settled into his preferred chair.

"Foul little ticks," he muttered.

And, *I've come not a minute too soon*, he thought.

He glanced down at the table at his elbow, where a copy of *Foxe's Morning Spectacle* lay. He took up the newspaper. His gaze settled on one column. His mouth thinned.

"Had it been Ashmont who overheard those remarks," came a quiet voice by his shoulder, "one of those two—or perhaps both—would spend the rest of the night wetting himself, in anticipation of an engagement at dawn with eternity."

That would not be half so satisfying as breaking Worbury into small pieces with one's bare hands. But that would be untidy. Blackwood must not make untidy scenes or set off even a hint of scandal. He needed to be discreet. The goal was to keep off the undesirables, not kill them.

He owed Alice that much.

"Duels are boring," he said.

The slender, dark-complected gentleman who spoke was the same who'd mentioned a litter. He took the chair on the other side of the table. "While humiliating one's enemies—"

"To call those creatures enemies would imply that I take them seriously."

"An annoyance, then. So much more satisfying to mortify these . . . let us call them human gnats."

"They're human, are they?" Blackwood set aside the paper. He had no objections to the Earl of Lynforde. Had he entertained any, his lordship would be fully aware of this fact, and would not be such a fathead as to plant himself next to a dangerous gentleman in a state of irritation.

The degree of irritation was by no means obvious, even to its owner, but Lynforde was a keen observer. Moreover, he had known Blackwood since their earliest school days.

The earl, who'd inherited his striking good looks from his Indian mother, was a tougher article than he appeared, as the Eton bullies had learnt the hard way. Far more important, it was he who'd brought three miserably lonely dukes' sons together. The principals viewed this act as an inestimable kindness. Others, a great many others, held a different opinion.

He took up the paper Blackwood had discarded. "No doubt you saw what led to their unfortunate remarks."

> *It is whispered that a marriage is on the tapis between a peer notable for his splendid weekly entertainments and the sister of a nobleman notorious for his riotous ones . . . The D____ of D____ danced twice with Lady A____ A____, who has become a favorite of the ton this Season.*

"What set their tongues wagging is beside the point," Blackwood said, and that wasn't entirely a lie. "What they said is the issue."

"Your restraint is admirable."

Blackwood's smile was sardonic. "Yes, that's what everybody admires me for. My restraint."

A gentleman does not give way to his passions. One of thousands of rules and regulations crammed into his brain from infancy.

Having only the one son, thanks to a second marriage late in life, the previous duke had poured all his energies into making that one Perfect. The strictures currently reposed in a gigantic tome in Blackwood's mind titled THE CORRECT BEHAVIOR OF A GENTLEMAN. One could break the rules easily enough. Forgetting them was impossible.

After a pause he said, "Why don't you join me for dinner?"

The earl glanced toward the doorway.

"Ashmont and Ripley will not appear," Blackwood said. "I had business in London that I preferred not to postpone."

His companion arched an eyebrow.

Blackwood shrugged. "I wanted a change of scenery, among other things. Your pretty face makes a change. Then there's your brain."

"And I'm a wonderful gossip," Lynforde said.

"That, too. You go everywhere and do everything—as we, owing to an unfortunate series of misunderstandings, do not."

Thanks to these misunderstandings, the ton's invitation lists these days rarely included the Dukes of Ashmont, Blackwood, and Ripley.

Not that they wished to be invited to respectable gatherings.

"In the usual way of things, this is not a problem," Blackwood went on.

"Ah, something unusual, then," Lynforde said. "And you want information. I'm delighted to be of use."

He truly did own an operating brain. A refreshing change.

Meanwhile, some streets away

"'PON MY HONOR, I thought my heart would give out," Consett said, clutching his chest. "When I heard that voice— Ye gods, who'd've guessed he'd turn up like that? For a minute I thought it was the Old Harry himself, took a mind to pop up from Hades to stand big as life in the doorway. One of us is a dead man, I thought. Or both. Only think if the other two had been with him. No, no, can't bear to think of it. He'll remember this, rely upon it. You know what they're like."

"What does it matter what he remembers?" Worbury said. "What do you think the chances are, one of them killing Ripley's heir? Talk of bad ton."

Had John Ancaster not succumbed to a lung inflammation, Worbury would have felt shyer about returning to London. Since then, however, he'd paid off the most dangerous of his creditors. The more respectable ones hesitated to decline the future Duke of Ripley's custom.

"You don't imagine there's a good chance, one of them shooting your ear off?" Consett said. "Or rearranging your face?"

"For what? Blackwood comes looming like the Angel of Death over us, over what? A few harmless remarks. He makes us look like the veriest cowards in front of every fellow in Crockford's drawing room. You know what that means."

"The tale's all over the club in five minutes."

"And in another few hours, all the world hears. Mockery in *Foxe's Morning Spectacle* tomorrow or the next day and satirical prints in every print shop window before the week's out. And we'll have to pretend to be amused."

All because of her, Worbury thought.

But one of these days, Ripley would get himself shot or get his skull broken in a drunken fight. Stabbed in the alley of a brothel. Trampled by a mad bull. Drowned in a lake or a river. He gave himself so many ways to die young.

Then Lady Alice would learn a lesson or two.

The trouble was, one of these days wasn't now. And Blackwood was in London, damn him to hell.

"I should rather feature in a satirical print than get my ear shot off, thank you," Consett was saying. "And what if his aim went wrong for once? Knowing my luck, it would be the day I was on the receiving end. By gad, by gad, what's he doing in London now? They were supposed to be safe away for months, rampaging over the countryside. My mother said so."

"Overbearing, sneering bully." Worbury slammed his stick against a lamppost. The blow's force made his arm vibrate with pain. "Walks into a room and everybody trembles. Nobody dares stand up to him, and he thinks he can do as he pleases. Thinks he can lord it over the world."

"Well, he can, actually."

"We'll see. We'll see. One of these days . . ."

A drunken derelict staggered out from a narrow alley. "Pennyworth o' gin, yer worships. Pennyworth o' gin fer a gennelman what's fallen on evil times."

"I'll show you evil times, you old sot," Worbury said.

He shoved the swill tub, making him stagger backward into the alley. Giving him no time to recover his balance, Worbury swung his stick at the fellow's legs. With a shriek, the drunkard toppled to the ground. While he lay there moaning, Worbury kicked him in the stomach. And in the head. And in the back.

Worbury smiled down at him. "Let that be a lesson to you," he said.

He left his target groaning and writhing on the ground and walked on. After a moment's stunned hesitation, Consett followed.

"I feel better," Worbury said.

Chapter 4

The new entrance into the Green Park, through the splendid archway erected a few years ago, under the direction of Mr. Burton, the architect, opens to the public today. The arch commands a fine view of the garden front of Buckingham Palace, also the fine and extensive plantations behind it.

—*Foxe's Morning Spectacle*
Monday 30 April 1832

Hyde Park Corner

Though the new archway's opening had occurred without ceremony, a crowd had gathered. The viewing platform was narrow, as was the spiral staircase leading up to it. At present the Countess of Bartham and her entourage occupied the platform. Consequently, Lady Alice Ancaster and her small party had decided not to ascend quite yet.

The afternoon was mild, the skies intermittently sunny. Lady Alice did not feel sunny. On the outside, she was a proper lady, garbed in the latest fashion. Her pink-and-grey moiré dress was French, the full sleeves ruffled in a novel mode that had elicited more than one envious stare.

On the inside she was restive. She stood, it seemed to her, among a flock of expensively dressed pigeons, her aunt's friends murmuring and cooing the same inanities she'd heard a thousand times before.

Worse, Cousin Worm and his minion Lord Consett, Lady Bartham's eldest son, had decided to loiter in the vicinity.

Alice moved away and turned her attention to the ever-changing drama of Hyde Park Corner.

Every day in this place, riders, pedestrians, vehicles of all kinds, livestock, stray dogs, and stray children made a great, heaving conglomeration, sometimes narrowly avoiding collision and sometimes not. On dry days a cloud of dust swirled and swelled about the scene. On wet days the masses roiled in a stew of fog and mud.

On this day, which had followed several rainy ones, excrement-infused mud prevailed underfoot, and the crossing sweep's task was no sooner done than it was undone. Vehicles raced through, throwing up mud, and sometimes throwing out passengers. Drivers' shouts and curses, horses' hooves clip-clopping, and wheels rattling on cobblestones made the music of the place.

London. When she went away, she missed it. When she was here . . . well, it depended.

Her gaze drifted back to her immediate surroundings, this time to meet a more piquant sight: a trio of young pickpockets. They were arranging themselves close to Cousin Worm in the approved manner: one for lookout, one to distract, and one to do the job.

One of them she recognized: The lookout was a street child known as Jonesy, among other nicknames and aliases.

She went cold inside. The Worm was the worst possible choice of prey.

She started toward them, to shoo them away, the footman Thomas shadowing her as he was required to do.

But before she could act, the tallest boy dipped his hand into her cousin's coattail pocket. In the instant the lad snatched his handkerchief, Worbury turned away from the young woman he'd been flirting with, saw the boys, tried to grab the nearest, and shouted, "Thieves! Get them! Get them all!"

The thief was already running, his long legs carrying him swiftly past Grosvenor Place. The second boy eluded Worbury and tore across the road toward Hyde Park. Jonesy shot the other way, in Alice's direction. His eyes widened as he recognized her.

She made a small beckoning gesture. He darted behind her.

"My lady," Thomas said.

"Hush," she said.

"That one!" Worbury shouted. "He's one of them!"

She put her hand behind her and motioned the boy to approach. As soon as he was near enough, she grasped his arm. He gasped and sent her an accusing look. No matter. She knew what she was about.

"This boy?" she said. "I think not. I saw it, and was about to warn you, Lord Worbury, but the pickpocket was too quick for me." The woefully thin little arm in her grip relaxed.

"This little bas— brat ran!" Worbury said.

"When somebody shouts 'Thief!' they run," she said. "It's instinct. This child had nothing to do with the others." She turned to Jonesy. "Or am I mistaken?"

"No, Yer Highness," he said, all blue-eyed angelic innocence. "Vat's how it were, like you said. Never seen 'em before. But I seen what was happening and was about to tell hizzoner to look sharp."

Her cousin apparently had no more trouble than she did in turning the strangulated vowels and misplaced consonants into something like English, because he narrowed his eyes. "That's a barefaced lie."

"Worbury, once more I find myself doubting my hearing. The lady explained the matter. Do you accuse her of abetting a falsehood?"

The voice, one of the last Alice might expect to hear at this moment, came from somewhere above and behind her. A sensation like electrical sparks raced down the back of her neck.

Those who'd drawn near to watch the show retreated several paces. Anyone with a modicum of intelligence would move out of the way. Even the boy, hardened to the London streets, tensed under her hand.

Ah, well, she'd wanted excitement.

To say that Blackwood had spotted Alice was to understate the case.

He saw her first and saw her only, the crowd and the hubbub of Hyde Park Corner fading into a stage background.

He saw her and felt a sharp, almost painful leap within, the way one might feel when the sun finally breaks through the clouds after weeks of cold and bleak days.

He told himself he felt only surprise, and that she was impossible to overlook, even in this busy place. He told himself he was simply reacting to the way she dressed. Thanks to his sisters, nieces, and a discriminating taste in mistresses, he knew more about women's attire than any man deemed necessary. He told himself that what had caught his eye were the refinements signaling the latest Parisian fashion.

Yet in his heart he knew that, for him, Alice would stand out in a crowd if she were dressed as dully as some of the ladies nearby.

Still, had seeing her been all, he would have made a detour. He wasn't here to further their acquaintance, what was left of it. He most certainly wasn't here to rejoin Society. He was in London to make sure nobody caused trouble for her and to be Ripley's eyes and ears.

Seeing her, however, had not been all. Once he regained his perspective, he noticed Trouble standing mere paces away from her, in the shape of Worbury.

And so Blackwood approached, to do what he was here for.

She looked up at him. "There you are," said she, quite as though she'd been expecting him. "Did you happen to see?"

"Yes," he said. "I heard as well."

"I believe the gentleman labors under a misapprehension," she said. Her expression was bored. Her green eyes held a signal he'd learnt to recognize years ago: She wanted him to play along.

He did not want to play along. He wanted to throw Worbury into the road, onto a fresh heap of horseshit in the path of a speeding vehicle.

Blackwood wasn't used to not behaving badly. He most certainly wasn't accustomed to taking orders from anybody, however subtly conveyed.

But he was here to protect Alice and not make untidy scenes. If he wanted to do Worbury damage, he must do it discreetly. No scandal must touch her. He must do nothing to hamper her matrimonial efforts. Ripley was counting on him. And Blackwood owed her this much and more.

Since he couldn't maim or kill Worbury, he must make London disagreeable for him.

"Sadly, Lord Worbury does misapprehend on occasion," he said. "And sometimes he speaks before he's fully thought matters through."

It was a narrow way out, but the Worm would take it. He'd know how much danger he was in. He wouldn't know how long Blackwood's forbearance would hold.

And so, as one would expect, the Worm's murderous expression swiftly reshaped into blandness and something like chagrin—as though he wouldn't have hanged the child himself from a tree in Hyde Park, had he only been able to do it at night, without witnesses.

"The duke has the right of it, Lady Alice," he said. "I do beg your pardon. I never doubted you for an instant and never would. I only doubted the brat had any intention of warning me—if, that is, I comprehended him correctly. I believed him more likely to laugh and call me a gull than to warn me. But one fact is beyond question: The culprit's been and gone with my handkerchief."

"Is that all?" Lady Kempton bustled toward them. "The noise

you made, I should have thought somebody had made off with your pocket watch, chain, rings, and fingers in the bargain."

"It's the principle, Lady Kempton," Worbury said. "Thievery is thievery."

"So it is. However, let us not bear false witness. If my niece says the boy was not involved, that ought to be sufficient. Do let the child go, my dear. We've no reason to detain him."

Alice released the little maggot, whom she ought not to have touched. He was ragged and filthy, and the smell spread about him like a toxic fog. That he crawled with vermin was beyond question.

He made off at speed, dodging Piccadilly's dogs, walkers, horses, and speeding vehicles with the finesse of an expert.

Blackwood watched him go until he'd disappeared into the crowd. As he turned back to the others, he saw Alice still looking after the boy, with an expression like . . . anguish?

It was there and gone in an eyeblink's time. It made him uneasy all the same. She was too softhearted where children and other defenseless beings were involved. Never mind that the boy seemed well able to look after himself.

Worbury's departure, on the other hand, left her unmoved. She watched coolly as he swaggered away. Consett, who'd tried to hide himself in the thinning crowd, hastily followed.

She brought her green gaze back to Blackwood.

"Neatly done," she said. She smiled up at him.

He was not in the least prepared for the smile, and for a moment the world went away.

He'd known her since she was a ten-year-old hoyden. He'd seen her up close, her face mere inches from his, only a month ago. But that morning drifted in a haze that the passing days and riotous living had only thickened.

Before that, when? Two years earlier? Had it been so long as that since Lord Charles Ancaster's funeral? He, Ashmont, and Ripley had drowned their grief in drink that day and in the days following, a process that had turned her into a dim, elusive figure in the clouded landscape of his mind.

And so the reality of Alice, here and now and smiling up at him, struck him very much like a hard punch in the head.

Ripley's hair and eyes, yes, inherited from their late, unlamented father. Ripley was no Adonis. Alice, though . . .

Her mouth was not a rosebud. It was not bee-stung. Hers was the wide, full mouth of an ancient Egyptian statue, and hers was the same enigmatic smile. For a moment, looking down into her extraordinary face, Blackwood forgot where he was. Who he was. What he was.

"Neatly done by all concerned," Lynforde said.

Blackwood had forgotten his friend was there. Caught in a smile, he'd forgotten rather more than he liked. He reminded himself—again—why he was here.

"Even the boy played his part," he said. "Harboring criminals these days, are we, Lady Alice?"

"That one isn't a criminal yet," she said. "A juvenile delinquent, perhaps. I'm sorry I had to let him go. I meant to give him a talking-to."

"Oh, really, Alice," said her aunt. "As though it would do any good."

"He's intelligent," Alice said. "He's . . . an interesting little puzzle."

As Blackwood had guessed, she'd seen a Defenseless Child.

"You can tell one of those wretches from another?" he said. "The smell made my eyes water. All I saw through the blur was an animate pile of filth."

"That's what most of our kind see," she said. "Nuisances. A lot of stray dogs underfoot. And no, I don't speak from sentiment. Most of these children are not angels, and I don't see how they could be. They'll only grow more hardened and hopeless as they grow older. I know this. But now and again . . ."

She looked away and shook her head. The ribbons and flowers and lace adorning her hat fluttered. "Good heavens, I was on the very brink of preaching. How ghastly."

"Speaking of ghastly." Lady Kempton nodded in the direction

of the arch's entrance. "That tiresome woman is coming this way. She must have noticed the furor and raced down the stairs."

"A pity she didn't break her neck," Alice murmured, so low that only Blackwood's sharp hearing detected it. That, or maybe he stood too close.

He moved away and turned toward the entrance. Consett's mother, bearing down on them like the warship she was, abruptly paused. Then, nose aloft, she veered off in the opposite direction at no slow pace.

"That is impressive," Alice said as they watched her ladyship's departure. "I vow, Duke, you're more effective than a pack of snarling bull mastiffs. I've never seen her turn tail before."

"Nor have I," said Lady Kempton. "How fortunate, your arriving at this moment."

"He can be useful sometimes," Lynforde said.

"When one wants to empty a room, for instance," Alice said. "A pity you are not there when one wants you."

"You've wanted me somewhere?" Blackwood said. "Apart from at the devil? This is a thrilling new development."

She turned her gaze away, but not before he caught a flash of something that was not boredom and nothing like the way she'd watched the boy run away.

"I should have welcomed the devil to Lady Drakeley's conversazione last night," she said. "Lord Tunstall droned on, at length and not altogether coherently, on every topic raised. I found myself wondering whether life was worth living."

"Alas, I was not invited, else I'd have hastened to your rescue."

He told himself he'd done his job. Worbury removed. Battleship Bartham in retreat. He'd attracted more attention than was desirable.

Also, Alice hated him, with good reason. As to the smile?

A momentary thing. He'd saved the Defenseless Child. The smile was a pat on the head, no more.

Good dog. You chased away the intruder. Go back to your kennel now.

Blackwood made himself look away from her compelling face. His gaze drifted up to the arch, and his brain malfunctioned and he heard himself say, "Have you visited the top?"

"It was overcrowded," Lady Kempton said.

"That does not seem to be the case now," Alice said. "The crowd has all but vanished. Even our friends have suddenly recollected previous engagements."

He looked about him. Men in uniform, mounted and on foot, came and went. Everybody else had found another place to be.

"I seem to have that effect, yes," he said. "Well, then, it appears that I've done as much as I can for one day."

He'd stayed longer than he needed to, longer than was good for him. He was about to lift his hat for a farewell bow when Alice said, "Why don't you gentlemen join us?"

He paused, hand on hat brim, and blinked.

AUNT FLORENTIA THREW her a look. Alice threw one back. They could argue about it later.

She was not a dolt. She knew Society had marked Blackwood as persona non grata. She knew being seen with him would remind people that her brother was cut from the same cloth.

But it wasn't as though Society forgot those sorts of things. Meanwhile the Countess of Bartham, owner of London's most poisonous tongue, had already observed the encounter. Her version of events, with nasty embellishments, would travel through the beau monde this evening. It would appear in the gossip sections of the papers tomorrow or the next day.

Blackwood had merely been passing by, but nobody would believe that when they could believe whatever lurid tale Lady Bartham fed them.

So the damage was done.

The question was, what was Blackwood doing here? Hadn't Aunt Julia told the three dukes to keep away? Not that he hadn't been useful today. But Alice could have managed without him, although less easily, and it was not convenient to have him about.

She would have to make that clear to him before he caused further damage.

"I daresay the gentlemen have already been," Aunt Florentia said, clearly hoping Blackwood would take a hint, since Alice wouldn't.

"Not yet," Blackwood said.

"We were at Tattersall's," Lynforde said.

The horse auctioneers stood round the corner behind St. George's Hospital.

"Settling-up day," Alice said. "You were at Newmarket with my brother last week. He wrote—scrawled—something about making his way to the ancestral mausoleum. One assumed you'd go with him."

"I had business in London that couldn't be postponed," Blackwood said.

"Bringing your will up to date, perhaps," Alice said. "In case of fatal accidents. I should have realized that only a matter of life or death could tear you away from your friends. How selfish of me to keep you from doing whatever it is. I shouldn't for worlds wish to delay your departure."

There. That was sufficient.

The sooner he did what he had to do, the sooner he'd be gone.

And she'd be glad when he was gone, she told herself.

Her mind, however, chose that moment to revisit Lady Bartham's abrupt exit. Keeping one's nose in the air while fleeing a scene was no easy task, but the countess had performed it admirably.

And all he'd had to do was stand there.

Alice turned away, biting her lip to keep from laughing aloud. She told herself that the Duke of Blackwood was no laughing matter and started toward the entrance.

"This day grows more interesting by the minute," Lynforde said.

"Do you think so?" Blackwood said.

"This is the second time in a few days you've defended the lady and thrown Worbury into a murderous rage."

"He's fortunate to have dealt with me, in a humor of forgiving loving-kindness. It might have been Ashmont, who would not have understood Lady Alice's subtle hint not to kill anybody. Or Ripley, who would have understood but ignored her."

"The lady has also hinted that we're not unwelcome," Lynforde said.

"Speak for yourself. That message was not clear to me."

"You ought to pay closer attention. For my part, I've discovered a craving to take in the view. But if you think the company of two respectable women will bore you witless, we can come at another time."

What Blackwood was not, at the moment, was bored. It would be better if he were. Following Alice was a bad idea. Leaving the scene—*now*—was a good idea.

The trouble was, he'd caught the hint of laughter as she turned away.

The trouble was, he'd fallen into the habit of pursuing bad ideas.

The trouble was, his mind flew to the past, and another scene at Camberley Place, a decade ago.

Alice gazing up at him, her green eyes sparkling.

"But you must teach me to shoot," she said. "Nobody else will. My brother laughs at me. Nobody else understands. Suppose a highwayman appears at the moment Cassandra and I are about to rescue a lady in distress. What am I to do? Throw my reticule at him?"

The right thing to do was refuse.

She was a girl of fifteen. She was a girl.

He could have told her that young ladies didn't travel without an escort. He could have told her that's what servants and outriders were for.

He said, "Meet me at the shooting gallery and don't tell anybody."

Years earlier, his father and Lord Charles had created the practice area for the three dukes-to-be. They had a place cleared on a part of the vast estate well away from the main house, surrounded by woodland. It was arranged according to Blackwood's father's rules for pistol shooting. These, like all of Father's rules, were Perfect. Young men must learn to handle all sorts of weaponry, after all. Duels were lamentable, but on certain occasions, unavoidable. Therefore it was crucial to learn how not to get killed.

The three friends had leave to practice here, under supervision.

Girls did not have leave. Girls did not fight duels. Girls were supposed to be shielded from danger.

But Alice believed that she would be called upon to perform dangerous deeds. And Blackwood thought it would be amusing to teach her, and one day surprise his friends with the new trick he'd taught her.

As though she were a pet.

She got off several reasonably good shots (for a beginner and a girl) at the target without their absence being noticed. It was not, after all, unusual to hear shots from this part of the estate.

The trouble was, he stood too close. He had to, in order to teach her the proper way to clean and load the pistols. The trouble was, he touched her. He had to, in order to guide her arm to the proper position and her hand to grasp the weapon correctly.

While he did all these correct things, he was drinking in the softness of her skin and the sparkle of her eyes . . . and he wouldn't have detected her scent if he hadn't stood too close. Then he wouldn't have got ideas he had no business getting, but he was seventeen years old and those ideas came all too easily.

And so he lost track of time, and somebody must have noticed at some point and decided this was not the usual thing, because they heard dogs barking and men tromping through the nearby woods and shouting.

"Go," he told her. "Run as though you're escaping an enemy army."

"But you—"

"I've simply decided to practice shooting on my own."

She slid him a conspiratorial smile, and made herself vanish.

And later, Ripley had caught Blackwood looking at her the Wrong Way.

"Blackwood?"

Lynforde's voice brought him back to the present.

"Ah, well," Blackwood said.

He started after her. With a soft laugh, Lynforde joined him.

Chapter 5

*I*t was, Blackwood decided, most assuredly a bad idea, because he could watch Alice climb the stairs above him. He ought not to look. He did it anyway. He was a man, after all, and no saint. And so he studied the way her black half boots' snug fit revealed the neat turn of her ankles. And because women's skirts were shorter these days (a small compensation for the rest of their overblown dress), he could discern a few inches of the pink stockings encasing her lower calves. He could imagine the rest.

Some would suppose that a glimpse of practically nothing couldn't possibly excite a man of his age and experience. Some would be wrong. A man's age and experience had nothing to do with anything concerning women. Furthermore, this was Alice.

He made excuses to himself: He needed to know more about the Defenseless Child, because complications could result, such as Murder and That Sort of Thing. He needed to know more about Doveridge and whether Ripley ought to take him seriously as a suitor. If not, if the man was only playing with Alice the way he'd played with so many other women, Blackwood would have to damage him.

Those were weak—nay—laughable reasons. Furthermore,

though Alice had invited Blackwood, she seemed to withdraw the invitation shortly thereafter.

Very well. He'd erred. He was a man, and a woman could disrupt his brain's proper operation, and Alice was better at that than any other woman.

They reached the viewing platform soon enough. There the ladies, clearly no worse for the climb, promptly attached themselves to Lynforde.

That explained the invitation and the apparent withdrawal. Alice had aimed the withdrawal at Blackwood. Lynforde was the one who was wanted. No surprise there. The widowed earl was handsome, charming, and welcome in Society. Aunts and mamas didn't view him as Undesirable.

Not that Blackwood wanted aunts or mamas to look kindly upon him. He'd devoted years to achieving the opposite effect. One day, he might be ready for a respectable girl and marriage, with its suffocating responsibilities and all the CORRECT BEHAVIOR these entailed. One day he might find himself in a suitable state of mind—or weary enough of life—to be a proper husband. That time was not today or, possibly, this decade.

An improper husband was out of the question. If a gentleman decided to do the Right Thing, he followed the Rules.

The matter being settled, he used his solitude to organize his thoughts. He pushed aside ankles and pink stockings and reminded himself why he was in London instead of carousing with his friends.

Worbury.

Murder or That Sort of Thing.

Unacceptable beaux.

The pink stockings hadn't fully dislodged themselves from his mind when Alice abandoned Lynforde and joined him.

Blackwood's heart gave a short, painful leap.

"Quite as described," she said. "I feel as though I'm on top of a cloud, looking down on London."

From where they stood, they could look out upon the royal

gardens, the vast circular reservoir, the lake, and the pavilion. London's smoke hung over the scene, though not thickly today. All in all a fine view.

The one closer at hand was better. He caught a faint scent, one he remembered all too well, of something fresh and green.

Which Alice was not, he reminded himself. She was no green girl. He wasn't sure she'd ever been.

With one brief, unhappy exception, she'd been educated abroad, primarily, safely distant from her parents. She was more sophisticated than other English maidens. He supposed she'd drawn legions of foreign admirers, in between whatever clandestine activities her best friend, Miss Pomfret, devised. Ah, yes. Miss Pomfret. That might explain the Defenseless Child.

"You seem to know more of London than most would suspect," he said. "The foul-smelling little boy."

Her expression softened. "Madame Girard's Minerva Society."

He'd heard of Madame Girard and her extensive philanthropy.

"Minerva, the goddess of trade," he said. "And strategy in war. Among other things."

"Madame's fortune derives from trade. The war she fights is for London's unwanted."

"And you and Miss Pomfret learnt their language, and very likely their ways, from Keeffe."

Miss Pomfret's tiger-cum-bodyguard had grown up in London's rookeries.

"It's been a help to Madame," Alice said. "I can talk to them and understand them, to an extent."

"Luckily for that boy today."

Her brow furrowed. "He had a narrow escape from my unpleasant cousin. If you hadn't turned up, the crowd would have pounced, and I should have had my hands full. Quick as he is, I'm not sure he'd be quick enough. As soon as somebody cries 'Thief!' all the world is ready to catch culprits, guilty or innocent."

"He was not innocent," Blackwood said.

"He did not pick Worbury's pocket."

"He was one of the distractions or lookouts."

"He did not pick Worbury's pocket."

"What does it matter?" Blackwood said. "The brat's vanished, and will lose himself in the stews easily enough. Does Doveridge know about your unsavory associates?"

She threw him a lazy glance, then turned back to the view. "You've been reading gossip."

He studied her profile and thought of Sphinxes. She hid something from him. He could feel it throbbing beneath the cool façade she presented to the world.

"Always, though unnecessary in this case," he said. "You're the talk of the clubs. Even as we speak, gentlemen die of despair, left and right."

"The Duke of Doveridge is fully aware of my involvement with the Minerva Society," she said. "He made a sizable donation only last week."

"And won your heart."

"He's generous. Intelligent. Witty. Kind."

"Oh, he's charming, no question," Blackwood said.

With so many decades of practice, the old flirt ought to be.

"Have you passed along the news to Ripley?" she said.

"Of your impending engagement? There's no great hurry. It may impend for a longer time than you anticipate. Other women have tried to lead Doveridge to the altar."

"Other women aren't me," she said. "Have you quarreled with my brother?"

"Hardly. We don't live in one another's pockets."

"You had me fooled."

"As I said before, I had business in Town."

"Then you'll rejoin them soon."

"Maybe. Or maybe I'll stay on, to follow your progress with your new—well, he's not so new, is he? Your progress with your beau, I meant to say. The question is, Shall I wager on your success or his?"

She lifted her green gaze to meet his, and once again he caught a flicker of emotion in her eyes, a hint of what thrummed beneath the surface.

He might have imagined it—a trick of the light, no more. It vanished as quickly as it had appeared, and all she gave him was the Egyptian statue smile.

"I recommend you wager anything you like on my being wed by the first of August," she said.

An ice sliver formed in the pit of his stomach. "You've set a date already? Does Doveridge know?"

"I set a date a month ago." She walked away.

"Well, Aunt, have you seen enough?" he heard her say. "I have."

Meanwhile, not far away

"BY GAD," LORD Consett said, wiping his brow with his handkerchief. "By gad, I thought—"

"Think later," Lord Worbury said. "For the present, I recommend you waylay your mother before she tells the world what happened at Hyde Park Corner."

Consett gazed at him in consternation. "Waylay Mother? I don't think—"

"Let me do the thinking," Worbury said. "Unless, that is, you want to act as my second in the very near future, and carry the bloodied remains away. If your mother makes an unflattering report about Lady Alice's doings this afternoon, Blackwood will blame us, and we'll pay."

"But we didn't—"

"He won't care whether we did or didn't. We'll pay, I promise you."

Consett all but ran to join his mother. They hadn't far to go, in any event, and as Worbury had supposed, they found Lady Bartham quite ready to share her barouche with her favorite son. Now that Worbury's prospects included a dukedom, she'd acquired an affection for him, too.

The barouche was more or less a coach with the top miss-ing. Since Lady Bartham's footman sat in front with the coach-man, on a seat raised well above the passengers, one needn't be concerned about servants following private conversations. Fear of eavesdropping wasn't what kept Consett tongue-tied. Like a great many other people, he was afraid of his mother. The pros-pect of telling her what to do terrified him.

She didn't intimidate Worbury. Growing impatient, he applied a surreptitious elbow to his friend's ribs, to remind him of his task.

Consett swallowed and said, "I must urge you, Mother, in the strongest terms, to say nothing to anybody of what happened today at the arch."

Her expression darkening, she looked from him to Worbury.

Worbury said, "You noticed, of course, the Duke of Black-wood, and wisely chose not to linger to chat."

"Chat, indeed," she said. "With that debauchee? He pollutes the very air about him. I wonder at Lady Kempton's allowing her niece to speak to him, brother's friend or no. But the girl is indulged to a shameful degree."

"He is by no means delightful company," Worbury said. "The caustic wit. The pranks. You will understand, then, our wish to avoid giving him reason to seek us out. For instance, if you hap-pen to report today's events in a way he construes as reflecting discredit on Lady Alice, he'll remember that Consett and I were on the spot."

Consett chimed in, "Truly, Mother, we—Worbury and I—have had a pair of exceedingly narrow escapes from a meeting at dawn. And this over the smallest things. Over nothing, really. But he—"

"Twice?" she said. "And the fiend back in London only—what? Three days? The man's unspeakable."

"Had to endure insult," Consett said. "No choice. *In front of my friends.*"

"Really, Alfred."

"What would you have me do? Fight him?"

Her eyes widened. "Certainly not. Duels are illegal. You know how your father feels about them."

What she meant was, the Duke of Blackwood was a deadly shot and dear Alfred was not. The duke's fists were not to be underestimated, either, a lesson he'd taught Consett and Worbury years ago at school.

"Would dearly love to keep in one piece, you know, Mother, with all parts in working order. Best if you overlook today's doings at Hyde Park Corner."

"This is not to be borne." The rose-and-cream complexion, so religiously maintained, darkened to brick red. "Those three dukes ought to be stripped of their titles. They belong in a lunatic asylum."

"I beg you will not distress yourself, Lady Bartham," Worbury said. "There are other ways to pay debts of honor. We shall do so, if you would be so good as to say nothing of today's events."

Her gaze moved to the passing scene while she considered. Finally she turned back to them, her countenance once more serene. "I was at the top of the arch," she said. "All I saw was some sort of commotion. Beggar children bothering people. But really, looking down on their heads from so great a distance, I could hardly make out who was there and what transpired."

Minutes later, close by a hackney stand, the two gentlemen disembarked from her ladyship's carriage.

"Now we shall square an account or two," Worbury said.

He summoned a hackney coach and directed the driver to the Temple.

"The Temple?" Consett said as the vehicle set out. "Don't you want a drink? I do."

"Later. At the moment, I want a lawyer."

"Not much else thereabouts, is there?" Consett said. "But whatever for?"

"You heard the brat, laughing at me. Mocking me."

"Well, not exac—"

"Pretending he was going to warn me, the little bastard."

"Yes, but I don't think a lawyer—"

"I'm going to teach that young criminal some manners," Worbury said. "I'll teach him the unwisdom of trying to make a fool of me."

"Yes, but how the devil—"

"I know. First we have to catch him." Worbury patiently outlined his plan.

Sussex Place, the Regent's Park
Early evening of Tuesday 1 May 1832

THREE WOMEN STOOD at a table in Lady Kempton's drawing room, their expressions troubled.

Before them lay a dozen handbills, all the same, headed *Missing Child.*

According to the text, eight-year-old George Foster, who had disappeared some weeks previously, had been seen on Monday afternoon at Hyde Park Corner. A ten-pound reward was offered for information leading to Master Foster's recovery. Those with information were invited to communicate with Mr. Maycock, solicitor, of the Fisk Building, Inner Temple. There followed a detailed description of the missing boy: height, build, coloring, and facial features.

Alice looked up to meet Liliane Girard's gaze. "It's Jonesy, beyond question," Alice said.

"It is most fortunate that you wrote to me yesterday about him and those boys," her friend said.

She had arrived at Lady Kempton's town house as Alice and her aunt were preparing to go out, to the theater.

"I didn't like his new friends," Alice said. "They worried me."

"You were right to worry," Liliane said. "You were right to tell me. Otherwise, I should have failed to perceive the connection. Who would expect him to be at Hyde Park Corner, so far from his usual haunts?"

Frowning, Aunt Florentia looked at Alice. "Maycock. We know this name, do we not? Was there not something in the newspapers recently?"

At the mention of newspapers, Alice remembered.

"A dispute about an annuity," she said. "We recall the name because he acted for Worbury." To Liliane she explained, "He's a cousin, not as distant as we'd prefer. Not a nice man."

"He's the one whose handkerchief was stolen yesterday," Aunt Florentia said. "The fuss he made!"

"He wanted Jonesy taken up for theft," Alice said. She tapped one of the handbills. "Hyde Park Corner. An exact description of the boy. Maycock is Worbury's solicitor. You may be sure this is no coincidence."

"So petty," Aunt Florentia said. "So unlike his father." She shook her head. "I can hardly credit it. To print scores of bills. To have them distributed everywhere."

"Not everywhere," Liliane said. "I found them in Covent Garden, but it seems they have been posted and handed out in neighborhoods where thieves congregate."

"Yet to go to so much trouble and expense!" Aunt Florentia said. "Over a handkerchief! The man seems to have satisfied his creditors, but he's hardly thriving. I wonder how he affords the house in Golden Square, and that a modest establishment compared to his father's."

"He's vindictive enough to go to any trouble, any expense," Alice said. "Not that he'd care what it cost. Peers can't be arrested for debt."

A month or so after Uncle Charles's funeral, Worbury had disappeared from England, and nobody knew where he'd gone. Apparently he was deeply in debt. Since he needn't fear sponging houses and debtors' prisons, he must have feared his creditors, which meant they were the sort who break arms and legs.

Once Worbury got money—however he got it—the dangerous creditors would be the only ones he paid.

"We must get to the bottom of this," Liliane said. "That child was never stolen from any family able to afford a solicitor. I am certain Jonesy has no family. I had better call on Mr. Maycock."

"That will not be a helpful conversation, supposing you can contrive to see him," Alice said. "A woman? Without a man to speak for her? Even you will have trouble getting past his clerk. And if you do manage the feat, you'll be dealing with a person whose ethics must be questionable, given his client."

"Yes, of course. I was not thinking clearly." Liliane gave a huff of exasperation. "What are we to do, then? You know these bills will get results. Ten pounds! A great fortune to ordinary people. And the thieves and such will sell their mothers, aunts, sisters for half this amount. If Jonesy is in a gang, he's a new recruit, expendable. If they believe he's a stolen child, they'll want to be rid of him. They will not want him calling attention to their activities. And we know what will happen once he falls into the hands of the authorities."

He'd be deposited in an overcrowded orphanage or workhouse, then farmed out to one of the so-called schools and asylums outside London.

The conditions in these places were too often unspeakable.

Alice knew, better than she ought to do, what they were like.

Even now she could see and hear it, as clear as if it played on a stage before her.

The Tollstone Academy in Yorkshire. Mrs. Tollstone smiling down at Alice, nine years old. Not a loving smile. Even the child she'd been had realized that.

"We make no distinctions here," the lady said. *"All of our girls are treated the same, and all are expected to obey. If they do not, they are punished."* She stuck the knuckle of her index finger under Alice's chin to make her look up at her, into that cold, smiling face. *"Do you understand, girl?"*

Alice remembered the hand, covered in rings. She remembered Mrs. Tollstone in her fine dress, while the girls all wore the same cheap uniform, too flimsy for Yorkshire winters. Girls fell ill and were punished for it. She had been terrified of falling ill. She'd been terrified and grief-stricken the whole time, but young as she was, she'd known enough to hide her feelings.

Only for three months. Only a lifetime before she was rescued. What had become of those who were not?

Alice shook off the recollection. Dwelling in the past accomplished nothing. She brought her mind back to the present problem.

Liliane didn't know about Alice's time at the Tollstone Academy. She didn't need to. She dealt with children in immeasurably worse circumstances. She'd lived in London long enough to understand both its underworld and the Poor Laws better than most Londoners did.

Not quite so well as Keeffe, though. What would he do in a situation like this?

"I doubt you'll find Maycock at his chambers now, in any event," Alice said. "A solicitor representing noblemen is unlikely to keep late hours. The bills appeared only a few hours ago, you said. We've time. Jonesy is safe for now."

So she hoped. She couldn't search for a street child at night. She wasn't sure where to begin. She wished Cassandra and Keeffe were here.

They were far away, but she had allies, she reminded herself. She had her aunt and Liliane as well as her own wits to rely upon.

"We've promised to attend the theater," Aunt Florentia said. "Lady Felpham will arrive soon to collect us. We cannot change plans at this late hour."

That would be unpardonably rude. Lady Felpham was sweet and kind, and her shy daughter, Emily, needed a friend.

Even if this hadn't been the case, Alice couldn't afford missteps. She needed to be everything her brother was not: responsible, courteous, rule-abiding. She needed to be a paragon, damn him and his two partners in crime.

"Nothing can be done until morning," she told her friend. "But I'll come early. By then, I'll have a plan, I promise."

Chapter 6

*T*he *laundress*? What the devil has the laundress to say to me? What time is it?"

Springate, Blackwood's valet, hovered at his master's bedside.

"Something after eight o'clock, Your Grace."

"In the *morning*?" Blackwood edged up onto his elbows to direct a baleful look at his manservant. "And you wake me for a washerwoman? Have you been drinking?"

The look would have sent other men scurrying for cover. Springate, however, had been in the duke's service for nearly a decade.

"Certainly not, Your Grace. But the woman said the matter couldn't wait, and I was to tell Your Grace . . ." The valet hesitated, his long, narrow face acquiring a pink tinge.

"What? Tell me what?"

"I do beg Your Grace's pardon. She said she hadn't all the day to wait, and to wake you, sharpish, or she'd do it herself."

Blackwood sat up fully. "The *laundress* said that?"

"Not Mrs. Hudgins. One of her minions makes the deliveries. But this person had Your Grace's shirts in her basket." Springate frowned. "Or somebody's shirts. I can't be certain because she wouldn't give them to me until I relayed her message. I suspect a prank, and yet—"

Blackwood held his hand up. "Wait. I need to think."

Like any gentleman careful of his appearance, the duke had his linen sent to the country—to Kensington, specifically—for laundering. Among other drawbacks, garments dried out of doors in London were liable to acquire a patina of soot and less-than-pleasing odors.

Mrs. Hudgins was a superior laundress. Annoyed as he was, he did not like to risk his linen.

"With the most profound apologies, Your Grace, I am uneasy about making the young woman wait. Her tone made me suspect that a brick through a window was a possibility. Not that she expressed this intention outright. Had she done so, I should have summoned the porter to throw her into the street."

"After you'd got my things, I trust."

"Certainly, Your Grace. However, one received the distinct impression—"

"Yes, yes." Blackwood waved off Springate's impressions. "I'd better see what this is about."

If a prank was in progress, somebody was going to be very, very sorry.

His valet nodded. "I shall ready Your Grace's toilette."

"No. If she's in such a bloody great hurry, she may take me as I am."

He threw back the bedclothes, revealing the nothing he slept in.

"Indeed not, Your Grace," Springate said firmly.

TEN MINUTES LATER, clad in shirt, dressing gown, and slippers, his face washed but still shadowed with morning stubble, his hair—despite Springate's objections—uncombed, Blackwood descended to the small ground-floor anteroom where the militant laundress waited.

She turned away from examining a framed sporting print and faced him.

He blinked. Twice.

She didn't. She looked him up and down and said, her voice very low, "A long night, I see."

He became acutely conscious of the fact that he was half-naked, his bare ankles showing below his dressing gown's hem. Warmth stole up his neck.

Embarrassed? He? Not in a decade at least. He was only reacting to being dragged out of bed at a barbaric hour, he told himself.

He opened his mouth to speak, then closed it. He turned away and closed the door.

"This had better be important," he said.

"Would I deprive you of your beauty sleep otherwise?" she said.

The initial shock subsiding, he in turn surveyed her.

If he hadn't known it was Alice, he'd never know it was Alice.

A white bonnet with a ruffled cap underneath concealed her black hair and part of her face. Over her dress's red-dotted green bodice she'd tied a patterned red scarf. Red stripes adorned her yellow skirt, over which she wore a blue apron. A dark red shawl completed this mad mélange.

Washerwomen had muscular arms, but the shawl and big sleeves concealed hers. Into his mind slid images of smooth, naked arms, muscles tensing . . .

And that was not useful thinking.

He shoved the images into the mental cavern and summoned his wits, no small challenge at this hellish hour after a long night of applying the usual remedies. Still, even with a barely functioning brain, he could see that she carried herself in a different way, not at all aristocratic. Pinning down what, exactly, she did to create the impression, however, was beyond him at present.

"Yes, it's a brilliant disguise, but we haven't all day for you to gawk at me," she said. "I wanted you to see this." From the laundry basket on her arm, she withdrew a handbill and gave it to him.

Head spinning, Blackwood read it and looked at her. "And this signifies what?"

"Maycock is Worbury's solicitor," she said. "The boy described is the one I misguidedly waylaid at Hyde Park Corner."

Into the quagmire of his mind came a more or less coherent thought: the Defenseless Child. Of course.

"I agree that you were misguided," he said. "You might have contracted any of a dozen diseases, not to mention fleas and lice."

"It was misguided of me," she said, with obviously strained patience, "because I allowed my cousin to get a close look at him, and against all odds, he took careful note."

"In spite of the smell, do you mean? And in spite of every instinct urging one to avert one's gaze and move as far away as possible?"

"The Worm does not possess your delicate sensibilities," she said.

"On that we agree. All the same—"

"He noted the boy's size and the color of his eyes and hair." She pointed to the handbill. "He noted the two scars over the right eyebrow and the bruise near the left. I daresay he could draw as accurate a portrait as I could, though I've seen and talked to the child many times. This does not bode well. We have to find that boy before Worbury does."

Blackwood stared by turns at the notice, then at her.

Obviously, he was still asleep. Obviously, this was a mad dream.

He stared at the handbill some more. No, this was Alice.

He was not ready.

He wanted to sit down. He wanted coffee. Well-dosed with brandy.

He held up a hand. "Wait."

"We don't have time to wait! Those notices have been posted in all the thieves' dens: Covent Garden, Saffron Hill, Seven Dials, and likely farther on, into Southwark and Limehouse."

"This makes no sense," he said, and there was a prime understatement. "It's a deuced lot of trouble and expense—and not even for the actual thief. Among other things, how did he learn the brat's name?"

She threw up her hands. "For heaven's sake, must I explain everything?"

"Alice, you woke me at the crack of dawn!"

"Dawn cracked hours ago."

"Noon hasn't cracked yet, and that's dawn to me."

She closed her eyes. She took a deep breath and let it out. His gaze—bloodshot, undoubtedly—slid to her bosom, in the ghastly bodice.

That will not help you think, he told himself. *You need to think. This is Alice.*

She opened her eyes and, visibly controlling herself, said, "The name doesn't matter. The sorts of people who inhabit the rookeries have various aliases and nicknames. What matters is the description and the ten pounds. Irresistible temptation, as Worbury well knows. If I truly were a laundry maid, it's as much as I might earn in a year. Giles, we must set out *now*."

Right. Defenseless Child, who could easily lead to Murder or That Sort of Thing if Alice was let to move on into avenging angel mode.

Blackwood wasn't remotely ready.

He'd had more than sufficient drink the previous night, or this morning, or whenever it was. He'd had less than sufficient sleep. He could not think clearly. That was well enough, even preferable, most of the time. At present he felt slow and thick, as though treacle filled his brain. The sensation was not agreeable.

She went on, "You know Worbury doesn't retaliate on those who can fight back. He chooses weaker targets. He's done it since your school days."

"Yes, yes, but this doesn't—"

"He was prepared to blame the child nearest to hand. You and I prevented that. You embarrassed him in a public place. This is his revenge."

What Blackwood did not want to do at this inhuman hour

was chase about London after young criminals who were headed for the gallows in any event. He told himself that Maycock had other clients. He told himself this could be what it seemed to be, parents searching for a missing child. One read every week in the newspapers of children stolen.

The trouble was, as far-fetched as it seemed, this was in character for Worbury.

The trouble was, Blackwood couldn't believe, as much as he wanted to, that it was simple coincidence, the bills appearing so soon after the episode at Hyde Park Corner and referring specifically to that location.

The trouble was, this was Alice, the reason he was in London.

The trouble was—

"Ye gods, how much thinking must you do?" she said.

He'd been staring at the floor while he made his brain perform a labor it was in no way fit for at present. He looked up to meet a flashing green gaze.

"Oh, I do beg your pardon," she said. "I forgot. You're out of practice with thinking. I should have realized you'd be useless. Never mind. I'll find another large, intimidating male to go with me."

He held up a hand. "Alice. Wait."

"I haven't time."

She marched to the door, and quite as though she wasn't a duke's sister but an ordinary washerwoman, she opened it herself and walked out.

He stood for a time, staring at the empty doorway.

The trouble was, his conscience was waking up.

"Goddamn," he said.

ALICE STARTED BACK down the passage to the tradesmen's entrance, wishing she'd thrown something at him.

She was a fool.

Her anxiety about Jonesy had addled her wits.

She was mad, utterly mad to expect Blackwood to care what

happened to a street child. Mad to believe he'd wake up from last night's debauches in order to help her.

Because he'd done one good deed on Monday—and that only out of contempt for Worbury—she'd imagined he'd perform further miracles.

The intelligent, sensitive boy she'd known in childhood, the boy she'd considered a friend and ally, had ceased to exist years ago. The boy she'd hoped—

"Will you wait, dammit."

She paused and turned.

He strode toward her, six-feet-plus of barely clothed male, his dressing gown flapping about his naked ankles and revealing a few inches of muscled, hairy lower leg. Beneath the dressing gown, she knew, only a shirt covered skin: a man's shirt, which ended somewhere above the top of his knees.

She stopped her mind from speculating about undergarments and the lack thereof and hastily brought her gaze to his rumpled black hair and the morning beard shadowing his jaw. He looked like the devil. He always did, perfectly groomed or not. This was why she'd come.

"I don't have time to wait," she said. She started to turn away.

"I've ordered a carriage."

"We don't have time for that. There's a hackney stand—"

He clamped one big hand on her shoulder. "Do you propose I come as I am? Because I will, if you're in such a bloody great hurry, though Springate will poison my coffee if I do."

She was keenly aware of the strength and warmth of his hand, and the awareness stirred memories. Her face heated, and the heat rapidly spread from there in all the wrong directions.

In her mind she swore and stamped her foot. Outwardly, she merely stared at his hand.

He took it away. "Will you think?" he said. "That would be helpful."

"I *am* thinking." She clenched her hands. "I'm thinking it will take you hours to dress. Ripley never completes his toilette in less than an hour. Two, more usually. I'm thinking I was deranged to come here."

"You are deranged, beyond question. You become furious and single-minded and you abandon logical thinking."

"Logical thinking! Have you examined your life lately?"

"This has nothing to do with my life, except that you've interrupted it. Under the circumstances, you might consider accepting a few facts."

"I am not in a humor for lectures."

"I don't care what humor you're in. Fact one, I'm not your brother. Fact two, I've ordered a carriage. Fact three, I must dress. Fact four, you will wait, because that is the intelligent method of procedure and you do own a brain, addled as it is at present."

What choice had she?

Who else could she turn to? Who else could cause hardened criminals to run away merely by standing there and—and *being*. Not Doveridge, certainly, or any other gentleman she knew. Not to mention the extreme impropriety of a young lady calling on any gentleman, no matter how desperate she was.

If only Cassandra were here, with her bodyguard, Keeffe.

But she wasn't. Alice was on her own.

"Yes, very well," she said. "But—"

"But me no buts," he said.

"Go," she said, waving him away. "Put some clothes on. And make haste. We haven't a minute to lose."

"Your gratitude overwhelms me."

He turned and left her in the passage.

BEFORE ALICE COULD kick anything, a footman arrived, who escorted her to a room in the wing containing household offices.

At least Blackwood had the good sense not to let her wait in one of the fine rooms in the main house, as though she were a lady. This was the proper choice, a section of the working area he might have occasion to visit, unlike most of the servants' regions.

Here she paced, aware that every passing minute raised the odds of somebody finding Jonesy and turning him over to Worbury's solicitor.

No choice, common sense told her. Where she needed to go, she couldn't go unaccompanied, even dressed as she was. Men assumed that women traveling on their own were fair game. She'd be prey to harassment at best, violence at worst. And that was only part of the complications.

She'd reminded Liliane of how difficult it would be to deal directly with the solicitor. Duke's sister or not, Alice would meet the same treatment.

And so she waited, fuming, while His Dis-Grace made himself beautiful.

Remarkably, according to the small watch she withdrew from the pocket of her skirt, little more than a quarter hour passed before Blackwood sauntered in and said, "The carriage waits."

Minutes later they sat in his sleek black cabriolet behind a powerful black stallion. The fashionable accessory, a tiny groom named Elphick, stood on his perch at the back.

She let herself imagine driving this vehicle with this fine horse, and going wherever she wished, with a man's complete lack of anxiety about traveling with only his little tiger.

She might as well imagine driving it to the moon.

"Needle in a haystack comes to mind," Blackwood said. "But I'm at your disposal. Where to?"

Needle in a haystack came to her mind as well.

She brushed the thought away.

"The Borough High Street," she said. "He's been working at the George Inn in exchange for food and a place to sleep in the stables."

"And nobody keels over from the smell? The horses don't bolt?"

"He isn't usually so rancid," she said. "He might have been dragged about in the river."

He said something under his breath—an oath, no doubt. He shook his head. "By gad, Alice."

"To make him join the gang," she said. "They knock the children about, or threaten someone they care about. There are scores of ways to force them into gangs or brothels."

"Keeffe," he muttered. "The murderous damned jockey. That's your expensive education, is it?"

"Part of it, yes," she said. "While I was keeping clear of my brother and his expensively educated friends."

"Ah, she bares her talons."

"She is disinclined to endure sermons about propriety from the Duke of Blackwood."

A pause, a low laugh. Then, "Very well. Let us keep strictly to the matter at hand. You wish to go to Southwark. Yet the brat was in Hyde Park Corner, well out of his territory, only the other day. And the bills appeared . . . when? Yesterday?"

"Late in the afternoon." She explained how Madame Girard had discovered them in Covent Garden. "She always takes note of signs for missing children. I'd written to her, saying I was worried about the boy getting into bad company. When she saw the handbill, she was sure something was wrong, and so she came to me last night."

"I should like to know what it is about the little beggar that awakens women's sympathy." He gave his horse leave to start, and they set out eastward.

"He's lost and utterly alone," she said, "yet he wears a cocky front, and somehow survives against enormous odds."

"Oh, Alice."

"Yes, I know what you're thinking. They're all lost. One can't save them all. So many criminals. Are they worth saving? But he's . . . different. He seemed to have potential. We tried to persuade him to attend school, but he balked. Fear, most likely. The children tend to associate the word *school* with ghastly places, and they're not wrong to do so."

"Then he can't read."

"No, he can't, and so no, he won't know what the hand-bills say." She started to wring her hands. She made herself stop. "Anybody might take him to the solicitor on this pretense or that. Still, he's a canny one. After the narrow escape from Worbury, I hope the boy had the good sense to abandon his companions. If so, it's likely he's gone to ground in familiar territory, where he feels safe."

"Hope," Blackwood said. "That's all you have to go on?"

"Yes. Do you have any other suggestions?"

"You know him better than I do. Southwark it is."

He urged the horses on.

Chapter 7

They had only about three miles to travel. Three miles in London, however, was not the same as three miles of a rural stretch of the King's highway.

Blackwood House stood on Piccadilly, two streets from Hatchett's White Horse Cellar, one of London's busiest coaching inns, as the scene outside attested.

Vehicles and riders crammed the road, vying for space. Harassed-looking passengers contended with pedestrians, street sellers, pickpockets, crossing sweeps, chimney sweeps, ticket porters. Dogs ran about, tripping the unwary and fighting with other dogs. Hereabouts even hackney cabmen, notorious for reckless driving, plodded along.

Normally, Blackwood would expect those clogging the road to remove themselves, and usually they had the wit to do so. When friends drove with him, they took their chances. He couldn't take chances with Alice.

Still, some human obstacles either recognized him or took stock of his powerful horse and dashing vehicle and got out of the way. As he passed Burlington House, the congestion eased, and he increased the pace.

His mind was clearing somewhat, though he retained a sense

of unreality, likely due to having been roused so rudely at an impossible hour. Or maybe it was her mad disguise that unbalanced him.

The fact was, nearly every word she spoke unbalanced him. He told himself he'd plunged blindly into numerous escapades, and nothing she devised could possibly match Ashmont, although His Grace with the Angel Face had grown rather predictable of late.

Blackwood made himself concentrate on the matter at hand: the plan, such as it was, though it was by no means the only half-baked scheme he'd ever engaged in. Didn't matter. He'd nearly got her brother killed. He owed her amends.

"The Temple's on the way," he said. "We could stop there first."

"I'm counting on thieves keeping later hours than even you do," she said.

"Good point. They can steal at any time. Why spoil their rest?"

"More important, I'd rather not alert the solicitor to our interest in the boy."

He shot her a glance, and his mind reeled again at the hodgepodge she wore.

"You're remarkably well-informed about the criminal classes," he said. "Well-trained, too, it appears. The disguise, for instance."

"I've learnt to observe," she said. "And I'm a fair mimic. Madame Girard helped me with my ensemble."

"And Keeffe has intriguing stories to tell. He's lived a colorful life."

"He has wisdom," she said. "And I want to be useful. I want a purpose that isn't . . . Oh, I don't know how to explain, and you wouldn't understand if I did."

Her tone made him glance at her again, but the bonnet and ruffled cap hid her expression. Not that her face was ever easy to read.

"Then tell me about this precious boy," he said. "Among other mysteries, I'm curious how you came to pick him out among the denizens of the Borough High Street. Not the most fashionable neighborhood. A long parade of coaching inns of varying degrees of squalor, amid hospitals, madhouses, and prisons."

She told him about the Minerva Society's visits to the Marshalsea Prison at Christmas and Easter and the dinners they provided for the debtors at the George Inn. "On Easter Sunday last, we were able to free more debtors than usual, thanks to Doveridge," she said. "They're left to rot there for the smallest sums. It's disgraceful."

"*Rot*, indeed. You've been spending your time in breeding grounds for typhus, cholera, and every other deadly disease. You can't help from afar but must distribute alms in person?"

"I've found it salutary to see for myself," she said. "The sixth Baron Digby went to the Marshalsea at Christmas and Easter, paid some of the prisoners' debts, then took them to the George Inn for a meal."

"He was a man," Blackwood said. "And those were different times. Some eighty years ago."

"True," she said. "These days we blame the poor for being poor."

Yet Doveridge had helped. Blackwood told himself this was simply to make a good impression on a fascinating young lady.

His conscience twinged all the same. It had a nerve, rising from the dead after all this time. But it would never die properly because the accurst tome, CORRECT BEHAVIOR, wouldn't let it rest in peace. In this case, it called his attention to several chapters on the topic of generosity to the less fortunate.

"But I won't bore you with my radical politics," she said.

"Very wise. A rude visitor interrupted my rest, and I might easily be lulled to sleep. Not advisable when driving in Piccadilly. Stray pedestrians could end up under the wheels, and they leave the deuce of a stain."

She turned slightly in the seat to look at him.

Between the revived conscience and her physical presence, he was not comfortable.

He wished she would keep still. The cabriolet's seat accommodated two people but without room to spare. He needn't look directly at her to be too keenly aware of her: the way she held her head and her hands, the rise and fall of the insane bodice, the maddeningly elusive scent of Alice. The side of his body barely touching hers had heated the instant he sat beside her. He felt her hips moving against his with the motion of the carriage.

He foresaw Satan's own headache, and not only on account of the alcohol he'd consumed the previous night.

"How I've missed our conversations," she was saying. "No, on second thought, I haven't."

"The feeling is mutual," he said. "Can we get to the part about the brat, whatever his name is?"

"He's had a few different ones in the time I've known him," she said.

"Aliases."

"I doubt he knows his name. I strongly doubt he was ever baptized. But let's call him Georgie, since that's the one we'll need to use today."

He caught the evasive note and wondered why. Then he wondered, Why not? Why should she trust him? She'd said she'd never forgive him, and if he were Alice, he wouldn't forgive him, especially for that morning at Camberley Place. She wouldn't have come to him if she'd seen any alternative. Had Ripley been about, she'd have gone to him.

"Georgie, then," he said.

"We helped him find work at the George. He wanted to look after horses, and he seems to have a gift. He wouldn't have been with those thieves if he hadn't been coerced. I'm sure of that. He's . . . different." She let out a sigh. "I should not let myself become attached to one child. I know what the odds are against them. But I think of Keeffe."

Tom Keeffe had somehow clawed his way out of the rookeries

and onto the turf, becoming one of England's finest jockeys, until a racing accident nearly killed him.

But Keeffe was the rarest of rare exceptions. Blackwood hoped Alice wasn't building dream castles for the sewer rat.

He recalled what she'd said about the boy earlier.

He's lost.

He remembered the nearly undetectable break in her voice when she spoke of the child's ignorance and how easily he might be led into danger.

He remembered the way she'd leant over her brother, the tender way she'd brushed his hair from his powder-blackened face.

He remembered the kitten she'd rescued all those years ago.

If they failed today . . .

They'd better not, because she'd murder Worbury. That could be awkward.

Among other things, it could spoil her marriage plans.

With Doveridge.

Blackwood shoved her antiquated beau into the mental cavern and turned the vehicle into Haymarket.

"Can't you go any faster?" she said.

"I can't risk breaking your neck," he said.

"Risk it," she said.

George Inn, Southwark

"Oh, he were here, missus," the stableman McClary said. "Some woman come and took him away."

"When?"

He shrugged. "Some while ago. Can't say, ezackly."

On the inside Alice screamed.

On the outside she was splendidly calm. "This woman: What did she look like?"

He took off his hat and scratched his head. "Well, we been

busy all morning, coaches coming and going, and it happened quick, you know."

And the woman was not the sort to hold his attention, apparently.

Alice glanced at Blackwood, who loitered by the stable door. She'd once watched him lift another boy straight up off the ground and hold him there, his feet dangling, while he quietly and calmly suggested the boy apologize to the youngster he'd bullied.

Alice was strongly tempted to summon Blackwood to lift this fellow off the ground and shake him until he remembered what she needed him to remember.

She summoned her patience instead. "Fair or dark?" she said.

"Couldn't say," McClary said. "Mebbe somethin' smaller 'n you and stoutish. She weren't no fine lady, but not shabby, neither." He considered. "Might've seen her before. Couldn't say for certain. Still, the lad, he went easy enough, like he knowed her. I reckoned she were one of them women come at Eastertime."

"Had she a servant with her?"

He shook his head. "None I could see. But like I said, we had our hands full then."

The Minerva Society's wealthy tradeswomen, like their aristocratic sisters, did not travel about London unaccompanied, and none of them would visit the Marshalsea alone. They went as a group.

Alice asked a few more questions, which elicited nothing useful. She gave the stableman a coin and returned to Blackwood.

She started to report the conversation as they walked out into the stable yard.

"I heard," he said.

Yes, of course. His hearing was sharper than most. The day at Camberley Place when he'd taught her to shoot a pistol, he'd heard the shouting and dogs before she did. Ripley always said that Blackwood had a dog's hearing.

"I can't believe we're too late," she said. "She wasted not a minute."

"Had I come naked and unwashed, as you wished, we should have arrived sooner," he said. "But Springate would not allow it. He's strict about these matters, I'm afraid."

Her face and other parts warmed, which they had no business doing. This was not the time or place or man, and she was not a naïve girl who blushed at the first hint of masculine attention. Yet her mind flitted back in time to a moment when she'd had every iota of his attention.

She snatched her mind back and reminded herself who Lady Alice Ancaster was. The bonnet shadowed her face, the stable area was dim, and like so many other ladies, she was adept at schooling her expression. If her face betrayed her in spite of this, it mattered not at all. It was nothing to her what he saw or believed he saw. She had more pressing concerns.

"Your valet's reputation depends on turning you out properly," she said. "It must have upset him very much not to complete the job." She drew her finger along her jaw, referring to the dark overnight growth adorning his.

Blackwood ran a gloved hand over his cheek. "I didn't want to keep you waiting. No telling what you'd do."

She could feel that long, capable hand again, on her shoulder.

It was a ghost of a feeling, and not remotely helpful at present. She needed her wits about her. She did not need to be reminded of her youthful errors and disappointments.

"You appear even more intimidating than usual," she said. "To say you look like the devil is no exaggeration. Unshaven. Bloodshot eyes. A general appearance of resentment at being roused against your will. Yes, that ought to help—if we can get to the solicitor in time."

"At least we know where to go next," he said. "We'll get the brat, never fear, one way or another."

She gazed up at him, into the hooded eyes, as dark as midnight and as unfathomable as the night sky—not that she needed to read his thoughts.

He was a man and a duke, used to getting what he wanted.

That alone was sufficient. He was one of Their Dis-Graces. That was even better.

"Then I recommend you risk my neck again," she said.

Inner Temple
A short time later

THE CARRIAGE HAD scarcely stopped in Fleet Street when Alice leapt from it and darted through the Inner Temple gateway, leaving Blackwood to follow.

This was not precisely the plan they'd agreed upon, but she was too anxious to wait while he gave his tiger charge of the vehicle.

Still, the duke wasn't far behind her. She was tall, but his legs were longer, and he caught up with her halfway along Inner Temple Lane.

"You agreed to let me go first," he said. "I'm the diversion, remember?"

"Yes, yes. But what if we're too late?"

"Worbury will not be there at this ridiculous hour," he said. "He'll leave it to Maycock to detect obvious imposters, and the lawyer will leave it to his clerks. Odds are he's in court or dawdling over his breakfast, like a civilized person. Everybody else has to wait, because nothing of any importance can be done without his approval."

There it was, the logic and precision and strict rules for doing this or that and the contradiction that was Blackwood: faultless manners and reckless behavior, sharp mind and childish pranks.

Yet she knew she could count on him in a crisis . . . once she woke him up—violently, if need be. She knew he'd stand by her the way he stood by his two friends, and the knowing eased her agitation somewhat on the way.

It was short enough. A minute's walk took them to the area southeast of the Temple Church where the Fisk Building stood.

In the court, about two dozen people waited on or near the entrance steps. The gathering comprised adults and a handful of older youths, all towing boys—and a few girls—of wildly varying ages and degrees of cleanliness.

Blackwood left her and moved to one side, a short distance from the group, drawing their notice. Easy enough for him to do.

He was big, dark, and dangerous-looking even when clean-shaven and rested. Furthermore, he was a duke, accustomed to commanding the world about him.

Alice, meanwhile, concentrated on appearing ordinary. This was easier with him in the vicinity. Still, she had to maintain her role. She had to make herself fade several degrees, and look and think and speak as a respectable working woman would do.

While he claimed onlookers' attention, she moved purposefully among them, searching for her target. The crowd, whether by instinct or distracted by Blackwood, didn't try to hinder her. She kept herself intently focused in the way a mother would do, trying to find her missing child.

At first she saw only a sea of faces, some clean and some dirty, and an array of clothing in various styles and conditions. She scanned them once, twice, thrice. No Jonesy in sight.

"How many have gone upstairs ahead of you?" she asked one of those close to the door, an older girl who had a very small boy in hand.

"Nobody," she said. "They said they wasn't ready, and tole us to wait outside, and somebody would come."

Good news and not surprising. Maycock and his minions wouldn't want the lower species of humanity stinking up the stairs and infesting his chambers. Out of doors, the smell of poverty abated somewhat.

Very well. Jonesy and his keeper either hadn't yet arrived or stood somewhere in this crowd.

She recalled McClary's vague report: a stoutish woman, somewhat smaller than Alice. Otherwise nondescript.

Only one woman here seemed to fit. She stood in the building's shadows near the entrance steps. Alice would not have described her as stout. She wasn't large or plump, but she looked strong, with no softness about her.

As Alice's gaze settled on her, the woman casually drew a boy behind her. Or tried to. He was not cooperating, and his attendant became less casual and a degree more forceful.

"Georgie?" Alice called. "Is that my son, my dear Georgie?"

No response. She debated what to try next.

Then, "Ma!" came a familiar voice. A neatly capped head angled out from behind the woman's skirts.

"Hush!" the woman said.

"Ma! Ow!"

"Stow it, you little bas— you naughty boy!" But he managed to pull away enough so that Alice had a better view. Her heart sank. Not Jonesy.

But yes, the blue eyes—the scars—the bruise. In a shockingly clean face. Wearing shockingly neat, clean clothes, not a hole or ragged edge in sight.

"Ma!" he called, and winced.

The woman was squeezing his toothpick of an arm, trying to push him behind her.

"Georgie!" Alice cried. "My dear lad!"

He strained to get free, but his captor held firm.

Alice marched closer.

"Ma!" Jonesy struggled, but he was no match for his watchdog.

"My poor Georgie!" Alice cried. She summoned her hours of studying and practicing lower-class accents. "I hardly know'd you, child, all skin and bones. What's happened to you?"

The woman was possibly Alice's age but possibly years older or younger. Whatever her age, she wasn't to be taken in so easily.

"Oh, no, you don't," she said. "I found him, and I recommend you don't mistake Maggie Proudie for no greenhorn. You don't steal him so easy as you think, Missus Whoever-You-Are."

Gazing into the hard, knowing eyes, Alice wondered if this was a gang leader, one who'd sent Jonesy with the other boys on the pickpocket expedition. In any case, Alice had better keep her wits about her.

She reminded herself that she was supposed to be a mother, a lioness protecting her cub. Drawing upon generations of patrician arrogance and the wisdom of Keeffe, she made herself big, and she was not a small woman to begin with.

She stalked nearer and met the woman's gaze. Others nearby gave way.

She was dimly aware of Blackwood looming nearby, but she kept her attention on the boy's captor.

"You didn't find that child under no cabbage leaf," Alice said. "That's my boy. You heard him. He knows me, don't you, Georgie? It'd be a funny thing if you didn't know your own ma."

"Ma!" he said. "Tell her to let me go!"

He was a quick-witted lad, no question. He'd recognized her, even dressed as she was. Or else he'd recognized Blackwood. In any case, Jonesy had put two and two together almost instantly, and calculated the better outcome.

His captor's eyes narrowed to slits. Like a viper about to strike, Alice thought.

"Nobody's goin' nowhere 'til we see that lawyer," Maggie said. She put her free hand to her bosom.

Heart pounding, hands icy cold but not visibly trembling, Alice managed to copy the gesture, pretending she, too, kept a knife concealed there. "I'd give him back now if I was you, Missus Proudie, because no lawyer's going to hold with child-stealing, and you could find yourself in a pot of trouble."

"So you say." The woman's gaze never faltered. "He was lost in the streets with nowhere to go when I found him and took care of him. The notice said to bring him to the lawyers, and I won't give him to nobody else. I'll have the reward, and you won't cheat me out of it. Then you can go up there"—she jerked her chin upward at the building—"and tell 'em he's yours, and swear your All-for-David to it, if you can."

This woman was no fool. She knew what an affidavit was, even if she hadn't the right word for it.

Her shrewd gaze took in Alice's costume, from bonnet to shoes. "Which I don't believe you can. You ain't his ma, any more than *him*." The sharp chin jutted toward Blackwood, who'd drawn nearer.

He was there, a large shadow in Alice's peripheral vision. She didn't need to see him. She could feel his presence, the back of her neck tickling as though his finger slid over it.

She heard coins jingle.

"Why don't we save the lawyer and ourselves time and bother," Blackwood said. "We'll take the brat off your hands for ten pounds, and add another pound for your trouble."

"Twenty," Maggie said instantly.

"I'll count to five," he said. "Then the offer disappears, and you get to explain, in detail, before witnesses, exactly where and how you found Mrs. Foster's son. Maybe you'll be paid the ten pounds. Maybe instead you'll find yourself explaining to a magistrate."

The other would-be George Fosters and their caretakers had crept closer at signs of an altercation. As Blackwood spoke, they crept a few paces back. Only a few paces. Nobody wanted to miss the show.

Maggie's jaw set.

"One," he said. "Two."

She held out her hand, palm up.

"Release the boy first," Alice said.

"Three," Blackwood said.

Chapter 8

Maggie let go of Jonesy. Before he could bolt, Alice grabbed him. She threw Blackwood one quick smile and hustled the boy away.

She was aware of negotiations going on behind her, but she left business to the duke. Bribery was one of Their Dis-Graces' specialties. If he couldn't manage Maggie Proudie, nobody could.

Alice wished she could be a fly on the wall, but the boy's safety came first.

"We need to get you out of harm's way—and no arguments," she said. She hurried the child along Inner Temple Lane, back to Fleet Street. Bypassing Blackwood's waiting carriage, she made for the nearest hackney stand.

Jonesy remained mute until they'd boarded the coach and she'd given the driver Madame Girard's direction.

Once the vehicle started westward, he found his tongue.

"Vat were a whisker she tole you," he said. "I weren't never lost. I were in the High Street, and vey was comin' from the Marshalsea. Five of 'em coves of hers and one of me. Vey brung me to her, and she said she'd take care of me. I didn't like it, but when I took off, vey come after me and half-drownded me."

More than once, Alice guessed, in order to break down rebellious inclinations.

"Vey watched me all the time," he said. "The only chance I got to get away was when you seen me t'other day. But she come after me today right when we was run off our legs in the yard. I had to go wif her 'n' do like she said. I was scairt what she'd do if I didn't." He scowled. "She made me have a baff! Vey rubbed the skin off of me!"

Maggie Proudie had not wasted a minute hunting down the boy and having him cleaned up for examination.

A good thing, too, that she'd taken the time to make him presentable, and that Alice had acted quickly and dragged Blackwood from his bed.

A few minutes' more delay and they would have faced extreme complications, not to mention greater danger.

But they'd succeeded, and in short order she'd put the boy in safe hands, she'd go home, and Society would be none the wiser.

Meanwhile Jonesy had no idea of the peril he'd narrowly missed. To him, the bath was the worst of his trials.

"You were right to be afraid," she said. "Is Maggie a gang leader?"

He shrugged. "You wanner watch out for her. She'll come for you."

"Let her try." True, the woman exuded menace. True, she might well be the most dangerous and frightening individual Alice had ever met. But Lady Alice Ancaster was not a small boy who had nobody to look after her. "Meanwhile you, my lad, are going on holiday, away from London."

He tensed, and his brow furrowed. "Away where?"

He was suspicious, as any intelligent street child ought to be.

"Putney," she said. "But first I'm taking you to a good friend of mine. You know her. Madame Girard."

He thought. "The brown lady? The one talks foreign? Her?"

"That one," Alice said. "She's the one who let me know you were in trouble. The man whose handkerchief the other boy stole? He's a mean one. He wants to catch somebody for it, and he picked you because he got a good look at you, which is my fault."

He rubbed his knuckles against his cheek. "I would've got nabbed if you didn't do nuffin'. Vem other coves, vey run off to let 'em nab me."

He was the new boy, expendable, as Liliane had said. Maggie wouldn't want a stolen child on her hands if she saw a risk of the authorities tracking him to her lair. If she could make an easy ten pounds turning him in, so much the better.

Alice said, "We didn't want you to swing for something you didn't do."

The child stared at his boots, not new, but not coated in mud and only slightly scuffed.

These days, children were rarely hanged, especially for a first offence. Still, influential persons could adjust the scales of justice to suit themselves. And some judges were notorious for severity.

"Had you been the one who stole the handkerchief, I wouldn't have bothered," Alice went on. "I don't help thieves. Do you understand?"

His blue gaze rose to meet hers, and he grinned. "Yer learnin' me a lesson, Yer Highness."

"Ah, you did recognize me, in spite of this." She indicated her disguise.

"Not straight off. But I fought I knew yer voice. Ven, when I seen the big gentry cove from t'other day, I smoked you."

"I counted on your being a clever boy, Master Georgie Foster or Jonesy or Jos or Rocket or Oyster or whoever you are."

He laughed. "Look who's talkin', *Ma*."

She swallowed a smile. It wasn't easy to tell where one stood with a street child, but he seemed to trust her.

"Then will you listen to your ma, and go away to Putney like a good boy?"

His eyes narrowed. "How far?"

"A few miles upriver," she said. "Several good coaching inns are there. Madame Girard will arrange for you to work at one of them."

She and Liliane had agreed that the prospect of another coaching inn, with all the horses coming and going and a bustle he was familiar with, would appeal.

All the same, he looked dubious, and Alice couldn't blame him. He probably thought Putney was in a foreign country. She'd met adult Londoners who'd never ventured beyond their immediate neighborhoods.

She remembered the stories Keeffe had told her and Cassandra about his London childhood and the methods he'd used to survive.

You don't trust nobody. If it looks like a favor, look again and then again. Everybody's watchin' out for hisself. When your gut tells you to get yourself lost, you do it, quick time.

"Or I can turn you loose wherever you say, Master Georgie Foster, et cetera, et cetera, and you can take your chances," Alice said.

"Lemme fink," he said.

THE DUKE OF BLACKWOOD retired with Maggie Proudie to the Cock, a tavern near Temple Bar. At this hour, the place was nearly empty. It was also dark, which was why Maggie preferred it. For Blackwood the attraction was what the *Epicure's Almanack* had once proclaimed "the best porter in London."

He and the gang leader had come to an agreement over the porter and a substantial breakfast. This was not the Cock's usual fare in the forenoon. But the Duke of Blackwood got what he wanted when he wanted it, and easily enough. All the world knew Their Dis-Graces were free with their money.

He wanted sustenance to restore his nerves to working order. He'd made himself stand by and watch, braced to intervene, while Alice confronted this woman, who wouldn't have thought twice about slashing her face to ribbons.

The encounter was like a duel, he'd told himself, and he was

not the principal but her second. The smallest word or movement could distract her. His job was to let her concentrate on
what she was doing.

Knowing this was the intelligent thing to do had not made it
a fraction less hellish. A part of him still reeled.

"We've a bargain, then," he said now.

Maggie nodded. "We do. Only we'd best make sure we're
plain about some things." She lowered her voice. "Like, you
oughter know, any o' them beak's men come botherin' me 'bout
this, I'll know why."

"When the law comes after you, I don't doubt you will know
why," he said. "But that will be none of my doing. Unless, that
is, you break the terms of our bargain. In which case the beak's
men will be the least of your problems."

He spoke softly, easily, but she sat back.

"Only making sure we're plain about some things," he said.

She gave a short laugh. "Oh, you're a one, ain't you?"

She bent toward him once more, and keeping her voice very
low, added, "You bein' so generous, I'll tell you something you
oughter know. The mort you come with: I can't say what she is,
but she ain't no washerwoman. She don't smell like one. And
her hands." She held out her own. "Too soft." Hers were clean
but not soft.

"I see." What he saw was how easily Alice might have been
maimed. Murdered. He swallowed the last of his porter.

"As to the boy," Maggie said. "Good luck with him. More
trouble than he's worth."

"On that we agree," he said.

Among other matters they'd settled, he'd paid her handsomely
to leave the young vagrant alone henceforth and to spread the
word among her confederates. With any luck, the brat would
stay in Putney, or decide to make an ocean cruise to New South
Wales.

She emptied her tankard and set it down. "I thank you kindly
for the vittles and drink. I'd like to stay and palaver, because

you're a funny sort of nob, but I got work to do, and best get doing it."

She rose and he did, too, because a gentleman is unfailingly polite. He watched her go out.

Then he summoned the waiter and took his time about paying the shot. When he estimated she'd put sufficient distance between them, he left.

ALICE LEANT CLOSER to the window of Madame Girard's drawing room, watching Jonesy and the groom in charge of him drive away.

"He is out of danger," Liliane said. "He will be away from the bad influences. He will have clean air and better food."

"And horses," Alice said, forcing a smile. She'd miss him, the naughty little urchin.

"And then, who knows?" Madame said. "With his skill, he could rise to become a groom, even a coachman. We offer an opportunity. We cannot control what he makes of it."

"That is more than true." All was well, yet Alice was not.

Liliane gently laid her hand on Alice's arm. "You were brave to do what you did," she said.

"Mad is more like it." Alice looked down at her hands. They trembled now, though they hadn't before. The aftereffects. "I couldn't let fear control me then. I had to pay strict attention. That woman. To find Jonesy in her hands." She shook her head. "You'd never notice her in the street. But up close, face-to-face, one feels it. She's formidable, Liliane."

"You had the Duke of Blackwood as chevalier," Liliane said. "You thought in the way an urgent situation demands. One throws aside ordinary considerations and seeks the most expedient means."

Chevalier. A knight. Alice smiled and shook her head. "Is that how I shall explain to the gossipmongers?"

"Who'll know what you did? Nobody could possibly recognize you. Who would be out and about at that hour? No member of Society, I promise you."

"It was well before Blackwood wanted to be up and about, certainly." The image came sharply into focus of the dressing gown lapping about his naked ankles . . . the few inches of muscled, hairy leg.

She smoothed her skirts and tried to smooth her mind. She'd reverted to proper attire while Madame bribed Jonesy with sweets and sent him to the stables with a manservant. Alice had suggested adding a visit to the coach house, where several fine vehicles might act as lures. The strategy worked.

All was in order, she told herself, and her life would continue as planned. Tonight she'd attend Almack's first assembly of the Season. Doveridge would be there, along with other beaux. She had a few wallflowers to look after. This was more than enough to think about. She had no time for inconvenient feelings.

Sussex Place
Midafternoon

BLACKWOOD SENT UP his card, then wondered what he was about. The servant would only return to tell him the ladies weren't at home.

He was supposed to keep his distance. He didn't need to see for himself whether Alice had arrived safely. He didn't need to come in person to assure her that the sewer rat was safe from Maggie Proudie henceforth. There were other ways. He wasn't thinking clearly.

He was about to do the intelligent thing and show himself out of the house when the butler appeared. To Blackwood's surprise, he was escorted not only into a drawing room but into one containing guests. A glance took in Lynforde, Lady Drakeley, Tom Drakeley, another matron, and a girl who must be her daughter.

They all faded to a stage setting when his gaze settled upon Alice.

Though he'd seen her mere hours earlier, he found it impossible to believe she'd ever been a washerwoman.

She sat back upon the cushions of the drawing room's L-shaped divan, the perfect lady. She wore a dress striped alternately with a color Blackwood's last mistress had called *Nile water green* and a sort of peach color whose fashionable name he didn't know. The dress's V-neck, which had extremely wide lapels, plunged nearly to her belt. A clear cambric chemisette filled in the V but only thinly veiled the creamy flesh beneath it.

Blackwood did not object to the scanty covering. What he objected to was the other gentlemen in the room having the same view. He crushed the feeling and said what he was supposed to say, precisely according to instructions in THE CORRECT BEHAVIOR OF A GENTLEMAN.

To his bewilderment, he found himself being made acquainted with the matron and her daughter: Lady Felpham and Miss Emily Felpham, an extremely shy girl whose color went from red to white and back again several times during the introduction, and who seemed in imminent danger of fainting. However, her mother bore her off shortly thereafter. Then, as so often happened when Blackwood appeared, others discovered reasons to depart. Lynforde dawdled, the last to leave. Flee. Whatever.

The leave-takings included promises to see Lady Alice and Lady Kempton this evening at Almack's.

Blackwood wouldn't see Alice there. He was banned.

Other men would dance with her. Other men would hold her hand. Other men would feel her skirts brushing against their legs . . .

Nobody's fault but his. She'd never dance with him again. After the goat incident at Almack's, she'd told him so. Furthermore, she hated him and would never forgive him or her brother or Ashmont for spoiling Cassandra's first Almack's assembly. She'd failed to mention the fact that they'd spoilt hers at the same time. It was all about Cassandra, whose feelings they'd hurt because not one of them had asked for a dance or even spared her a few minutes' conversation. They were boors. They were immature and selfish. They didn't deserve to breathe the same air. Etc. Etc.

She wasn't wrong, and Blackwood couldn't go back and make it right. He dragged the memory to the mental cavern and reminded himself why he'd come. All he needed to do was say what he had to say and get out. He told himself this while her guests busily pretended they weren't running away.

He told himself he wasn't tired of people running away from him.

"It seems we owe you thanks," Lady Kempton said once the room had cleared. "We were in a considerable quandary last night after we'd seen the handbills. But here is Alice, who did not, as I truly feared, get herself murdered. And the boy is in good hands." She let out a sigh. "For the moment."

"You did a good deed," Alice said. "Aunt nearly fainted when I told her."

"As though I had a choice." He walked to a window and looked out at the lake.

"You might have had her thrown out of the house," Lady Kempton said. "You'd no idea who it was."

"In fact, I planned to throw her out bodily myself. Why should the porter have all the fun? But then the sleep destroyer turned out to be Alice, about to do something deranged, and I was obliged to save her from herself and tidy up afterward. Not for the first time."

"Choice or not, you did us a great service," Lady Kempton said.

He turned away from the window, and his surprise must have shown—he wasn't himself, after all, having enjoyed almost no sleep—because Alice said, "You needn't be anxious, Giles. It isn't as though we're going to tell anybody."

"In short, the brat's been taken care of," he said.

Her expression softened. "He's probably in Putney by now."

"He'll be safe from Maggie Proudie as well as Worbury," he

said. "She and I reached an agreement. That's what I came to tell you. There will be no further trouble from that quarter. In fact, she's undertaken to declare the boy out of bounds to the rest of the vermin who form her acquaintance."

"Good grief." Lady Kempton shook her head.

"She wields a great deal of power, then," Alice said. "I guessed as much. She seems the type nobody would notice. But at close quarters . . ." She looked away, as though seeking words. "It's like facing a viper. A crocodile. One does not feel safe, to say the least."

"You needn't give her another thought," he said. "As to Worbury—"

"He's only grown worse. Cringing and smirking to our faces, then going after a child. I should like to take a horse-whip to him."

She would do it, too.

"You needn't exert yourself," he said. "By tomorrow, he's likely to decide London no longer agrees with him. In any case, you may leave him to me." He started to turn away, then paused. "On second thought, I *insist* you leave him to me. You're too reckless. Ladies." He bowed and made his escape.

Aunt Florentia turned to Alice. "He isn't wrong. Had I known precisely what you planned—"

"I didn't know what I planned," Alice said. She didn't add, *Not that you could have stopped me.* "I only knew I had to do something. When I reached Liliane's, it simply became obvious that somebody had to find Jonesy before any criminals did, and who else but me? It was so early in the morning, I never supposed that a gang leader would be up and about."

"But the children go out in the daytime to pick pockets," her aunt said.

"Rarely in the forenoon." Alice glanced down to make sure her chemisette was properly in place. She'd felt Blackwood's gaze there . . . and sliding away, the lightest touch. It was as though his hand had brushed the chemisette and it dissolved under the touch. She'd felt it on her skin, and within she'd felt a tug, low in her belly.

She recognized the sensation too well. She wanted to feel that powerful pull to somebody else, somebody who was the right choice. She told herself to be patient. Uncle Charles had not made Aunt Julia's heart flutter at first. She'd wanted another gentleman. She'd never gone into detail, merely mentioned this as an example of youthful infatuation versus mature affection. She'd married a worthy man, and her tepid feelings had warmed and deepened into powerful love.

Aunt Florentia brought her attention back. "I do wish you were not quite so well-versed in these matters, my dear."

"I can't shut my eyes," Alice said. "At any rate, it's too late. I've learnt and I can't unlearn. What matters is, I came away unhurt, the child will work at a respectable coaching inn, and Blackwood assures us that Worbury won't trouble the boy again. I wonder what he has in mind for the Worm."

"I wonder what business Blackwood had in London that his secretary or steward or solicitor couldn't manage for him. I thought Julia had told the dukes to keep away."

Alice rose from the divan and crossed to the window Blackwood had looked out of. "Jonesy and I were lucky he was here. I *might* have managed on my own, but not so easily or so well. I was in such a state, I never thought of bribery, the obvious method. I was too busy wishing I'd remembered to carry a weapon and deciding how to defend myself if she tried to cut my throat."

"Good grief, Alice."

Alice laughed and turned back to her aunt. "And tonight we shall attend Almack's first assembly of the Season, we and some three or four hundred other elite persons. How many, do you think, in their wildest dreams, would guess where Lady Alice Ancaster was this morning and what she was doing?"

"None, I fervently hope, my dear."

Which was as it should be, Alice told herself. This morning had constituted an emergency, a crisis. It wasn't her life. It wasn't the life she needed.

She didn't regret what she'd done this day. In truth, she'd felt more alive during those morning hours than she'd done in what seemed like a very long time. She'd made herself truly useful to somebody, and it had been dangerous and exciting and satisfying.

Almack's was bound to seem tame in comparison, but *tame* was the life she sought: the opposite of her parents' turmoil and her brother's chaos. She would become a settled matron, and do more good that way than with a hundred disguises and brushes with death.

Late afternoon

LORD WORBURY STORMED out of the Fisk Building, Consett on his heels.

"Impossible," Worbury said. "The notices were everywhere. Ten pounds! And nobody tries to claim it? *Nobody?*"

"The boy could be dead," Consett said. "Or, you know, maybe his mother or father saw the notices and came and got him before the lawyers were ready. Maybe somebody found him before the notices went up."

"Mother! If the filthy little bastard has one, she's a street slut with no idea who his father is or what parts of London her numerous spawn are infesting."

Worbury paused and looked about him at the ancient structures surrounding the court. "There was a small crowd, Maycock's clerk said. Then it dispersed. Nobody knows why, and nobody is inclined to look into it."

"Don't see how they could, if everybody left," Consett said.

"They preferred not to look into it, more likely. Too much bother."

Possibly Maycock hadn't swallowed Worbury's tale of wanting to assist, anonymously, a family whose son had been stolen. Or maybe the apathy resulted from Worbury's failure to pay recent legal fees.

Who cared why? Couldn't trust lawyers—pettifoggers, all of them.

"Maybe somebody will turn up tomorrow," Consett said.

"That I doubt. Something's wrong here, damn them all to hell!"

Worbury left the court to storm along Inner Temple Lane. Before he reached the entrance to Fleet Street, a common-looking female emerged from a doorway and bumped into him.

"Watch where yer goin'," she said.

"Get out of my way," he said, and knocked her aside.

The blow threw her back against the building, her head struck the bricks, and she sank to the ground.

Consett, trying to keep up with his friend, paused, gaped at the fallen figure, then hurried on.

When the pair had disappeared through the gateway, she stood up, straightened her bonnet, and brushed herself off. She drew from her pocket a gold watch and chain, complete with seals.

"Not a bad day's work, Maggie," she said. "Lost a boy but won twenty quid from the big swell and more to come later, got a good look at this pair, and had an easy dive for gold in the bargain."

She bobbed a scornful curtsey toward the gateway her accoster had gone out of. "Much obliged, sir."

With a laugh, she set out in the opposite direction. She made her way eastward through the maze of streets to Blackfriars Bridge, collecting handbills as she went.

Chapter 9

Early morning of Thursday 3 May 1832

Fog obscured the sun floating up from the horizon as Aunt Florentia's town coach turned into Piccadilly. Gazing out of the window, Alice told herself she had nothing, really, to complain of. She'd danced twice with the Duke of Doveridge.

This was no small achievement. Since he always made sure that ladies did not languish, neglected upon the red sofas, he rarely had time to dance with any lady more than once. Yet tonight, despite the shortage of gentlemen, he'd found time for a second dance with her.

Furthermore, the notably fickle duke's continuing interest roused her other suitors' competitive instincts. Despite the night's thin attendance, she'd not only never lacked for partners but had seen her small collection of wallflowers—including Emily Felpham—partnered for most of the evening.

Under the attention, Emily's shyness receded somewhat. Of course, after the shock of meeting the Devil Duke of Blackwood in person, other fears must diminish to near-nothingness.

"Good heavens, he did her a favor," Alice said with a laugh.

"Which *he*, my dear, and what was the favor?" her aunt said.

Alice turned back to her. "Blackwood. Emily Felpham."

Aunt Florentia laughed, too. "I'll admit I was astonished when he sent up his card. But I could hardly turn him away, after all he'd done."

Alice shrugged. "You could, easily enough. He's accustomed to my ingratitude. But what a treat it was, to watch his face when Emily was allowed to make his acquaintance! It was all I could do not to laugh out loud."

"I was taken aback as well. I never thought Lady Felpham would consent to the introduction."

"Perhaps the shock of seeing him scattered her wits. It scattered mine, certainly." More than that. A great deal more than that. A mad urge to throw her arms about his neck and thank him. The echoing voice in her head: *Why can you not be this man?*

Hope. The small, flickering light that refused to snuff itself out.

A night so long ago. His arms about her. His mouth on hers and the world she knew falling away at the first taste of him. The scents of the night and the warmth and strength of him, surrounding her. The haven of his arms and a moment of fierce happiness, then his voice, low and choked as he broke from her: *We can't do this. I can't do this.*

Then he left her, and she stood, shattered, watching him go.

Above her head, stars glittered. For a moment, in his arms, she'd felt she was there, among the stars.

Aunt Florentia's voice called her back from the past. "He managed well enough, shocked or not. He did not put a foot wrong."

"His manners are impeccable when he chooses to apply them."

But he didn't choose to live among those who prized such qualities. He chose to apply his brain and skills to pleasure-seeking and juvenile pranks.

A waste of his life. A waste of all he could be.

She couldn't undo the damage, and she certainly had better things to do than let gloom about him darken her mind.

She added more briskly, "At any rate, Emily survived, and the experience might have done her some good. She'll have noted, one hopes, that the Duke of Blackwood does not sport cloven hoofs, but is simply a man like other men, merely big and dark and intimidating. But many gentlemen of rank can be intimidating when they choose. Even Doveridge. Girls like Emily need to understand their own power, and not let men make them feel uncertain of themselves."

"I should not say that Blackwood was like other men, Alice."

"I'll admit he can change the atmosphere merely by standing there." Alice returned her gaze to the carriage window. "As to atmosphere, I wonder if this fog ever means to lift. And is our carriage moving at all? I don't recall Piccadilly being so crowded at this hour. We traveled more quickly through King Street, so we can't blame Almack's crowd. Not that we constituted any great crowd tonight. Is there an accident ahead, do you think?"

DESPITE THE FOG, Lord Worbury's carriage had made its way from one of St. James's gaming hells with little difficulty. Although Almack's had begun emptying at about the same time he set out, the journey proceeded smoothly until his carriage entered Golden Square. There he found a host of adults and children of every age and the lowest levels of squalor.

They swarmed and settled like flies, crowding the pavement in front of his house and spreading out over the west side of the square to Upper John Street.

He sat, stunned, in his stalled carriage, aware of irate neighbors glaring down from their windows.

Somebody must have summoned the police, yet he saw no sign of them.

No surprise there. The Reform Bill disrupted everything. Mobs rioted across London and other towns. Thanks to a lot of softheaded radicals—Doveridge and his ilk—the police were busy everywhere but here.

One of the taller wretches pointed at Worbury's carriage, and the crowd surged toward him.

"Found him, yer 'onner," somebody shouted.

The others took up the cry, with variations. Sometimes it was "Found 'er." He became "yer worship" and "yer 'ighness" and other barely intelligible honorifics.

The stench of poverty penetrated his carriage's interior. He tried to close the window fully, but his hands shook too much.

This day had begun happily enough. Then came the infuriating news at Maycock's chambers. Shortly thereafter, Worbury happened upon a satirical print, stuck in a print shop window for all the world to gawk at. It depicted him with tears streaming down his face as he knelt before Blackwood and begged, "Please don't hurt me!" Then, when he was nearly home, he discovered he'd lost his pocket watch, chains, seals—the lot.

Now this, on his very doorstep.

"Drive on, damn you!" he shouted.

The carriage inched on, hemmed in by the hordes who escorted the vehicle as it rounded the corner toward the mews. Grimy hands waved handbills, the ones he'd ordered printed and plastered about the neighborhoods where thieves roosted.

He dared not disembark. Cholera ran rife among the poor. They carried its miasma, and here they were, a cloud of disease filling Golden Square.

"Send for a constable!" he screamed. "Somebody read the Riot Act! Do something, damn you!"

Not that anybody could hear him above the crowd's chant: *Found 'im. Found 'er.*

With a furious struggle, he got the window fully closed. One after another fiend lunged at him, holding up a pile of rags—possibly human—and shouting, "This 'er 'im, innit?" or "This 'un!"

"Fetch a constable!" he shouted, again and again until he was hoarse.

"A TO-DO IN Golden Square?" Alice said, when the coachman had explained the constant stopping and starting. "Worbury lives in Golden Square."

What had Blackwood said?

By tomorrow, he's likely to decide London no longer agrees with him. In any case, you may leave him to me.

"I want to see," she said.

"Alice, it may well be a riot," her aunt said. "Between the cholera and the Reform Bill—"

"In Golden Square?" Alice said. "Not in Whitehall or under the Duke of Wellington's windows?" She told the coachman to drive to Golden Square.

Her aunt countermanded the order. "Are you mad, child? A public disturbance—and you mean to plunge into it?"

She couldn't sit in the coach another minute.

"I want to see for myself." The carriage had stopped again. Alice put down the window and reached for the door handle.

"Alice!"

In a moment she was on the pavement, stumbling a little from the jump, but she quickly regained her balance and hurried through Lower John Street.

She heard footsteps behind her. Thomas, as usual, required to guard her.

"My lady!"

"Hush." She quickened her pace.

She heard the chanting voices first. When she reached the corner of Golden Square, she saw the source. A crowd of what many would call London's refuse milled about the western side of Golden Square, the greater part in front of Number Twenty-One.

Worbury's house.

She started to move nearer when she felt a hand on her arm. "I'd keep out of it if I was you, princess."

The hairs on the back of her neck lifting, Alice turned. She had light enough to make out Maggie Proudie's unremarkable face.

A GROAN MADE Alice glance downward. Behind them, Thomas struggled to rise from the pavement.

"What have you done to him?" Alice started to push past Maggie. One might as well try to push an ox out of the way. Her hand was like a manacle.

"Well, you're a bold one, ain't you? There's some'd pay good money for little girls who run about looking for trouble." Maggie eyed her dress up and down. "And that frock don't suit this party."

Large as it was, Alice's cashmere shawl couldn't conceal her white gauze ball dress. It was a costly article, embroidered in green silk, with matching green silk bows on the shoulders and the back of the waist, whence floated ribbons.

People could be murdered for their clothes, she knew.

She adopted her washerwoman's mode of speech: "It suits me well enough, Missus Proudie, and I recommend you take your hand off of me, if you don't want some fingers broke."

A short, tense pause. Then Maggie laughed. "Oh, it's you, is it? Got up like a queen."

"My lady." Thomas had risen to his hands and knees.

"Oh, Thomas, are you hurt?" Alice said.

"Nah, he only tripped over somethin'."

"Your foot, no doubt!"

"*My lady*, is it? Well, you're a one, ain't you?"

"Where is he?" Alice said.

"Where's who?"

"You know who I mean. This has his handprint all over it." With the hand not encumbered by Maggie's iron grip, Alice gestured at the crowd, all chanting and holding up children or signs.

"That would be me," came a low voice behind her. "She's always chasing me about. You may let her go, Maggie. I'll see that she doesn't hurt anybody. Kindly help the footman to his feet. It looks as though he went down hard, poor fellow."

"Well, how was I to know what they was about?" Maggie said. "She come raging through the street, and him behind her. Mebbe he had something bad in mind for her, you know, and mebbe I was lookin' out for her. I look out for girls, you know."

For the brothels, most likely.

"You may leave her to me," Blackwood said.

BLACKWOOD SENT THOMAS back to the coach to let Lady Kempton know that Alice was safe and would return shortly.

Then, when a highly amused Maggie and a greatly shaken Thomas had gone, Blackwood led Alice deeper into the shadows of the square.

His heart was pounding, and he wanted to shake her. He made himself very, very calm and said, "Did I not tell you I had everything in hand?"

"There was a to-do in Golden Square, the coachman told us," she said. "Worbury lives here. Did you think me incapable of putting two and two together?"

"You couldn't do that from a distance?"

"I wanted to see."

"And what about those who might see you? You are not inconspicuous." He gestured at her dress, a froth of white, dotted with green. He was near enough to detect the scent of greenery that belonged to her and nobody else.

"I was sitting in the carriage forever! I've been smiling and pretending half the night. Three partners insisted on performing the steps to the wrong dances, mainly on my toes, but I danced on, as one must. One of the Season's fair damsels was beastly to Lady Olympia Hightower, but I could not knock the spiteful cat against one of the mirrors she was so fond of looking into or even swat her with my fan. I made do with a setdown that probably went over her head. And that isn't the half of it. You don't know what it's like. I only wanted to get home and out of my dress and to bed. But we were stuck in the Quadrant this age, and when I guessed why, I wanted to see."

He wasn't sure what to make of the rant, and decided not to try. This had been a long day and night.

He looked down at her feet. "You are wearing dancing slippers."

"What should I wear to Almack's? Galoshes?"

"Your slippers are made of silk. Men have danced on your toes, which must be begging for mercy. Yet you run through the filthy London streets like one of the urchins you're trying to save."

"I don't care!"

She all but jumped up and down. Inside, she was probably doing so. He knew this Alice very well. This was the girl who climbed down ivy-covered bricks from second-floor windows. This was the girl who beat unpleasant boys until they begged for mercy, then dragged them into a river.

He clasped her arms. He wanted to pick her up and kiss her until she melted and clung to him the way she'd done so long ago.

That was the past, and a mistake. What he ought to do was shake her.

"Now you've seen for yourself. Being a clever girl, you grasp my cunning scheme."

The myrtle sprigs sprouting from her coiffure bobbed as she lifted her head to meet his gaze. "You enlisted Maggie Proudie to do your bidding."

"She rules a vast criminal network. She did in a few hours what would have taken me a week or more to arrange, and she was delighted to do so."

"For a price."

"Certainly. That is not to say she hasn't enjoyed herself. Meanwhile I've performed a public service, you see, in directing her extensive powers to rid London of a menace."

"Another good deed, Giles? Will this not bring on dyspepsia? Or an attack of megrims?" She looked from one to the other of his hands. "You may release me now. I shouldn't dream of disrupting your elegant mise-en-scène. I cannot wait to hear the gossip this afternoon at the Queen's Drawing Room. And when the topic comes up, you may be sure I shall seek details and be as eager as anybody else to discover what it was all about."

He was a fool, the greatest fool. Touching her was always a mistake. Letting go was painful. He didn't want to. But she was here to find a worthy husband, and he was here to make sure nothing got in her way. He owed it to her.

He stepped back a pace. He could still feel the warmth of her skin through his leather gloves. He drew in her scent with every breath. "Then you'd better go home and get some rest. I shall walk with you back to the carriage."

His mind drifted to beds, to the image of a certain young woman in bed, her black hair streaming over the pillows . . .

He hauled the image into the mental cavern.

"It isn't a very long walk," she said.

"You are not going alone."

"If that's the case, you might tell me all the lovely details on the way."

"It's a prank, Alice. You hate pranks."

"Not when done for a noble cause."

"Nobility has nothing to do with it. Duels are tedious and murder is scandalous, and I'm not supposed to make scandal that could possibly be connected with you. Unnecessary, in any event. You are perfectly capable of creating a disturbance with no help from anybody else."

But he did tell her. All the lovely details. She listened appreciatively. And when he handed her up to her aunt's carriage, and the door closed, he felt regret and regret and regret.

AFTER WHAT SEEMED like years, the crowd in Golden Square melted away as though they'd never been, and the fog began to lift. Then, at last, when he could be of no earthly use, a constable appeared, apologetic.

A cartload of bricks had spilled in Beak Street, blocking the way. A drunken brawl had erupted in Warwick Street. A wagon had got stuck at the corner of Brewer Street. In short, many residents of Golden Square and its environs had been unable to get home, thereby slowing travel in Regent Street.

Lord Worbury scarcely heeded the excuses. He was too frightened even to abuse the constable. Nigh weeping with relief, he entered his house. As he crossed the vestibule, he heard a whispery sound behind him. He turned in time to see a folded piece of paper slide toward him from under the door.

With trembling hands, he picked it up and unfolded it. The paper was cheap, and the message was written in pencil in a rough hand. Still, the coarse black capitals were clear enough:

**LEAVE MY LADS ALONE OR NEXT TIME IT
GOES WORSE FOR YOU.**

When Maggie's legions had gone, Blackwood joined her in the shadows of Golden Square's east side.

"Neatly done," he said.

"Easy enough when a girl has coin enough to manage it."

"Money works magic," he said.

"You know that trick well enough, from what I been hearing."

He and his friends had grasped the simple rule long ago: Pay enough, and people become wonderfully forgiving and cooperative.

Not everybody. Good Society tended to look askance at the pranks, melees, and other rule-breaking.

Their Dis-Graces did not give a damn about Society. That wasn't where the fun was.

This prank wasn't for the fun of it.

Maggie didn't care what it was for. She cared about the money he paid her to bring it off successfully. She'd done so, sending out a team to follow Worbury and report his whereabouts, summoning minions to block access to the square and a host of wretches to play their parts within it.

She was formidable, and Blackwood could have throttled Alice for placing herself in this woman's path again.

"I've heard nothing about you, and I don't require enlighten-ment," he said. "It's enough to know you keep your bargains, for which I thank you. All the same, I believe we'd do well not to become better acquainted."

"Right. Don't want to put your pretty mort's nose out of joint. Got yerself a handful there, I see." She laughed. "I'm good at not being found, yer worship. But if you ever do need me, I reckon you'll find a way to let me know." She strolled away.

He, too, walked away, in the opposite direction.

If tonight's scheme succeeded, Worbury would move to a safe distance. Then, once the Worm was out of the picture . . . Then what?

Lynforde could be Ripley's eyes and ears. He knew London. He knew Alice.

Better to leave the rest to him. Better to go back—to Ripley and Ashmont and the life Blackwood had chosen. He told him-self it was the life he wanted, where he and his friends made their own rules. He told himself it was fun. Horse races. Boxing and wrestling matches. Brawls. Gaming. Pranks. Women. Wine. And more of the same.

Fine remedies for every malady. Repeat as needed.

He returned to Blackwood House and went to bed.

Chapter 10

*T*he letter from Newmarket arrived as Blackwood was in the last stages of dressing for the evening.

Lynforde, who'd arrived some time earlier, had poured himself a glass of sherry and settled onto the sofa.

"Ripley," Blackwood said as he took the missive from the tray.

"I recognize the scrawl," Lynforde said.

Blackwood waved the footman out of the dressing room and dismissed his valet.

When they'd gone, he said, "Since he isn't the most diligent correspondent, we may expect a matter of urgency. Ashmont's run amok again, very likely. As though I could do anything about it. As though anybody could."

He broke the seal and unfolded the letter.

No date, no salutation. Typical.

Aunt Julia's got the wind up and commands us to appear at headquarters. She heard you're in London. No surprise. Try keeping anything from her. She's like Ashmont's Uncle Fred—spies everywhere, and she knows all that's happening and sometimes before it happens. To put it plain, my aunt is in a fine twist. The letter scorched my fingers. No point in answering. I never do well, trying to explain in letters. Best to appear as ordered. I'm setting out as soon as I settle a few matters here. You can guess at one of them. What do you reckon the chances are, Ashmont making matters worse if he's with us? Damned good odds I'd say. Auntie sees through his charm. He'll have to stay behind. Look for me to land at the Lovedon Arms in Kensington by Saturday night. Meet me there. Can't turn up in London or she'll have my head. We'll set out for Camberley Place on Sunday morning. Make sure you've a good story to tell her. Keep in mind that she's cleverer than the three of us put together. No difficult achievement, now I think of it.

R

Blackwood passed the letter to Lynforde, saying, "The timing could be better."

"When is the timing ever right in life?" Lynforde read the letter through, squinting now and again to make out the words. He gave it back.

Blackwood set it on his dressing table and poured himself a drink. He stared at it for a while before lifting it to his lips.

"I can play spy for you," Lynforde said.

Blackwood drank and set down the glass. He returned to the dressing table, opened the velvet box Springate had set there, and removed the sapphire stickpin it contained. He turned to the dressing glass and inserted the stickpin in his neckcloth precisely where it ought to sit. "I should be easier in my mind if I were certain Worbury had left Town."

"He can't do that so soon after the event. He's put it about that what happened on Thursday morning was a political demonstration, caused by his opposing the Reform Bill. To leave immediately afterward would look cowardly."

"He *is* a coward, as we and many others are well aware."

"This is why we can be certain that he's too shaken to make

trouble for anybody at present," Lynforde said. "He'll leave London as soon as he can devise a suitable excuse, I'll wager anything."

Blackwood had shared with his friend the broad outlines of recent events: Worbury had conceived a vendetta against the boy Alice had shielded at Hyde Park Corner, Alice had alerted Blackwood, and he'd arranged the demonstration in Golden Square to make Worbury believe he'd run afoul of a criminal overlord. As Alice had said, the scene bore Their Dis-Graces' handprint. The dukes had contacts in low places. Lynforde had a brain. That was sufficient.

"It's only for a few days," Blackwood said. "Once I explain the Worbury problem, Lady Charles will understand. As Ripley realizes, however, the business ought to be done face-to-face."

Not to mention that Blackwood would never put into writing all the details, any more than he'd confide them to Lynforde, much as he trusted him. Without these details, Lady Charles would worry. He'd done damage enough. He would not add anxiety to her sorrow.

The morning of the thirtieth of March haunted him still.

What is wrong with you? Drunk, shooting off pistols, so close to the house—and this house, of all places. Do you three think of anybody else, ever? . . . And you . . . You let this happen.

No, he hadn't thought. Yes, he'd let it happen, and his best friend could have died in Lady Charles's garden. He couldn't leave this to Ripley, who was in the dark about recent events, and therefore unable to reassure his aunt.

Blackwood was the one who'd decided to go against her wishes. He had to be the one to explain why. At least he had proof he'd done the right thing in returning to London. A small amends but better than nothing.

"If anything happens, I know you'll send a message immediately," he said.

"Of course," Lynforde said. "Camberley Place is only a few hours' journey from London. You can be back on the spot in no time. But I strongly doubt you'll need to be. By the time you return, Worbury will be gone, beyond a doubt."

Gardens of the Zoological Society,
the Regent's Park
Saturday 5 May 1832

"ONE OF THE most useful peculiarities of the camel is its power of passing many days without drinking," the Earl of Tunstall was saying. "This has long since been recognized as dependent on a cellular apparatus connected with the first and second stomachs, and capable, to quote the expressions of Monsieur Cuvier, 'of retaining water or of continually producing it.'"

"Lord Tunstall is fully capable of continually producing words," Alice murmured. "He does not seem to be aware of the quantity."

"It would appear that he's memorized one of the Zoological Society's publications," the Duke of Doveridge said in the same low tones. "One wishes we had encountered him not quite so early in our visit. Still, he means well, I'm sure. He is simply a little naïve."

Alice glanced back at the bespectacled young man. His was not the most prepossessing figure, but he wasn't unattractive. "He is so earnest. Do you know, I believe he's trying to impress Miss Emily Felpham."

Tunstall had turned up as they were leaving the bear pit, the first stop on their tour of the gardens, and had attached himself to their party. He wasn't the only one.

At Almack's on Wednesday night, Doveridge—who, naturally, was a member of the Zoological Society—had invited the Ladies Kempton and Felpham, Alice, and a trio of debutantes for a tour. Since the young ladies were bound to mention it to somebody or other who would mention it to somebody else, several enterprising gentlemen had discovered a compelling need to visit and had applied to members of the society for orders for entry. Consequently, the small group had enlarged.

"She does not seem to be bored," Doveridge said.

"Maybe she understands that he seeks her admiration," Alice said.

While Lady Felpham was growing desperate about her twenty-one-year-old daughter's lack of social success, the daughter had her own views. Shy though she was, Emily was not so anxious for a mate as to encourage the first male who displayed interest.

Lord Tunstall was a reasonable choice, however. His behavior was gentlemanly, his rank and income acceptable. The spectacles did not detract from an amiable countenance.

Doveridge studied the pair. "She does not hang raptly on his every word, but she seems to be paying attention."

"Possibly she comprehends that he, too, is shy, and tries to burst out of it in an awkward way. Perhaps she feels sympathy. He doesn't mean to be boring."

"Good heavens, what man does?" Doveridge said. "We all like to imagine we're fascinating fellows. Let us move on to the aquatic birds, and give the pair a moment to themselves. If she hurries to catch up with us, we'll know he's failed to captivate."

As they walked on, Alice looked up at him. "You're matchmaking."

"It is the besetting vice of a man who has failed to make his own match for some twenty years."

"I suspect you weren't trying hard enough."

He lifted his eyebrows and regarded her for a moment. Then he laughed. A few heads turned their way.

"That wasn't meant as criticism," she said. "The trouble is the world we live in, which seems to encourage incaution. Most people marry on the thinnest acquaintance, and that's because they're not allowed any more. There is Miss Emily, who must decide on altogether flimsy evidence whether she can find happiness—*for the rest of her life*—with a gentleman with whom she's had only snatches of conversation, and virtually no privacy."

"What do you recommend, Lady Alice? Ought the chaperons to look on from a distance, perhaps with spyglasses?"

"They would need to be able to read lips," Alice said. "If, that is, we young ladies are to be protected from the ignorance imposed upon us."

"I detect the voice of Mary Wollstonecraft."

She shook her head in mock sorrow. "Alas, I'm found out for the radical being I am."

"I found you out ages ago," he said. "The first—no, second—well, the first time we met when I was paying attention."

It was her turn to laugh, and she thought, *He is so like Uncle Charles, and one can be friends with him, and is that not an excellent basis for marriage?*

Impossible to imagine her parents ever being friends.

But Uncle Charles and Aunt Julia had had that kind of marriage. Private jokes. A private language. They understood each other.

Doveridge seemed to understand Alice well enough, considering how little time they'd had for anything like real conversation. A minute or two here and there. While dancing. At dinner.

The present gathering was different. With two matrons chaperoning, the other members of the party could walk along in changing constellations, some pausing here, others there, but never straying too far. And so, one or another pair might enjoy a brief opportunity to talk more freely than was usually the case.

He hadn't disappointed her.

She remembered Blackwood's provoking comment: *Maybe I'll stay on, to follow your progress with your new—well, he's not so new, is he?*

Not so new, perhaps, but compassionate, liberal-minded, and *civilized.*

And that's enough, is it? an inner voice demanded.

It will suffice, she answered.

Yet the memory returned of Blackwood's hand on her shoulder and the sound of his voice and the way she'd wanted—what? Disappointment? Heartbreak?

Excitement.

She pushed unwanted thoughts away and looked about her and listened. The noise of the streets didn't reach here, except as a distant murmur, and she seemed to be in a Garden of Eden. The sounds of birdsong, along with bird talk and argument—squawks and honks and shrieks—and the sound of water splashing in the fountains and ponds washed over the human voices.

Then she saw him.

At the cage holding the birds of prey, Blackwood stood, hands clasped behind his back, and riveted, apparently, upon one of the creatures within. The crowd of spectators at the cage, with their hats and umbrellas, had hidden him from her before.

But the crowd quickly thinned, as crowds tended to do when the tall, dark figure appeared among them, and a few whispers here and there alerted the ignorant to his identity.

She didn't need to be alerted. She felt her pulse quicken and her senses sharpen with anticipation.

Of what? Frustration?

She told herself to continue in the other direction, where Doveridge would politely continue with her, but she hesitated a heartbeat too long.

Blackwood turned and looked at them. He nodded and tipped his hat.

DOVERIDGE CURSED IN his mind, but on the outside, he was his usual urbane self. He had no valid reason to cut the Duke of Blackwood, he told himself.

Not that he wouldn't have given a great deal at this moment to possess one.

He'd spent time with Lady Alice. Not as much as he'd like, but as much as he could without putting her reputation in danger or placing himself in a compromising position before he was absolutely certain. As she clearly understood, intelligent young woman that she was, one's choice of spouse was no trivial matter.

And he'd lived a bachelor life for a very long time.

Still, he was sufficiently acquainted with her to notice the change in her now, as though the air about her had grown heavier somehow, and vibrated.

Invisible yet palpable. And undeniable.

He reminded himself that certain people possessed a personal magnetism to which others responded instinctively, on an animal level. Was that not the way he'd responded to her on that day in the bookshop?

Blackwood possessed something, certainly. It wasn't entirely Their Dis-Graces' notoriety that made people retreat, as though expecting an explosion.

Or an uninvited goat.

Remembering the goat, Doveridge recovered his good humor. He smiled and said, "Why, here is the Duke of Blackwood. I'd no idea he'd taken an interest in zoology."

"I wonder who let him in," Lady Alice said. "Then I ask myself, Who could keep him out?"

This was encouraging.

Not that Doveridge needed encouragement. He was, after all, a man of the world, a gentleman of two score and two, hardly one of the unseasoned young fellows who languished after Lady Alice and her circle. He was a courtier of long standing, an intimate of both the previous and the present King, not to mention the Tsar of Russia. He was a hardworking member of the House of Lords. He'd dealt with snakes and scorpions in human form since his minority.

He was not afraid of dangerous young men. He'd been one himself, once upon a time.

He returned Blackwood's acknowledgment. Then there was no choice, really. As a member of the Zoological Society, one must welcome His Dis-Grace to the zoo.

BLACKWOOD WAS AWARE of her before he saw her, in the way that one senses an approaching storm. Or, more prosaically, he'd probably noticed her out of the corner of his eye. She always did dress to be noticed. That was enough to break the spell the golden eagle held over him, and to make him turn away and look straight at her.

And there she was, the orchid amid domestic flora, fully encased up to her neck today in a walking dress of thick violet silk. The upper part appeared to continue below the belt, to create the effect of a shorter coat over the skirt. Her hat was the same color, of watered silk, with a gold moiré lining. The gold enhanced her green eyes. In the fitful sunlight, it seemed to create a halo about her face.

For a moment he saw his hands cupping her face while he bent his head toward the enigmatic smile. He remembered the feel of her mouth against his and the taste of her and the sensation of falling and drowning . . .

But he'd been a boy, nineteen, infatuated for the first time. The only time.

If he'd thrown away an opportunity—but he hadn't, really. He couldn't be the man she needed and deserved.

Doveridge is that man, Conscience said.

Blackwood shoved Conscience into the mental cavern.

"There you are," he said when the pair drew near. "Lady Alice." He bowed. "Duke." Another bow.

Which was returned with equal courtesy.

Doveridge, too, must have a volume of CORRECT BEHAVIOR stuck inside his brain forever.

"This is a most welcome surprise," Doveridge said. "You take an interest in zoology?"

"I'm partial to wild animals."

Doveridge smiled. "Then you'll be agreeably entertained, I trust."

Blackwood contemplated the agreeable entertainment of feeding the duke to the nearby vulture.

Which was childish. Doveridge wasn't Worbury but the oppo-

site. Furthermore, not being dead yet, the duke was unappetizing
to vultures.

Doveridge was a damned paragon. Only his political foes had
anything bad to say about him, and most of them were blockheads.

Alice had done the intelligent thing in captivating him. Not
that he was her only victim. A handful of puppies hovered—
though at a safe distance—gazing at her as though at Venus
rising from the waves. And while these half-fledged beaux could
hardly compete with a man of Doveridge's rank and stature, he
was, like them, a man. No person of sense could blame him for
being infatuated with her, and Society, according to Lynforde,
had no doubt the man had fallen into that condition.

And so, having no excuse to do otherwise, Blackwood said
what CORRECT BEHAVIOR required. "A fine collection—what
I've seen of it so far. I shall have to make a proper tour at another time. Today, however, I only came to have a word with
Lady Alice. I went to Sussex Place and was informed that she
and Lady Kempton were here."

He was aware of Alice all but visibly vibrating with something.
Anger, no doubt, at his turning up to interrupt her enslavement
of Methuselah.

"A message from Ripley," he said, and felt her anger or whatever it was change to something else. "A family matter. I only
want a moment."

BLACKWOOD LED HER a short distance away from the others.
They didn't need to go far. The vociferous birds and talkative
humans thwarted eavesdropping.

"I'm sorry to keep you from your lover," Blackwood said. "I
realize he hasn't much time, and we oughtn't to fritter it away.
I'll be brief."

Her green eyes narrowed. "A message from my brother, you said."

"In strict truth, Ripley's message was to me. But I knew you'd
want to be informed. First, to ease your mind: He isn't near
death or even damaged."

"Or wasn't when he wrote."

The late March morning scene played in his mind. He pushed it back into the mental cavern.

"Yes, let's be precise, shall we?" he said. "To the best of my knowledge, he's thriving. However, it seems I've got him into trouble with Lady Charles, and he's been summoned to Camberley Place for an inquisition."

She grasped her umbrella more tightly, preparatory, no doubt, to braining him. "Plague take you, Giles. You know you are not to upset my aunt."

"Do you suppose I did it on purpose?"

"I suppose you rarely think."

He wished he could stop thinking.

"Lady Charles ordered Ripley to keep out of London while you set about subjugating the male population," he said. "She was concerned that he might frighten away potential captives. But I couldn't put off my business in Town." That wasn't a lie, exactly. Worbury was urgent business, and Blackwood had arrived not a minute too soon.

"I assumed the injunction didn't apply to me," he went on. "An error of judgment."

Not his first. So many errors he couldn't undo. So many bridges burnt.

"You split hairs very fine," she said.

"Lady Charles seems to see it that way," he said. "Word reached her that I was here, and now your brother's in her black books, and I must go with him and take my punishment."

There it was, the spark of strong emotion in the green eyes. It came and went like a flash of lightning, yet he was sure he hadn't imagined it.

"I see." She stared at the vulture. It stared back.

Her gaze returned to Blackwood. "Thank you for informing me. I shall endure your absence as best I can."

She walked back to her ancient beau. She did not look back.

Chapter 11

Camberley Place
Afternoon of Sunday 6 May 1832

Lady Charles still wore mourning. She still mourned. The sadness lingered in her eyes, though it by no means dulled them. Her mind was as dagger-sharp as ever.

She did not interrupt once during Blackwood's explanation, though it was long and detailed. He felt she ought to know everything, or very nearly everything. He simply couldn't prevaricate with Ripley's aunt. She'd been an aunt to Blackwood as well. Like Ripley, he loved her dearly and respected her. Ashmont felt the same, he knew.

Moreover, she knew Alice better than he did, and couldn't possibly be surprised, let alone scandalized.

She sat listening, her elbow on the arm of the drawing room's scroll sofa. Her head rested on her hand.

No, *rested* wasn't a proper description. She held her index and middle fingers at her temple and her thumb at the angle of her jaw under her ear. He recognized the pose, and knew it was not a relaxed one. It was the look of one struggling for patience and, possibly, words.

Because she said nothing, Ripley kept still, though it was clear he was poised to jump up and hit somebody or break things. Blackwood had told him the full story when they met at the

Lovedon Arms last night. Today they'd traveled some thirty miles—this following Ripley's sixty-mile journey from Newmarket. Nonetheless, Ripley's anxiety about Alice and rage at his swine of a cousin hadn't quieted much.

Blackwood understood.

When his tale was done, what felt like a year's silence ensued before Lady Charles said, "Worbury is tiresome."

"We should have let him drown when we had the chance," Ripley said.

His aunt's eyebrows went up.

"Long time ago," Ripley said. "Not important."

They had never revealed the facts of the fishing house episode to anybody, even Ashmont.

"Florentia never dropped a hint of these matters in her letters," Lady Charles said. "She would not want to worry me, though she must have been worried to death. I grieve to think of what she's endured. But she's had charge of Alice these last few years, time enough to develop a degree of resilience. All the same, I do not understand why other girls can go on the Marriage Mart without becoming involved with murderous gang leaders."

"To be fair, that encounter could not be avoided," Blackwood said. "Alice only wanted to keep the foul little boy out of Worbury's clutches. Perhaps you believe I ought to have put my foot down."

"Refused to help my sister?" Ripley said. "As though you could stop her, short of locking her in a cage. And good luck trying that. Aunt, you remember what would happen whenever she was confined to quarters. It was a matter of pride and principle for her to break out, even if it meant breaking her neck. One doesn't stop Alice. Can't be done, short of violence. Even then it's a tetchy business. All we can do is try to contain the damage."

"I'd believed the warrior business was a phase she'd outgrow," Lady Charles said. "Clearly there was more to it than children playing Let's Pretend."

"There's more to it," Blackwood said. "That's who Alice is."

One could blame the company she kept: Keeffe. Miss Pomfret. But they only supported her in what she believed in, didn't they?

Blackwood found himself wishing he'd been the one supporting her. All these years, and what had he accomplished, compared to her?

Well, then, how was he to have known that when he was seventeen years old? Or nineteen. Or twenty-one. Or a month ago?

He became aware of Lady Charles's penetrating gaze. Her eyes were hazel, changeable, but always keen. Even in sorrow, her formidable mind seemed to catch the smallest clues.

"Her life would be easier if that were not the case," she said. She smiled faintly. "Finding a spouse would be easier, I daresay. Most gentlemen would prefer their wives perform heroic acts without calling attention to themselves or inconveniencing their husbands."

"I'll wish them good luck in achieving that dream," Ripley muttered.

"Given the circumstances, I don't see what else she could have done," Blackwood said. "She was deeply distressed about the boy. I cannot say why. He's one of the most unpromising specimens I've ever had the misfortune to come within smelling range of. All the same, even I couldn't relish the prospect of his falling into Worbury's hands."

Lady Charles closed her eyes. "Please tell me she isn't making plans to teach him a lesson."

"Whatever for?" Ripley said. "She knows Blackwood took care of it, as he described. Very neatly done it was, too."

The lady's eyes opened and her gaze fixed, like a bayonet, on Blackwood.

"I saw the note in *Foxe's Morning Spectacle* about the mob in Golden Square on Thursday morning," she said. "A Reform Bill demonstration, they claimed."

"What could be neater than that?" Ripley said. "Everybody

else thinks it's politics, and the Worm thinks he's come up against a crime lord! Ha-ha!"

"He has, actually," Blackwood said. "If he'd gone after one of Madam Proudie's senior boys, rather than a recent acquisition, I believe Worbury would regret it very much."

"I should rather my niece not become involved with felons, Giles."

Too late, he thought.

"We'd all like that," he said. "Still, her charity isn't merely for show, and one can't deny her courage. I wonder how many other members of the upper orders would risk their lives for a street child."

"In which case I must be glad you were on the spot," she said.

Blackwood did not swoon with relief, but he felt it wash through him, a slight cooling and quieting of the inner turmoil.

"What could've been better?" Ripley said. "Blackwood's the one of us three with finesse, and this proves it. No scandal. No lovers running away in terror on account of him, either. Nobody who signifies, at any rate."

"Indeed, you or even the three of you at once are unlikely to frighten away a man like Doveridge," Lady Charles said. "To him you are mere striplings—ill-behaved ones, to be sure, but little more than naughty boys to a man like him."

"Ouch," Ripley said. "I knew Auntie would bare her talons sooner or later, didn't you, Blackwood?"

Whether he'd expected the jab or not, Blackwood felt it.

"Sad to say, your revered aunt speaks no more than the simple truth," he said. "Unlike nearly everybody else, Doveridge failed to turn pale at the sight of me. Instead of slinking away, he advanced in the most amiable manner and welcomed me."

Alice had not, but she wouldn't. She couldn't wait to be rid of him.

They'd been partners in crime briefly, but what did that signify? He'd helped her retrieve the boy. He'd helped her in the past. That didn't make him her hero. If, on occasion, she found his general worthlessness and bad behavior useful, that didn't mean she forgave him or had stopped hating him.

He'd hurt her badly—once, most certainly. Very likely he'd hurt her on other occasions without realizing.

He knew he'd hurt her a few weeks ago.

He couldn't blame Ashmont. Blackwood had been as drunk as the other two. He'd participated. Then, angry with himself, he'd slunk away in shame. Promptly thereafter he'd done the usual to stifle those disagreeable feelings.

They'd left Camberley Place, and then . . .

For a moment the drawing room seemed to dissolve into a hazy landscape while thoughts raced through his mind like wind-driven clouds.

And then . . .

Alice had gone to London.

And then . . .

Instead of returning to the Continent and her best friend, she'd gone on the Marriage Mart.

I set a date a month ago, she'd said on that day at Hyde Park Corner.

A month would make it the thirtieth of March.

He looked at Ripley, who might have died that day, who might even now be sealed away in the family vault at Castle Ancaster, or here at Camberley Place, next to the uncle he'd loved.

With her brother dead, Alice would find herself at Worbury's mercy. Then, no matter what the law said, no matter what Ripley's will said, Worbury would find a way to make her life a purgatory. He'd dispute every last legal detail and do everything else his filthy mind could devise to punish her and everyone who tried to help her.

He was a reckless profligate who'd destroy the dukedom, in any event. He'd complete the ruination her father had begun and Ripley had spent years repairing.

That was why.

That was why she was ready to throw herself away on a man who didn't know her and would have no idea how to deal with her. Worbury wouldn't dare to tackle Doveridge. The duke would crush him like the worm he was.

My fault, Blackwood thought. *This is all my fault.*

THE TWO DUKES departed Camberley Place on the following day, leaving Lady Charles to the melancholy that nobody and nothing could assuage, except, perhaps, time. At least she'd forgiven Blackwood and understood why he needed to remain in London until Worbury left it.

"Remain *discreetly*, if you please," she'd said.

The hard part was persuading Ripley not to hang about in Kensington, waiting for word or plotting his cousin's demise. Patience wasn't Ripley's greatest skill, and while not as volatile and unpredictable as Ashmont, he could be single-minded and heedless when Something Was Wrong.

Not altogether unlike his sister.

Blackwood sent a message to Lynforde, inviting him to join them for dinner at the Lovedon Arms. The earl was a calming influence. Equally important, since he always knew the latest gossip, he'd be among the first to learn of Worbury's doings.

When they reached the inn, they found Lynforde awaiting them. They adjourned to Ripley's rooms, and dinner was sent up. Once the food was served, Ripley dismissed his valet, Snow, to give the gentlemen complete privacy. His servants were discreet and trustworthy. All the same, he'd rather they didn't overhear certain conversations.

"Can you credit it?" he said to Lynforde as they began dissecting their chops. "Going after a child, to spite my sister, merely because she protected the brat. And he a street child, no less, ignorant and ragged and half-starved. Somebody needs to teach my cousin to pick on somebody up to his weight."

"If you try to teach him, he'll only nurse a grudge, and go after another unfortunate, to get even," Blackwood said. "Let the demonstration and Maggie's message do the work."

"It seems that's been accomplished," Lynforde said. "Worbury told Lady Bartham that he intends to visit an invalid aunt in Bath. He and Consett mean to set out on Tuesday or Wednesday. In the meantime, he's playing least in sight."

"I should rather he set out for the Outer Hebrides," Ripley said. "Excellent chance he'll drown en route. Will somebody please explain to me why I can't kill him?"

"We're not to make scandal, remember?" Blackwood said. "Killing your heir is Not Done." The rule was bound to be somewhere in CORRECT BEHAVIOR.

"There'll be a scandal only if I get caught," Ripley said.

"You've never killed a man in your life," Blackwood said. "You're sure to bollix it up."

"Leave it to Blackwood," Lynforde said. "He's already frightened the fellow out of his wits without uttering a word to him."

"Right," Ripley said. "Finesse." He raised his tankard. The Lovedon Arms was known for its ale. "Here's to the finesse of my friend and brother by bonds thicker than blood, and whom I've missed, actually. Let's have another toast, then, to Blackwood's rejoining his brothers at Newmarket in the very near future."

Tuesday or Wednesday, Blackwood thought. *So soon.*

More toasts were drunk as the evening wore on.

But it wasn't the usual drunken debauch, lasting into the small hours. Ripley had a long journey ahead of him tomorrow, and Blackwood wanted to be in London in case Worbury devised any parting atrocities. They left Ripley soon after dinner.

"I thank you for coming on short notice," Blackwood said as he and Lynforde rode back to Town. "As I'd hoped, his mood improved markedly when you turned up."

"He was right to be furious," Lynforde said. "I fear we didn't beat Worbury often enough and hard enough when we were at school. Now I'm reluctant to dirty my hands."

"One of these days he'll annoy the wrong person," Blackwood said. "Somebody free of our delicate sensibilities and exquisite principles. For now, I only want him far from London."

"Then you can rejoin your friends."

Blackwood glanced about him. They were approaching the King's Arms. Here the granite paving stones ended, as did the inns and taverns that clustered along this portion of the road. They'd meet another cluster as they neared Hyde Park Corner . . . where it had all started.

The episode with Alice and the pickpockets played in his mind. He could hardly believe it had happened only a week ago.

He drew his attention back to the present and said, "Once Worbury's gone, there's no compelling reason for me to remain—although I'll miss your company. Why don't you come with me?"

Lynforde laughed. "I grow old. I haven't the stamina."

"You're not thirty."

"Perilously close, my friend. Another few weeks only. And truly, I no longer have the wherewithal to keep up with you three."

He no longer had the desire, more likely. Blackwood had caught hints here and there that, after some five years of widowhood, Lynforde, too, was beginning to contemplate marriage.

A lot of that going about. Alice. Doveridge, the confirmed bachelor. Lynforde, the longtime widower.

Too bad. Blackwood had enjoyed spending time again with Lynforde. He was good company and not demanding. One needn't always remain braced for battle to erupt or be prepared to deal with whatever uproar had to be dealt with.

Blackwood had hoped—well, what?

Whatever it was, he'd think about it another time, or never.

"Then we'll make the most of what time remains to me in London," he said.

"Can you endure an hour or two of nearly pure idleness?" Lynforde said. "The Society of Painters in Watercolors has mounted a new exhibition. I'd planned to attend tomorrow."

"Do nothing but look at pictures?" Blackwood said.

"I'm afraid so."

"No children likely to be kidnapped? No criminal acts on offer? No crises?"

"Unlikely, I'd say. One or two persons demonstrating their ignorance in loud voices is about as much excitement as we can expect."

"Sounds perfect," Blackwood said.

Blackwood House
Tuesday 8 May 1832

THE MIDDAY VISIT to the exhibition passed peacefully.

Blackwood's arrival home did not.

He entered his house to find his butler in a high state of emotion.

This was unheard-of.

Dawson was never agitated. His normal self was wooden.

The butler had Views, and in his View, servants were to keep Feelings to themselves, reserving them for their leisure time, which, by the way, they ought not to have too much of, because it put Ideas into their heads. It was not a servant's business to have Ideas. They encouraged Feelings.

At present Feelings seemed to have overcome him. His face was red. His usual stately manner had deserted him. Speech burst out of him in rushes, not altogether coherently.

"Snow was here?" Blackwood repeated, unsure he'd heard correctly.

"He left not half an hour ago, and I assure Your Grace that I did my best to detain him. It was of no avail. He was in a shocking state of nervous upset. He *would* go to Lady Kempton, though I endeavored to explain that this was highly inadvisable. Whatever the trouble was—and I must apologize, Your Grace, because it was exceedingly difficult to make heads or tails of his speech, so agitated he was."

Gone to Lady Kempton.

This wasn't good news, in a hundred ways.

Blackwood bit back some extremely bad words. "I take

your meaning," he said. "But the main points, Dawson, if you please."

With visible effort, the butler composed himself. "As I understand it, Your Grace, the crucial point is that Snow has lost his master."

At first Blackwood thought that Ripley had dismissed Snow. But that was impossible. Snow was a paragon among valets. Ripley was no more likely to part with him than to dismiss his brilliant French chef, Chardot.

Then light dawned. "Do you mean Snow can't find him?"

"That seemed to be the gist of it, Your Grace."

"And now he's gone to Lady Kempton."

"I remonstrated with him, Your Grace. I told him he ought to know better. 'Their Graces will have their little jokes,' I told him. To no avail."

Unlike Ashmont's valet, Sommers—who cried at the drop of a hat or a handkerchief and sobbed over fluff on a coat sleeve—Ripley's man was a steely fellow, as unlikely a candidate for hysteria as Blackwood's valet, Springate.

Blackwood thought quickly, something he was accustomed to do, given his friends' propensities for sudden starts and whims, not to mention accidents. "Thank you, Dawson. I shall want the mail phaeton as soon as may be."

Ripley might be perfectly well. He might be the opposite. In the latter case, one needed a larger vehicle than the cabriolet. In the mail phaeton, one might safely though not very comfortably stow incapacitated persons. Dead drunk persons. Post-melee persons.

"I took the liberty of ordering it, Your Grace. In the circumstances, and expecting you momentarily, as I tried to tell Mr. Snow."

It wouldn't be the first time Blackwood had needed to retrieve one of his friends. His servants were old hands.

After taking a few minutes to make suitable changes to his attire, Blackwood went out again. He found his carriage drawn up at the door, his powerful matched bays, Circe and Sappho, in harness. In lieu of a footman, a more useful though less decorative groom by name of Pratt accompanied the duke's tiger, Elphick.

Dawson had thought of everything, as he was exceedingly well paid to do.

That was the easy part.

Chapter 12

Sussex Place

"A hackney, Alice?" Aunt Florentia cried. "Have you taken leave of your senses? You cannot simply—"

"Somebody must go."

"But where?"

Alice was not at all sure where to begin, but begin she must. "Kensington, it seems. Blackwood will know, but where is he? Not here when needed. Out all night, no doubt, and recovering from the wretched excesses in a brothel or opium den."

"My dear, there is bound to be a reasonable explanation. Or an unreasonable one. That is more likely. But regardless of the reason, it is quite, quite mad to suppose you can find Ripley—on your own, no less. For all you know, it's meant to be one of their jokes."

"Snow was beside himself!"

They'd sent him down to the servants' hall for tea or brandy or whatever the senior servants deemed necessary to settle his nerves.

"Ripley failed to enlighten him, that is all," Aunt Florentia said. "You know those three do not always consider others. They act first and compensate afterward. You have no idea where your brother has gone or why. If he's done it for a prank, you'll have made a spectacle of yourself for nothing. You cannot afford a scandal—and that is the least of the dangers. Heaven only knows what sorts of people you'll encounter. I do wish you'd take a moment to think in a rational manner."

Alice drew on her gloves. "Somebody must do something. I cannot sit here stabbing a needle into linen when my brother may be in danger. I cannot."

Had she been certain Worbury was well away in Bath, she would worry, but not nearly as much.

If only Keeffe were here. And Cassandra. But they weren't. Neither was Blackwood. Thomas would have to suffice as protection. At least he was large.

"But we are promised to dine at Doveridge House," her aunt said.

Doubt twinged. Was this madness, after all? Making mountains of molehills? Impossible to know, and one couldn't take the chance.

"I can't promise to be back in time," she said. "I'm truly sorry to disappoint the duke, but it can't be helped. Make my excuses, but you are not to deceive him. He deserves the truth."

If this sort of thing turned his mind against marrying her, it was better to know that now.

She hurried out of her aunt's sitting room, down the stairs, and into the vestibule. She heard footsteps behind her: Thomas in hot pursuit, as required. Another footman standing at the door hastily opened it. She hurried through—and ran straight into Blackwood.

The impact might have thrown another man back, down the steps and onto the pavement. He staggered slightly, then grasped her arms, his big hands crushing her sleeves. He set her firmly on her feet inside, and let her go.

She stepped back a pace, aware of the ghost of warmth and pressure on her arms, aware of the size of his gloved hands. For a moment she forgot what she was about. But in the blink of an eye she came to herself, and fear and rage crashed against surging relief.

Blackwood closed the door behind him.

"I knew this would happen," he said. "I thank my lucky stars for Dawson. Another minute and you'd be charging away in your chariot like Boadicea, leaving me in desperate pursuit."

"Where have you been?" she cried. "You're never there when one wants you."

He waved away the hovering footmen. They went away, Thomas weeping tears of relief, she didn't doubt.

"Shall I follow you about like your devoted footman, watching for the next cataclysm?" Blackwood said in a low voice. "Thank you, but I have enough of that with my friends."

He was so infuriatingly calm, she wanted to choke him.

A part of her knew she was being unfair, but anxiety fought with reason.

For Snow, of all people, to come here in a panic because Ripley had disappeared? Unheard-of, even in Ripley's life of extremes. And for this to happen when Worbury was reported to have left London—in the dead of night, no doubt, headed supposedly to Bath, which would mean traveling the same road where Ripley lodged? A coincidence? Not likely.

"You were with him," she said. "Last night. Snow said so."

"I was. And left him in perfect health and cheerful spirits."

"Drunk, you mean."

"No, he planned an early bedtime in order to make an early start today."

"He never went to bed, according to Snow."

"Then he found a girl," Blackwood said.

"She was the bait. For an ambush. I knew it."

"That I very much doubt. Alice, you've let Snow's panic affect you. If you would take but a moment to reflect—"

"I've taken moments! I've been waiting this age! Aunt said there was an explanation, but nobody seems to have one. Snow was altogether in the dark. And when he went to your house, hoping you'd enlighten him, you weren't there."

"Lynforde and I decided to view an exhibition of watercolors.

If Snow had waited not half an hour, as my butler tried to persuade him to do—"

"If he'd done so, you wouldn't have told me."

"Not until I was certain we had reason to be anxious."

She wanted to scream. She clenched her hands instead. "Is
Snow not reason enough? He owns nerves of iron. Otherwise
he couldn't have survived two days in my brother's employ, let
alone nearly a decade. He knows him. He wouldn't panic if he
hadn't a good reason. He said that after you left, Ripley was too
restless to go to bed. He went down to the taproom. Snow fell
asleep waiting for him. This morning he learnt that Ripley had
ordered his horse last night. He rode out. And that was the last
anybody knew of him."

Finally she perceived a faint crack in Blackwood's calm demeanor. "He took his horse?"

"Yes. Do you see now? Why should he take Lucetta out at all
hours, when he planned to ride to Newmarket this morning?
Would he not want her fully rested for the journey?"

Silence fell, rather in the manner of a roof collapse.

IN SPITE OF Snow's out-of-character panic, Blackwood had
told himself that this was no more than the usual thing. Among
Their Dis-Graces, unexplained disappearances were nothing
new. Most often they involved women.

"I was not in possession of details," he said. "Snow was not
as coherent as he might have been when he spoke to Dawson."

"If we might start out now," she said, "I'll be happy to supply
such details as Snow conveyed."

"*We* are not starting out. I shall do the searching. Having
you along will only complicate matters. You'll remain here
quietly—or unquietly, as you choose—with your aunt, and let
me find your brother. I always do."

"No."

"Alice."

"You will not leave me behind to go mad with worry."

Lady Kempton burst into the vestibule, huffing a little. "Blackwood, thank heaven you are here. You must make her see reason."

"What I see is time passing," Alice said. "My brother is in trouble, and we stand here, talking."

The scene flashed in Blackwood's mind again, of the morning at Camberley Place.

Ripley infuriated her, but she loved him dearly.

He remembered the letters she'd written so faithfully to her brother nearly every day, though Ripley was not so faithful in answering. That was how Blackwood had first discovered Alice, months before he met her: through the letters her brother shared with his friends—because they were brothers *by bonds thicker than blood.*

If he were in her place, how would he feel to be left behind?

"Alice had better come as well," Blackwood said. "She'll search for him, with or without me, Lady Kempton, no matter what we say or do. Better with me."

He turned back to Alice. She was dressed more simply than usual, in a fawn-colored walking dress, and carrying a plain green umbrella. She still looked expensive.

He gestured. "The hat. Send for something unexciting. Let's try to attract as little attention as possible. While you do that, I'll speak to Snow."

THE INTERROGATION OF Snow added virtually nothing to what Blackwood and Alice already knew.

"He was calmer and coherent, but it was simply the same story in more intelligible form," Blackwood told Alice as he turned the carriage into Baker Street. "I don't doubt we'll make sense of it by the time we reach the scene of the crime that didn't happen."

"You don't know that it didn't happen."

"Experience tells me that what happened was a woman," Blackwood said. "Ripley met up with her and changed his plans. Easy enough. He wasn't urgently needed at Newmarket. He'd intended to set out early, but a pretty girl made him set aside his intentions."

"If that's the case, I'll slap him until he cries," she said. "I'm so tired of worrying about him. I wish I could stop. It does no good. It changes nothing. You'd think I'd have learnt by now."

Blackwood glanced at her. She'd exchanged the exciting hat for a more subdued one of deep violet silk. Ruffles framed her face, and a ribbon wrapped about the crown, but no sprigs or flowers sprouted from the thing. The deep brim cast her face in shadow. He hoped it offered concealment enough, and he cursed Society for making concealment necessary.

She ought to be able to search for her brother without worrying about causing scandal and ruining her marital chances. It was all so ridiculous.

But one couldn't change the world they lived in. Men could escape it without much trouble. A woman who escaped lost everything.

He'd simply have to keep her as safe as he could, including safe from scrutiny. With the vehicle's hood up, onlookers would have to crane their necks and peer inside to recognize her. He didn't intend to give anybody the opportunity.

All the same, if he didn't smuggle her back to Sussex Place by nightfall, her reputation would be in tatters.

He silently cursed Ripley for disappearing. In answer, his mind busily painted pictures of the worst possible outcome: Ripley set upon by an armed gang of ruffians . . . Ripley lying in a ditch . . . Ripley under an overturned carriage.

"I'll hold him while you slap," he said. "He's ruined my day. I'd planned a peacefully amusing few hours before dinner. Lynforde and I were to visit Crockford's new bazaar in St. James's Street. You might enjoy it. Pickpockets abound. I saw something in the paper about a fellow caught in the act and sentenced to hard labor. One of your friends?"

"I saw that, and no, my friends, as you call them, are more highly skilled than that sad excuse for a thief. The report said one of the bazaar's officers as well as the inspectress watched Mr. Williams make several attempts. He's been caught before, more than once. He ought to take up a profession better suited to his limited abilities."

"I hear the voice of Keeffe."

"You hear correctly. If you plan to commit a crime, be sure you can do it competently."

"Madam Proudie's boys do it well enough, judging by what I was able to observe at Hyde Park Corner," he said.

"They were splendidly trained," she said. "If Keeffe hadn't taught me how they work and what to watch for, I shouldn't have realized what they were about. I was amazed that Worbury noticed. Talk of light fingers!"

"And you wish Maggie would teach the boys instead to read and write and aspire to a career less likely to end in Newgate Prison."

A pause. Then she turned in the seat to look at him. "I do wish it, yes. Great Juno, the demonstration she organized for you in Golden Square! That is a formidable woman. Imagine what she could do if she applied her talents to philanthropy."

"Crime is more profitable." He was aware of her knee touching his, and of the rustle of heavy silk when she moved, and of the pull of longing. Too bad. He would simply have to endure it. He needed to make amends. If this was punishment, he'd earned it.

"I envy her power, Giles."

The words jarred him from his descent into self-pity.

"Maggie lives her life in the shadow of the gallows," he said. "It isn't romantic."

"Who said it was? You can't understand. You're a man and a nobleman. You do exactly as you please."

"Not *exactly*." She had no idea, and it was better that way.

"Indeed, my heart breaks with pity," she said. "A few rules about honor—pay your gambling debts, though not necessarily your tailor and other tradesmen."

Before he could contradict, she waved a gloved hand. "Yes, I know you three pay everybody because it keeps life running smoothly for you. It encourages service and loyalty. It keeps people quiet and happy. What other ghastly strictures do you labor under? Oh, yes, the onerous rule about viewing gently bred maidens as the Black Death. Because otherwise you might find yourself entangled and—heaven forfend!—inconveniently married . . . although it's likely you could wiggle out of the difficulty if you throw money enough at it. But why take the chance, when there are so many willing women in the world?"

"Now I know what this day lacked," he said. "A lecture."

"I should lecture a brick with equal result," she said. "I simply point out how oblivious you are to your circumstances, how easy it is for you to do what you do. Really, how many rules can't you break? How many broken ones can't be mended with money or influence?"

"Meanwhile, Maggie Proudie breaks all sorts of rules yet commands legions of not merely boys but desperate and dangerous men," he said. "I see, Alice. It took a while—I'm rather thick, as you know—but I do see. If it's any comfort to you, I believe you would have made a superior criminal overlord, if only Keeffe could have supervised your education from the beginning."

The laugh broke from her like ice breaking, and he could feel the thaw set in. She turned away, yet out of the corner of his eye he caught the lingering hint of her smile as she faced straight ahead.

He wished he could take that smile full-on, in the way one lifted one's face to the sun. He wished . . . oh, when she looked at him . . . he wanted to look back, and look forever, as though he could never get enough of her, of simply drinking her in.

But looking could never be enough, and wishing was worse than pointless. Wishing was a reminder of lost chances.

Not to mention he'd nobody to blame but himself for being here, sitting beside her, looking and wishing, like a besotted schoolboy.

Still, it was Ripley's fault, too, for not staying put and doing what he said he'd do, and when they found him, Blackwood was going to slap him until he cried.

Then they'd both get very, very drunk. And break rules. Because that was so much fun, wasn't it?

SHE HAD BEEN wishing precisely what Blackwood said—that Maggie would teach the boys reading and writing instead of pocket-picking—and it made Alice wild that he could do this so easily at times. It might be simple coincidence. It might be a clever guess. But it might be something he did more easily and often than she realized. She might find him inscrutable at times, but she, apparently, was transparent to him. He could find a way under her guard and make her laugh even when she wanted to throttle him.

She had thought, once upon a time, that they were allies, even kindred spirits. Rules had caged him, very much as they'd caged her. But he'd broken free of the rules because he was a man and a duke. She, a duke's daughter, could never break free without losing the little power she had.

Money was power. Position was power. But a woman's money and position stood on the shakiest ground, because they depended on a man. So the world commanded.

The Great World. Good Society. The beau monde.

Her world now.

If that world found out what she was about at this moment and who she was with, she could lose everything she'd spent the last month struggling to achieve. She'd worked so hard to be respectable. To keep all radical thoughts and opinions to herself. To say and do nothing to set gossip mills grinding.

Men didn't want wives who caused talk. Society ostracized women who were too outspoken—or at all outspoken.

Only look at what had happened to Cassandra last year. She'd had to go abroad again, because she'd embarrassed her family. True, she'd set off a riot, but that was because she was a woman who'd contradicted a man in public.

Women were supposed to keep out of it, whatever it was.

Not this woman, Alice told herself. Maybe Blackwood could find her brother without her help. But she and he could do it more efficiently together—the way they'd rescued Jonesy.

She sat quietly now, to let him keep his mind on driving, preferably at breakneck speed. She had plenty of time to think second thoughts, if she needed to.

Once they'd turned into Oxford Street, Blackwood urged the horse to greater speed. He was a prime whip, because he was perfect at everything. That was how he'd been trained, he'd told her long ago. All the same, even he needed to pay full attention in order to make his way as swiftly as possible around slow or stalled vehicles while also dodging two- and four-footed wanderers. After that they had a short distance to the next turn, at Park Lane.

They soon reached Piccadilly and entered the chaos of Hyde Park Corner. They endured only a brief slowing, though, before they broke out of it into Knightsbridge. The way was busy but not so crowded now as it would be at night when the Royal Mail coaches set out, all at the same time, with stage and post coaches joining the procession.

They passed a series of inns and taverns and the Horse Barracks, where the granite paving stones ended. They sped past the Halfway House and the One-Mile Stone.

Having traveled this way from time to time on the journey to Camberley Place, she knew that many fine houses stood behind the walls, trees, and shrubberies bordering the southern side of the road. Otherwise what she observed was foreign territory. She was still relearning London and its environs after her time abroad.

They sped through Kensington Gore, came to a stop to pay at the tollgate, then continued to the Kensington High Street. Though it felt to her as though they crept along, the swiftly passing landscape told the opposite story.

"Another time I'll point out the sights," he said. "Such as

they are. But we've not far to go. The inn stands on the corner of the road to one of the Earl of Lovedon's country places, Castle de Grey."

She looked about her, and her spirits sank. Buildings clustered along the road. Beyond them, however, was not a bustling town. "It's a great deal of countryside. I've been this way time and again, but never considered what I was seeing."

"Some dozens of inns and taverns and shops huddle along the Uxbridge Road, as you'd expect," he said. "North and south of it lie a number of fine estates. More and more areas are being built upon all the time. Still, the place is mainly rural. Fields and gardens. Acres of farmland. A great deal of productive countryside. It also holds substantial stretches of wasteland where one finds potteries, piggeries, and brickmakers."

"Ripley could be anywhere," she said. "Talk of a needle in a haystack."

"Good thing we've had recent practice with that sort of thing," he said. "This time we've a few advantages. Not so many people. No venturing into London's rookeries. Equally important, a man like Ripley attracts more notice than a street child does. For all we know, we'll find him at the inn, all amazed at the fuss we've made."

"If we find him at the inn, you will help me drag him to the nearest horse trough and hold his head under water until he gurgles for mercy."

"Agreed. But first things first. We've raced here with no plan. To begin with, you can't be you, and I can't be anybody but me."

"*You* may have no plan," she said. "I made one before I left Sussex Place, and dressed for the occasion. I thought carefully about everything, including the hat you insisted I change. But I couldn't bear to waste time arguing with you."

"Since when?" he said.

Chapter 13

The Lovedon Arms
A short time later

Mrs. Jagg, the innkeeper, hurried into the parlor with tea. A maidservant bearing a plate of cakes followed her.

"*Mais, c'est impossible!*" Alice cried.

"Pray calm yourself, Madame," Blackwood said. "We'll get to the bottom of this."

"But how does this happen? How does *un duc* vanish—pfft! Like this!" She waved a hand. "Into the air."

She was a French actress, having adopted for the occasion Madame Girard's Parisian accent—exaggerated for effect, she said. She was the *très chère amie* of *le duc de Reeplee*, who had appointed to meet her last night after her performance and failed to appear.

Blackwood had never been to Paris, and he wasn't sure how well Alice mimicked Madame Girard in particular, but the accent matched those of certain Parisian women he'd met. Her manner, meanwhile, was so wonderfully *French* that he could scarcely maintain his composure. Nearly as difficult was keeping his mind on what they were doing.

"I wish I could tell you more, Madame, Your Grace," Mrs. Jagg said as she arranged teapot and accoutrements upon the table. "We've been asking about His Grace all day, ever since his man came to us in a dreadful state. But you know, His Grace had a trifle to drink last night, and he said he wanted air. And that was the last I saw of him. We asked in the stables, as you may know, and it's true he took his horse out."

She frowned over a spoon before setting it down.

Blackwood sensed hesitation. "Mrs. Jagg, if you've any ideas, hints, suspicions, we should be grateful."

"Why should you be so quiet? Is this because *Monsieur le duc* has another *chère amie?*" Alice waved her hand. "Bah! What is this to me? A great surprise? I supposed him to be a monk, do you think? Do I look to you like the fool?"

"Pray recall that Madame is French," Blackwood told the innkeeper. "A Parisian, furthermore."

Following another short hesitation and after sending the maid out of the parlor, a red-faced Mrs. Jagg admitted that the Duke of Ripley knew a handsome young woman originally from the neighborhood. It was possible he'd gone to visit her.

"I see," Blackwood said. "And, as was his custom, he distributed certain monetary gifts to keep his doings quiet."

"Since when is my brother so secretive?" Alice said to him in rapid French.

"He might have been uncertain whether the young woman has acquired a beau or a husband recently, and he didn't want to make trouble for her and complications for himself," Blackwood said in the same language.

To the innkeeper, in English, he said, "Where, exactly, might one find this young woman at present?"

SOMETIME LATER, ALICE sat at a table by a tavern window while Blackwood charmed the proprietress of the Two Swans, no onerous task, she supposed. One must admit that her brother had fine taste in women.

Margery Ronse was a curvaceous young widow, blessed with

a cloud of red-gold hair and deeply blue eyes. About Alice's age, or not much older, she kept a clean, well-run tavern in Kensington Gravel Pits, a village on the Uxbridge Road.

Unfortunately, Mrs. Ronse was as baffled as they. The duke, she said, had left the premises at eleven o'clock last night, when she closed the tavern. Here, too, he'd had "a trifle to drink." She appealed to her customers for information.

Some private discussion followed before one old fellow said, "If he were goin' back to London, he took the wrong way. Maybe got east mixed up with west."

"Well, he were bung-eyed, weren't he?" said another. "Drunk as a lord. Meanin' drunk as a duke. Ha-ha."

This witticism mightily amused the other patrons.

"It were dark as your pocket last night," another volunteered. "What odds he lost his way?"

"He's a duke! He went to Castle de Grey and slept on a feather bed. Him and Lord Lovedon being cousins."

"No, they ain't."

"All them nobs is cousins."

After a few minutes of these exchanges, Blackwood rejoined Alice. "This sort of discussion might go on for hours and still result in nothing useful," he said in an undertone. "I recommend we move on."

Alice shook her head. "That one," she said. "By himself in the corner."

Blackwood looked toward the lone youth scowling into his tankard. "He's a boy."

"I've been watching his expression while the others talk. He seems to have something bothersome on his mind." Alice rose. "I think he's shy to speak in front of the other men. Find a pretext to get him outside. I want to know what's troubling him."

BLACKWOOD'S PRETEXT WAS a coin, surreptitiously conveyed, and a murmured suggestion.

Then he took Alice outside to the carriage.

They waited, but not for long.

After about five minutes, the young man emerged from the tavern.

"You there, lad," Blackwood said. "What's the shortest way to Castle de Grey?"

The youth approached the carriage. His name was Sam Pryke. He didn't know what had become of the missing duke, he said, but the tavern talk made him think about what he'd heard today.

"This morning," he said. "At the blacksmith. I went to fetch the tools he mended for my father. I caught some talk but I wasn't listening so close. They was talking about a fine horse, fitted out like for a king and on its own. Somebody said, 'Did he catch it?' and somebody else said it took a while, her being skittish. But she was tired, and they got her."

He didn't know who, precisely, had captured the animal, but he knew the men who'd been talking about it, and gave their names.

"Only they didn't steal her," he said, clearly anxious. "I didn't want to say nothing in there." He jerked his chin toward the tavern. "Sound like I was blabbing on fellows. And there's more than one in there, you got to be careful what you say if you don't want a fight. But the men talking about the horse, they were farmers. The mare was running loose, and one of them caught her, same as he'd do with any stray, especially a fine one. They wouldn't want to risk her coming to harm. There's bad places thereabouts. The clay, you know. All the digging, they make holes the rain fills up. Big as lakes, some of them."

He provided the men's names and where to find them, and went on his way, enriched with an additional coin.

Alice looked at Blackwood. "Lucetta was running loose."

"If Ripley was as drunk as they say, he failed to tether her securely. Lucetta has a mischievous streak. She might have run off while he was answering Nature's call."

"Or being sick into the bushes," she said. She closed her eyes briefly and opened them. "When I get my hands on my brother, I shall throw him to the pigs."

"I'll help."

NEARLY TWO HOURS later, they found Lucetta.

"We looked everywhere for her master," Jonas Hodge said. "She'd wandered into Porto Bello Lane, and we thought he couldn't be far away. Fine animal like that, we thought she'd come from one of the big houses. We sent word, but nobody's come for her."

The mare was uninjured. The farmers had taken good care of her. She recognized Blackwood, a generous giver of treats, and nickered at him. He didn't disappoint her. Alice caught one of Blackwood's rare smiles when he petted the horse and gave her a carrot.

Always prepared, Blackwood was, to bribe man or animal. But she supposed he'd been taught that way. His father was strict about such things, she knew. He'd have rules for the proper way to treat horses and dogs.

Not a bad man, Ripley had said of Blackwood's father, *but rather exacting and suffocating. Still, at least one knows what to expect.*

One couldn't say the same of their own bewildering sire, with his fits of rage and fits of penny-pinching and fits of remorse and a dozen other species of tantrum. Day to day, sometimes hour to hour, one never knew which father would be there.

Alice shook off the past and focused on *now*.

The once-suffocated son's dark eyes were as readable as onyx at present, but as Blackwood turned away from Lucetta, Alice discerned the tightness about his mouth. He was more worried than he let on.

Like her, he'd be imagining a hundred scenes, none of them pleasant. She couldn't let herself think that way. It would cloud her reason.

"I'm told she gave you more than a little difficulty," Blackwood was saying.

The men grinned.

"That she did," one said. "She's a lively girl. But we couldn't let her run loose. There's too many places where she could get hurt. You want to be careful once you leave the main road, Your Grace."

"The Duke of Ripley will be grateful," Blackwood said. "On his behalf, I hope you'll allow me to make you a small gift."

Coins changed hands, and he arranged for them to return Lucetta to the Lovedon Arms stables. There was further murmured conversation. Alice didn't try to eavesdrop.

They'd stopped several times in recent hours and interrogated dozens of people. They took turns, depending on the circumstances. This was his turn.

She moved away, back to the carriage, and let Elphick hand her up. Her distress must have shown, because he spoke.

"We'll find His Grace, my lady. We've lost one or other of 'em before—mostly His Grace of Ashmont—and they always turn up sooner or later."

"I'm sure we'll find him very soon," she said. She only wanted to find Ripley alive, no matter how long it took.

Blackwood returned to the carriage minutes later, and Elphick rejoined Pratt in the dickey.

"How does a man more than six feet tall, a man who looks, at his best, like a wolf in expensive clothing—how does such a man vanish?" she said. "This area is not heavily populated. You'd think somebody would have seen him."

"They've seen him. The trouble is, they haven't seen him at the right time, when he and Lucetta parted company." He looked at her. "We can expect more of this tedious stopping at local gathering places. It could go on for hours. It's unlikely you've been recognized so far, but that sort of thing is unpredictable. I can take you back to Sussex Place at any time you say."

She shook her head. "I know I'm supposed to sit patiently at home and wait for news, or go out to dine at Doveridge House tonight and pretend I've nothing else on my mind. Aunt Florentia would prefer that. But I told her to tell the duke the truth. He'll understand or he won't, but I cannot act according to what might or might not upset him or any other man. I cannot. I will not. You know me, Giles. You, of all men."

He turned away, offering a stiff profile. "Very well. Let us continue to accost the locals."

YOU KNOW ME, *Giles.*

You, of all men.

A dagger to the heart.

His vicious mind displayed the scene for him, undimmed by time.

Late summer. A garden of Camberley Place. The annual party for the young people, to end their visit. Lamps twinkled in the dusk, while he and Alice danced. There were others, also dancing, who might as well be part of the shrubbery. He had not seen Alice for two years. Now he saw and heard nobody else.

She wore a fine white muslin dress. Short, puffy sleeves threaded with pink satin ribbon left her arms bare above the long white gloves. The same ribbon bordered the bodice under the low, ruffled neckline and at the waist—or what fashion designated a waist, directly under her bosom. Fashion called further attention to the area, thanks to a line of pink satin ribbon between her breasts, effectively framing them.

He knew he had a weakness for her. He knew he ought to keep away. But he'd missed her, and he'd had so little time with her during this visit, and she spoke to him in the same way she'd always done—confiding and teasing and all else she did that made him feel he was special to her. He wanted to be special to her. That was the trouble, part of the trouble.

And so they danced, and at the end of the dance they moved away from the others and farther into the garden's shadow, through an arbor, because moving away from the others was what they'd used to do, as though he and she had their own private club with their own special rules.

"I'll miss this," she said. "There's no other place in the world like Camberley Place."

In a few days she'd return to the Continent with Cassandra Pomfret, to finish their schooling.

"You must go," he said. "You want more Continental polish. You aren't yet quite insufferable enough. You must come back with French airs, and always use an inadequate French word to replace a perfect English one. You must learn to be a coquette."

"I'm learning other things," she said. "Useful things."

"Don't you want men at your feet?"

"That I might step on them?"

"Miss Pomfret is not a good influence," he said. "I must speak to your guardian."

He stood too close. He'd never known Alice to wear strong scent, but they'd been dancing, and the night was warm, and he detected a fragrance, maddeningly faint, that drew him closer still. He saw the satiny skin of her face and the curve of her cheek and neck and shoulders and the soft swell above the pink ribbon and ruffled neckline.

He felt his head dipping that way, and very nearly made a terrible mistake, but a noise from the party woke him to what he was doing. He stepped back and started to turn away.

She caught his arm. "Giles?"

He looked down at her hand and said, "Don't."

She looked up at him.

Her face, her remarkable face, as though she came from another place and time. It hurt to look at her like this, to be so close and to know she'd soon be far beyond his reach.

To know she'd always be beyond his reach.

His choice. The right choice. He knew that, but he had the scent of her in his head and dusk was shading into night, the shadows lengthening and spreading, so that it was as though they were completely alone.

"Alice." He needed to move away, to put space between them

so he could think, but he looked into her face, upraised to his, and didn't want to think. He closed his hand over hers, the one holding him and keeping him without exerting any pressure at all. Then he pushed down the glove and bent his head to press a kiss to the inside of her elbow.

She gave a little gasp. "Oh." So soft, a whisper in the night. "Giles."

He drew her into his arms, and she came easily. He kissed her, and the taste of her went to his head like strong wine. The taste of her was Alice and summer, all their summers, a string of moments spent together.

This was what he'd given up with the choice he'd made: Alice in his arms and he dizzy with the scent and taste of her, the softness of her. He, weak with longing, falling and falling endlessly.

One kiss, that was all. One clinging kiss that sent the world whirling away, along with promises and choices. He fell, spinning in happiness, while she grasped his arms, holding on as though she'd never let him go, never let him sink unless they fell together. She kissed him, innocently answering, without hesitation, as though all their moments together had naturally led to this.

Innocent.

She was seventeen, still a schoolgirl.

He was no innocent schoolboy. He'd made a choice, and he'd cheated.

Only one kiss. Only one wrenching moment of happiness before he broke away, shattered and heartsick.

"We can't do this," he said. "I can't do this. By God, I must not."

He walked quickly away from temptation and set out for the place where he, Ripley, and Ashmont always went, especially in times of difficulty: the fishing house, their refuge.

In short, he ran away, caught up in his own turmoil. He never considered her feelings, a seventeen-year-old girl who cared for and trusted him, who'd come so willingly into his arms and would have willingly given herself.

He dragged a mental curtain over the scene and summoned his wits. His memories and dreams and desires didn't signify. He needed to find his friend, his brother. *Her* brother.

After an overlong, throbbing silence, he found his powers of reason and his voice. "We could investigate every lane and path where a man might go astray. I believe, though, that keeping to the main road and continuing our current method makes more sense. Sooner or later somebody will offer a clue."

"People do seem willing to help," she said.

"So far. Until now we've met up mainly with respectable persons. As we move nearer to the less prosperous areas, that will change. My mind will be easier if you remain in the carriage with the servants."

He braced himself for the inevitable argument. She said nothing, and he went on, "They're tougher characters than they appear—like your tutor Keeffe, whom you no doubt wish were here, instead of this great, useless ox of a duke."

"You annoy me," she said. "Yet you are not without intelligence."

Oh, Alice.

He laughed inwardly and smiled a little outwardly, and the shell of misery about him cracked a degree. "Thank you. Allow me to return the compliment."

"You may. And may I return it again by saying I presume you have a weapon in the carriage?"

"Alice."

"Tough servants are all well and good, and I did bring my sturdiest umbrella. Still, an object more obviously deadly can be of use to a lady. One ought not to underestimate the element of surprise. Also the element of terror. A woman waving a loaded pistol is extremely alarming. She might fire it accidentally, or be so lost to human feeling as to aim a few inches below the waist."

He had himself to thank. Or blame.

He was the one who'd taught her how to clean, load, and fire a pistol. The first, aborted, lesson hadn't been the last. Eventually, he'd shown her off to his two friends. They were vastly amused, watching Ripley's little sister fire at a target. She'd turned out to be a competent shot.

Still, even the moving targets his father and Lord Charles had devised were not the same as living human beings. There were so many ways to go wrong with guns, especially in unexpected situations.

"I'll leave you the whip," he said. "The pistol case is under the seat, and the pistols will need to be loaded. We left in haste, and I hadn't time to fully prepare for problems."

"And you don't trust me to load them properly," she said.

The moment flashed into his mind when the pistol had misfired and Ripley fell.

"In ordinary circumstances, I'd trust you," he said. "This is not ordinary. It's different when you're acting under duress, which might easily be the case."

"And you'd be uneasy, leaving me alone with loaded pistols." She smiled suddenly, and his heart twisted in his chest. "I'm not sure I blame you. In fact, I might congratulate you on learning a lesson. Very well, then. I'll make do."

Chapter 14

They made their way westward toward the too-swiftly descending sun, or what one assumed was the sun, behind a vast bank of clouds. Though nightfall was a few hours away, the clouds would bring an early twilight. Searching would become harder, then impossible.

Alice told herself it was no use fretting about the darkness until it came.

Meanwhile she waited in the carriage.

Blackwood and Pratt, the larger of the two servants, had entered a ramshackle establishment called the Blue Sow nearly half an hour earlier.

Elphick stood patiently at the horses' heads, as he'd surely done countless times before.

"You and Pratt must be hungry," Alice said.

"I thank you, my lady, but it's these girls we got to look out for." He patted them affectionately. "Me and Pratt had sandwiches before, at the Lovedon Arms, and got more for later. Servant girl there packed 'em up for us. What with leaving London so sudden, and not sure where we'd be going, His Grace made sure they took care of things at the inn. They did it properly, too. Good corn for these fine mares. And carrots for treats."

Undoubtedly the Lovedon Arms proprietors would have packed up the contents of the wine cellar if needed. Clearly Their Dis-Graces had spread their largesse there, as they did over all the establishments they frequented.

Very well. The dukes might have been worse human beings. True, their motives were selfish: They required cooperation and comfort. Yet others, ostensibly better-behaved, treated those who served them rudely, unkindly, even brutally.

Generosity to others was all well and good. Nonetheless, it did not undo the damage the dukes did to themselves, day after day. It didn't ease the anxiety of those who cared about them.

They had not always been like this. The process of three mischievous boys turning into a trio of reckless pleasure-seekers had been a gradual one. Perhaps it had started in their Eton days. Then or shortly thereafter.

Her mind was drifting into the past when Blackwood emerged from the Blue Sow and strode to the carriage.

She watched him greet the horses and murmur praise as he petted them and rewarded their patience with carrots. These were powerful, spirited creatures who could not love the slow pace and the constant stopping and starting. Yet they behaved beautifully.

Their owner understood them, and they liked him, clearly. Even Keeffe wouldn't find fault in this category.

As Blackwood climbed onto his seat, her mind made pictures of the boy he'd been, the boy who thought of everything and knew how to do everything. The boy she'd admired. Adored.

But that sweet boy was gone. Only tantalizing hints seemed to remain in the saturnine man beside her.

She kept her sigh to herself.

"It's gossip, but it's recent and it fits," he said as he took up the ribbons. A long pause followed. Then, "One of the local ne'er-do-wells has acquired an expensive shirt. His bosom companion sports other finery. Both have been flashing their blunt, and everybody is speculating about where and how they acquired these garments and the coins they spend so freely."

It took Alice a moment to absorb the news. Then, as she took in the implications, she thought she would be sick.

And being sick would accomplish what? she asked herself, as Keeffe would have asked. After all, this was *Ripley* they were looking for. Losing his clothing did not necessarily mean what it seemed to mean. He'd done mad things for a wager. Naked adventures were not unheard-of. His clothes might have been stolen while he slept . . . wherever he'd slept.

She collected herself. "Any idea where we might find this fine pair?"

"To my surprise, informants were not only many and willing but have also kindly provided directions to the suspects' lair." He nodded westward. "It lies north of the main road, among the potteries and piggeries."

"You were in there for so long, I assumed the people were uncooperative."

"On the contrary, they were surprisingly forthcoming. Messieurs Bray and Moss are unpopular."

"Dangerous men, then?"

He shrugged. "Dangerous or pestilent. I suspect the latter. Dangerous men create fear, and fear breeds silence. All the same, I believe we need to be cautious."

"Does that mean I'm to wait in the carriage again?" She didn't like it, but quarreling with him only wasted time. He could be extremely pigheaded.

So could she, but that was different. A woman had to hold her ground or she'd be mowed down.

"You've had a long wait," he said. "You must be bored witless."

She wished she were bored. She wished she could stop her mind from imagining terrible things.

"I whiled away the time reviewing my grievances against my brother and imagining suitable punishment for the trouble he's caused me."

There was a silence. It lengthened. He gave the horses leave to start.

At last she said, "I'm not a fool, Giles. I know there are a number of explanations, and not all happy ones."

"Yes."

"You believe he's in trouble."

"I'm allowing for the possibility."

"Then the sooner we find him, the better," she said.

THE COTTAGE WAS larger than others in the vicinity, but no more elegant. It stood at an inconvenient distance from the broad lane they'd traversed, but at least the ground was relatively dry, sparing Blackwood and Pratt the need to trudge through the muck.

Smoke drifting from the chimney told him somebody was at home.

Pratt knocked on the door while Blackwood stood a little to one side. A tall, gangly fellow opened the door. Before he could react, Blackwood grabbed him by the front of his coat. Ripley's coat. Blackwood had only to touch it to recognize the fine wool. He yanked the fellow through the door and out into the yard.

"Get off of me!" the thief screamed. "Murder! He's murdering me!"

Blackwood heard shuffling and thumping from within.

"Go!" he told Pratt. "Don't let the other one get away."

The groom ran inside the cottage.

A minute later, he ran out again. "Climbed out of the window," he gasped, and raced round the side of the house.

Blackwood shook his captive. "Your friend won't get away. All the world's looking for him. What sort of half-wit robs a nobleman?"

Any number of half-wits, he knew. Even royalty wasn't immune. The late King had had his pocket picked in Manchester.

"Get off of me! I don't know nuffin'!"

It wanted every iota of Blackwood's self-control not to throttle the man, or throw him down and stomp on him.

Ripley's coat.

He thrust the villain against the side of the cottage and lifted him up until his feet dangled.

"Can't breathe! Get off! Oof!"

Blackwood knocked his head against the cottage wall, then dropped him.

"Ow! You broke my leg!"

"Get up."

"You broke my leg!"

"I don't care. Get up or I'll twist your head off your neck."

The fellow scrambled upright. "You can't go about—"

"I can do what I damned well please." Blackwood grasped the coat lapels with one hand, pulling them tightly together.

"I can't breathe."

"You're talking. Now tell me which one you are. Bray? Moss?"

"You got the wrong one. Never heard of—"

Blackwood tightened his grip, heedless of creases or any other damage. The coat would have to be burnt in any event. The man hadn't bathed in some time, if ever. "I'm going to count to five. Then I'll start breaking your fingers until you remember your name. One."

His name was Lewin Moss. He claimed he'd won the coat in a card game.

Blackwood dragged him into the cottage. He did not have to search. The goods were heaped on a table. He had light enough to see a pair of pantaloons. A hat. Neckcloth. Handkerchief. Purse. They must have been counting their treasures and deciding how best to dispose of them when he and Pratt turned up.

"Quite a profitable card game," he said. "Did you leave him anything?"

"I dunno what—"

Blackwood backhanded him, and Moss fell.

"Get up," Blackwood said. "There's a sack. Put those items into it. All of them. We're going for a walk."

Moss started screaming that he hadn't done anything. He didn't know anything.

If only he knew how close to death he was.

"You're wasting precious time," Blackwood said. "My patience is running thin. You can cooperate, or you can die a slow and agonizing death, after which your corpse will feed the nearest pigs. If you cooperate, I will leave you to His Majesty's justice. In that case, depending on what exactly you've done and what the judge and jury determine, you might hang, or you might be transported to New South Wales. Or maybe you'll be lucky and win a few years at hard labor. Choose. I will count to five. One."

Moss hurriedly collected the sack and started shoving Ripley's belongings into it.

Meanwhile

"DID YOU HEAR something?" Alice said.

"Shouts, like," Elphick said.

They both looked in the direction Blackwood and Pratt had gone.

"He must have found them," she said.

I hope he doesn't kill them, she thought. Not, at least, until they found Ripley.

More noise, from the same direction.

She was debating whether to climb down and make her way to the cottage to try to prevent murder when a half-dressed, scrawny young man burst into the lane. He stopped short, gave the carriage one startled look, then took to his heels.

In the moment he'd paused, she'd taken in the shirt and waistcoat, too large for him. Too rich for him.

"Elphick!" she cried. "He's one of them!"

She reacted instinctively, gathering up the ribbons, straightening and separating them.

"My lady, I don't think—"

She gave the horses the alert, and loosened the reins. "Go along, girls," she ordered crisply. "After him."

Keeffe had trained her and Cassandra to maintain absolute

calm while driving. No shouting, whipping, jerking on the ribbons. No panic. No hint of anything less than complete self-control. Horses sensed uncertainty and fear. It was the driver's or rider's job to exude confidence and mastery.

That came from practice and practice and practice. In this case, she had a pair as well-trained as she. They came promptly to attention and started, though a stranger held the reins and a strange voice issued orders.

She was vaguely aware of men shouting behind her, but her attention was on her prey and the cattle. Circe and Sappho were eager to be on the move again, clearly, after so much stopping and starting. Very likely this wasn't the first time they'd set out in pursuit of somebody. They needed little urging to pick up speed. They seemed to know what she expected of them.

Chariot races, that was why. Their Dis-Graces would compete for which of them would come closest to a fatal collision with a tree, a fence, a wall, the ground . . .

The thoughts flew through her mind, mere wisps, while she concentrated on her quarry.

The thief—for thief he surely was—turned abruptly into a lane she hadn't realized was there, and she nearly overturned the carriage when she rounded the corner. The way was narrower and deeply rutted. A part of her mind was aware of the risk she took, driving a vehicle made for a man who owned longer legs and arms and a great deal more muscle. In this tight place, the work would be challenging even for Blackwood. She was more than likely to lame the horses or break an axle, a shaft. Endless possibilities for catastrophe.

Too late to worry.

She couldn't turn back. She wouldn't.

GRASPING MOSS'S ARM, Blackwood led him back to the lane where he'd left the carriage. He would have preferred to drag the cur along the ground and kick him in the head a few times on the way. That would be satisfying but not productive. One must remain calm. One must exert self-control.

They reached the lane.

But no, this couldn't be the place. He'd got turned about somehow.

The carriage. Not there.

Alice. Not there.

But there was Elphick, staring, as one dumbstruck, down the road.

"What?" Blackwood said. "Where is she?"

The tiger started, and shook his head as though to clear it. "It happened so fast, Your Grace, I—"

Blackwood went cold inside. "What. *Happened.*"

Elphick explained.

ALICE HAD NEARLY caught up with her prey when he turned into another lane. Though not much more than a cart track and badly rutted, it was somewhat wider. The horses trotted on, easily gaining on the runner.

"Good girls," she said. "Let's get him."

The young ruffian ran, but not as fleetly as before and more unsteadily. Drink as well as fatigue were getting the better of him. He was no horse, let alone a match for Circe and Sappho. Soon they were neck and neck with the thief, then drawing ahead. She turned the mares aside to block the way and brought the carriage to a halt.

Stymied, the wretch turned to go back the way he'd come and stumbled. He staggered on, gasping. She laid down the reins and climbed down, whip in hand, and went after him.

He tried to run, tripped, fell, and picked himself up.

She marched on, heart pounding. "You'd better stop," she said. "Before you make me truly angry."

He glanced back at her. "You keep off of me! I didn't do nuffin'!"

"Then why do you run from me?"

He didn't answer. He tried to jog along, but he was limping now.

Alice noticed people coming out of buildings to stand in doorways. They watched. It was strangely quiet but for her and the runaway's footsteps and his gasping. The onlookers were mute.

He looked about him for a way out. Every door was blocked. No signs of sympathy. Only blank faces.

He turned suddenly, lunged at her, and shoved her aside. She staggered and started to topple toward a wall. She pushed herself back upright, spun toward him, and swung the whip at his legs.

He shrieked and went down.

She marched toward him.

"You keep off of me!" He struggled to get up. "I didn't do nuffin'!"

"Down," she said. "You stay down. I'm done playing with you."

He rose unsteadily.

The whip lashed again at his legs, and he toppled.

"You bitch! You broke my leg!"

She scarcely heard him. She saw the shirt clearly now. Fine linen. The ruffles at the neck opening. The finely sewn cuffs, fully visible at the bottom of his shabby coat sleeves, because the shirtsleeves were much too long for him. The pearl buttons.

The whip fell from her hand, and she forgot everything else in the world except her brother.

Ripley's shirt. Expensive, superior quality. He was so particular about his linen. He would fuss for hours over buttons.

She launched herself at the horrible creature wearing her brother's shirt.

But he'd already got back onto his feet.

"You keep off!" he shouted. He pushed her away.

She stumbled backward but found her footing and swung out at him. He dodged, laughing, and lifted a hand to strike her. She threw a punch, wildly, and caught him hard on the nose. Blood spurted. He screamed and staggered backward, clutching his nose.

She stalked toward him. He tottered and fell.

"You. Filthy. Cur. What have you done? Get up and tell me or I'll pummel you to a streak of grease. Where is he, you miserable swine?"

"Alice."

She was dimly aware of the low voice, but it was far away, on the edges of a cloud of rage and grief. She clenched her hands, nails digging in.

She stood over the wretch. "My *brother*, you disgusting excuse for a man. Where is he? What have you done?"

"Alice."

Big hands took hold of her and pulled her back, before she could fall on the—the thing who wore her brother's shirt, and pummel him senseless. She wanted to hurt him. *Needed* to.

"I'll kill you," she said.

"Not now, Alice. We need him to talk."

Blackwood drew her away.

She went, numbly.

"No," she said. "No, no, no."

She turned to him and set her face against his chest. And wept.

Chapter 15

For an instant, Blackwood was too stunned to react.

Alice didn't cry. Alice raged and fought.

But this was she, leaning upon him.

Great, gasping sobs against his chest.

He froze. One dark, helpless moment.

Then he came back to himself and wrapped his arms about her.

He held her, that was all, as she grieved a terrible, desperate grief. He didn't try for words of comfort. He knew there weren't any. He could only hold her while the storm raged.

And abruptly ended. In a few heavy heartbeats it was over. She set her palms against his chest and drew back.

He did not release her. His mind came back from wherever it had gone to during that first, dumb instant. With it came flashes of the past few minutes: of bewilderment and fear and the frantic search for her. A short search, though those few minutes had passed like eternity in Hell.

She tried to pull away.

He let go, but only to lift his hands to her shoulders and grasp her firmly.

"Never," he said. "Never without me, Alice. Do you understand?"

She looked up at him, through lashes glistening with tears.

"Never without me," he said.

She was safe, unhurt. His heart still beat too hard. The panic was slow to subside. He needed to crush her to him. He needed . . .

He made himself release her.

"We're going back to collect the other thief," he said. "Then we'll deal with this in a rational manner."

She rubbed her eyes with the back of her hand. She fumbled at her pocket. He drew out his handkerchief and gave it to her.

She blew her nose briskly and stuffed the handkerchief into her pocket. Her lip trembled. She bit it and took a deep breath. "I didn't have time to be rational. He was running away." Her voice was choked and thin, nothing like the voice he'd heard a moment ago, so cold and deep and dark.

Like Ripley's when he was in a dangerous mood.

Like Blackwood's.

But they were men and she was a woman. She'd pursued a drunken poltroon. Another sort of man could have laughed at that dangerous voice. Another sort of man could have easily disarmed and assaulted her in the short time before Blackwood caught up with them.

He told himself it hadn't been another sort of man. He told himself she hadn't cried because she'd suffered violence, but because of Ripley. He told himself that What Ifs, after the fact, were nonsensical. Here she was. Alive. In one piece. Apparently undamaged.

Apparently.

He said, very, very calmly, "Did he hurt you?"

She looked up at him, and he caught a glint of humor in her eyes. "He tried. But I hurt *him*."

He looked down at the thief, who remained on the ground, curled up, whimpering.

"I think you hurt him very badly in his pride," he said.

"I hope I broke his nose." She rubbed her gloved hand.

"The way he carries on, you must have done. Good work. But your hand might swell. I should have recommended the whip handle. You are not practiced in bare-knuckle boxing."

"I know how to throw a punch. The whip was too far away. My fist was handier."

"Good point. It worked. Come. Let's do what we can."

She started walking toward the carriage, head high and body stiff.

"Get up," he told Bray.

"My nose is broke!"

"I don't care. Get up or I'll drag you by one ankle."

Bray hauled himself upright, and they followed Alice. Pratt, who'd chased after them, stood by the vehicle, as Blackwood had ordered. It did not look to be in prime condition. Clearly it had endured a few knocks. The horses seemed to have suffered no injury, though.

He focused on cattle and carriage because if he thought about what might have happened to her, he'd kill somebody.

He wanted to kill Keeffe. If not for Cassandra Pomfret's be-damned jockey-groom-bodyguard, Alice would not assume she was a match for gang leaders and ruffians and possible murderers.

His uncooperative mind said, *Keeffe's the only one to blame? What about you and her brother and Ashmont? What about the example you set, never thinking about what you might be teaching her? Because she's only a girl.*

It was no use asking his provoking mind what other girl would have followed their example, and so he didn't.

He told himself—again—that it was pointless to stew over what might have happened to her had Bray been a larger and more vicious article. It hadn't happened.

What mattered was, she had not suffered any injury. She'd inflicted some.

Keeping this in mind, he focused his rage on the young idiot she'd chased through these rutted byways. An unwashed, gawky youth, who'd probably had more than enough to drink recently, judging by the smell. He'd been celebrating with his friend in their cottage while they gloated over their treasures.

A broken nose wasn't suffering enough, but it would do for now.

After he put Pratt in charge of Bray and stowed Alice safely in the passenger seat, Blackwood gave the mares a quick examination. No visible injuries.

He stroked them and told them what good girls they were. Under his breath he added, "Thank you for not letting her break her neck."

As to the carriage: Apart from scratches in the previously pristine paint, he discerned no obvious damage. That didn't mean it was in perfect condition. Later he and the two servants would examine the cattle and vehicle more thoroughly.

Meanwhile, he'd simply have to take care. They couldn't afford further delays. They had to find Ripley soon.

Not long thereafter

"BUT HE WERE here!" Moss said.

"Swear he were," Bray said. "We was at a friend's last night, like we told you. We come down the lane, goin' home. We stopped right here. That big old tree, see? To do a piss. And tripped over him."

His face was streaked with dried blood. If his nose had been straight before, it wasn't any longer. When he spoke, he sounded as though he had a severe head cold. His right eye was swelling.

Alice must have hit harder than she'd thought. That would explain why her hand ached.

She wasn't sorry. She'd do it again if she had to.

But Bray had had enough of her, and his friend wasn't eager to test Blackwood's patience. After a halfhearted attempt, the pair had given up protesting their innocence and led them to the spot. Not happily. Not willingly. They were truculent. They whined about their injuries. They whined about having their hands tied together. They whined about having to walk in front of the carriage.

Now they stood with their captors and the two servants, all gazing at the place where Ripley was supposed to be.

It lay at the end a footpath that opened into the lane they'd traveled, not far from the main road.

Dead men did not get up and walk away.

Relief made Alice dizzy. For a moment she came perilously close to fainting. *Absolutely not*, she told herself.

She and Blackwood turned to stare at their prisoners.

"He were there!" Moss said. "Big as life, early this morning, I swear. We called to him. Shouted. He never moved."

"And so you robbed him," Alice said. "A man lying there, helpless."

"We thought he was dead," Bray said.

"What's a dead man want with clothes and money?" Moss said.

"Was he breathing?" Blackwood said.

"I wasn't going to get in his face to find out, was I?"

"You must have touched him to get his things. Was he cold?"

"It weren't full sunup yet, so still *dark*, weren't it, and cold?" Bray said. "How could we tell? Didn't move or nuffin'. From all we could tell, he were dead, weren't he?"

Two drunken men as conscienceless as Worbury, Alice thought. They'd descended on their victim like vultures. Yet there was no body.

She had no trouble imagining all too many ghastly scenarios. They applied better to London, though, and this wasn't a London slum or a graveyard. No resurrection men here. While some places were unsavory, the area seemed, for the most part, to be pleasantly rural.

Kensington was where Ripley sent his linen to be washed, she remembered. Thanks to clean air and a clean spring, Kensington Gravel Pits was home to laundresses. Even the Blue Sow was the resort of people scraping by, according to Blackwood. Some kept pigs. Others made bricks. Still others farmed. Not all of the local population were criminals.

She turned her attention to Blackwood.

Brow knit, he was studying a place on the ground. "Something is there," he said. He bent down and retrieved the object from the tangle of undergrowth.

"He was here," he said. "They're not lying about that."

He handed her the item: Ripley's watch, chain, and seals.

He turned to the thieves. "I'm curious. How did you miss these valuable articles?"

"Didn't miss 'em," Moss said. "Dropped 'em, didn't I?"

"You had too much to carry?" Blackwood said.

He shook his head. "He made a noise. Godawful sound, like a banshee wail. Scared me out of my skin."

"Then we hopped it, didn't we?" Bray said.

A short, stunned silence ensued.

Blackwood's shout of laughter broke it.

THE LAUGH SIMPLY erupted from him, a shout of relief. Only at that moment did Blackwood realize how deeply he'd despaired.

Alice stared at him.

If he were Alice, he'd stare, too.

He drew her a few yards ahead, to thwart eavesdropping.

"I cannot promise he's perfectly safe or well," he said. "But when this pair of bacon brains tripped over him, he was in a deep, drunken sleep. Anybody who's heard that snore won't forget it soon. The first time I heard it, my blood ran cold."

"Snoring. Well." She let out a long, shaky breath. Her gaze turned to the place where Ripley had supposedly lain. It was a gloomy spot a few yards from the road, under a clump of ancient trees. In the deep shade, lying among the weeds and brush, Ripley wouldn't be easily visible even in broad day. Small wonder Bray and Moss hadn't seen him until they tripped over him.

"Either he fell off his horse or dismounted to answer Nature's call," Blackwood said. "He must have sunk into slumberland before he could remount. Once he's in that state, there's no rousing him. We've shaken him. We've shouted at him. We've tried emptying buckets of cold water on him. He only snorts and turns over and recommences the aria."

At last her green gaze came away from the shady spot. It did not return to him but to the watch in her hand.

She put him in mind of the grubby little girl he'd watched pummel Worbury all those years ago.

Strands of black hair dangled from under her hat, which had tipped to one side and lost one of the ribbons adorning the crown. Dirt speckled her face. Though the dress's brown color hid a multitude of sins, it was undoubtedly dirty and clearly wrinkled. The dark spots might simply be the dust of travel or filth the horses kicked up when she chased Bray. That, or Bray's blood.

She needed a bath. Her clothes needed to be burnt. His hands itched to put everything right, to smooth and brush and rearrange.

"Do you believe my brother is wandering, naked, somewhere among the fields and clay pits?" she said.

He made himself stop fretting about her appearance and how much worse it might have been. "He'll have taken shelter somewhere."

"Then why hasn't he sent word?"

"I don't know," Blackwood said. "What I do know is, if he was sufficiently intoxicated to fall into that particular state—and this is not as frequent an occurrence as you might imagine—he mayn't have recovered yet."

"Yet he must have recovered sufficiently to leave."

"It's possible that persons possessing charitable impulses found him and transported him"—his gaze swept over their bucolic surroundings—"somewhere."

"So we hope."

"A well-founded hope, enough to put your mind at rest," he

said. "We've talked to dozens of people hereabouts. Apart from our petty larcenists, who happened on easy pickings, villains don't seem to infest the place. When those two were done with him, Ripley had nothing left worth stealing. Why kill a man for nothing?"

She looked about her. "True. I had Worbury in my mind. But he's too cowardly to stalk my brother, too devious to ask about him openly. Had Worbury done the normal thing and enquired, as we've done, somebody would have told us."

"You might also want to ask yourself why anybody would make off with the corpse. Why go to the trouble? Why not leave him here? Those two numbskulls wouldn't have found him if they hadn't tripped over him. He might lie in this place unnoticed for days."

"True enough."

"He'll be somewhere in the vicinity," Blackwood said. "Still asleep, very likely. He usually needs a full twenty-four hours to recover."

"Juno grant me patience." She rubbed her forehead, spreading the dirt into dark streaks. "I don't understand. Perhaps I never shall. I've never understood what drives you three. But this confounds me utterly."

At last she turned to him. "He was to return to Newmarket. He meant to leave early this morning. Why, instead, did he go out to visit a former mistress? And then, why did he not stay with her, instead of going out to who knows where with who knows what companions, and reduce himself to that extreme state of drunkenness? And where are these companions?"

Why why why why.

Women. So many questions.

He shrugged. "What does any of that matter? The evidence points to his being alive. We shall bestow our two miscreants upon the local constabulary. Tomorrow, with or without the help of the police, I'll organize a search party."

"Tomorrow! And what do you propose in the meantime?"

He swallowed a sigh and several bad words. For a precious few minutes, she'd seemed to be reasoning as he did. But the combative tone was all too familiar, as was the lift of her chin and the shift in her stance. Defiance stared him in the face. Not for the first time.

He wished he'd left her with her aunt. He wished he'd left her tied to a chair, in a locked room, with armed guards outside doors and windows.

Remain calm, he told himself. *A gentleman does not give way to his passions. The man who lacks self-control cannot control others.*

He moved a step closer. Voice quiet and even, he said, "I propose that we accept the facts. It grows late. The area is thinly inhabited. Farmers and such do not keep late hours. We don't know the neighborhood. Once darkness falls, we can do nothing except get ourselves lost. I propose instead to take you back to Sussex Place."

"No." She folded her arms.

No surprise there.

He gathered his patience. "Alice, be sensible. Depending on the condition of the carriage and the number of vehicles clogging the roads, I may need an hour, even two or more, to get you back."

She shook her head.

Be calm.

"You cannot remain here," he said.

"I won't go back. I cannot bear it."

He was at a loss. She kept throwing herself into danger, and he didn't know how to stop her. He'd been sick with fear while he hunted for her, and the feeling lingered. She made chaos of his mind, and he hated the confusion.

He wanted to shake her. He kept his hands at his sides and his frustration tamped down. "I will find him, Alice. I always do.

This mad adventure has gone on long enough. I ought never to have let you overcome my and your aunt's good sense. I do not understand why I indulge your whims."

"Whims." Her expression hardened.

He was distantly aware that he'd blundered. But the thought was faint and fleeting, crowded out by frustration and worry and other emotions he would not examine now or in this lifetime, if he could help it.

And so he said, "I wish you would use your intelligence, not your feelings. I'll find him. I don't need your help, and I don't need the added bother of running after you and worrying about what's become of you."

"Bother."

"You were supposed to wait in the carriage. You might have been injured—assaulted—killed!"

"Oh, might I, indeed?" The green eyes flashed. "So might you, every day and every night. So might Ripley. So might Ashmont. Yet I'm obliged to sit by helplessly, with my anxiety to keep me company. Indeed, my heart grieves for the *bother* I've given you. I vow, I'm altogether desolated to learn I've caused you the least inconvenience."

She threw the watch at him and turned away. She stomped along the lane in a flurry of skirts. She threw up her hands. She kicked a stone into a ditch.

"Alice."

"I'll find him myself," she called over her shoulder. "You may go to the devil."

He stood for a moment, watching the tempestuous exit. He clenched and unclenched his hands. He picked up the watch and dropped it into the pocket of his waistcoat.

He went after her.

Chapter 16

She was behaving irrationally. This fact had not escaped Alice. She did not know how to go about finding her brother. She might as well be in China, for all she knew of this place. She was on foot. She was a woman. And the sun would set soon, as Blackwood said.

Everything he said was correct, and she hated this and wanted to kick him.

She stormed on. She ought never to have come. He didn't want her help. He could find Ripley without her—more easily without her. But to come this far, only to go home and pretend she had nothing more important on her mind than a dinner party . . . to attend a party and behave prettily, making sure to keep Doveridge amused and intrigued . . .

Oh, certainly, he was kind and intelligent. He was charming, beyond question. So many fine qualities. The perfect choice, truly.

Yet not her choice.

Worbury had made the choice for her. All she did was because of him and dread of what he'd do. He was a kind of cholera personified: a disease in human form that spread over everything, contaminating and destroying whatever happened into its path.

Even now, he controlled her. If she stepped wrong, she'd lose her carefully built place in Society. The Great World would close ranks against her. Gentlemen would lose respect for her. Her plans would fall to pieces.

If the worst had befallen her brother, her plans wouldn't signify. It was already too late.

She thought of Cassandra and Keeffe and wished she were with them, far away, where life made a kind of sense and offered a kind of freedom.

She wanted very much to sit down on the nearest wall or stump or large stone and cry.

She marched on . . . and tripped. And fell face-first.

She lay there, dazed. Her ears rang.

"Damnation, Alice!"

"Oh," she said.

Blackwood crouched beside her. "Don't move."

She was too stunned at first to move. She needed a moment to grasp what had happened, and another to sort out details.

Her face, she discovered, was partly turned into her hat brim rather than smashed against the ground. She'd thrust out her arm instinctively to break her fall, and she lay partly upon it. The hat seemed to have taken the worst of the impact.

Very well. She seemed to be in one piece, physically, at any rate.

She started to push herself upright.

"Confound it, Alice, did I not just tell you not to move? You might have broken something."

"I'm not broken." She was a little short of breath. "Merely . . . surprised." She started to turn over onto her side and winced.

"What?" he said. "What hurts? Your arm? Broken? You fell on it." He ran his gloved hand over her shoulder and down her arm. She felt the touch keenly, in spite of sleeve puffs and layers of fabric. Tingles raced up and down her arm, then inward and onward, everywhere. Her body had merely suffered a shock, she told herself.

Her self would have none of it. *You big liar*, it said.

She said, "My arms are inside pillows, as ought to be obvious."

The sleeve puffs were stuffed with down, but it was enough to cushion the impact. Of the ground. Not of his hand. She still quivered inside.

"You went down hard. You might have broken a rib." He pulled off his gloves.

"No! You don't need to check. I'd know. I'll be bruised, no more." She added hastily, "I did fall hard, but it's not the first time. I've fallen off horses and walls and fences. Luckily, women's clothing these days is more well-padded than in my mother's time. This is an awkward position to rise from, though, and I should be glad of a hand up, if you'll be so—oof!"

He lifted her up off the ground and carried her.

She could have struggled. She didn't.

He was large. All Their Dis-Graces were large men. She was by no means a small woman, yet he lifted her as easily as if she'd been a bundle of clothes, carried her along the rough uphill road, and didn't gasp for breath when he set her down, on one of the thick roots of a tree.

She did not want to be set down. He was strong and warm. She could feel the hard muscles of his body in places where she was accustomed to feel only her clothing. She could smell his clothes and his skin. She detected traces of the various places he'd entered, hints of smoke and ale and spirits. She caught whiffs of horses and leather and faint scents of soap and wool and starch. She wanted to bury her face in his shoulder. She wanted to put her cheek against his. Her mangled hat was in the way, luckily for her.

She was deeply wrong in the head.

No no no no no, Alice. You gave up this nonsense years ago, because you're not a fool.

They're the fools, reckless, catastrophically immature.

They're the problem.

That's why you're here, and not with Cassandra.

Here. With him.

He paced in front of her.

Surprise drove out self-pity. She could not recall seeing Blackwood pace before. He wasn't the restless sort. She could not remember when before she'd seen him so untidy, either, even a month ago, after the drunken incident.

Mud and scuffs dulled his boots' polish. Dirt spattered his trousers. A button dangled from his coat. His rumpled neckcloth hung limply. Dust coated his hat.

"Do I, too, look as though I've been dragged behind a cart?" she said.

He stopped, and his dark gaze settled on her.

She felt it, as though he'd put his hands on her. Which he'd already done and which she wanted him to do again because, obviously, she'd suffered a concussion.

She hated herself. She wanted to run away.

"This will not do," he said. "It's impossible to think clearly when I have to deal with you. Mere hours have passed since we left Sussex Place, though it feels like months. In that short time you've nearly killed yourself twice. Had I not happened along, you might have killed Bray. Admittedly his absence from the world can only improve it, but he was a source of information. I am trying to do the right thing, and you . . ."

He threw up his hands. "You hate me, and you have ample reason, but can you not set that aside for a time, and stop colliding with me at every turn? Do you not understand that I want to go on searching, too? But doing so would only increase our difficulties while accomplishing nothing. Why can I not make you understand that the longer we delay, the more difficult it will be to get you back to London without setting off a scandal?"

"I own a brain," she said. "I understand perfectly well. Excruciatingly well. Scandal comes so easily for women. For men, it's nigh impossible."

"Do you imagine I'm unaware of that? Why the devil do you suppose I'm such a brute as to insist on getting you back? I can break rules, but I cannot change them. I cannot make the world the way you want it to be. And at this point, I'm not at all certain what you want."

She was no longer certain, either.

She stared at her scuffed half boots. Ruination stared back at her.

So unfair. She hadn't done anything wrong. If she were a man, she might stay away from home for as long as she needed to, and nobody would raise an eyebrow.

If she were a man, she wouldn't be in this obnoxious position in the first place.

"I had a plan when I came to London," she said. "It was a good plan. But you and Ripley—"

"We've ruined it, have we? Your plan was rubbish."

She looked up at him. "You don't know what it was!"

"Do I not? Pray credit me with a little intelligence—or at the very least, the ability to put two and two together. You leapt onto the Marriage Mart mere days after Ripley nearly shot off his face. Admittedly I was slow to comprehend. But matters became exciting so very quickly after the Hyde Park Corner episode that I lacked the mental wherewithal to discern the obvious. By gad, Alice, I find myself wondering why in blazes I'm fighting with you about taking you back. Society and your beaux are your problem, not mine. Must I remind you that, if you insist on staying here, you'd better forget about Doveridge."

She needed a moment to collect her wits. He knew. But of course he knew. This was Blackwood, the man of logic and precision and rules.

She found words. "He isn't as narrow-minded as many. He of all people will understand."

"He can be as broad-minded as he likes. That changes nothing. He has a position to maintain, and no ordinary one. This isn't the Prince Regent's day. Society is a deal more intolerant and hypocritical than it used to be. He cannot overlook your disappearing overnight, even if he wants to. If he marries you in spite of the scandal, he'll be pitied and laughed at. His prestige will sink, and with it his influence."

He spoke nothing but facts, and she felt as though she was falling on her face and slamming against cold, hard ground.

Doveridge's influence was prodigious, and he used it wisely. He had the King's ear and the Queen's. He was a force in the House of Lords, fighting a Sisyphean battle for a measure of reform. She knew of no other peer who had so much compassion for the lower orders. Liliane Girard was a mere tradeswoman in the eyes of the Great World, yet Doveridge treated her with the same courtesy he gave queens and princesses.

He'd already done so much good. He could do a great deal more.

Or he could be mocked and pitied. People like Worbury and Lady Bartham would leap at the excuse to belittle him. Alice had no trouble picturing the satirical prints and the jokes in *Figaro in London* and elsewhere.

"I wish you would use the brain you own," Blackwood went on. "Even a man like Doveridge must be circumspect or pay a great price. And if he's off the list of prospects, your other lovers will shy away. If we leave now and get you back to your aunt at a reasonable time, you can continue your husband-hunting. There may be a little talk, depending on whether you were seen leaving with me, but nothing so bad as if you're gone overnight."

"But Ripley—"

"You want to see him for yourself. You want to punch him in the face for worrying you. Understandable. He's your brother. But can you not wait until tomorrow to do that?"

"We don't know! We don't know what's become of him. We only surmise." She clenched her hands. "This is intolerable. It's so absurd for you to have to take me back now instead of continuing. Who knows what will happen while we're away? How do we know he isn't ill? How do we know he hasn't met with an accident?"

"We don't," he said. "What I do know is, if you insist on remaining here, you'll have to marry me."

Chapter 17

The world tilted. Alice gripped the tree trunk she sat upon, and she was glad she was sitting. She couldn't have heard aright. She was concussed. Delirious.

"What?" she said.

"I'm looking at the facts," Blackwood said. "You might try doing the same. What difference will it make to you which duke it is? I'd serve the same purpose as Doveridge. If you want be in a position where the Worm can't trouble you, then you might as well marry me and spare yourself the charade."

Marry me. He'd said it. Twice.

"Did you fall on your head, too?" Her heart surged to double time.

"Face facts, Alice. Two choices."

Two choices. Like choosing between Scylla and Charybdis.

Yet it wanted scarcely a heartbeat to decide.

She leapt up so quickly that her head spun. She was so flurried, she barely heeded it.

"Very well," she said. "You. I choose you. I choose to remain. Now can we find my brother?"

He went very still. Had she not been so wild with frustration, had she not endured an excessive degree of emotion this day, she would have laughed at the expression he wore. She was far too agitated to take any notice.

He put up a hand. "Erm . . . one moment. I believe—"

"Yes," she said. "As you said, what difference does it make? May we set our minds to finding Ripley?"

He opened his mouth to speak. Then he shut it and cocked his head, listening.

It took her a moment to make out the sound through the tumult in her mind. Then she heard it, too.

Somebody was shouting.

He and she turned their heads in the direction of the sound.

The grooms were shouting and pointing.

"Now what?" Blackwood said.

"I don't know."

They stepped farther to one side of the road and made out a pair of figures, hands joined, swiftly shrinking into the distance.

ABSORBED IN THEIR private upheaval, the duke and Alice had forgotten they had an audience, a most attentive one.

The scene had captivated the two grooms, who'd been standing by the horses, pretending to be deaf, as good servants ought to do in such situations. What they observed, however, was too thrilling to resist: His Grace in a temper on account of her ladyship; her ladyship ringing a peal over His Grace.

While unable to hear precisely what was said, Elphick and Pratt had no trouble comprehending facial expressions, gestures, and tone of voice. Her ladyship stormed down the lane. His Grace stood, clearly at point non plus, before retrieving the thing she'd thrown at him and setting out after her.

This was a once-in-a-lifetime scene, and the servants were riveted upon it.

All the same, they did not forget their responsibilities altogether. They led the cattle cautiously after the couple while maintaining a discreet distance. After all, the vehicle ought to be near at hand when the time came to depart.

What they did forget temporarily were the two thieves.

Moss and Bray, on the other hand, were on high alert, survival at the front of their minds. The prospect of meeting with the local constabulary failed to enchant them. With even less delight did they anticipate a close acquaintance with, say, a stint of hard labor, a voyage on a transport ship, or a swing on the gallows—all distinct possibilities.

While not the cleverest fellows, they could recognize an opportunity when it presented itself. They looked at each other.

As one—not much choice, since their hands were bound together—they took a cautious step backward. Then another and another. A few more steps brought them behind the carriage and concealed them from their captors' view.

At which point they turned and ran.

BLACKWOOD STOOD WATCHING them go.

It did not seem very important at present. His heart beat as though he faced a firing squad. What had he said? What had he said? Not what he'd thought he'd say.

But there it was.

He'd said what he'd said and could not take it back.

He waited for Alice to come to her senses, laugh in his face, throw something at him. All three and more.

She was still gazing after the two figures as they grew smaller and smaller. Then they pivoted left, presumably into a footpath, and disappeared altogether.

At last she turned away and looked up at Blackwood. "The thieves said Ripley was in a place between the two-mile stone and the turnpike. We've passed the two-mile stone. What do you think the odds are of our finding a tavern or inn near the turnpike? The farmers and their friends will not have gone to bed yet. We might as well stop and continue our enquiries."

"Alice."

"I've crossed the Rubicon," she said. "You offered two

choices, and I chose. I will not turn back. If you wish to continue arguing, we can do that in the carriage. I should like to reach the next stopping place before everybody goes home for the night."

Marry. Alice. He'd said it. She'd said yes.

He would think about it later, when his mind came back from wherever it had escaped to.

He returned with her to the carriage and his two red-faced servants.

"I'm that sorry, Your Grace," Elphick said.

"We took our eyes off of 'em," Pratt said. "It's the sad truth. And them sneaks took off."

"Right under our noses." Elphick's color deepened to brick.

"They was well down the road before we noticed," Pratt said. "They won't have gone far, though, battered like they was, thanks to you and her ladyship, and tied right tight. But I ought to've run after 'em, all the same."

"I don't care about them," Alice said. "They're no use to us anymore. They don't know where Ripley is. Why waste our time and fray our tempers further trying to find them? Let the police deal with them."

Blackwood looked about him. Clouds, heavy and nearly black, obscured the sun. What fading light penetrated this blanket told him it was touching the horizon.

"Lady Alice has summed up the situation correctly," he said. "They know the area. We don't. We're losing the light. We'll have the devil's own time trying to find them now. I'm not even sure I could find their dratted cottage again."

"Then let's not waste any more time," Alice said.

Meanwhile in London

"Newmarket!" the Duke of Doveridge said.

"I see no alternative," Lord Frederick Beckingham said. "One cannot leave Ashmont there on his own, and at the moment, I've nobody to send. His two companions abandoned him on Saturday, it seems. An urgent matter, I daresay." He smiled wryly. "Or, possibly, plain fatigue. One cannot blame Blackwood and Ripley altogether, and I do believe they've grown rather old for this sort of thing. Wild oats, Doveridge. We've sown them ourselves. Still, one would hope my nephew and his two friends would be done with the foolishness by now."

He'd called at Doveridge House to explain his inability to attend Parliament this evening. His lordship had more on his agenda—he usually did—but this was his ostensible reason.

The two men sat before the fireplace in the duke's study, where they met at least once a week to discuss Parliamentary or royal strategy or gossip. They were both courtiers of long standing, with Lord Frederick the elder and more experienced—some would say the wilier—of the two.

"This is a day of disruptions," Doveridge said. "My dinner party is all to pieces. Perhaps that's for the best. I had expected the Reform Bill to be passed by now. When I planned my little party, I did not foresee the obstinacy of the forces of obstruction. In hindsight, I ought to have done."

"These things are impossible to predict."

"Sussex will speak tonight, beyond question, yet I ought to speak as well."

His Royal Highness the Duke of Sussex was one of the Reform Bill's staunchest supporters.

Doveridge rose from his seat by the fire. "It won't do. I cannot cancel my party at this late hour, though our numbers are so sadly reduced."

"Somebody is ill?" Lord Frederick said. He had a good suspicion what the problem was. As his nephew Ashmont often complained, Uncle Fred knew everything about everybody. He knew, for instance, that there had been a to-do this morning at Blackwood House, and another not long thereafter at Lady

Kempton's at Sussex Place. He had not yet learnt all the whys and wherefores.

Meanwhile, he could not leave Ashmont alone to run amok at Newmarket. He was a profound pain in the arse, but he had to be kept alive—at least long enough to find a suitable girl, marry, and produce a legitimate heir.

"I've only minutes ago had a message from Lady Kempton, apologizing for the late notice," the duke said. "She's unable to attend."

"Ah. In that case, Lady Alice will not appear."

A longish pause ensued before Doveridge said, "I am not easy in my mind." He sat down again and briefly described the scene on Saturday at the Zoological Gardens.

"I never interfere," Lord Frederick said. He smiled a little. "Actually, I do. All the time. Let me say a few words, which you are free to discard as nonsensical."

"That is something I rarely do, as you well know. After all, you are my elder. Not by much, admittedly. As I recall, you counseled me regarding a lady some years ago, and I had reason to be grateful."

"It could have gone the other way," Lord Frederick said, though he doubted this very much. "At present I offer two recommendations. First, I recommend that either you cancel your dinner party or leave your sister and her husband to host it. Anybody owning a grain of sense will realize that tonight's session will not be a short one. You must be there. You are crucial to the business. Second, I advise you to call on Lady Kempton as soon as may be." He glanced at the clock on the mantel. "You have time."

THE BRIDGE INN was a substantial establishment that stood on the north side of the Uxbridge Road, next to, appropriately enough, a bridge. By the time Alice and Blackwood entered, darkness was falling.

As one would expect, all conversation ceased when two strangers entered the bar.

Alice and Blackwood looked as though they'd recently enjoyed a melee. Still, nobody would mistake them for ordinary people. The quality of their attire and the way they carried themselves revealed their place in the social hierarchy, even before they spoke.

The first words Blackwood uttered did this and more.

"Landlord," he said, "the lady and I have been on this road, on a compelling errand, for some hours, and we perish of thirst. May we trouble you for a drop of something to wet our throats? And while you're about it, kindly do the same for the others present." He gestured to indicate the other customers. "Our servants wait outside with the cattle, all equally parched. I wonder if you can spare somebody to attend to them?" He laid several coins on the counter.

And this, Alice thought, showed why Their Dis-Graces could break so many rules with impunity. This was why so many jumped eagerly and happily to do their bidding. It wasn't simply because they were dukes, although that certainly contributed. It wasn't even entirely because of the generous bribes, although those smoothed the way, beyond question.

It was the dose of courtesy they added.

He did not march into the place in state, demanding this and that. He didn't have to. He knew he had wealth and rank on his side. He had nothing to gain by treating other human beings as less than human. He had nothing to prove to anybody.

Beyond question it was plain bribery to get prompt and undivided attention, but he did it with courtesy. At the same time he did not pretend to be anything but what he was.

They received prompt and undivided attention. Alice couldn't hear the rest of Blackwood's conversation with their host. This was conducted in quiet tones. But soon thereafter, a maidservant named Mary led Alice to a room where she could wash her face and hands and put herself to rights, insofar as this was possible, with the maid's help.

While this futile endeavor proceeded, Alice began the interrogation.

"We're looking for my brother," she said. She'd long since given up the French actress pretense. "He was last seen lying deeply asleep under a tree not far from the two-mile stone."

Mary let out an exclamation, incomprehensible.

Alice turned away from the horse dressing glass she'd been looking into—and wondering who was looking back at her, because she was no longer sure who, exactly, she was. "You've heard something of this?"

"Oh, yes, miss. They been talking about it ever since Mr. Vickery brought word. Oh, miss, it's a terrible shame."

Alice's heart went icy cold and seemed to stop.

"The sleeping man," she said through stiff lips. "My brother. What's happened to him?"

"It's a wicked thing, it is. They found him, naked as the day he was born—begging your pardon, miss—"

"I'm not missish. Say what you mean."

"They didn't leave him nothing, miss, whoever it was. And him . . . well, dead, they thought he was at first, but then they could tell he was breathing. Dead asleep, they said. Like maybe somebody knocked him in the head, but there wasn't any lumps or bruises they could see."

Alice breathed then, cautiously.

"Who said? Who found him?"

"Why, Abel Pulbrook and his son Jonas. It was the dog found him first, and barking his head off. Otherwise, they say, they might have missed him and he could've been left there in the morning wet and took his death. But they got him into the cart and took him home. Last we heard, he ate a spoonful of gruel. Then he went back to sleep, poor gentleman." The maid shook her head. "I hope they catch whoever left him there like that. Shameful."

Alice's head spun. She grabbed the back of a chair and sat down hard.

"Miss?"

"Yes. Yes. Oh, Juno." She looked up at Mary. "Alive. He *is* alive? Yes?"

"Oh, yes, miss. He— Miss?"

Something crashed and somebody cried out, and that was the last Alice heard before the walls closed in on her and the world went away.

Chapter 18

$\mathcal{A}$lice opened her eyes to find herself in Blackwood's arms again. He carried her to the bed, set her down carefully, and propped up pillows behind her.

"What's happened?" she said. "Did I faint? I never faint."

"I did not knock you on the head with a chamber pot, though the temptation was strong," he said. "I merely tapped on the door. The maid cried out. I burst in to see you subsiding to the floor, and Mary trying to hold you up. In short, you swooned all of your own accord, and I hope it's a lesson to you. All this long day, taking no rest and next to nothing to eat, then driving a pair of mares too powerful for you, then stopping for a boxing match with desperate criminals. I might as well spend my time with Ashmont."

"Your horses are not—"

"Luckily for you, Circe and Sappho have withstood the shock admirably," he cut in. "Mary has gone for a glass of port to strengthen the blood. I've ordered a dinner, which will be sent up soon. Kindly stay where you are, and do not force me to tie you to the bed. This is neither the time nor place for jollity. Really, Alice, this will not do."

"Ripley's alive," she said.

He went on fussing: He rearranged the pillows. He smoothed the bedclothes about her. He made sure her dress covered her ankles.

While he fussed, he talked. "He is. One of the men in the taproom saw the invalid for himself not two hours ago. Ripley was sleeping, soundly and loudly. My informant attempted an imitation. Had I entertained any doubts, those horrifying sounds crushed them. You may now stop being impossible. Good gad, what am I saying? I might as well tell the Thames to part for me."

He straightened and went to the window. Heavy pattering against the glass told her the threatened rain had come. She could see his reflection there, ghostlike against the night-black glass.

"You know where he is," she said. "Nearby?"

"Pulbrook's farm is northward of here. Unanimous opinion declares the area unsafe for traveling at present. Even if it were not raining furiously, we should have no moonlight. Our host assures me that even locals become lost on dark nights. No surprise it happened to Ripley, if that is what happened. Too bad he fell asleep when he was practically upon the Uxbridge Road. But it was dark. Easy to lose one's bearings in places like this."

"Especially if one is profoundly intoxicated."

He came away from the window. "Do you know, I'm asking myself the *whys* you asked before. If it were Ashmont who'd done this, I shouldn't wonder. One can seldom account for his actions. But it's pointless to try to ascertain whys and wherefores. It's possible we'll get answers when we see your brother. I shouldn't count on it, though, if I were you."

He pulled up a chair and sat beside the bed. He folded his hands against his stomach and looked at her. "I believe we still have time enough to get you back to your aunt. The stage and mail coaches will clutter up the Uxbridge Road in a short while, but we might reach Sussex Place at a reasonable hour."

She ought to take time to think twice. She didn't. She saw

all too clearly what lay ahead if she returned, if she married Doveridge or anybody else.

She'd been so careful to seek good men. She'd wanted a marriage like Aunt Julia's. But she wasn't Aunt Julia. She wasn't fit to be a proper wife. That had become clear in the past week, and especially in these last few hours. Doveridge didn't deserve to be saddled with the likes of her.

And she did not want to spend the rest of her life trying to be somebody she was not.

Spare yourself the charade, Blackwood had said.

"Don't you want to marry me?" she said.

He blinked once, twice. "Certainly not. Who'd want to marry you? A lunatic, perhaps. An ancient duke with one foot in the grave."

"He's two and forty!"

"Pitiable, doddering thing. If he marries you, he may look forward to an earlier-than-anticipated demise. As do I. But I at least am used to you. No shocks in store. A strain upon the nerves, certainly. Excessive fatigue, absolutely. But you'll have to work harder to kill me. Still, if you'd rather not take on the challenge of reducing me to a drooling half-wit—"

"On the contrary, I look forward to it," she said. "Among other things, it will offer a species of revenge for the anxiety I've endured."

Before he could answer, a sound made him look toward the door. Footsteps approached. Then came a cautious tap.

Blackwood went to the door and let in Mary, with the port. He took it from her and brought the glass to Alice's lips.

"I'm not an infant," she said. "I can hold it myself."

"Promise you won't dribble it all over your dress."

"The dress is ruined."

"But it doesn't smell of drink yet. You see, it is in fact possible for you to appear even more disreputable than you do at present. Still, your face is clean and your hair is somewhat less

Medusa-like. That's an accomplishment. Thank you, Mary. You may carry up the lady's dinner when ready."

Mary went out, closing the door behind her.

He gave Alice the glass. Her hand was only a trifle unsteady, and that, she told herself, was hunger and the daylong strain on her nerves. She drank. It felt good, better than she'd expected, warming her as it went down. As the warmth spread, she could feel herself calming. Only then did she understand how acutely uncalm she'd been.

Mad with anxiety was a figure of speech, yet uncannily accurate. How impossible it had been to think clearly or care about anything but finding Ripley. How frightened she'd been, without realizing how deep the fear went. She'd been angry as well—with him, with men, with the world.

"That's better," he said. "Your color begins to return. You looked ghastly. Ashen-faced doesn't become you."

"One of the things I've missed about you is your honeyed speech," she said. "The sweet way you have of making a girl believe she's the most delicious thing you've ever seen."

"You've missed me?"

"It's the brain injury," she said. "One of the times I had to climb out of prison at Camberley Place, I must have fallen on my head."

"I have not missed you," he said. "Not in the least. You're nothing but a bother."

"Excellent. You raise my spirits no end. I shall bother you for the rest of your life."

"The rest of my markedly short life."

"If I'm going to send a husband to an early grave, I prefer it be you."

He gazed at her steadily for a time. She let him. She finished the port and gave him the empty glass. He set it down on the table next to the bed.

"You're thinking," she said. "I can always tell when this momentous event occurs. Your eyes become very black."

He folded his hands again, on the bedclothes this time, and looked down at them. Then he raised those coal-black eyes to hers. "I want to make one detail clear," he said. "I am not a Turkish sultan. I get only one wife at a time. If we wed, ours cannot be a marriage in name only. Ours cannot be a business arrangement. Ours cannot be a marriage of convenience. If we're to take this step, it cannot be a sham. My current heir, unlike your brother's, is more than acceptable. Nonetheless, I should like to have my own family."

Her heart decided to skip a few times, then break into a run.

"I broke a man's nose without even trying," she said. "According to you, I drove horses too big and strong for me. Do you imagine I'm afraid of your bedding me?"

He looked away and bit the corner of his lip. A smile. He bit back a smile. Her spirits rose.

"I wanted to make sure we understood each other," he said. "No screaming on the wedding night."

"That's unfair, Giles. I had hoped to start wearing on your nerves at the first opportunity, and screaming on the wedding night—"

He leant in, cupped her face, and kissed her.

She forgot to breathe.

Eight years.

Since *that* kiss, the one endless yet too-short kiss, the one she couldn't forget and hadn't wanted to, though she knew better.

She trembled inwardly, and her heart beat hard, like the rain against the window. It had beat this way long ago, and the long ago came back:

Camberley Place and the gardens in the deepening twilight, the stars beginning to show themselves, faint glimmerings in the gold-streaked, ultramarine heavens . . . he pulled her into his arms and kissed her, and it seemed he'd lifted her off the ground, off the earth altogether, and she was tumbling into another, dark and dizzying and inviting world. She'd wanted to tumble forever. She hadn't looked for it or realized she wanted it until that moment, and then she was lost.

Now, the first touch of his mouth called it all back.

He started to draw away, but she grasped his lapels. "Ah, no, my lad. You don't get away this time. This time I'll put up a fight."

His eyebrows went up. The glint in his dark eyes told her he knew what she was talking about.

"I was a boy," he said. "Nineteen. A callow youth."

"You were afraid."

"An ignorant boy, yet not altogether brainless."

"And not altogether heartless." He could have taken advantage of her youth and innocence. He hadn't.

"As to that, Alice, I—"

"Not so much talking, my lord duke. The sweet kiss was a good beginning, but I know you can do better. You may try again, but with more concentration, please. You are not to trifle with my affections."

"You have affections? For me?"

"Mere seedlings," she said. "You'll need to cultivate them. Let me offer a helpful hint. You might start by kissing me again. How long will you make me wait this time?"

THE WORLD COULD change in an instant.

His world slipped, fell, and came right again altogether differently.

Blackwood was not sure he understood, although he was reasonably sure he'd acted correctly, at last.

He didn't stop to ponder. He did as he was told.

He kissed her cheek. He heard her breath catch and felt her tremble, and his heart turned over.

"Giles." A murmur.

"Give me time," he said.

He drank in the scent of her skin. He felt its softness against his mouth. He let his arms close about her and draw her nearer.

He slid his mouth to her jaw and kissed the place near her ear. He kissed her neck. Then he turned her face to his and kissed her the way he might have done all those years ago.

He hadn't been altogether wrong to stop then, but he'd done it badly, like a fool of a schoolboy. And he'd hurt her, then and more than once thereafter.

He wasn't a boy anymore. He wasn't the man he'd thought he was, either. He was not sure how that had happened. He knew only that his life was changed and could not be put back the way it used to be.

He didn't want to put it back.

This man, in this new life, held her and drank in the taste of her and the way she felt in his arms and the reality of her, the woman she was now. He let the feelings, good and bad, rise and fall about him, waves breaking upon a rocky shore.

She held on to his lapels, and her mouth pressed to his, following his lead without hesitation, as though she'd been waiting for this, as though she'd been waiting for him to come to his senses.

She responded in the way the seventeen-year-old version of Alice had done so long ago, tipping her head back for more, her lips slanting against his as she clung to his coat, as though she were drowning.

He was drowning.

He shifted onto the bed to hold her more closely still, and warm, turbulent waters closed over him, a sea of feelings. She tasted the same and different. The girl was there and the woman, too. She pressed her body to his, her full curves shaping to fit against him. He deepened the kiss. Her mouth was soft and yielding, unlike her character, and the kiss was like that, honey and fire.

He drew her down onto the pillows with him. He pulled her closer. He let his hands slide down, over her back, her bottom. His brain, the one in his skull, began to close up shop, and leave business to the little one lower down. He brought one of his legs over hers, entangling himself with her, while he slid his fingers toward the fastenings of her dress.

She stiffened.

Jolted, he stilled, while his mind shook itself awake and tried to run a dozen different ways at once. Too soon. He went too fast. She was an innocent, in spite of appearances and sophistication, and he was an idiot. The most inconsiderate of idiots. A boy, a lust-addled boy.

Then he heard the rap at the door.

He dragged his mouth from hers and disentangled himself from her. "Damn and damn," he said.

She gave a soft laugh.

He looked at her, into her shimmering green eyes and full into her smile. He laughed, too, and hastily slid from the bed, to open the door to Mary and the dinner tray.

THE DUKE OF Blackwood dined in one of the private dining parlors. He needed to think, and he knew he couldn't manage it in proximity to Alice. In normal circumstances she was no small challenge: clever and willful and all too fearless.

Current circumstances were abnormal, even for a man who'd spent most of the past fifteen years in the Duke of Ashmont's company. Blackwood had never, after all, lusted for the Duke of Ashmont, and therefore never suffered such extreme mental confusion, even during their most drunken episodes.

He thought, *What am I to do about Ashmont? I can't leave him entirely to Ripley. We can't leave him to himself.*

He thought, *What am I to tell Ripley about Alice?*

I did mean to shield her from Worbury but matters became . . . complicated.

It turns out that my feelings for her are not as brotherly as I believed . . . wanted to believe . . . pretended to believe.

Do you mind very much? I hope not, because I shall marry her, and I had rather that didn't mean you and I must meet at a ghastly hour to shoot each other.

He shook his head. Not the most intelligible explanations, and that was hardly surprising after the day's events. At this point, trying to arrive at logical conclusions was a waste of what reasoning powers he retained. He and Alice needed to agree on what they'd say. They'd both think more clearly after a night's sleep . . .

Not with her.

Not this night.

But they would be married—married!—and one night . . .

"I don't believe it," he murmured. "I don't believe this day. I must have wandered into an opium den without realizing, and I've dreamt it all."

He didn't believe that, either, but he set his mind to his dinner, which he very nearly fell asleep into.

And when he went to bed—at the same ridiculously early hour as a farmer—he slept dreamlessly.

Meanwhile in London

As the day waned with no word from Alice, Lady Kempton gave up trying to read or do needlework. She took to her writing desk.

Sussex Place
8th Instant

My dear Julia,

I should have been happy to keep you abreast of Alice's doings had I seen any value in your sharing my headaches. At present, however, I discern no way to protect you from the truth. All the world will be made aware by tomorrow or the next day or very soon, at any rate, that she has driven away with Blackwood to search for Ripley in Kensington or thereabouts. I am quite sure that Lord Frederick Beckingham is apprised of this matter, because he left it

to me to break the news to Doveridge. You will know I'm
not joking. Lord Frederick, having heard this and that—
more, I don't doubt, than I could hope to hear in a lifetime
of listening—advised the duke to call on me!

We were to dine with Doveridge this evening, as you
know. It was to be an intimate dinner party, with his most
trusted family members in attendance. Anybody can read
these signs, of course, and draw the obvious conclusion:
He was on the brink, at last, of offering.

Alice's abrupt departure obliged me to send a message
informing him that we were unable to attend. He called—
yes, as Lord Frederick advised—that dratted know-all—
ostensibly to ask after my health. In the circumstances, it
seemed most unkind to send reassurances through a servant. I felt obliged to speak to him directly. Alice told me
not to deceive him, and I did not. I explained that Ripley
had gone missing in Kensington, that we should not have
worried had his most trusted manservant not been genu-
inely alarmed and that, consequently, she had gone with
Blackwood to find him. Doveridge's first words were,
"Dear me, how anxious she must have been! I wish she
had come to me with her trouble. But that is my fault, I
daresay. He who hesitates is lost."

Indeed, as much as I dislike Alice's placing him in this
embarrassing position, and greatly as I sympathize with
his disappointment, it is true that he hesitated for too
long. Nonetheless, I am now compelled to believe it is for
the best, for all concerned. Alice likes and admires him.
She holds him in great esteem, as he well deserves. In some
cases, this is sufficient to build a marriage upon, as we
both well know. In her case, however, it struck me as insufficient. That is to say, I was struck with the insight when
she was on the brink of exploding from the house—to go
heaven knows where to do heaven knows what, for she
had no more inkling what had become of her brother than

the man in the moon. She, to search for him! Alone but for a pair of servants! Then Blackwood appeared.

My dear Julia, I have tried to counsel myself about jumping to conclusions, but it has been quite impossible to watch them together and not discern what one may call an undercurrent. Indeed, Doveridge has not failed to notice it. He may be infatuated with our niece, but he is not blind. He mentioned it, tactfully, of course. He'd observed them at the Zoological Gardens, and it is clear that the sight made an impression. All the same, who would have believed there was any danger of Blackwood stealing her away? None of those three is ready for marriage, and nothing less is acceptable in Alice's case. Ripley would tear his friend limb from limb—and we know how precious that friendship is. And so we are in a predicament, and I see no possibility of getting out of it easily. It is now past nine o'clock and she has not—

I broke off because of a tumult downstairs. I thought Alice had returned. She has not. She has sent a message. My dear Julia, you had better prepare yourself to think impossible things.

She and Blackwood mean to wed!

There is more, of course, but the rest is anticlimax. To spare you additional anxiety, let me assure you that they have discovered Ripley's whereabouts. Unfortunately, the lateness of the hour and the weather have made it impossible to go to him. However, she writes that he is well, and they mean to collect him tomorrow morning.

At least she and Blackwood plan to do what they ought. All the same, the talk will be terrific. But no more this night. My head is a jumble. I must make an early bedtime and try to sleep.

Your most affectionate,
Florentia

Chapter 19

Pulbrook Farm
The following morning

They found Ripley pouring slops into a trough. Pigs pushed about his legs, which sported overlarge breeches and rough stockings, all stained. With what, Alice chose not to consider too closely.

He wore an equally coarse smock, much mended and patched, and thick, mud-encrusted boots.

His hat was even more battered and shapeless than hers.

When Ripley at last looked up from his task, his expression was blank at first. Then his eyes narrowed, and his gaze went from Blackwood to Alice once, twice. "What the devil?" he said.

Alice ran at him and pushed him into the trough.

Ripley swore. The pigs grunted their own displeasure.

Blackwood dragged her away. "You are not to hold his head under."

"I said I would."

"A horse trough. I distinctly remember. This one is for pigs. Completely different. Now look at you. Muck has splashed onto your dress."

"It was already ruined, because of him," she said. "He has no idea what he's made me endure. Nor does he care. Well then, if he's so insensitive, let him be insensitive to pig slops."

Meanwhile Ripley managed to scramble up and out of the muck. He nudged a pig aside with his boot and stepped over the fence. To add to the previous attractive picture, he was wet, and the smell was nearly as bad as Jonesy's everyday aroma.

"What?" he said. "What the devil, Alice?"

"What is wrong with you?" she said. "You disappear without word to anybody, including Snow, who thinks you've been murdered—"

"Murdered." Ripley regarded her in the way one contemplates a Bedlam escapee.

He turned to Blackwood. "Has she been drinking?"

"Snow didn't know what had become of you," she said. "You took out Lucetta late at night, on the night before you were planning an early departure for Newmarket. You never went back to the inn. Nobody knew anything about you until we reached Kensington Gravel Pits—and even your former *chère amie* was baffled. You ask *me*, 'What the devil?' Have you lost your mind? Or what remains of it?"

His gaze reverted to his friend.

"Alice has summarized correctly," Blackwood said. "Had it been Ashmont—a different story, obviously. But it was you, you see. Even I grew uneasy."

"Did it not puzzle you in the least to find yourself in a farmhouse, naked?" Alice swept her hand over their surroundings. "Did none of this seem at all unusual to you?" She stamped her foot. "I should like to know how you have the effrontery to stand there staring at me as though I'm the one who's the problem."

"Actually—"

"I wouldn't, if I were you," Blackwood said. "I'm going to marry her, by the way."

"What?"

Alice glared at him. "That is not the way we agreed to break the news."

"I remember perfectly well what we agreed," Blackwood said.

"But look at him. He isn't in the least incapacitated. He doesn't need nursing. He's well up to surprises."

"Surprises," Ripley said. "Is that what you call it? Well, yes, a bombshell is a bit of a surprise. An earthquake, too."

"Better he knows now," Blackwood said. "You see? Give him time to digest it."

Ripley looked from Blackwood to her and back again. "*You're* going to marry her."

"Yes."

A long pause.

Ripley brushed muck off his cheek. "Are you sure?"

"Quite. She amuses me."

Alice kicked Blackwood in the ankle, turned her back on the infuriating pair of them, and walked away.

THE TWO MEN watched her go.

When she was out of sight, Ripley turned to his friend.

"What the devil?" he said, and threw a punch.

Blackwood blocked it. "Don't be an idiot."

He braced himself, but Ripley backed away, shaking his head.

"My sister! You're not Sir Bloody Galahad."

"No."

"My sister. You." Ripley swore vividly and profanely.

"Don't you love me anymore?" Blackwood said.

"I thought she was going to have the other fellow. Doveridge. *He's* Sir Bloody Galahad. Even my aunt says so. Everybody says so."

"I did ask her to choose between us."

"And she chose you."

"Yes."

"Was she drunk?"

"You're hurting my feelings," Blackwood said.

"Were *you* drunk?"

"No. Were you?"

"What have I got to do with it?"

"What do you think?"

After a lengthy silence, Ripley took off his hat and stared at it. Then he put it back on and gazed down at his borrowed attire.

"Because Alice has a point," Blackwood said. "Did it not strike you as odd to find yourself in this place? Frankly, I find it deuced odd. The whole business. Odd for you. Nothing is odd where Ashmont's concerned."

"I don't . . ." Ripley considered for a time, then nodded slowly. "Here's the thing. The night before last? Hazy. I was in no mood to sleep, that much I know. Thought I'd get some fresh air. Then Margery came into my head. You remember her. Handsome, buxom girl, and hair like a glorious sunset. Found her without much difficulty, but I couldn't seem to settle to anything, and she had her hands full that night. It seemed to me that what she wanted was a good night's sleep and not tumbling about with an old lover. And then . . ."

He frowned.

Blackwood waited.

"Then I went out again," Ripley continued. "I meant to go back to the Lovedon Arms. Went the wrong way. Couldn't find the right way. Rode about endlessly. Got thirsty. Stopped somewhere. Don't know where it was. Do you know, I think I drank more than I meant to. That damned Worbury." He rubbed a knuckle along his nose, smearing whatever was there. "What to do with the cur? Makes me sick to think of him inheriting. And there's Alice. I hadn't really grasped what it meant, you know: John Ancaster dead. The consequences. By gad."

"We were rather slow to comprehend," Blackwood said.

They'd attended the funeral. They ought to have considered what it meant, but they were too busy not thinking.

Ripley scowled at his borrowed boots, as well he might. They were unspeakable. "There's the nub of it. I didn't see the complete picture. Not until I heard your story about the street brat. Then I couldn't get clear of my accurst cousin and what this signified for the future: John Ancaster dead, me dead, and what about Alice? What about the dukedom? It gnawed at me, a maggot on the brain. So galling, not knowing what was best to do."

He looked down at the creatures crowded about the trough. "Feeding pigs, now. That's simple. Straightforward. Reminds me of the home farm at Camberley Place. Life was simpler."

"Do you mean to stay here?" Blackwood said. "Where it's simpler?"

"I thought of going back to Camberley Place to talk to my aunt," Ripley said. "Among other things, she'll enjoy telling her provoking nephew what to do, and I should like to see Aunt Julia more cheerful. But what the devil I'm to say about you and Alice . . ."

"Lady Charles will understand the necessity."

"Yes. Now I do. Alice kept you hunting for me, didn't she?"

"No, I meant to keep at it. I couldn't get her to let me do it without her."

"Right. She was out, away all night, with you. And now you're being heroic."

"Gad, no."

"Are you sure? Because I can't stomach that. Love my sister and all, but I know she's more than a handful. She wants a bodyguard. That's what the footman Tom was supposed to be."

"Ashmont needs a bodyguard," Blackwood said. "Alice needs a henchman. An accomplice. Not Sir Bloody Galahad. One of the other ones. There must have been a disreputable knight in there somewhere. Rusty black armor. But useful for dirty work."

"Ah."

"I'm not respectable. I realize that."

"Maybe it's too late for respectable, for her," Ripley said. He shrugged. "Well, she isn't a naïve little girl, and I reckon she knows what she's about. But you? Will you be all right? Because it's marriage, and when it comes to Alice—"

"I never meant to do it until I was ready to do it properly,"

Blackwood said. "I didn't know I was ready until . . ." He quickly reviewed recent events in his mind. "I don't know. Maybe it dawned on me suddenly yesterday. Was it about the time Alice planted the thief a facer? Not that he didn't deserve it. Don't they always? Where was I? Oh, yes. It must have struck me at some point that it was time I wed. And there she was, conveniently at hand, thus sparing me the ugly necessity of going out and finding a bride. When I suggested she forgo all further rigors of husband-hunting and accept unworthy me for the position, she was kind enough to acquiesce."

Ripley laughed. "Yes, that tale will do. It came upon you sudden-like."

"The sudden part is true. I can't quite explain, that's all."

"Time you wed." Ripley looked up at the cloud-riddled sky. Then he moved away to the pump. He gave himself a dousing, hat and all, and shook off the wet like a dog.

"That does not improve your appearance," Blackwood said.

"It feels good. Clears my mind. I'm still . . . fogged in." Ripley fell silent.

Blackwood waited. He knew his friend and therefore knew he was digesting an upheaval. Of everything, including, especially, their friendship.

A brother by bonds thicker than blood.

Finally Ripley said, "There's always been something between you. I don't know what the right words are. You and Alice. Even when we were schoolboys. Last week you were the one who realized somebody had to look out for her while Worbury was about. You were the one who did it. Took care of matters." He grinned. "With finesse. I don't doubt that all this hunt-for-Ripley today—and I'll wager there's a story there—it's her doing, Alice driving the chariot, like Boadicea. Once she gets a thing into her head—but you know as well as anybody what she's like. Best to let her do as she wishes because she'll do it anyway, only then it will get more complicated."

"I'm aware of that."

"At least you have an idea what you're in for. Not like those other fellows. Lambs to slaughter was my thought."

"I am not a lamb," Blackwood said.

"Neither is Doveridge."

"Yes, well, maybe. But I gave her a choice and she chose me."

"Don't get all prickly on me. I only meant I supposed he was old enough to know what to do. But maybe not. You probably won't know what to do, either. Still, she does like you. I think."

"She has confessed to finding me not without intelligence."

"Ah, well, then, you have my blessing," Ripley said. "You'll probably need amulets, though. Good luck charms. That sort of thing."

"Never mind the amulets," Blackwood said. "What are we going to do about Ashmont?"

By the time Blackwood approached the carriage where Alice waited, her temper had cooled, partly thanks to the memory of Ripley's face when Blackwood announced the marriage plans.

"Did you drown him in the pig trough?" she said.

"I considered it. Then I recollected that, thanks to him, I shall have a handsome, stimulating wife without having to go to a great deal of bother to get her. Well, a little bother, but nothing to signify."

He collected the ribbons and climbed onto the seat, so smoothly that it seemed but a single movement. "Am I forgiven, then?"

Excellent question. Forgiven for what? A few minutes ago? The past eight or ten years? She was not at all sure of the answer.

She said, "I remembered that men have their own peculiar ways of communicating. I reminded myself that you are moderately intelligent. It occurred to me that a gentleman able to manage gang leaders ought to be able to manage my brother. Does he mean to stay with the pigs, I wonder?"

"He'll borrow a horse from the Pulbrooks and meet us at the Lovedon Arms. Folding him into the box struck me as unwise. The smell, among other things. He needs a bath. Badly."

She knew that Blackwood had sent for Snow before they set out this morning. Doubtless the innkeeper would be ready— nay, eager—to supply whatever else might be necessary to make Ripley presentable.

As to herself and Blackwood, they were as presentable as they were likely to get, although, knowing him, she wouldn't be surprised if a change of clothes magically appeared at the inn.

Blackwood did think ahead. He thought logically. He could be useful as well as agreeable to look at and entertaining to converse with.

Could be. Whether one could depend upon him was another matter. But then, many husbands were not dependable. Few took their marriage vows seriously, or their wives. Or any women.

Still, it wasn't as though she had a choice at this point. She'd burnt her bridges.

"Is he forgiven, by the way?" Blackwood said after he'd given the horses leave to start. "These last four and twenty hours have thrown all of your arrangements into disarray. Not to mention your future."

She looked down at her dress. Mary had done her best to clean and mend it, but it would not tempt Maggie Proudie. What would Doveridge make of her now?

Never mind him. What would his friends and colleagues make of her? They'd say he'd had a narrow escape, and they wouldn't be wrong.

"I've had time to reflect upon my future while you and Ripley communicated in the primitive manner of men," she said. "It isn't what I envisioned yesterday morning. And I'm not done being exasperated with Ripley on general principles."

"I believe he's begun to comprehend your reasons."

"Maybe I should have pushed him into a pig trough long before now, if it's had that positive result." She paused, collecting her thoughts, her most recent thoughts. It was remarkable, the sharpening effect an impending marriage had on one's mental processes. What had Dr. Johnson said about being hanged?

When a man knows he is to be hanged in a fortnight, it con-centrates his mind wonderfully.

She said, "It dawned on me that what's happened in the past month, the past week—none of that was Ripley, really, was it? Worbury's at the bottom of it all. If not for him, I should have returned to the Continent. I should not have cultivated Doveridge or any other eligible *parti*, and at present I should not be in the disagreeable position of appearing to have taken leave of my senses."

"By marrying me."

She brushed at her beyond-reclaiming skirt. "Exactly."

"It will give the gossips more excitement than they've had in months."

"It's some consolation to know I shall brighten the dreary days of the *ton* in my own small way," she said. "There's also comfort in the knowledge that you will be marrying *me*."

"Ripley was comforted, too, to have you off his hands. He was concerned about me, though. He wondered whether I was making a martyr of myself to protect your honor."

"Men like you three are bound to see marriage as martyrdom."

"I don't. At present."

She turned to look at him. He was no more his usual elegant self than she was. One of the inn servants must have made his own attempts at cleaning, with mixed results. While Blackwood had bathed and shaved, his clothing was far from pristine. His neckcloth, no longer gleaming white, hung limply. Though the loose button had been sewn into place, his coat bore battle scars. While this must cause him grief, he wore his battered attire with his usual confidence. Arrogance.

And she was drawn to him, as she'd always been. He touched her, and hard-earned wisdom left her.

He met her gaze briefly, then returned his attention to the road ahead. "You and I have an affinity," he said. "I believe that's the word Ripley was searching for a little while ago."

"An affinity."

"Yes. Or call it a degree of understanding. I'm not sure, but that's what comes to mind. Here's what else comes to mind: I could have tied you up and taken you back to London, whether you liked it or not. I did not have to bring you with me in the first place. Departing without you would have called for drastic measures, but I could have taken them. I'm not the long-suffering sort. My nature is neither complaisant nor compliant. Yet I yielded. One may discover a clue in this."

"Or maybe in the back of your mind was the thought, 'What if she escapes? She always escapes.' Better to have me where you could keep an eye on me."

"And the instant I turned my back, you escaped to engage in reckless and violent acts."

"You know I couldn't wait for you."

He shrugged. "Whatever it was that stopped me from leaving you behind, I don't regret it. Whatever it was that led me to offer to marry you—whether I was in a sort of frenzy or panic or disorder of mind—whatever it was, I am not in that state at present, and I do *not* regret it."

Did she?

She remembered the leap of recognition and the relief when he suddenly appeared, exactly when needed, at Hyde Park Corner. Was he not the one she turned to when she was in a quandary?—as she'd used to turn to the boy she'd known and trusted and loved.

He was not that boy anymore. He was a man, and changed. But he knew her. He at least would not expect her to change or conceal her character.

Spare yourself the charade.

That's what it had been, hadn't it? She'd shaped herself to fit others' standards. For her part, she understood his character better than that of any other gentleman she knew.

Then there was the kissing.

Last night, and the way he'd touched her, the way he'd held her face, as though she were a precious object. The kiss that took her breath away and made her come so intensely alive, lit up within like a Roman candle, but the light and fire were feelings, all for him.

And the way it had felt when he wrapped his long, powerful body about hers.

This is where I belong. Yours.

She could feel it still, a tug like an ache in the pit of her stomach. An ache for more. Dangerous, and yes, she wanted more. A risk, a great risk, and she would take it.

"I had two chances to retreat," she said. "I didn't. I may live to regret it. So may you. But for the present, I do not."

"That will do, don't you think, to go on with?"

It was not the most romantic exchange.

Did it need to be?

Romantic pairings did not always turn out well. She'd seen many fall apart, some extremely unpleasantly: her parents, for instance. On the other hand, Aunt Julia had not married for love. She'd never dwelt on the details, but that much Alice understood. Others in the family were aware.

Yet love had come, and it had come powerfully, by all indications.

Marriage was a gamble. That was a fact of life. But Alice had taught herself to dare, to not be afraid.

And there was the kissing.

"That will do," she said.

Chapter 20

*L*ady Kempton awaited them at the Lovedon Arms. She'd brought Alice's maid, Vachon, and a box containing fresh attire. Vachon eyed her mistress's present ensemble, took a long, deep breath, and adopted a stoical expression.

Blackwood's valet, Springate, who'd arrived with Snow, did not turn a hair. He'd seen worse sights by far than the one that greeted him.

Lady Kempton sent Alice away with her maid. For once, Alice did not argue, but went off peaceably enough to be made elegant again.

But Blackwood's and Ripley's transformations had to wait. Lady Kempton led them into the private parlor she'd commandeered.

She stood by the window, arms folded. "I expect a full explanation. The scribbles I received from Blackwood and Alice were far from satisfactory. I cannot arrange a proper strategy without knowing precisely what happened. Blackwood, you will begin. You will provide the facts of the case, as though you speak at a trial—because that is precisely what Alice faces. A wedding, while crucial, does not solve everything."

Blackwood told his tale, leaving out what he deemed irrelevancies. Lady Kempton did not need to know about the intimate and all too brief interlude last night, for instance. She did need to know about Alice's punching the thief and breaking his nose, because there had been so many witnesses.

Lady Kempton closed her eyes from time to time during the recitation. Once she put her hand over her eyes. But in the main, she bore it well enough.

Ripley's story followed. That was simpler. When he came to the part about Alice pushing him into the pig trough, his aunt said, "I can well understand the provocation."

At the end she said, "I see. It might have been worse. Still." She pinched the bridge of her nose. "Well, I shall deal with it. As to you . . ."

She turned to the window and looked out, tapping the sill. "Worbury is living on his expectations. He would not be in London otherwise. Tradesmen hesitate to deny credit because they feel reasonably certain he'll inherit soon."

"Why does everybody think I'm going to die in the next five minutes?" Ripley said.

"Use your head, nephew. That hollow thing on your neck, which you might crack open in the course of a brawl or a mad race. You could be dead at this moment had those farmers not happened along with an observant canine. Worbury knows the odds are greatly in his favor. As do his creditors."

"Change your will," Blackwood said. "You can do that when we attend to the marriage settlements."

"I can't stop the swine from inheriting—and I'm not going to dash off to find a bride on his account, by gad! He's a pestilential bother, and every bit of trouble lately traces back to him. I should like to break every bone in his body. One at a time. Slowly."

"So untidy," Blackwood said. "Amusing, but bound to lead to complications. I suggest lawyers instead."

"You want me to sue him to death?"

Blackwood shook his head. "You can't prevent his inheriting the title. You can't prevent his inheriting entailed property.

But you can arrange a great deal else. That was what my father did when he gave up hope of having a son. His heir at the time, my Uncle William, was a wastrel. My father decided to arrange matters to restrict the amount of damage Uncle William could do. Father tied up everything he possibly could in trusts and I don't know what else. Your solicitor will know what can be done and how to go about it."

Ripley's expression brightened. "Do you mean I might leave him with only the title and a portion of property?"

"Something like that. It will depend on a number of factors. But I suspect you'll be able to contrive an elaborate set of restraints specifically for Worbury. Better yet, this is an arrangement you can enjoy before you enter the family tomb for the last time. Imagine the effect on Worbury's creditors should word happen to leak out of the changes to your will—exaggerated, of course, as rumors so often are."

He became aware of Lady Kempton's sharp gaze fixing upon him. "Your head is not quite so hollow, I perceive."

Ripley regarded him with plain admiration. "A wonder, this fellow's brain. Finesse, Aunt. That's what it is. Finesse."

"He'll need it," Lady Kempton said, "if he hopes for a happy marriage."

AUNT FLORENTIA WHISKED Alice away shortly after she'd emerged, transformed, from her room. The men decided to go to Newmarket to collect Ashmont and break the news to him.

Alice was reflecting upon this and other matters as her aunt's carriage started eastward.

"They will not have an easy time with Ashmont," she said when the carriage stopped to pay the turnpike toll.

"When does anybody have an easy time with Ashmont?" her aunt said. "I vow, at least half the fracases start with him. But he's so beautiful and charming that people forgive repeatedly, while his two bosom companions aid and abet."

"And clear away the damage."

"We must trust Blackwood to manage matters. He sorted out Ripley's troubles neatly enough. Your affianced husband can be astute when he chooses."

Husband. Alice's heart tossed and tumbled in her chest. She waited for it to settle down and said, "It won't be easy, even for him. I'm prepared to accommodate. To a point. The bond between them is strong, Aunt. I understand very well what it means to them. It's the way I feel about Cassandra: a connection stronger than kinship." She shook her head. "But our friendship would change, no matter whom I wed. She and I will manage, too."

"I wish that were all in need of managing. This latest episode of yours presents no small challenge. I shall have to consult with Julia. We'll have at the very most three days, by my calculation, before Society lights up like a bonfire."

"Society is welcome to go to blazes in it," Alice said. "I see no reason to trouble Aunt Julia. I refuse to live my life accommodating the gossips. I shall be the Duchess of Blackwood. The ton may like it or lump it."

"Alice, you punched a man in the face after taking a whip to him. There were witnesses."

"He nearly killed my brother. He robbed Ripley and left him for dead. What ought I to have done?"

"You ought not to have been there in the first place."

"But I was, and was observed, and that can't be changed. People will say I'm a monster. In that case perhaps they'll know not to get in my way."

"Really, child."

"Yes, really. I'm only sorry that Doveridge will be affected. The papers will ridicule him. That is most unf-fair." Her voice began to break. She bit her lip and turned her gaze to the window.

He had been kind, and he was intelligent and amusing and charming and easy to talk to. Now he'd pay for it.

She could not forget what Blackwood had said about her scandals affecting Doveridge's influence and prestige.

"You're fatigued, and no wonder," her aunt said. "You've been under a great strain."

Alice managed a laugh. "Indeed, trapping and fighting villains is not as easy as one might suppose."

"You were worried about Ripley. Doveridge understood that." She told Alice about the duke's visit on Tuesday.

"You needn't fret about him," Aunt Florentia said. "He's no dreamy-eyed boy. He'll recover from the infatuation soon enough. As to any talk or teasing—"

"They'll make a mockery of him. He doesn't deserve that."

"He knows what to expect. He's had decades of practice in sailing those waters, and he'll coast along smoothly enough, rely upon it."

Newmarket
Thursday 10 May 1832

BLACKWOOD AND RIPLEY found Ashmont relatively sober in the coffee room of the Rutland Arms.

Since one could seldom predict his reaction to anything, they took him to one of the private parlors on the first floor and ordered emollients in liquid form. The parlor overlooked the busy courtyard, where many fine specimens of horseflesh came and went.

He wasn't in the best of tempers. This was not because he was more or less sober but because his Uncle Fred had turned up. "It's no end aggravating," he told them. "He keeps his distance and pretends he's here for the races, but there he is, a great black cloud hanging over the place."

"Since he's spoiling your fun, you might as well return to London with us," Blackwood said.

"I thought we were supposed to keep clear of London. Well, it seems I was to keep clear of it, as you two have found something interesting to do there that doesn't include me."

"Now it does," Ripley said. "Blackwood's going to marry Alice, and we want you back for the wedding."

"What?" Ashmont looked from one to the other.

"I thought we were going to break it to him gently," Blackwood said.

"That wasn't gentle?"

"What?" Ashmont said.

"Alice has very kindly agreed to marry me," Blackwood said. "I'm thoroughly pleased. I hope you'll be pleased, too."

"But she's not supposed to marry us." The excessively blue eyes were bewildered. "We're unworthy."

"Alice didn't know that rule," Ripley said.

Ashmont's gaze shot from one to the other of his friends. "But we're not getting married yet."

"It seems we are," Ripley said. "One of us, at any rate."

Ashmont stared at his tankard as though the mystery's solution were written there in a language he was not familiar with. Still, he knew what to do with the contents. He lifted it and swallowed ale. He put the tankard down very gently. "This is very . . ." He shook his head.

"Yes," Ripley said. "It is. You could have knocked me over with a feather. But there it is. These things happen, and one must make the best of them." He summarized the events of recent days.

Blackwood watched Ashmont during the account. He did have a brain. He simply chose not to employ it most of the time. But he seemed to realize that this was one of the times he needed to bring it out of retirement. After a while, his incomprehension gave way to something like amused resignation.

"By gad, she led you a merry chase," Ashmont told him at the end. "If I'd been in your shoes, I'd have offered, too. What a fine girl she's turned out to be! Planted the turd a facer! That's our Alice. I wish I'd known about Worbury, though. Immense, stinking turd. But I'd only have beaten him to a lump or taken a horsewhip to him. Well, maybe I'd have shot him. What Blackwood did . . ." He laughed. "Oh, very well. You get the best girl in the kingdom. I reckon you've earned her."

"Unless my sister undergoes a radical change of character, he'll go on earning her for the rest of his life."

Ashmont patted Blackwood on the shoulder. "You'll do what needs to be done. You always do. But if things go awry, we're still your brothers. Well, he'll be your brother more than me, but—"

"No," Blackwood said. "We'll always be brothers."

"By bonds thicker than blood," Ripley said. He lifted his tankard.

They drank to that. And to other things. Many other things.

It appears that those who have wagered on the nuptial date of a certain peer and another's beauteous sister will lose their stakes. The lady, we have recently learnt, has exercised the fair sex's right and inclination to change her mind. In a reversal that has turned Society on its ear and overtaken the Reform Bill as a sensation and source of speculation, the lady has given her hand to another peer of equally high rank and altogether different reputation.

—*Foxe's Morning Spectacle*
Friday 11 May 1832

Camberley Place
12th Instant

My dearest Cassandra,

What a beast of a friend am I, to send you cryptic messages and leave you to wonder, but that seems to be the nature of my life lately. Half the time I imagine this is all a dream, but here is Aunt Florentia making lists of all the things that Must Be Done and all the things One Cannot Do Without, and arguing with me about what I may and mayn't do between now and the wedding. I'm sorry to be such a trial to her, but she loves me and is obliged to think when I do not.

Have you had time enough since my letter of the 10th to make sense of my choice of bridegroom?

Did I have a choice?

Certainly. The choice was plain, and mine is very likely a bad one, which has occasioned any number of second and third thoughts. As I've informed you more than once, I hold Doveridge in high esteem. He's perfect, everything I believed I wanted in a husband. Thus regrets begin to form. But then come the third thoughts, and I see the future stretching ahead of me, dinners and balls and appearances at Court and entertaining the King and Queen and the Royal Dukes and all the FitzClarences. Imagining it, I ought to feel stimulated and challenged. Instead I feel as though I face a lifetime in a cage, with no hope of escape. Clearly, I am not correctly designed for the position of Duchess of Doveridge.

Restrictions and obligations of that kind, we may rest assured, will not occur with Blackwood. Not, at any rate, while my brother and Ashmont are alive.

My future husband will break my heart sooner or later, but he's done that before. You and I had our hearts broken a few times, until we decided to put our infatuations behind us, as far behind and as far away as possible. We chose to adopt and adapt Shakespeare to our purpose: Women have died from time to time, and worms have eaten them, but not for love.

This in no way lessens my concerns about Aunt Julia's melancholy. We drove down this afternoon to explain the business and discuss it with her. She did not seem overly troubled by my engagement. Or troubled at all. She said,

"*Blackwood cares about you. That was obvious when I saw him last. He is by no means perfect, and the other two constitute a problem, but there is a great difference between infatuation and caring. I should prefer the latter, if I were you.*"

She calmed Aunt Florentia and had good advice for both of us. But she will not attend the wedding. She is not yet ready to leave Camberley Place. "*Forgive me and give me time,*" she says.

Sometimes I wonder if she will die of a broken heart. At other times I know she's much too sensible. Women have died, etc. . . .

As to your attending my wedding, she says there is no question of it, as do I. While I care nothing about heaping more scandal upon the pile I've already made, I will not have you leave your grandparents, and it is both pointless and ridiculous to make them curtail their travels for a wedding that will be done in an hour or less, and a wedding breakfast from which I shall very probably be absent. You and I will be reunited next year, by which time I expect to be settled in my new role.

It seems I must stop now. We have company, Vachon says. As she is laying out a fresh ensemble, it must be somebody important. I hope it isn't one of the royals. They call on Aunt Julia from time to time or send Lord Frederick Beckingham or another courtier to enquire after her health. No doubt, these deputies do what they can to entice her back to London. Let us wish them luck. And do wish me patience under their politely concealed curiosity.

Since I do not foresee further opportunities to write while I'm here, I'll close now and promise more after we return to London on Monday.

Your ever affectionate,
Alice

P.S. Not a royal, I have just been told, but a courtier. And whom do you suppose it is? My discarded duke, no less! I vow, the Fates are playing pranks on me.

LADY ALICE OFFERED both her hands when she greeted the duke. He took them.

"You were so kind to come," she said.

"I wanted to be among the first to wish you happy," he said.

She withdrew her hands to clasp them at her waist and raised her eyebrows at Lady Kempton, who took the hint and made an excuse to step out of the drawing room.

"I know this is most improper," Lady Alice said. "But I am improper, and I hate a rule that doesn't let me behave like a gentleman." Her brow knit. "Although, if I were a gentleman, I suppose we might have to fight it out at thirty paces."

He laughed. How could he help it? It was this sort of thing that had charmed him in the first place, and she charmed him still.

"Let's not pretend," she said. "Let's look at the thing, and please let me say I'm deeply sorry for any trouble I've caused you. Perhaps I've caused none. Perhaps a great deal. I don't know. I can only say I'm sorry, because you have been nothing but good to me."

He guessed that this cost her something. Her stance, the hands folded at her waist. But she did it, brave girl, and he had to admit it was well done.

"Would it be ungentlemanly of me to say I wish I'd followed my instincts and lured Blackwood to the bear pit and pushed him in?" he said. "Completely by accident, of course."

"I believe I can promise you that, at the time, marrying me was the last thing on his mind."

"Perhaps, then, I ought to have held him over the bear pit by his ankles until his thinking adjusted," Doveridge said. "Because, you see, it was annoyingly clear to me that he strongly objected to me and all the other fellows about you. But he's come to his senses, and I'll give him credit for that. And since you've been so brave as to arrange for us to speak privately, I shall speak my mind."

She stiffened as though to brace herself.

Yes, this exchange cost her a great deal more than she showed. Normally he had no inkling of her feelings, she hid them so well.

"Here's the thing," he said. "I do not mean to give you up. You are too interesting, and so many of our aims agree. I cannot afford to let your marriage estrange us." He paused. "I am not a young man, and you needn't fear that I speak impulsively. I've had a few days to absorb the news, to reflect and become philosophical."

Her stance eased. "I'll give you some philosophy," she said. "You had a narrow escape. We shall be good friends, if you like, but I should not have made a satisfactory wife for you. I did not intentionally mislead you. I misled myself. I flattered myself that I could do it. But you deserve better."

"Different, possibly. Better does not enter into it."

"You *are* kind," she said. "Thank you."

She gave him a full smile then, and the spark of humor was back in her green eyes, telling him he'd done the right thing. She was young, and she deserved to have the man of her choice. Only a great blockhead could fail to recognize who that was or how much better suited to her he was.

The Duke of Doveridge was not a blockhead. All things considered, he reckoned that having the lady as a friend would be more useful and a deal less nerve-wracking than having her as a wife.

Chapter 21

*T*he winner of Lady Alice Ancaster's hand called at Sussex Place in the afternoon. Alice and her aunt were standing at table in the library, arguing about her trousseau, when he entered. Sketches and lists covered the table.

"Thank heaven you've come," Alice said. "My aunt deems my current wardrobe insufficient. I disagree. It makes more sense to wait, because we have no idea what role the new Duchess of Blackwood will play in Society."

He looked startled. Then the mask came down, and his eyes became unreadable black. "Not a great role at Court for the foreseeable future, I suppose. I hope you're not disappointed."

"I'll try to bear this tragic turn of events with fortitude," she said.

"As to the rest . . ." He frowned. "Something to talk about. For the present, I thought we might go for a drive and sight-seeing. Or a walk, if you prefer. It isn't far, about a mile. The Colosseum. Or have you visited already?"

Though he didn't display it, she sensed tension. She wondered if the conversation with Ashmont had gone badly. Ripley hadn't written, but then, he wasn't the most reliable correspondent.

"I should like to take a walk and sightsee," she said.

She turned to her aunt. As much as Alice wanted to interrogate

Blackwood privately—which would want considerable skill and probably torture devices—she supposed a chaperon was required.

"Unless Blackwood insists—I know *you* will not—I see no reason for me to accompany you," Aunt Florentia said. "It will do no harm for you to be seen in public as an engaged couple." She turned to Blackwood. "Naturally you will take care to remain in public."

The mask cracked slightly, and Alice caught the flash of irritation. "Naturally, I'd rather not face her brother at thirty paces over a damp heath, and spoil my boots," he said.

"For heaven's sake, Aunt, this is the man who did not want to be seen with me in broad day not six miles from here, and acted as though we'd traveled to the ends of the earth for weeks. He's the one who fussed about my reputation. This is *Blackwood*, Aunt."

"Really, Alice, Lady Kempton is only—"

"Yes, only, but you don't know what it's like to be a bride-to-be," Alice said. "You'd think nobody ever got married before, the way my aunts carry on. I realize my situation is complicated, and I'm grateful they care so much about me and wish to protect me from gossipmongers, but I vow, if I hear another word on the subject, I shall scream. Kindly talk to my dear aunt, and make her feel better, as you know how to do, while I change into something suitable for walking and gawking. And yes, I shall be delighted. I've never been to the Colosseum, though I've been meaning to visit for weeks."

A ROLE AT Court.

Blackwood ought to have realized. He was a duke. He was about to be married. His wife would be presented at Court as the new Duchess of Blackwood.

The three dukes were not favorites there. He couldn't remember the last time he'd attended one of the King's levees. Was it during the previous King's reign, when Lord Charles was still alive? Certainly Their Dis-Graces were not familiar figures at St. James's Palace . . . unlike Doveridge.

He remembered what Alice had said about envying Maggie's

power. A woman in good standing at Court wielded considerable power. Certainly Lady Charles had done so and continued to do so, regardless of her self-exile.

While his mind reviewed relevant chapters of CORRECT BEHAVIOR, he made conversation with her aunt, with little idea of what he was saying.

Though it seemed to him that they'd been talking since the time of the Flood, Alice reappeared in what the drawing room's mantel clock told him was remarkably short order.

She'd donned an emerald-green pelisse of heavy silk, with a lot of silk ornaments adorning the bodice and skirt fronts and the decorations over the sleeves. Black lace made a large X over the dress: a V from the tops of her enormous sleeves to a point at her waist, then an inverted V below the waist to somewhere about the area of her knees, wherever they were, to create the effect of a coat over the dress. A lacy white ruff encircled her throat. Gauzy white bows framed her face, and ribbons flowed from the white bonnet. The green matched her eyes, and the style focused one's attention upon the oval of her face, which constituted about all the skin on view.

It was ridiculous, and he wanted to kiss her.

But then, he'd been wanting to kiss her for a large part of his life.

Soon, he reminded himself, if he didn't muck it up.

"Try to behave in a civilized manner," Lady Kempton said. "No fisticuffs, if you please."

"None that anybody will find out about, I promise," he said.

At last they left the town house, and he felt he could breathe properly again. As they started southward, he said, "Are you so disgusted with wedding business that we must throw the subject into the lake?"

Alice gazed at the lake. He wondered if she was considering throwing herself into it.

She was unhappy, clearly. Second thoughts, no doubt. Ice formed in the pit of his stomach.

"May we elope?" she said.

He gave her a quick glance. Her profile—what little he could discern of it—told him nothing. "That will save me the bother of getting a special license," he said.

She looked up at him, and the bows and ribbons fluttered. "I'd forgotten. In that case, we might be married anywhere."

"A clergyman will be required."

She waved this away. "It's only that I don't want a great fuss, and I don't see the point of creating one."

"It's considered rather a special day."

"It will be more special to me if it's simple. I shall order a pretty white dress to be married in, of course. Is that not sufficient? I brought scores of dresses from Paris, but Aunt tells me the Queen wants us to wear clothes of British manufacture to Court events. I said I'd wear my bridal dress to the Drawing Room when she presents me, the way my mother did and she did and Aunt Julia did. It seems wasteful to run up dressmaker bills when I've more clothing than I can wear as it is. Then I shan't have to listen to Ripley's jokes about how expensive I am. I shall listen to your jokes instead. Kindly make them wittier."

The inner ice began to melt, and his spirits made a cautious movement upward.

"My dear girl, you might have the wedding in whatever manner you prefer. The prospect of marrying me is trial enough for the nerves. How you do it is entirely up to you."

She stopped short and looked up at him. "Will it be a trial for you? Hard for Ripley and Ashmont? Because I'm not oblivious, you know. Those two are your brothers, in the same way that Cassandra is my sister. You're used to being with them."

Before he could respond, she went on, "I imagine it was especially difficult for Ashmont."

"Ashmont was Ashmont. After the first series of shocks, he bore the news better than expected. I told him of your recent activities. He listened, enthralled. After he heard how you planted Bray a facer, he opened his eyes very wide and—"

"I know that look," she said. "I've watched women melt under it. Actually, they melt under all his looks. Most unfortunate."

"I don't melt easily. His objections did, though. He patted me on the shoulder and congratulated me. Then he became philosophical."

"After how many bottles?"

"I don't remember."

"That many," she said.

A pair of ladies on horseback nodded at them. They nodded back.

"They've had their delicious thrill for the day," Alice said. "Now they can tell their friends." She started walking again, and he went with her.

Then he had a glimpse of what troubled her. His was no deep comprehension, certainly. Women were profoundly complicated puzzles, so far beyond most men's deciphering skills that they rarely attempted the feat. Furthermore, he normally dealt with women who did not require much in the way of solving. Jewelry was an effective solution.

He had sisters, though—much older, but sisters nonetheless. From time to time he'd had to do more cogitating and less shopping—although gifts never made anything worse, in his experience.

"I did have wedding questions," he said. "The logical first question is, When shall we be wed? Then I should like to know whether you would like to escape London for a time and take an extended honeymoon. Six months, if you like. A year. We could travel about England, Wales, Scotland. We might spend time in Brighton. Or the Lakes. Or the Peak. You've traveled extensively abroad, but not here."

If what she needed was to get away from the ton, he understood that, quite well.

She slowed and came to another stop. She turned to him. "You think of everything."

"Sometimes."

"I should like that very much," she said.

The inner ice melted a little more.

"Then let's have a farewell look at London from the Colosseum, and plot our escape," he said.

THE BUILDING BORE no resemblance to Rome's Coliseum. Still, it was imposing enough externally: a sixteen-sided polygon, some four hundred feet around, and one hundred twelve feet from the top of the glass skylight to the ground, Blackwood informed Alice.

She'd seen it time and again, of course, from the outside. One could hardly miss it. The outside did not prepare one for the wonders of the interior.

One entered a saloon filled with works of art, which Blackwood promised they might study at another time.

"I want you to see the panorama," he said. "It's impressive."

He led her to a wooden tubular structure in the center of the building. "We have two ways of ascending. We might climb the stairs. They're not taxing, and one might view the lower parts of the picture through a scaffolding like the one the original artist saw when St. Paul's was being repaired. Or we might float upward, as though rising in a balloon."

Alice had read about the Colosseum in various magazines. She knew that a Mr. Horner had made the drawings about ten years ago from various rickety contraptions at the top of St. Paul's. He'd also invented the elevating device or whatever it was. She'd wondered how it worked, and what it would be like to soar upward in it.

"I should like to float," she said.

They entered a small room in the center of the structure.

It rose, not as quietly as a cloud, but gently and slowly.

"This is a strange feeling," she said. She giggled. "How odd it is!"

"Like being hoisted in a room-size bucket."

"But more smoothly. This is so much better than arguing

about trousseaus." She looked up at him to find him gazing down at her, his head tipped slightly to one side, his dark eyes intent.

"When you look up at me in that way, your remarkable face framed by all that nonsensical—" He waved a hand. "Whatever it is. When you look at me in that way, as though I have performed a mighty feat, I feel, very strongly, that I must kiss you."

Everything inside her came suddenly alive, as though galvanized by an electrical device.

"If you must," she said.

She tipped her head back.

He leant toward her. His mouth touched hers. Then it was more than a touch. They came together quickly, as they'd done that night at the inn. His arms wrapped about her, and his mouth invited. And she went, without the smallest qualm. The opposite, in fact. She wanted the taste of him and the scent of him and the feel of him and she didn't hesitate, but gave all he seemed to ask for, because it was what she wanted, too.

Kissing him was like drinking strong brandy. Shocks ran through her, little fires that seemed to race through her veins. She pressed closer, and he tightened his embrace, drawing her against his powerful body. While he ran his hands down her back and over her bottom, she could feel his arousal, despite all the layers of clothing between them.

He backed her up against a wall of the little room, kissing her all the while, his tongue doing wicked things inside her mouth, and her own tongue learning how to be wicked, too.

The room stopped moving.

It took her time to notice, and for a while it was no more than a distant awareness, as one is dimly conscious of the sky being overhead and the ground under one's feet.

He broke the kiss, though his mouth hovered over hers. His eyes were very dark.

"Have we stopped already?" he said. His voice was rough.

"Have we?"

He blinked, then gently drew back. When his hands slid away, she felt bereft.

"I hate when we stop," she said.

"Then I recommend you set an early wedding date," he said.

THE MACHINERY HAD carried them to the first gallery. Alice stepped out—and instinctively stepped back from the balustrade. Below and before her lay London, from the top of St. Paul's, looking down Ludgate Hill, but so sharply distinct and *real*. Even from the top of the Green Park arch, on a relatively clear day, drifting smoke had obscured the view. She was so accustomed to mists and fogs and smoke, though, that she'd hardly noticed.

This was a crystalline view, the original sketches having been made very early in the morning. No pall of smoke hung over the place, obscuring its buildings and beings. Only a few wisps, here and there, rose into the blue sky from chimneys.

The Thames wound its way through London and beyond, a blue snake sparkling in sunlight, her bridges and vessels crisply detailed. As one moved round the gallery, the vast canvas presented the great streets—Oxford Street, the Strand, Piccadilly, the Mall, the Borough High Street—and row upon row of buildings great and small, magnificent and miserable. Before one lay the parks and gardens and palaces, the warehouses and factories, the churches and monuments. London, all of it and more, stretched out for twenty miles in every direction.

She could not stop looking. Blackwood pointed out particular places, and she felt as though they were celestial beings looking down on the metropolis.

There was more, another gallery higher up, which this time they reached via stairs. It offered a different perspective, equally marvelous. Blackwood handed her a pair of spyglasses, conveniently provided for visitors, which allowed her to make out even finer details.

He pointed out objects he thought would interest her. He had answers for every question, it seemed.

"This is splendid," she said. "I've seen panoramas, but this—such an undertaking. Every street and building and bridge, carriages and boats." She waved a hand at the vast scene. "Everything. It's wonderful."

"If you care to undertake another set of stairs—a short ascent, this time—we might visit yet another gallery, this time out of doors, where we shall have a fine view of London as it is today, not quite so sharply clear."

She went up the stairs with him, and it was altogether different. As he'd said, the view was not crystalline. Smoke, constantly moving, shortened and dimmed the vista. Still, it was thrilling to feel as though one stood atop the world, like gods.

They two might be Jupiter and Juno, gazing down from Olympus.

They were not unlike that pair, both strong-willed.

"You liked the sensation of being at the top of the arch," he said. "I deduced that you'd enjoy this."

"I do, very much." She gazed up at him. "You've made me forget all the petty irritations and squabbles. You've given me something much larger to think about. Thank you."

All the galleries had benches, since many visitors had trouble with dizziness.

He gestured for her to sit, and she did, and realized that though she wasn't exactly tired, she did feel rather overwhelmed.

He took the place beside her. "Now that I've softened your mind, I've something for you." He reached into the breast pocket of his waistcoat and drew out a small red leather box.

Her heart beat very hard then.

"We set about this marrying business in the strangest manner," he said. "But I want it to be right. And here is my promise." He opened the box. "It was my grandmother's. Old-fashioned, I'm afraid, but—"

"Oh, Giles." Inside its white satin nest, a large diamond sparkled in its gold setting. Two smaller though not very small diamonds stood, one on each side, like attendants. These each had a pair of tiny emerald attendants.

"It's perfect." Her throat closed up, and her eyes filled. *Watering pot*, she scolded herself.

"We can't expect it to fit, but—"

"Try." She put out her left hand.

He slid it onto her third finger. "A little loose. That can be mended easily. The whole thing can be mended. We can reset the stones. Or buy you another."

She looked up at him. His face shimmered through her tears. "I don't want another. I want them as they are. But you are making me cry, and . . ."

"I don't want another," he said. "I want you as you are, and you are never to think otherwise." He cupped her face and kissed her.

She would have climbed into his lap, to continue what they'd started in the elevating room, but he broke the kiss.

"I arranged for us to have as much privacy as possible," he said. "Still, it's difficult and awkward to keep visitors away for any length of time at a popular site like this one. In any case, if we continue in this manner, I shall lose my head and forget to be a gentleman, and this is not the most comfortable location for the rites of the wedding night."

She smiled down at the ring on her finger. His grandmother's. That told her a great deal. The kissing told a story, too, as did the time they'd spent together this day. She widened the smile and turned it upward, at him. "We'd better set a date, then."

Chapter 22

York Hotel, George Street, Bath
Saturday 19 May 1832

Lord Worbury's doddering maternal aunt was planted at last, having dragged out the dying business for an eternity.

This morning he'd attended the will reading. She'd left her riches to be divided among several Bath charitable institutions: the Female Orphans Asylum and House of Protection, the Puerperal or Child-bed Charity, the Society for the Relief of Lying-In Women, the Children's Friend Society, and the Servants' Friend Society.

Upon Worbury she'd bestowed her extensive collection of sermons.

He wished he'd held a pillow over her face.

While tradesmen were still willing to extend credit to a rackety duke's heir presumptive, credit wasn't ready money, an article even a titled gentleman required. One might ignore the tradesmen's bills, of course. Bets, however, must be settled promptly. Furthermore, a great many establishments catering to gentlemen's pleasures expected pounds, shillings, and pence, not IOUs.

Worbury pushed the money problem aside for the time being, because a letter from Lady Bartham had arrived in today's mail from London. He and Consett had retired to a sitting room overlooking George Street to enjoy it. Consett's mama, whose mission in life was collecting and spreading scandal, had proved quite useful, and her letters could be amusing.

The previous one had been full of the scandal about Lady Alice and Blackwood, including various rumors about her unchaperoned, overnight visit to Kensington with His Dis-Grace. Worbury would have been happier with eyewitness accounts of her having been brutally assaulted by a gang of criminals and thrown into a brothel for the amusement of the patrons.

He wasn't thrilled, either, with the change of intended spouse from Doveridge to Blackwood, though he would have preferred rather less formidable mates for her. Still, one might take comfort in one certainty: If she and Blackwood did actually wed, theirs would be a marriage made in hell.

If they wed. According to Lady Bartham, the nuptials had not yet taken place. With two dukes involved, a great deal of legal business had to be settled first. And of course the trousseau required time and thought.

"Trousseau, my foot," Worbury said. "They're only delaying because they mean to cry off. Mark my words, one of them will balk. He'll never give up his friends and whoring for any woman, and she hates men. They'll wait until the talk about the Kensington orgy dies down, then decide they don't suit. It happens all the time."

Consett glanced down at the letter. "Mama says they've set a date. Settlements signed and . . . Oh."

"What?"

"I don't think—"

"Don't think. You know it doesn't agree with you. Plague take it, what's that look for?"

"It's only . . . It's not good."

Worbury snatched the letter from him and found the place where he'd left off.

I have it on the best authority that the Duke of Ripley has made extensive changes to his will. He and his solicitor have contrived sufficient entanglements to leave Lord Worbury with what amounts to an empty title. They have tied up the properties and restricted the income by so many conditions that he will be hard-pressed to make anything of it. In short, Ripley has left your friend as near penniless as a duke can be.

The news is already making the rounds of the ton, and tradesmen will get wind of it within days. In the circumstances, Lord Worbury may soon find his creditors baying at the window and clawing at the door. Were he my son, I should advise him to find an heiress without loss of time.

THE DUKE OF Blackwood and Lady Alice Ancaster were married by special license at Sussex Place on Tuesday 5 June.

The bride changed into traveling attire not long thereafter, and the couple set out for Brighton, leaving their guests to enjoy a sumptuous wedding breakfast.

As the coachman turned the traveling chariot into Regent Street, Blackwood said, "It's done. I began to think it would never happen."

"Changing Ripley's will complicated matters," she said.

"Among other concerns, we had to make certain Worbury had no way of touching anything to do with you. We were obliged to become Machiavellian."

"You've relieved my brother of a great worry."

"My desperate desire to marry his sister as soon as possible spurred my imagination, and so I spurred the lawyers."

She laid her gloved hand over his. "Now you're stuck with me."

He gazed into her green eyes, and the moment came back to him when the minister asked the fatal question and Blackwood had looked down at his bride. She'd worn white then, something frothy and fanciful, but all he saw was her wondrous face. He simply fell into her eyes, as into a sparkling sea, and said, "I will."

At present she wore a pink-and-green dress. A pleated cambric chemisette filled in the low neckline and effectively covered the skin beneath. The overly enthusiastic flower and lace hat decorations matched the green of the dress. It was all very silly and excessively feminine and altogether too inviting. Getting all those layers off, for instance. So tempting.

"I regret nothing," he said.

"If you do have second thoughts—"

"Too late for that now."

"It's never too late. One might do away with unwanted persons in scores of ways."

"Doubtless you've thought of them."

"Women warriors need to employ guile and cunning to compensate for lesser physical strength than men."

"After all the bother I've endured, I might as well keep you," he said. "At least for a time."

"Let's pretend, though. We've a longish journey ahead, and it will help while away the hours."

He had fine ideas about how to pass the time, but those constituted Incorrect Behavior. She was the Duchess of Blackwood. He was not going to deflower her in a traveling chariot on the Brighton Road. He'd married her properly, and he'd endure six or so hours of travel in order to perform the wedding night rites correctly.

What an idiot he'd been to suggest Brighton.

Why not Twickenham or Richmond?

But he wanted her to know England's beauties and wonders. Then, perhaps, she wouldn't miss the Continent so much.

"I could always leave you in one of those lanes in the northern part of Kensington, where you might wander for hours and never be found," he said. "I'd say you'd run away from me, and everybody would understand why."

"That's clever. But people might point out that traveling through Kensington is an odd route to take to Brighton. What about a brewery? You might take me to visit—there must be one on the way, or not far out of the way. Then I could accidentally fall into a vat of ale and drown."

In his mind appeared an image of this concoction dropping down into a large vat, rather like a balloon landing. "Not in that dress. You'll float."

She looked down at the dress. "It's French. The Queen would not approve. But Parisians have infected my taste, and I haven't yet found the perfect London modiste. There was a splendid shop in Paris, but the dressmakers closed it during the cholera and riots. They never reopened, and I don't know what's become of them."

"I am not the Queen," he said. "Furthermore, I'm a man, and I don't give a damn about your dress."

"But your duchess must look like a duchess."

"My duchess is free to wear whatever she likes, the world's or the Queen's opinion may go to the devil, and her spouse will merely make witty remarks about the expense. I believe it would be wise to stop talking about your dress because I find myself debating the quickest way to get it off—or not necessarily *all* off—and—"

"What about kissing?" she said. "Can there be kissing?"

"Of course there can be."

"Now?"

"I'm not sure that's a good—"

"Because it seems to me that there has not been enough kissing of late."

"I've been busy," he said.

"You're not busy now."

"I'm busy thinking about the wedding night, which will happen in a *bed*, not in a vehicle."

She looked about her.

It was a ducal carriage, furnished in the height of luxury. Nonetheless, it was not the correct location for the business.

On the other hand . . .

"However, it's true that you haven't had much practice," he said.

"No, I haven't had anybody to practice on since our visit to the Colosseum. While that was exciting, it was insufficient."

"I don't doubt that any number of men would welcome the opportunity to be practiced upon."

"That may be, but for some reason, I've felt disinclined to offer it."

He sighed heavily. "Then I suppose it will have to be me."

She smiled up at him, and down he went, to drown in the sparkling green sea.

BLACKWOOD DIDN'T TAKE her in his arms and kiss her, as Alice expected.

He lifted the hand that rested on his. He pushed back the edge of the glove and kissed her wrist.

"Oh." Not a word but a tiny gasp of a word. It was a wonder that so small a touch could do so much, making her insides tighten and quiver.

He drew the glove off, finger by finger, and slipped it from her hand.

He did the same to the other glove. He brought her naked hands to his mouth and kissed the palms. He brought her hands to his jaw, and she held him that way and looked up into his eyes and found herself falling into midnight.

"I wish you would kiss me, in your own amateurish way," he said.

She slid her fingers into his thick hair and drew his head down and brought her mouth to his. The merest touch, yet she felt it deeply. Tiny shocks skimmed along her skin and set her alight.

She pressed a little more, and he brought his arms about her and drew her closer while his mouth moved against hers. As soft as velvet but potent, it brought a rush of warmth and joy. All this, from no more than a meeting of lips. It was like another sort of speech between them, another secret shared.

A kiss, an endless kiss, and the feel of his mouth and the scent of his skin, the whisper of their clothing as they drew closer. Her lips clung to his, and she let her hands slide down to grasp his coat, the way she'd done so long ago, holding on while she fell, deeper and deeper.

This time he didn't draw away.

This time he made a sound like a low growl and pulled her onto his lap.

She knocked off his hat and dragged her hands through his hair and along the back of his neck. She felt the muscles tighten under her fingers, and her insides tensed in sympathy, as though invisible cords tied his body to hers. He brushed his tongue against her lips, and she opened to him, easily and unthinkingly. The intimacy of it brought a wash of inner heat that hurried everywhere, outward and downward and into her brain to make her drunk. A drunken being inside her whispered, *I want I want I want*.

She dragged her hands up over his shoulders, and down along his arms, and *mine mine mine*, the drunken being whispered. It was a shadow, a feeling, and the whispers were feelings more than words.

She broke the kiss to let her lips touch his cheek. She brushed his cheek with hers and took in the familiar man-scents of starch and wool and shaving soap mingled with whatever it was that was this man's alone.

"Good God, Alice." His voice was a groan.

"I know you," she said, letting her mouth graze his jaw. "Why do I know you?"

Because I love you. I've always loved you.

It played in her mind, the whispering feeling, telling secrets she kept even from herself.

"Affinity," he murmured.

She nuzzled his neck—the precious bit of it she could get to, between his neckcloth and ear. The way he smelled was an intoxicant. She needed more. She wanted to touch more of him.

He moved his hands over her in the same way she did to him, learning and claiming him. He slid his hand down her back to the bottom of her spine and pressed her closer.

She let out a little gasp. "Oh, when you touch me . . ."

She might have said that. She might have simply made noises. She didn't care. He filled the carriage and the world, and she wanted only to be in that world, close to him and part of him.

He eased his hold and made the growling sound again.

"This won't do," he said. His voice was hoarse.

She laid her head on his shoulder, aware of her breath coming and going so quickly, her heart beating a gallopade.

This will do very well, she thought. *This ought to go on doing.* That was virtually all she could think. That and, *Why do we stop?*

"I don't want to stop," she said.

"Neither do I," he said. "That's the problem."

"That is not a problem."

She felt rather than heard his laugh.

"This time it is. Another time, not at all."

She lifted her head to look at him.

He was not a beautiful golden angel like Ashmont. Black-wood was dark and not angelic. The angles of jaw and cheek-bone were sharp, the nose commanding, the mouth sensuous now, but she'd seen it hard and unforgiving.

His eyes were even more intriguing. They could be soft or amused or stern or dangerous. Sometimes looking into them was like looking into nothing. This was not one of those times. They were gentle now, with a hint of laughter and something more that she wasn't sure of but rather liked.

"That hat," he said, shaking his head. "That hat has taken leave of its wits. It thinks it's a hat but it's gone too far. It's much too much hat. I want to take it off. I want to take off the rest of your excessive clothing. But."

"I believe I should like for you to take off the rest. But leave the hat on. So many pins."

"Alice."

"Giles."

He smiled. "You'll make me dote upon my own wife."

"Is that so wrong?"

"It's very difficult to think while you sit in my lap," he said.

"Why are you thinking at a time like this?"

He put his lips against her ear. She shivered.

He said softly, "I had in mind a large, well-appointed bed-chamber in my Brighton town house. A grand ducal bed. Champagne and a bite to eat. But if we continue in this way, the lovemaking will happen awkwardly, uncomfortably, and far too quickly—in a carriage. All very well in its way, that sort of thing, but I had wanted our wedding night to be special."

She wanted the wedding night to be this minute. Sitting in his lap, she was fully aware of his desire for her. The awareness was making her have feelings she wasn't used to and needed assuaged. She had a reasonably good idea how this might be done.

Aunt Florentia had explained wedding night matters on the previous night. Alice was already schooled in the basics. She'd seen animals mating. She and Cassandra had closely studied pictures they were supposed to know nothing about. Even so, she'd insisted that her aunt provide all the particulars. At present she felt not at all afraid, except of not knowing exactly what to do when. But Blackwood knew, and he'd teach her.

"You have a point," she said. She eased herself off his lap. "How much farther have we to travel?"

Chapter 23

Alice's French maid and Blackwood's valet had left London at the same time they did, in a separate carriage. They were to make their way with all necessary dispatch, while master and mistress followed at a more leisurely pace.

The house in Brighton would be prepared for their arrival.

As always, Blackwood had planned for everything.

Except the Duchess of Blackwood. His wife.

He had a *wife*. Alice. And Alice was Alice.

She'd always been fierce, especially when anybody or anything she cared about was threatened. She was sharp-witted and strong-willed and defiant. He knew all that.

Her lack of inhibition was not altogether a surprise. She'd never been prudish.

But the trust! After all this time and the way he'd lived his life for the last decade and more, she had ample reason to keep her guard up. Yet when it came to physical intimacy, she hesitated not at all. She gave herself wholeheartedly and spoke frankly about what she wanted.

There has not been enough kissing.

Even a man who'd avoided good girls from the time he discovered girls knew how they were expected to behave. The standards appeared in reviews of books, operas, plays, and even circuses, as well as in gossip sections of the journals. Young ladies were modest and circumspect. They maintained a quiet demeanor, a dignified reserve, etc., etc.

Boring, in other words. One of many forceful reasons to shun their company.

This sort of being might be Alice at Almack's, but it was not Alice in his lap in a carriage.

Alice in his lap meant exerting every last iota of his willpower *not* to relieve her of her virginity en route. It meant reminding himself that he was not a callow youth of nineteen but an experienced man of seven and twenty.

Most important, this was the only wedding day and night they would ever have. It had to be special. Alice deserved no less.

What he needed to do was thank Fortune for placing him in this uncomfortable position.

The capricious goddess had smiled on him. She'd somehow tricked him into doing the intelligent thing before he realized how intelligent it was. Brilliant, actually. An act of pure genius.

He kept these considerations in mind and restricted himself to conversation. For sixty long miles.

They talked about the passing sights, unfamiliar to her. He had stories. She had comments and her own stories of Continental travels, and she told him a great deal she hadn't included in her letters to Ripley.

They reached Brighton before sunset, to find the staff awaiting their master and new mistress, and all in readiness.

There were ceremonies to be got through: introductions and preliminary tours of the gleaming white mansion on the Steine. It was the second most impressive residence in Brighton, the Royal Pavilion being the first.

All the while, Blackwood asked himself why he hadn't chosen instead to spend the wedding night during the wedding afternoon, at an inn on the road. Better yet, why hadn't he bought a cottage requiring only a handful of servants?

But at last the rituals were done, and the newlyweds retired to their separate apartments to change out of their traveling clothes.

The duke and his new duchess did not dine in state in the handsome dining parlor, but in Her Grace's boudoir.

In fact, they dined very little, hardly touching the food he'd been so particular about ordering.

After staring at her plate for a time, Alice rose. He did, too.

"This is a sad waste of beautiful food," she said. "But I am too—" She waved a hand. "I can't. I'd better find something more productive to do, like changing out of this . . ." She looked down at herself. "And into something less."

"Wait, please." He circled the small table and caught her in his arms and kissed her, long and deeply, until the blood was hurrying through his veins and heading downward and he forgot who and what and where he was.

Then he collected the last threads of his self-control and released her. "I only wanted to make sure you don't forget," he said.

She gazed at him, her eyes soft and dazed. "Forget what?"

She laughed, rather unsteadily, and went out.

An hour later

ENTERING ALICE'S BEDCHAMBER was like entering a dream.

Amid billowing white bedclothes she sat, propped up with pillows. Though the night was mild, Blackwood had ordered a fire lit. Sea air was all well and good, but it was damp and more chill than London air, if some degrees clearer.

Embers glowed in the fireplace. A pair of lamps on the mantel cast their soft light over the room. One lamp at the bedside table shed its glow over her.

A lacy cap, as fine as gossamer, confined her hair. Lace edged her nightdress, framing a creamy expanse of neck and shoulder and the soft curves of her bosom.

He found it hard to breathe.

She set aside the guidebook she'd been perusing and looked up at him.

"That is something a great deal less," he managed to say.

Her green gaze swiftly took him in. "I might say the same of you."

He wore a black silk dressing gown, embroidered and trimmed in gold and green. And slippers. And no more.

It was not the first time she'd seen him in a state of undress. The previous time, however, he had not been quite so undressed. He'd worn a shirt under his dressing gown.

"I know you won't faint," he said. "But I might."

Her skin, so much smooth skin. No vast pillows of fabric concealed her arms. Only the fine muslin veiled them, leaving their outlines clearly visible. He could imagine the rest. Soon he wouldn't have to imagine.

"You're beautiful," he said softly. "I do not at all regret my temporary loss of mind some weeks ago."

"We'll see about that." She smoothed the bedclothes. "This may be rather tedious for you. I need instruction. In theory, I understand the proceedings. In practice, my ignorance is complete."

"I'm prepared to persevere," he said.

He moved to the bed. He was tall enough not to need the step. He sat and took her hand, the one wearing the betrothal ring and the wedding ring he'd had made to match, because she liked his grandmother's ring as it was.

He kissed the back of her hand and the knuckles, one by one. He turned her hand over and kissed the wrist. In the room's quiet he could hear her breath quickening. His quickened as well.

He released her hand to unfasten his dressing gown. "You've seen naked men before."

"Naked boys, a long time ago. And naked statues, but . . ." She stilled as he shifted out of the dressing gown. He could feel her gaze as though it were her hands moving over him.

"Well, it isn't quite the same," she said. "Statues don't

breathe, and their muscles don't move, and *that* . . ." Her gaze had dropped. "The membrum virile is *much* larger in real life."

His swelled with pride, not to mention anticipation. He was quietly going mad, yet he laughed a little. "Really, Alice."

She took a deep breath. "This is going to be interesting."

He moved to take her in his arms. "I should like it to be more than that for you. I should like it to be pleasurable. But if we don't quite manage that the first time, we can try again."

"Stop talking," she said. "Kindly kiss me, as much as you please. And the rest as well."

HE OBEYED ORDERS. He held her in his arms and kissed her.

This kiss was altogether different from those before. This was the wedding night kiss. This time the only barrier between them was the fine muslin of her nightdress.

This time the bare palms of her hands curved over his naked shoulders, skin to skin. The pleasure of that simple touch and the trust it conveyed swept through him in waves of feeling, nearly unbearable. Yet he wanted what he felt to go on forever.

He drank in the taste of her and the scent of her, and he might as well have taken opium. The world slipped away. There was only this place, wherever it was, warm and inviting and impossible to escape, and no, he didn't want to escape, ever again.

He deepened the kiss, and she quickly began to learn the way of it, playful at first, a sort of teasing, but soon becoming something else, stronger and hotter.

She moved her hands over his chest and shoulders and arms, and his muscles tightened, but what he felt was more than physical. Women had touched him before, and that was pleasurable and arousing. Alice's caresses were another experience altogether, shockingly powerful. His entire being responded. Everything in him marveled and stirred at the same time.

He dragged his hands over her shoulders and arms and over the swell of her breasts. Muslin whispered secrets under his fingers.

He wanted skin, more skin.

He broke the kiss and murmured, "Too much clothing."

She shifted to help him get the nightdress off. No shyness. No hesitation.

And then there was Alice, naked.

He caught his breath. "Ye gods," he said. "Ye gods, Alice."

Lust was murdering his mind, yet he had to take a moment to simply look at her.

The lamplight turned her skin golden. He might as well be looking at an ancient goddess.

He drew the bedclothes back a little more.

So beautifully formed she was: the perfect swell of her breasts and the graceful curve of waist and hips and long legs.

His wife. This was his wife.

"With my body I thee worship," he said softly.

Tears glittered in her eyes. "Giles."

He brought his hand to her cheek and gently brushed away the tear. He stroked her neck and downward, touching her and discovering her.

He ached, and every animal instinct wanted possession—*now*—but he couldn't bear to hurry.

"We'll never have another wedding night," he said. "I want to make the most of it."

She smiled the Egyptian goddess smile.

He kissed her neck and her shoulders. He slid his mouth lower, to draw paths of kisses over the tops of her breasts, then lower. She squirmed and reached for him. "More," she said.

"Yes." He took the bud of her breast into his mouth and she made a little sound, like a moan.

He suckled the other breast, and she writhed under him.

He slid down and kissed her belly, then lower. She made little sounds of pleasure and excitement. She didn't hold back, but let herself be pleasured. When her body arched upward, he slid his hand to where his mouth had been. He shifted himself upward again to kiss her cheek and below her ear and her mouth while he moved his hand between her legs.

"You're a wonder," he murmured. "There's nobody like you."

He stroked her and kissed her until her body shuddered and shuddered, and release came, with a surprised little cry.

She opened her eyes very wide. "Good heavens."

"I hope so." He brought her hand to his impatient cock pressing against her thigh.

"I've done what I could, but I'm afraid this will hurt," he said, his voice rough.

"I'm not afraid of you," she said. "Don't stop now."

Gently he drew her legs apart and pressed himself into her.

He felt her tense at the intrusion and the discomfort, and heard her breath catch. He paused, though the blood was racing through his veins and he was sweating and his brain was going black.

"Don't stop," she said. "You're not supposed to stop."

In spite of himself, he let out a choked, short laugh. "Alice."

"Do it," she said. "More. I want you."

Thinking was in another land, another universe. The sound of her voice. *I want you.* He pushed inside her, and she gasped, but she grasped his arms. "Don't stop."

He kissed her, on the mouth, on the nose, on the cheek. He kissed the top of her ear. He felt the tightness give way slightly.

He pushed in, and the feel of her body closing about him, holding him, was new, all new. He didn't wonder at it, because he had no mind for that. He tried to fix on taking care, and that was growing impossible. He began to move inside her, as slowly as he could.

She grasped his arms. "Giles."

"Yes." He kissed her again and again. Her eyebrows, her forehead, her mouth again, deeply, and her body made way for him.

Her eyes opened very wide. "Oh, my goodness. Oh, Giles. *Yes.*"

The last thread of control gave way, and all he knew was the woman whose body was joined with his, and the need to possess her entirely. She began to find the rhythm of it, and they moved together, as though they'd always done so. It was the way they used to dance once upon a time, so long ago. It was the way they played with words and the way it had always been with them. Even when they were apart, even when they clashed, there was a bond.

Affinity.

These weren't thoughts in words but a bone-deep knowing.

She trembled and cried out—but not in pain—and he felt a surge of triumph. His heart crashed against his chest again and again, and the need built and built like a great wave surging ever higher, until there was nowhere left to go. His body shuddered, and he let out a low, hoarse cry. Then came release and a dizzying descent.

"Alice," he said, a breath of a word. "Ye gods, Alice." He lay, spent, upon her for a moment, his cheek against her breast.

He felt her shiver. He shivered, too.

After a time, he gently eased from her and drew her into his arms. He kissed the top of her frivolous nightcap, then drew it off and kissed the top of her head.

Later, when they'd lain, more than a little stunned, in each other's arms, and their breathing had quieted to something like normal:

"Giles."

"Yes. I'm here. Not going anywhere."

"I believe we'll do well enough."

"I believe you are right."

THEY DID WELL enough again that night and the next morning.

They did well enough for a fortnight in Brighton. They did well enough as, over the following months, the Duke of Blackwood took his bride on a grand tour of England, her own country, of which she knew not very much. They visited his estates and smaller properties. They toured the Peak and the

Lake District and the various fashionable watering holes. They sailed on his yacht.

The honeymoon lasted for six months.

And they lived happily ever after.

Until.

Chapter 24

April 1833

Maybe the trouble started with the rabbits.

Though a mere half a dozen of them were involved, the number proved sufficient for the Duke of Ashmont's purposes.

He hadn't been invited to the royal fête for the Grand Duchess of Volldenham. He hadn't been invited to respectable gatherings for some time.

Not inviting him was one thing. Keeping him out was another altogether.

They'd made the mistake of holding it on April Fool's Day. He got in. So did the rabbits, also not invited. The event dissolved into chaos. Women shrieked, men tried not to laugh and failed, servants ran about, and a lot of shouting prevailed generally.

The Grand Duchess, who prided herself on not speaking a word of English and hadn't a sense of humor in any language, failed to grasp the concept of April Fool's Day. Believing she'd been grossly insulted, she stalked out.

She was one of the Royal Family's numerous distant cousins and by no means King William's favorite. Furthermore, having spent his youth in the Navy, he was a better sailor than diplomat. But like it or not, he had to swallow his resentment and pacify her. Lord Frederick Beckingham learnt His Majesty's true feelings at the levee on the following Wednesday.

"I've borne enough of your damned fool of a nephew's non-sense," the King raged. "I will not be placed in this ridiculous position again. You tell that goddamned Ashmont that I'll hang him by the yardarm if he comes within a mile of any member of the Royal Family."

It was no use telling Ashmont anything.

Instead, on Thursday afternoon Lord Frederick told the Duke of Blackwood, who told his wife that evening as they set out for Lady Tunstall's dinner party, the former Emily Felpham's first entertainment since her marriage.

"What did you suggest?" Alice said.

"A strait-waistcoat," Blackwood said.

"Ashmont is at loose ends," she said. "I wish he'd gone abroad with Ripley."

A few days after their arrival in Brighton, Ripley had sent a letter, saying he intended to make a belated Grand Tour with Ashmont. Two days before they were to depart, Ashmont changed his mind. Too many foreigners, he said.

"I wish it, too," her husband said. "He's running amok, worse than ever, thanks to the company he's keeping lately."

Though Blackwood spoke coolly enough, Alice knew he wasn't untroubled. In the dim light of the carriage, she discerned the mask he'd worn all too often in recent weeks, mainly at so-cial events.

He was bored, among other things. Ashmont was one of the other things, she was sure.

She swallowed her frustration. *The other two constitute a problem*, Aunt Julia had told her. Alice had understood the problem when she chose to marry Blackwood. All the same, she wanted to throttle Ashmont.

"I suppose you feel as though you've abandoned him," she said.

"No. Yes. There has to be a limit. A man ought to be able to marry and make a married life without feeling guilty."

"And bored. And impatient."

He stared at her. "Not with you. It's this life."

"And you find this life boring."

"Is it not? Do you not find yourself spending far too much time at social events where courtesy dictates making conversation with an endless parade of fools and gasbags?"

"And you never encountered fools and gasbags before?"

"I could get away from them before. Now I must pretend I don't want to throw them out of the nearest window. You have your collection of wallflowers and social failures to keep you happily occupied. Business, too. Winning important people over to your causes. You need to employ skill and subtlety. You've stimulants, in other words. Rewards."

"And you haven't."

"Apparently not. My life is not as exciting as yours, strangely enough. You have the Minerva Society. You have Miss Pomfret's return to look forward to. I, too, have friends, good friends. But Ashmont finds them dull and goes off with people I despise. And there am I, standing idly by. There am I at Lady Eddingham's rout. Dinner with the Orbys. Endless chitchat with uninteresting people. All the while knowing my friend is out there, behaving like a madman."

"And there am I at Lady Eddingham's or the Orbys' or St. James's Palace, aware of how discontented you are."

He turned his gaze to the window. "I hadn't realized it was so obvious."

"To me. I can't speak for others. And even I didn't realize how deeply discontented you were."

"Not with you, Alice. Never with you."

"But this is our life!"

"Your life."

She felt cold inside. Was that true? Her life, not his? Not theirs?

"It isn't perfect, certainly," she said. "It isn't what I expected. The Minerva Society demands my time. But one can't isolate oneself from Society if one wishes to have any influence. And one can't abandon Court life for the same reason. I never imagined

I'd be running hither and yon for the Royal Family's whims and tantrums. I never guessed they would make me a substitute for Aunt Julia. How does one break free of that claim?"

"I don't know, but here we are."

The carriage was slowing. For another party he wouldn't enjoy.

She couldn't make him enjoy it. She couldn't stop doing what needed to be done. She couldn't abandon the children who needed help. She couldn't make him stop fretting about Ashmont.

She didn't know what to do.

THE DUKE OF BLACKWOOD was cursing himself for not holding his tongue.

He cared deeply for his wife, yet he'd hurt her feelings.

Being somewhat respectable wasn't as dull as he'd expected. At times it wasn't dull at all. There was Lynforde, for example, and his circle. And Doveridge, of all men, had become a friend. He'd been among the first to call on the Blackwoods when they returned from their honeymoon. He'd dined with Blackwood at Crockford's, admitting that the club's chef, Ude, was superior to his own chef. He'd invited the Blackwoods to his entertainments and in other ways quietly eased Blackwood's way into the world he'd abandoned.

Alice and Blackwood were welcome at Court. They were invited everywhere, or nearly everywhere. Blackwood still made some people nervous. Well, everybody. But the ton admired his wife, and many wanted to make use of her, and so they bore with him. A mixed blessing.

Good for Alice and her causes. Not as good as it might have been for Blackwood, when every day and night he heard of Ashmont's doings.

He told himself he wasn't his friend's nursemaid. He told himself that Ripley hadn't felt compelled to give up his trip on Ashmont's account.

He shoved Ashmont into the mental cavern and did his best to enjoy Lady Tunstall's party. Lord Tunstall, whom he'd always viewed as a prodigious dull gasbag, turned out to have a dry sense of humor. His wife must have discovered this little gem about him and polished it, because the man made Blackwood laugh, more than once.

Yet on the way home afterward, the worries flooded back. Finally, as they neared their house, Blackwood said, "I'm going out for a while."

"You need air after the stuffy party, I suppose," Alice said.

"It wasn't stuffy. But I need to walk about. Clear my head. You'd better not wait up. It may take a while."

He escorted her into the house and saw her safely in the servants' care.

Then he went out again and walked. He walked from Piccadilly to Park Lane. He walked along Park Lane, past Stanhope Street, which led to Ripley House. He continued northward, and turned into North Grosvenor Street. He walked to Ashmont House.

He knew a handful of Ashmont's servants would be up and about, awaiting the master's return.

"Not come back yet, Your Grace," the porter told him.

No point in asking when Ashmont would return. No one ever knew.

Blackwood walked back the way he'd come. He walked past his house and on to St. James's Street, thence to Crockford's. Ashmont wasn't there, either.

Blackwood visited several more haunts. The sun came up, to shed no light on his friend's whereabouts.

He went home.

LATE THE FOLLOWING morning, Blackwood entered Alice's bedroom. She was in bed, a tray on her lap, and a tedious amount of paper about her. Invitations. Notes. Letters. Though she had a secretary, she liked to attend to certain correspondence herself. This lot fell into the category.

"You look like the devil," she said. "Have you slept at all?"

He drew up a chair and sat.

"I spent the night looking for Ashmont," he said. "He's still in Town, according to his servants, but where in Town, nobody seemed to know. None of the usual haunts. Worse ones is my guess."

"Yes, very likely."

"I've got to do something."

Her heart sank. She set down the letter she'd been reading. "I'd rather it were Lord Frederick."

"My preference also, but if he could rein in Ashmont, he'd have done it by now."

"Which leaves you."

He rose abruptly. "I don't see a choice. Not one I can live with." He walked to the fireplace and scowled at the grate. "If you saw Cassandra Pomfret headed toward destruction, what would you do?"

Her mind went black for a moment, and she had a sensation of sinking. She'd lost already, and she hadn't begun. She managed a short laugh. "Of course you know. I'd don my armor and run to the rescue, even if she fought me, kicking and screaming."

He turned his attention back to her. "Even now that you're a married woman, a duchess with responsibilities and the troubles of the world on her shoulders. And a husband who wants you by his side."

Logic. Inescapable. She'd never win this debate. "Even now, yes."

"It's a choice," he said.

"And you choose your friend, and I can say nothing because I'd do the same, if it seemed to me a matter of life or death."

"How else ought I to see it?"

She remembered too clearly how she'd felt, watching the three of them racing toward their own funerals. She had no trouble recalling the helplessness and frustration. She'd been ready to risk everything she'd worked for—not only the Perfect Wife designation, but the Minerva Society, which gave a purpose to the husband-hunting as well as her life. She'd been ready to risk everything that mattered to her in order to recover her brother.

It wasn't fair to make Blackwood stand by doing nothing.

Yet the prospect of facing Society alone chilled her. She would not be able to look across a room and see Blackwood. They would not share a conspiratorial smile and later, observations and jokes. She'd grown used to having her chevalier near at hand.

"I can't rescue him," Blackwood was saying. "I can't force him to behave reasonably. All I can do is keep him within certain bounds. That means keeping him company." He returned to the chair and sat.

He was not a restless man. The way he couldn't seem to sit still told her the inner turmoil was worse than she'd supposed. She was in turmoil, too, because she understood and wished she didn't. She didn't want to be reasonable. She wanted to throw something, break something. She wanted to cry.

She reminded herself that she'd known this was a possibility. A probability. A strong likelihood.

The other two constitute a problem.

"I need to keep him company," he said.

"Yes."

"It isn't forever. Ripley plans to be back in a few months."

"Yes, I know."

"What's the alternative, Alice? Do I stand by and do nothing? Could you do that?"

"No." She met his gaze. "I never could, and you know that. But right now, I hate Ashmont. It isn't fair—to you, to me, to us. I want to tell you to choose differently, but I can't. If anything happens to him, you'll never forgive yourself. I'll never forgive myself. So I'll simply hate him—and maybe you, a little, because I'm not reasonable, and it's unreasonable of you to expect me to be."

"Then I shan't expect it." He put out his hand. She wanted to knock it away. But she gave him hers.

"I only ask you to believe this," he said. "I'd much rather climb into your bed than watch Ashmont's servants wrestle him into his. I'd rather not leave you alone to indulge the whims of a lot of spoiled royals. I'd rather not leave you to do what you need to do in Society. I know people will talk, and it won't be pleasant."

"Oh, they're talking already, some of them," she said. "Any excuse will do. Rich and poor, people love gossip. I do, certainly. Annoying, but it won't kill me. I can manage without you. Ashmont can't."

He lifted her hand to his lips and kissed the back of it and the knuckles, and then he turned it over and kissed the palm.

That night when they made love, she knew it was goodbye.

Not many hours later, he went to Ashmont House again and found his friend. The following day, the two dukes set out for the Newmarket Craven race meeting.

The D____ of B____ was observed at Newmarket this week with one of his former companions and without his bride. It seems the leopard cannot change his spots. Married in haste, repenting at leisure—such seems to be the case for the pair whose nuptials ten months ago caused so great a stir in the polite circles.

—*Foxe's Morning Spectacle*
Saturday 13 April 1833

So it began.

No surprise, really.

Alice went on with her life. She knew some would gloat and others would pity her. It was easy enough to know, since a number of people didn't try very hard to hide their reaction. The pity was more provoking by far.

She refused to pity herself, though she missed Blackwood more than she ought to do. She'd grown used to having the tall, dark, dangerous man at her side, across the breakfast table, across a crowded room. In her bed. It galled her to know that Ashmont had all his attention.

More galling, though, was realizing that she and Blackwood had acted in the very nick of time.

He wrote daily. The weather had turned miserable at Newmarket, he reported. Cold and wet on Thursday and Friday, with torrential rains at times and furious hail at others. Ashmont took ill and by Saturday was too unwell to leave his hotel bed. This was an unheard-of state of affairs, though not unexpected, given years of hard living.

"I've no choice but to stay on," Blackwood wrote. "He's a terrible patient. He'll be up and about long before he ought, unless I sit on him. That isn't a figurative turn of speech—although a strait-waistcoat might be the simpler solution."

A few days later, an influenza epidemic struck London, bringing widespread closings and cancellations. It shut down whole households, including Blackwood House, with most of the servants incapacitated.

"I urge you to keep Ashmont away," Alice wrote to him. "The influenza hasn't killed many. It isn't at all like the cholera, and you needn't be anxious on my account. However, it has hastened the deaths of several who were already weakened by other ailments. I shouldn't risk Ashmont if I were you."

The following week was Newmarket's First Spring Meeting. Since he and Ashmont were already there, Blackwood decided they might as well remain.

When he finally came home, a week later, Alice saw him only briefly, because she was summoned to Windsor, thence to Camberley Place with a message and gifts from the Queen to her aunt.

"Letters are all well and good but not entirely satisfactory," Queen Adelaide had told her. "Lady Charles assures us that she is quite well, but she would. You are so observant, Duchess. You will visit her and tell me how she does. And I wish you would use your persuasive powers, to the extent you deem wise, to send her back to us. She is not an old woman, to shut herself away like that. It is not right, and I do not believe Lord Charles would like it. But there, I trust to you to say and do what is needed, and to tell me plainly how it goes with the dear lady."

That wasn't the only errand, albeit one of the harder ones. But Alice would do the royals' bidding, because it meant power and influence to expand the Minerva Society's reach. This is what she told herself while she tried to think and act as Aunt Julia would do, and while she wished her beloved aunt would return to London and leave Alice time for the work she truly valued.

Liliane Girard wanted to establish schools, proper schools, not the ghastly places where pauper children so often found themselves. The ones she was developing in London she could oversee herself, but she deputized Alice to seek suitable spots outside Town, so that the less robust children might breathe cleaner air.

It needed to be done. Somebody must do it, and Alice knew better than most of her peers why.

Nine years old.

The Tollstone Academy.

Three months in purgatory.

She'd been one of the lucky ones. She'd escaped. She could hardly object to making sacrifices now.

And so she did favors for royals and others she needed to cultivate. She attended the necessary entertainments. She worked for the Minerva Society. This, coupled with Blackwood's frequent absences, meant she saw almost nothing of him until the middle of May, when for once they were in Blackwood House at the same time.

That night, after the lovemaking, he told her that Ashmont had fallen in love with Lady Olympia Hightower and was determined to marry her.

"THE POOR GIRL!" Alice said. "It won't do, Giles. You must put a stop to it."

"A stop to it! Whatever for?"

He'd risen from the bed to refill their champagne glasses. They were celebrating their reunion. How long had it been?

An indecently long time. A miserably long time. Nonetheless, he had not lifted her in his arms and carried her up the stairs—or debauched her upon the stairs—as soon as he was home, though the urge was powerful.

Still, their gazes had only to meet, and she had only to smile, and in a few minutes they were in her bedchamber and he had her against the wall.

After that, they'd made love more comfortably in the bed.

Then he told her what he'd assumed was good news.

He refilled the glasses, carried them back to the bed, and gave one to her. She was dressed in his favorite attire: nothing. Her long, curvaceous body seemed to glow in the afternoon light.

He carried his own glass to his side of the bed, but remained standing there.

"Lady Olympia isn't a green girl," he said. "She has a head on her shoulders. That seems to be part of the attraction—the initial attraction, at any rate."

Alice had already heard about the way, a few days earlier, Lady Olympia had saved Ashmont from falling into the path of a furiously driven hackney cabriolet.

"How many other girls would have the presence of mind to do such a thing?" Blackwood said. "She hauled him back onto the pavement with the crook of her umbrella. She subdued the dog that attacked him. She insisted on taking him home in her coach. Her *kindness*—as he put it—brought him nearly to tears. You must know who she is, Alice. Do you not believe she's up to his weight?"

"I know her well enough to hope she's too intelligent and sensible a girl to lose her head over him. She has numerous brothers and inattentive parents. She'll be accustomed to leaping to the rescue of reckless boys, and he is a little boy, in so many ways. I don't doubt she acted instinctively."

He drank as he took this in. It wasn't the reaction he'd hoped for.

"I believe she'll be a steadying influence," he said. "She isn't at all his usual thing."

"She wears spectacles, and she's bookish to an extreme. Quite different from his usual thing, I agree. You say he's determined to marry her. That tells me she hasn't yet succumbed to the angelically innocent blue eyes."

"I hope she succumbs to something. I've never seen him so taken with a young woman—a young, *respectable* woman. It gives me hope for him."

"They have nothing in common."

"Don't you want to see him settled? I do. I'd rather not spend my days following him about, making sure he doesn't kill anybody or himself."

She moved restlessly against the pillows. "I'd much rather you didn't spend your days that way, as you well know—and I seem to be making a fuss over nothing. She's not a child, as you say. She's intelligent. She's been out in Society for years. I only worry that the novelty will wear off and he'll tire of her."

"That I doubt. You are no longer a novelty. Ye gods, we've been married an eternity—nearly a year. And yet, curiously enough, I feel not in the least tired of you."

"That's because you see me so rarely."

"Good point. Perhaps seeing you is a novelty. Now I think of it, I wasn't sure who you were when I entered the house and you appeared. 'What a fine-looking woman,' I thought. 'I wonder if I can lure her into bed.'"

"It's possible." She patted his pillow. "Come and persuade her."

He went, of course. He climbed back into the bed and drew up the bedclothes and brought his arm about her shoulders. She leant against him.

"Perhaps it's for the best," she said. "Lady Olympia is a capable young woman. No doubt she can manage him."

"With any luck, they'll be wed soon, and he'll be her problem.

In the meantime . . ." He stroked Alice's beautifully bare shoulder. He slid his hand down her arm and lower, and his brain began to close down.

"In the meantime, let us drink champagne and express our frustrations with each other in the time-honored fashion," she said softly. "I have missed you, sir."

"And I you, madam."

He stopped thinking about Ashmont and Lady Olympia.

He was a man. His wife was naked in bed beside him and she was willing and he wanted her, as he'd always done.

All will be well, he told himself.

Chapter 25

*J*onesy has run away," Liliane said. "He has been gone for a fortnight, and I only learnt of it last night. This is most distressing. He seemed to have settled well in Putney, and the reports of him were all good."

Alice had called on her before setting out for Camberley Place. On the way there, she'd planned to stop at the White Lion, where Jonesy worked, to deliver messages and gifts from Liliane, and to see for herself how he fared.

After that she needed to consult with her aunt regarding the care and handling of the Duchess of Kent, mother of the King's heir presumptive. Thence Alice was to proceed to the Drakeleys' for a house party.

"I'll stop at the inn and make enquiries," she said. "I wish I could do more, but my time is not my own at present."

"I hope you will find answers," Liliane said. "I have not the slightest idea where to look for him—and now we have lost so much time. I do not understand. He has been there for a year and more, and he seemed happy."

Alice remembered what Keeffe had said: *When your gut tells you to get yourself lost, you do it, quick time.*

If Jonesy felt unsafe, he'd make himself vanish.

"Something must have happened," Alice said. "Still, I don't

imagine he'll go farther afield. To him, Putney was across the world. He's likely to return to London, familiar territory."

"If he is in trouble, I hope he will come to me," Liliane said.

Alice hoped so, too.

For the moment there was little she could do, and nobody she could turn to. Blackwood still kept watch over his friend. Cassandra had returned to England earlier in the week, but she'd stopped in London only overnight before going on to Hertfordshire to look after one of her sisters-in-law. Of course Keeffe had gone with her.

"I daresay Miss Pomfret will be back by the time I return," she said. "If he hasn't turned up before then, she and I and Keeffe will hunt the boy down. But with any luck, I'll find answers today in Putney."

She did not.

All she learnt there was that Jonesy had gone off without a word, leaving most of his belongings behind.

THE FOLLOWING WEEK, all hell broke loose among Alice's friends and family, and she could do nothing, because Aunt Florentia, who joined her at the Drakeleys', caught a severe cold. She didn't need nursing so much as watching, because she had a streak of Ancaster stubbornness along with a belief that giving in to illness was a sign of moral weakness. Or something like that. At any rate, Alice was obliged to stand guard, rather as Blackwood had had to stand guard over Ashmont while he was ill.

Meanwhile, the letters came—from Blackwood, Aunt Julia, Cassandra, two of Blackwood's sisters, Cassandra's sister Hyacinth, and, of course, the Queen.

By the time Alice was able to return to London, the situation had resolved itself. Lady Olympia was married, not to Ashmont but to Ripley, and Ashmont was now determined to win Cassandra.

A great deal more had happened, some of it nearly catastrophic, and most of it infuriating. But Ripley was safely wed to an intelligent girl who wouldn't stand for any nonsense, and Cassandra belonged to the same general category.

This allowed Alice to devote her exasperation to her husband. Blackwood had found Jonesy . . . and let him get away.

He wrote faithfully, though sometimes the letters were cryptic.

This wasn't.

He wrote:

I didn't recognize him. He was with a lot of other boys in Kensington High Street, and I could not tell one from another. Ashmont was the one who singled him out as the leader of the ragged youth group. It was only when we arrived in Battersea that I began to wonder if I'd encountered him before. Jonesy, the other boys called him. But the only name I knew was George Foster or Georgie, and that was a year ago. Truly, Alice, I doubt you'd have recognized him. Well, maybe by the stench, but I've not refined my smelling ability sufficiently to discriminate. He smelled like a cesspit that hadn't been cleaned since the time of Queen Anne. It was not until he vanished that the possibility of his being your special juvenile delinquent dawned on me. Ashmont and I had been speaking of continuing to Putney, and it was then I remembered you'd sent the so-called George Foster there. But we came upon him in Kensington, miles away. Why was he there? And why did he not recognize me? He must have done, though he gave no sign, the cunning brat.

Oh, Jonesy had recognized him, beyond question. But the boy was far too sharp to let on—because he'd run away and didn't want to be found. He'd gone on with the two dukes as long as he felt safe. Blackwood's failing to recognize him must have amused him. Meanwhile, the child got to ride with Blackwood on a fine horse while getting paid to help the dukes find their quarry. When they mentioned Putney, though, he must have sensed that Blackwood was beginning to catch on. A look. A raised eyebrow. A word or two. The boy would need no more than a hint. And by now he'd moved on, to who knew where.

Blackwood House
Evening of Thursday 20 June 1833

ALICE HAD DINED with Cassandra Pomfret's family, and Blackwood had dined with Ashmont and Humphrey Morris, a younger brother of Worbury's minion, Lord Consett. Morris, however, had turned out to be a different article from his repellent elder brother, and an unexceptionable companion for Ashmont.

Now, at last, Blackwood and his wife had a few hours to spend together, and he did not want to spend it quarreling about the sewer rat. She did, apparently.

True, she'd come to his bedchamber and was dressed or semi-dressed appropriately, but she did not seem to be in a loving frame of mind.

"Men are idiots," she said as she climbed onto his bed. "I tell myself you can't help it, and I try to forgive you on that account, but I had deluded myself that you were above the common herd of men."

"Ye gods, no," he said. "I'm there in the herd, taller than most, perhaps, but otherwise indistinguishable from the rest."

"Giles, that child was there today, at the fancy fair at the Hanover Square Rooms. Cassandra recognized him, though she hadn't seen him since before we left England last year. She wouldn't have let him go if she'd known I was looking for him. But she had her own problems, and I saw no reason to trouble her with this one, especially in the little time we've had together."

Ashmont was one of the problems. He'd used the boy to

commit a prank at the fancy fair, a prank that Miss Pomfret turned back on him. Now Ashmont loved her more than ever.

"My dear girl, I was some distance away, in a suffocating crowd—though that might have been due to the boy's aroma thickening the atmosphere. I caught a bit of the exchange, but I never had a close look at him. All I saw was an animate rag heap. Miss Pomfret dealt swiftly with matters, and the boy ran off—with riches, I might add."

"And you didn't try to catch him."

"I am not a rat catcher." He frowned. "Do I insult the rats by saying that? I would as soon catch a mound of horse manure, on grounds that it's more wholesome."

"Oh, Giles." She put a hand to her forehead.

He slipped into the bed alongside her. "I wish you wouldn't fret about that boy."

"You think he's a hopeless cause."

"I'm more sure of it than ever. He's cunning, and he has his own peculiar charm and winning ways—once you get past the filth and translate whatever language it is that he speaks. But this is a street child. He's run away from respectable employment, a safe place to sleep, and regular meals. Clearly, domestication doesn't suit him. Not all of those children can be reclaimed. Surely you realize this. You must have seen enough cases."

"He was content for more than a year. He would not have run away unless he was frightened."

"He doesn't strike me as the kind who frightens easily."

"You don't know what it's like for those children."

He didn't. His childhood had not been ideal. She and Ripley, though, had had a miserable time of it. Their father had been a man of sudden and extreme changes of temperament. Without reason or warning, he'd fall into terrifying rages and bouts of remorse and bewildering delusions of poverty and persecution. Their mother had eventually retreated into the laudanum bottle.

While such a childhood was nothing like the wretchedness paupers faced, it helped account for so much that Alice did, especially her ferocious determination to rescue Defenseless Children.

"I don't know what it's like," he said. "That's my good fortune. But knowing or not, we're not going to find the brat this night. Given that he seems not to want to be found and is a genius at disappearing, the search will take thought and time. Tomorrow we'll have only a few hours. We do need to dress for Ripley's ball. We're supposed to be celebrating his marriage."

"We must also attend the state ball," she said.

"On the same night?"

"You've forgotten, in all the excitement about my brother and Ashmont. I received and accepted the invitation before Ripley announced his plans. But Aunt Julia and others are in the same predicament. She's spoken to the Queen. We'll attend the supper so as not to disrupt those arrangements. We're excused from the ball."

The *excitement* about her brother and Ashmont: That was putting it mildly. Last week had been hellish.

"I'll wager anything that your brother's supper will be better," he said.

"Of course it will be. Chardot is the best chef in London." She paused, studying his face. "You're disappointed. And displeased with me."

"Not with you. With this." He waved a hand. "This life of ours. Your aunt has returned and we're not free yet."

"She's been back for only four days! I'm no happier than you are, but we can't have everything precisely as we like it."

"We seem to have nothing as we like it."

And so they quarreled, and in the end she slept in her bed and he in his, and the next day when he rose, very late, having spent a restless night, he was told that Her Grace had gone out, and had not said when she would return.

Friday 21 June 1833

"TRY TO PRETEND you don't hate me," Blackwood said as they set out for the state ball. "At least for the duration of your brother's party. Then, when we return home, you may throw things at me."

They'd been sitting as far apart as the carriage permitted, Alice at one window, Blackwood at the other. The atmosphere had been chilly from the time she came home in the late afternoon. Not a pleasant experience.

She turned toward him. "Oh, Giles."

"It wasn't even a proper quarrel," he said. He held out his hand.

She took it. "I'm not always reasonable."

"That is because, unlike me, you're not perfect. It isn't your fault. You didn't have my father."

That won him a small laugh. "No, I had an altogether different one."

"Had I wanted a reasonable wife, I should not have married you," he said. "Come."

She drew nearer, and he brought his arm about her shoulders. Carefully. The dress was white, with a great deal of lace, and decorations on the lace. An embroidered green cashmere scarf circled her neck.

"I would hold you more tightly," he said, "but then I'll crush the lace, and everybody will think we had a tumble in the carriage."

"I'm so tired of what everybody thinks," she said. "There are moments when I want to run away, to simply travel about England as we did before, more or less carefree."

"I should like that above all things, but at present, responsibilities are rather in the way," he said.

"How did this happen?" she said.

"It's other people. They refuse to behave as we wish."

"I haven't the right personality for a courtier, Giles. Meanwhile, I can't stop fretting about Jonesy. I tell myself he's a street child. They can't all be domesticated, as you said. I know this. All the same, I can't stop being anxious."

"He's a winning little sewer rat, I'll give him that."

"And there's Cassandra. She has problems enough without having to deal with Ashmont."

"He's grown excessively fatiguing of late. I daresay I could find a pretext for taking him away for a time. That will be more difficult than usual. He seems fixed on her."

"I should feel more optimistic had he not also seemed to be fixed on Olympia."

"As would I. Last week was not the most comfortable of my existence."

He might easily have lost one of his two closest friends, possibly both of them. She might have lost her brother.

"I have not quite forgiven them," she said. "Either of them."

"Let's see how Ashmont behaves tonight," he said. "Frankly, I'm bloody tired of watching him and trying to protect him from himself. Can't we leave it to Miss Pomfret?"

Before she could retort, he put up his hand. "Please hear me out. Consider her character. Do you not deem her perfectly capable of putting him in his place? Of all the women he might take it into his head to pursue, I should say she was the last to fret about."

"She may be capable, but she has a great deal burdening her mind at present. And he's a handful, even for her."

He knew she wasn't wrong. That didn't make him any happier. "If you want him away, I'll get him away. At the moment, I've no idea how to accomplish the feat. But I'll do it."

"I suppose that isn't the soundest thinking." She paused. "But nothing is right at present. If I could remain here, on the spot, I shouldn't fret so much."

He was aware of a churlish anger welling. "You're going away *again?*"

"Liliane has asked me to inspect two sites for the schools."

He kept the curses to himself. "More productive than dealing with the Duchess of Kent, I don't doubt," he said as mildly as he could.

She looked up at him. "If you'd rather I didn't, say so."

"Of course I'd rather you didn't," he said, too sharply. "I'm rather fond of my wife and want her nearby. I'd rather not be saddled with the nigh impossible task of prying Ashmont away from Miss Pomfret. I don't want to tax my brain with clever schemes for luring my friend out of London. I do *not* want to attend this damned supper. But Duty calls. Personal inconvenience doesn't signify. Even the King can't do exactly as he pleases. He probably doesn't want to attend, either. I'm sure he'd much rather go to Ripley's ball, but kings aren't allowed to have that much fun."

As it turned out, Blackwood didn't have much fun at Ripley's ball. Between holding his breath, waiting for his erratic friend to set off an explosion, and racking his brains for a clever way to divert said friend from his pursuit of Miss Pomfret, Blackwood had neither patience nor attention for much else.

He said and did the proper things, thanks to CORRECT BE-HAVIOR. He didn't need to be fully present for that. Even when he danced at last with his wife, he simmered with frustration, his mind wandering to Ashmont and Miss Pomfret and the accurst brat.

He was sufficiently attuned to Alice, though, to be aware that she was in no better frame of mind.

So much for affinity.

Two days later, he and Ashmont left London.

Camberley Place
23rd Instant

My dear girl,

The uncanny Lord Frederick has saved my brain from burning up into ashes. He summoned Ashmont yesterday and counseled him on the wooing of Miss Pomfret. His lordship advised Ashmont to leave Town for a time—and take me with him. I was dumbfounded when Ashmont agreed. To our further astonishment, when we called on Lady Charles to say goodbye, she invited us to stay at Camberley Place on our own. My heart leapt, as you can imagine. We'd planned to go to the races, but neither of us hesitated to accept her kind offer. As you can guess, we stay at the fishing house, living rough, as we prefer. It will be good for Ashmont and even better for me, since it will be easier to keep him occupied and out of trouble. I must say, he seems in some ways another man, and I can't help but ascribe the change to the effect Miss Pomfret has had on him. I hope this view of matters will not grieve you overmuch. I believe—and it seems that your aunt and Lord Frederick take the same view—my friend is on a path to reform.

Is it fanciful of me to wonder whether the two courtiers have been plotting together? At Ripley's party I gained the impression that Lord Frederick and Lady Charles were in league. The night is a blur for the most part, but I do recall their dancing together, and now I wonder whether they, too, have an affinity. Fanciful, no doubt. It's the air of Camberley Place. We arrived only a few hours ago, and already my spirits improve. They would be more improved if you were here instead of Ashmont, but one can't have everything.

I remain
Your humble and obedient husband,
B

A young couple of high rank have developed a remarkable talent for not being in the same place at the same time. When the one is in London, the other has urgent business elsewhere. Little more than a year ago, the lady's sudden change of heart and decision to give her hand, not to the highly esteemed nobleman it was assumed she'd choose, but to another of altogether different reputation, shocked members of the polite circles. In the betting books at the time, we are told, odds leant heavily toward the failure of this puzzling union. At present it appears that the principals have already deemed their marriage inconvenient, thus proving the naysayers more perspicacious than the optimists.

—*Foxe's Morning Spectacle*
Wednesday 3 July 1833

Chapter 26

As Blackwood and Lynforde were leaving the Haymarket Theater, a tall youth wearing a shiny top hat, a coat two sizes too large, and trousers six inches too short accosted them.

"Message, yer wership," he said, and added in a lower tone, "Maggie sent me."

"This is for me," Blackwood said.

Lynforde eyed the young fellow dubiously. "Are you quite sure?"

Blackwood nodded.

Lynforde took the hint and stepped out of earshot.

Blackwood signaled to the boy to move aside, toward the shops adjoining the theater, and out of the way of the emerging crowd.

The boy gave a furtive look about him.

"Nobody will trouble us," Blackwood said. When he wasn't with Alice, a great many people still tended to shy away.

"Wot she says is, vem traps took up vat lad of yours on account of springin' 'is plant and d'yer want 'er to stall 'im orf or do it yerself, only yer better be quick."

It took Blackwood a moment to make sense of these sounds, because this boy's speech was even less penetrable than Jonesy's. It took another moment to grasp the meaning through the cant: The police had caught Jonesy with stolen goods, and did

Blackwood want Maggie to get him out or did Blackwood want to do it?

"I'll do it," Blackwood said. "Where are they holding him?"

The boy jerked his head eastward. "'atton Garden."

Blackwood gave him a coin, and the messenger promptly vanished into the crowd.

When the duke rejoined his friend, he said, "You'll recollect the incident not a year ago, at Hyde Park Corner?"

"How could I forget?" Lynforde said. "It led you down the path to matrimony."

"The boy Alice defended that day has been taken up. He's at the Hatton Garden police office. I suspect they caught him with the goods he obtained during the recent incident at the Hanover Square Rooms."

"And they assume he stole them. A natural conclusion to jump to, in the circumstances."

"They jump quickly, indeed. Last year, as I recall, these same Hatton Garden geniuses took up a boy on suspicion of picking pockets. He had no stolen items upon him, but a police officer said the boy had been in trouble before. On this non-evidence he was immediately sentenced to time in the house of correction."

"I suggest we make haste," Lynforde said.

Thursday 17th Instant

My dearest girl,

I've got him!

The little beast got himself taken up in Holborn with the heap of fine goods lawfully obtained at the fancy fair. Luckily for Jonesy, our dear friend Mrs. Proudie sent another young criminal to alert me. Lynforde and I raced to the Hatton Garden police office, arriving in the nick of time. I explained matters, and Lynforde provided another eyewitness account. In short order—by police office standards, which is to say, early this morning—they released the brat, and I took him into custody.

Over his vociferous objections, we went straight to the nearest baths. After leaving him in the hands of the largest and strongest of the attendants, I sent another in search of clean clothes.

I recovered your favorite sewer rat this afternoon. He was not happy, but he was clean. Then I had to decide what to do with him. Finding myself short of brilliant ideas, I took him to Keeffe. This turned out to be a brilliant idea, if I may congratulate myself. The boy can't read or write, but he knew who Tom Keeffe was. The famous jockey is a legend in the back-slums and stews, as you are no doubt aware. Overawed, Jonesy was a strangely subdued and obedient version of himself.

After a lengthy private discussion with the lad, Keeffe suggested I try him in my stables. I daresay Jonesy will corrupt the rest of the grooms and stable boys, but I did not like to turn him loose without your consent. Keeffe did warn me that Jonesy mayn't stay. "He's young, maybe nine or ten, but he's got the habit of being independent," I was told. "If he starts feeling crowded or maybe told to do this or that too many times, he'll be off. Same if he don't feel comfortable about something or somebody. Just warning you." These are not Keeffe's precise words, but I don't know how to render his unique speech into the King's English.

He also said he thought the boy's face was familiar, but he couldn't place it. Given his being nearly trampled to death during the fateful race, we might consider it a miracle that Keeffe has any memory at all.

Undoubtedly you know as much about the progress of Ashmont's courtship as I do. Probably more. I try to keep out of it. Miss Pomfret summoned him while we were at Camberley Place, he obeyed the summons with alacrity, and I left him to it while I lingered to enjoy several more days of laziness and peace in the fishing house. I even read without interruption a book I found there: a thought-provoking, well-worn tome by a Mrs. Wollstonecraft. Most enlightening. All in all a refreshing and heartening change of pace. No doubt the revival of my spirits contributed to my quick and clever thinking today.

They will revive further when you return.

I remain
Your humble and obedient husband,
B

Tuesday 23 July 1833

A LITTLE FRAUD here. A little card cheating there. A false identity. A slight misrepresentation. The trick was to keep moving.

This was the way Lord Worbury kept himself in funds in the year and more that had passed since he was cheated of his inheritances, as he saw it. Not the best year of his life. He had avoided showing his face in London, sure that everybody would be laughing at him.

He'd done fairly well since, at various races and elsewhere, thanks to making friends with a few extremely sharp men. The trouble was, one or two had turned out sharper than he, and he'd found it prudent to move on, not back to Town, but near it. At present he resided in Chelsea, and not as comfortably as he'd like.

This evening, as happened several times a week, Lord Consett dined with him. Tonight they met at the White Horse Inn on Church Street, and Consett had news, as he always did.

"My mother says Blackwood's taken in a beggar child to work in his stables," Consett told his friend. "She says it's the same boy Ashmont had with him at the fancy fair at the Hanover Square Rooms last month. It seems the brat was taken up for thievery not long ago, and Blackwood actually went to the police office and had him set free."

This was news, indeed. Worbury knew about Ashmont's prank at the fancy fair, again thanks to Lady Bartham. She'd been present at the event, and provided her usual scathing observations.

"I wonder how Blackwood found out the boy was at the police office," he said. "Was it in the newspaper?"

"Not likely. The duke got him out only a few hours after they brought him in. Lynforde was there, too."

"That's interesting."

"Curious, isn't it? My mother says somebody else saw the new stable boy the other day, and told her he's fair."

Worbury's attention sharpened.

"Don't know why, but it made me think about that pickpocket you tried to find," Consett went on. "They're all so dirty, I can't tell whether they're fair or dark. But you said that one was fair. Blue eyes."

"Blue eyes. The scars. The nose. The chin. Oh, I'd know the cunning little bastard anywhere, clean or dirty." Worbury poured himself more wine while he turned the matter over in his mind.

"I wouldn't, no matter how close I looked. Not that I'd want to look close. Rather not breathe the same air, to tell the truth. Don't know where they've been. Like I told my mother, they all look the same to me. You've the sharper eye by far."

And the sharper ear. And brain. Worbury remembered all three pickpockets. He could pick out any one of them in a crowd.

The brat Alice had protected, though, remained distinctly clear in his mind, thanks to the fuss she and Blackwood had made over him.

But that little troublemaker was under the protection of

criminals who'd frightened Worbury sufficiently to make him leave London and stay away.

All the same . . .

"I should like to get a look at this felon they've rescued," he said. "He must be special, for them to go to so much bother about him. Then, to take him under their own roof is extraordinary."

"Mother says they're asking to be murdered in their beds. The boy will have accomplices, she says, and show them the way."

Worbury did not object to this outcome. He strongly suspected Blackwood's having a hand in the changes to Ripley's will. Ripley lacked the Machiavellian turn of mind to devise such schemes on his own.

Sadly, the chances of the Blackwoods' being murdered were minute to nil. Only the boldest, cleverest, and most vicious villains would consider it—then reconsider, most likely.

He knew all too well what the villains would be up against.

He'd experienced Alice's temper years ago. He'd never forget the experience, or the humiliation. Both Blackwood and Ripley had watched two little girls beating him until he wept. The ruffian whose nose she'd broken last year wouldn't forget that, either.

As to Blackwood, most men would as soon tangle with the Old Harry himself.

None of which meant that revenge couldn't be had, especially for a man with years of grievances stored away, not to mention the more recent indignities he'd endured.

The boy, whoever he was, was the chink in the Blackwoods' armor.

"If it's the same boy, the one we saw at Hyde Park Corner, there's no question he has dangerous confederates," he said. "Your mother may well have the right of it. You know I don't love my cousin Alice, and I'm no friend of Blackwood's. All the same, we can't stand idly by when there's likely to be murder in Mayfair, can we?"

"Well, I—"

"One crime begets another," Worbury said. "If one set of villains succeeds, the others will grow bold. Then none of us will be safe. I'd better get a look at this boy."

THE LETTER HAD arrived while Alice was away. Her secretary had sorted the correspondence as usual. This was among the many applications for help Alice received weekly.

This was not like the others. Not remotely like the others.

Heyshaw, Yorkshire
2 August 1833

Madam,

I take the very great liberty of writing to Your Grace, in hopes that your considerable experience will help guide our group in establishing the Heyshaw School for Girls.

Aware of the many claims on Your Grace's time, I shall be as brief as possible. Our society, which we have modeled upon London's Minerva Society, aspires to carry out, here in the West Riding, Madame Girard's good work. We intend the Heyshaw School for Girls as an equally inexpensive alternative to the Tollstone Academy nearby, whose distressing reputation Your Grace may already be aware of. Suffice to say the conditions in that place are deplorable and have only worsened in recent years.

We have found a suitable building with sufficient surrounding land. Thanks to generous benefactors, we have begun the process of acquiring the property. It is small, but one must begin somewhere. Regrettably, small as this beginning is, Mr. Tollstone has raised endless objections and used his influence to create every possible stumbling block. At present we find ourselves stymied.

Naturally we are aware of the many obstacles Madame Girard and the Minerva Society have encountered. Rather than repeat methods that the Society have already discovered to be unhelpful, we apply to Your Grace for guidance.

I keep this short on purpose. No doubt ours is but one of many applications for aid that cross your desk daily, any number I daresay more urgent than this one. If, however, you can find the time to make suggestions or direct us to those who can help resolve our difficulties, we—and a number of young girls—will be most grateful. I shall be more than happy to send particulars, if desired.

I have the honor to be,
Madam,
Your Grace's most obedient,
and most humble Servant,
Eliza Eccles

Alice set down the letter and covered her face with her hands.

Hyde Park
Friday 9 August 1833

"YORKSHIRE?" BLACKWOOD SAID. "You've been home not two days."

"I shan't go straight away," she said. "I won't miss Cassandra's wedding."

He knew the two friends hadn't spent as much time together as they'd hoped. Alice had too many calls on her time, and Miss Pomfret had her own problems, which consisted mainly of Ashmont.

But His Grace with the Angel Face had performed what amounted to the Labors of Hercules, and the nuptials would take place tomorrow.

And when, Blackwood wondered, would his marriage become what he wanted?

He and Alice had ridden out before breakfast, to avoid the heat of the day. While Rotten Row was by no means deserted, it was emptier by far than it would be by late afternoon. The equestrians present were here for the exercise, not gossip and gawking.

"Why the devil must you be on the spot, every time?" he said.

"Because I can be intimidating. Because I'm effective. Because I'm a duchess."

"Teach or find somebody else to be effective," he said. "I have competent people as my agents. I don't manage the details of my household, nor do you. We have superior senior servants for the purpose. In this case, especially, I see no reason for you to become directly involved."

"Giles, it's the Tollstone Academy for Girls," she said.

"And?"

For a time she said nothing. Then she let out a shaky sigh. "I was there," she said. "For three months. My father sent me because I was 'incorrigible,' he said. It was a cheap and easy way to make me somebody else's problem. Cheaper than nursemaids and governesses. One must not only pay their wages but provide bed and board, you see. I wasn't worth the expense."

Blackwood remembered. Ripley had spoken of it, more than once. He'd mentioned it during Blackwood's first visit to Camberley Place, the day they'd watched Alice climb out of the window. What had Ripley said? The school *didn't agree with her.*

"Ripley said you weren't there for long."

"Oh, not long, unless one is a child. I was nine, Giles. And it wasn't Eton. You know Ripley never had enough money. You know how shabby he was. But he was at a fine public school, with other boys of the upper classes. He had regular meals. He had a proper education. He was not ill-fed and ill-housed, and those shabby clothes were of good quality. He had you and

Ashmont and Lynforde and others. You had proper fires in your rooms and servants. You had sports and camaraderie. Shall I tell you what I had, what we girls had, no matter who we were or where we'd come from?"

She didn't wait for his answer but told him, briefly and sharply, anger throbbing in her voice, and grief, too.

He listened, while sorrow and outrage built inside, so fierce that he found himself utterly at a loss what to think, let alone what to say.

He looked about him. The Serpentine glistened in the early morning light. The pall of smoke hanging over London had begun to thicken. A pall seemed to hang over them as well.

"My aunt and uncle rescued me," she was saying. "After that, they arranged to keep me away from my parents. I went abroad with Cassandra and her grandparents. She, too, was a difficult child, but her grandparents have never seen her in that light. I was extremely fortunate, you see."

"Yes, I see," he said.

He didn't want to see. He understood now, too well, too painfully well.

"I don't want you to go back there," he said.

"Giles! Were you not listening?"

"I was, and I don't want you to go back there. You'll accomplish nothing, and that will hurt you. You're a duchess. Impressive. The Tollstones and their minions will bow and scrape to your face. The instant you go away, the trouble will recommence. There are hundreds of such schools. They're cheap, and they keep unwanted children out of the way, all the year round. 'No holidays,' they advertise, and that's one of the attractions, along with the low fees. I've seen the advertisements. I'm not oblivious."

"You can't expect me to ignore this."

"What do you imagine you can do? The schools are notorious. Complaints are made. Inspectors dutifully inspect. They find a few minor problems. They make excuses. Nothing happens."

"Kindly remember that I own a brain," she said tightly. "Even I understand that the school won't change. But what's wrong with the ladies of Heyshaw establishing another inexpensive school in the area? You'd think there were unwanted children enough to supply any number of schools, but Tollstone is doing everything he can think of to drive them out."

"And your appearing will accomplish what, precisely?"

She stared at him. "You propose I do nothing?"

"I propose you turn your attention to more promising missions. I thought Madame Girard wished to establish her schools in and near London. Haven't you enough to do for her? Is it necessary to go to Yorkshire? The lady wrote seeking advice. She didn't ask you to ride in on your charger and rout the dragons. My dear girl, there's injustice everywhere. Can you not put on your shining armor and kill the dragons already at hand?"

"This is *my* dragon," she said.

He was silent for a time. He had no answer. He was lost.

He shook his head. "So it is. And you suppose only you can destroy it. Very well. Go. I cannot stop you."

They rode home in a taut silence.

Chapter 27

*B*y the time the Ashmonts' wedding breakfast was over, Blackwood thought it would be a good idea to bash his head against the nearest wall.

Thickhead. Dolt. Clodpoll.

But that would be theatrical, and he was not theatrical. Also, it would not improve matters. And so he made himself wait calmly and put intelligible words together. When at last he and Alice were in their carriage on their way home, he was ready to speak. Grovel. Whatever was necessary.

"I chose my words stupidly yesterday," he said to her stiff profile. "No, *stupidly* is an appalling understatement. But it can't be helped. Let me try again."

She said nothing.

"I don't want you to be hurt," he went on. "I don't want you to reawaken bad memories by being on the spot. I know it's not very intelligent of me, but I keep wanting to protect you from . . . everything. Sewer rats and malign cousins and gang leaders and wicked schoolmasters and anybody else who might hurt you in any way. I want to protect you from the world. All I could think of yesterday was not letting you go near that place."

"But I'm safe now," she said. "The children are not."

"No, they're not. And it's absurd to expect you to turn your back, simply because you might be hurt. With you, it's the opposite: You want to meet the trouble head on. I cannot believe I was such a monstrous thickhead as to fail to take that into account."

A pause while he waited, heart unsteady.

At last she said, "You've always seemed to me less thickheaded than most men."

He started to breathe again. "You're all the more disappointed, then, when I fail so badly."

"Yes." She threw him a glance, and he felt the wall between them begin to give way.

"Do you know," he said, "I remember, vividly, the first time I saw you. It was my first visit to Camberley Place. You were ten years old, climbing down from a window. Ripley said you meant to become a warrior or a knight or maybe both. He said you'd been to a grim sort of school earlier in the year. That was the Tollstone Academy for Girls, obviously."

"Yes. The worst January, February, and March of my life."

"And after that experience, you determined to learn to take care of yourself, in case you were ever again confined against your will."

"Yes." She was watching him now, still tense.

"I ought to have realized that your feelings about such places must be all the stronger because you deal these days with so many unfortunate children. No, it's more than that. You open your heart to them. You see yourself as one of them, one of the lucky ones."

"But I'm not a child anymore. I don't need to escape. I'm the one who can make a difference for them."

"You are a child," he said. "You're all the children. You've had a glimpse of what they endure, and it breaks your heart, and you want to mend it, and— Oh, what does it matter? What more need I say? I was shockingly wrong. You need to do this. And I'll go with you."

She turned fully toward him. "To Yorkshire? Truly?"

"I meant what I said a lifetime ago when we were in Kensington and you broke that fellow's nose. I said, 'Never without me.' Starting new schools is one thing, and it's a joyous thing for you, I know. Returning to the scene of a crime is another altogether. I can't and won't let you face it alone—that is to say, without me."

She was studying his face. She couldn't always read it, he knew. But most people, including his nearest friends, couldn't read it at any time.

"This is so frustrating," she said. "I keep hoping to catch you not being perfect, but I fail, again and again."

"Keep trying," he said. "You might find a flaw somewhere. A minuscule flaw, to be sure. But if you persevere, I daresay you'll find it."

"Oh, Giles." There was a flurry of rustling fabric, and she closed the few inches between them and climbed onto his lap.

His heart lifted. He brought his arms about her.

"You are an excellent husband, no matter what anybody thinks," she said. "No, more than that. When you make a mistake, you admit it. You are a *superior* husband."

"As long as you think so, I'm content."

"I think so, and believe it or not, I have reflected on what you said yesterday. I did want to gallop onto the scene and slay dragons. But I should only end up singed. What's needed in this case is a scheme, and that is your forte."

"I'm glad to hear that you recognize my genius," he said, "because I already discern the glimmerings of an idea. A little dangerous, perhaps. Possibly not precisely legal."

She smiled, and mischief sparked in her eyes. It was the mischief he'd seen all those years ago as she ran past him. It was the same conspiratorial smile he'd seen so often before, directed at him.

"How clever of me to marry a man with a brain," she said. "You've no idea the weight you've lifted. I didn't want to leave you again. I loathe all these separations. But this was worse. I dreaded the prospect of returning to that place. All the same,

I couldn't turn my back on them. With you, I know we'll succeed. Then we can return to London, and I'll direct my attentions to Liliane's schools, closer to home, where I can truly be effective."

"If you would come closer still, my dear, I believe you can be extremely effective," he said.

London
Monday 12 August 1833

GROUSE HUNTING SEASON had begun. This year, the grouse had to do without Blackwood. Instead, on the "glorious twelfth," he summoned his solicitor to Blackwood House, and Alice had her first glimpse of the elaborate planning employed for Their Dis-Graces' infamous pranks.

They met with Mr. Furnell in the duke's study.

Upon hearing their mission, he shook his head. "Difficult business, Your Grace. Exceedingly difficult."

"Over the years I've followed several of the cases reported in the newspapers," Blackwood said. "I'm fully aware of the difficulty."

Alice had followed them, too, while she was abroad. "We know that criminal complaints fail repeatedly," she said. "In the teeth of the evidence, the juries find the school proprietors not guilty." Even though children died of illnesses brought on by neglect and starvation, it was the fault of the illnesses, not the abysmal conditions. "When one considers the kinds of cases that have failed, one can hardly hope for a different verdict for the school in question. It isn't the worst, by far."

"But it's bad enough," Blackstone said. "What we need, Furnell, is another route. The ladies of Heyshaw ought to be able to establish their school without interference. We'd prefer to avoid criminal acts if possible."

"Then I'm obliged to inform Your Grace that burning down

the Tollstone Academy is out of the question," Furnell said in his dry voice.

"And no throwing headmasters out of windows, I've told him," Alice said. "They tend to create a bother about such things, and Mr. Tollstone is extremely litigious."

"Our difficulty is the location," Blackwood said. "We're miles from the spot, and we haven't spies in place. It's crucial to give no warning. At the same time, everything must appear more or less aboveboard."

"We don't want to taint the Heyshaw ladies' efforts," Alice said. "We must appear to be acting on our own."

"What I want from you," Blackwood said, "is ideas of what to look for. We also want clarification as to what is and isn't out of bounds. I had some thoughts about money matters, and I don't doubt you do as well."

"Not bribery, though," Alice said. "We refuse to enrich those people."

Furnell considered. They let him review the material they'd gathered, including Mrs. Eccles's letter. He had questions. Eventually, he had suggestions.

When he left, Alice looked at her husband. "It's going to be complicated."

"That's what makes these sorts of things so much fun," he said.

ON THE FOLLOWING day, they met with Keeffe. The next day they spent with Madame Girard. Then there was research: reviewing various Acts of Parliament, the *Police Gazette*, and journals like *Figaro in London*. Blackwood wrote to Mr. Crade, a solicitor in the West Riding whom Furnell had recommended.

Alice wrote to Mrs. Eccles, asking in strictest confidence for the further details the lady had offered to provide. "The Duke and I have decided to look into the matter," Alice wrote. "However, given the legal difficulties you've faced, I must urge you in the strongest terms to share this decision with nobody, even the members of your society. In the meantime, you may rest assured that we will do everything in our power to assist you."

She could only hope the lady was discreet. Some people could not keep a secret if their lives depended on it. But there were bound to be risks. Any number of them. Alice had always been willing to risk. Now she'd have Blackwood at her side. They'd risk together.

Now all they had to do was succeed.

Rehearsals began the following week.

The Duke and Duchess of B_____ and party honored the Haymarket Theater on Wednesday. Along with the opera of *Clari* and the drama *The Housekeeper*, they witnessed the new farce, *Pyramus and Thisbe*, by the junior Charles Mathews, which proved a great success. While perhaps too improbable even for farce, the piece is excessively amusing, and the noble couple were seen to laugh heartily as well as indulge in their own exchange of secrets. We are led to suspect a reconciliation, one which has long been hoped for among their families and friends.

—*Foxe's Morning Spectacle*
Friday 16 August 1833

Chapter 28

A two-storey grey stone building housed the Tollstone Academy. In late summer, this wasn't the cold, damp place Alice remembered. Not that the present climate was healthier. The chinks and rattling windows let in the moor winds, which carried with them the aromas of the adjoining barn and stable, the pigs and chickens wandering about through muck, and the nearby cesspit. The smell was all the more oppressive in the warmth of the day.

Apart from the time of year, all was as Alice remembered.

She and Blackwood had done what they could to appear to be an ordinary couple of the middling classes. They stayed at an inn several miles away, rather than at Castle Ancaster. There the locals were all too likely to recognize them, in spite of their attire and the side whiskers and beard Blackwood had let grow during the preceding weeks.

Fortunately, he was unknown in the isolated village housing the Tollstone Academy—if one could call it a village. A few poorly maintained cottages stood here and there. The place boasted a bridge over a stream, shallow, murky, and slow at this time of year. Unlike the environs of Castle Ancaster, this piece of Yorkshire demonstrated what would have happened to Ripley's villagers had he not spent large sums restoring what his father had let go to rack and ruin.

Alice wore widow's weeds, veil included. All was of a quality in keeping with her identity: She was the Widow Smithers, saddled with two orphaned nieces whom she wanted off her hands as inexpensively as possible. Blackwood was her late husband's friend, Mr. Rookwood. If people believed that she wanted the girls off her hands so that she could marry, unencumbered, the bearded fellow accompanying them, all the better. He stood behind her chair, his hands on the back of it. He wore the benign look he'd practiced for several days.

The office they occupied was elaborately furnished, suggesting luxury throughout the establishment. In fact, the Tollstones reserved luxury for themselves.

Mrs. Tollstone was expensively if soberly dressed. Under the profusion of lace constituting her cap, a series of stiff rolls of curls framed her long, narrow face. A large gold watch on a heavy gold chain was pinned to the pleated bodice of her costly brown satin dress.

Mr. Tollstone was much as Alice remembered, if a few degrees greyer and plumper. A stiff white collar and black neckcloth. Side whiskers that had seemed to nine-year-old Alice to be made of metal wire. A top-notch tailor had made his dark green coat.

He gazed benevolently upon the two girls Alice had brought with her. Polly and Hannah, ages nine and eleven, looked very much the worse for wear. This wasn't entirely because of the long journey from London. Certain cosmetics were involved. They were street children Liliane had rescued two years earlier. She and Alice had chosen them for their intelligence, diligence, and acting talent.

"Promising girls," Mr. Tollstone said. "Very promising, indeed. But in need of proper instruction, no doubt."

"Well, as to that, naturally they ought to learn to be useful," Alice said. "Was my husband alive—bless his memory—we might put them to work in the shop." She sighed heavily, drew out her black-trimmed handkerchief, and dabbed under the veil at her eyes.

"There, there, Mrs. Smithers," Blackwood murmured. He patted her shoulder. "Courage, now."

"Indeed, indeed, we do not wish to bring up sad memories," said Mrs. Tollstone. "Our dearest wish is to help."

"You are too kind, I'm sure," Alice said with a sad little sniff. "I have been at my wits' end what to do with them. With my dear Mr. Smithers gone, I was obliged to turn to his good friend Mr. Rookwood for advice." She patted the big hand on her shoulder. "This gentleman was good enough to look about for me. He assured me that your school would suit."

"You need have no fears about your girls," said Mrs. Tollstone. "We'll look after them like they was our own. You may rely upon us absolutely. What dear things. Good girls, I'm sure, yes?"

She reached out a heavily beringed hand, put a knuckle under Polly's chin, and stared deep into her eyes.

She'd looked at Alice in the same way. Impossible to forget. She didn't want to forget, ever. Those hard knuckles and the rings and the cold voice.

We make no distinctions here . . . Do you understand, girl?

"I'm sure they will be," Alice said.

She smoothed her gloves, the agreed-upon signal.

Polly gave a little cough.

Mrs. Tollstone stepped back.

She was a hard woman, but she had an Achilles' heel: a morbid dread of illness. When children fell ill—which was often enough—she kept well clear of them, leaving the staff and other children to look after them. When measles or any other such disease ran through the place, she took a long holiday at the seaside.

"Pay her no mind," Alice said. "The child took a chill along the road."

"Not used to all this fresh air, eh, Polly?" said Blackwood.

Polly coughed some more and rubbed her nose.

"But she was coughing before, Aunt Essie," Hannah said. "Ever since—"

"Now, now," Blackwood said.

"These girls," Alice said. "Spoilt, I'm sorry to say. But they won't be shirking no more, will they?"

Hannah persisted. "But the doctor said—"

"Hush," Polly said. "Aunt Essie said not to say."

Hannah stared at her. "Say what?"

Polly gave her a warning look, then started coughing. "I need to use the privy," she said. "*Now.*" She jumped up from her chair. "Where is it?"

"Dobbs!" Mrs. Tollstone shouted.

A young girl hurried in. She was a very little, shrunken child, wearing an enormous, dirty apron and no shoes on her still dirtier feet. "Missus?"

"Take this girl to the privy, and be quick about it!"

Dobbs grabbed Polly's hand and dragged her from the room.

"That's how Amy was," Hannah cried. "She's got it, I know."

"Got what?" said Mrs. Tollstone, eyes wide.

"A trifling chill, no more," Alice said quickly. "These girls imagine things."

"Too much time on their hands," Blackwood said. "Idleness. The devil makes work—"

"She turned all blue, and she was sick horrible!" Hannah shrieked. "Doctor said it was the cholera!"

"Cholera!" Mrs. Tollstone grasped her husband's arm.

"First Papa, then Mama, then little Amy," Hannah cried. "Now poor Polly, and what shall I do?" She burst into tears and flung herself at Mrs. Tollstone, clutching her skirts.

"Get off me!" the schoolmistress screamed. "Don't touch me!"

"Help me, please!" Hannah sobbed.

"Stop that noise, girl," Blackwood said.

"Don't pay them any mind," Alice said. "It's all in their heads. They didn't want to come to school. My brother spoilt 'em shameful. It's no more than tantrums."

Hannah began coughing into Mrs. Tollstone's skirts.

Mrs. Tollstone managed to pry the girl loose. She looked down at her skirt, where a wet spot was spreading.

Hannah made retching noises and ran out of the room.

"Her face is turning blue!" the schoolmistress screamed. "It's the cholera, Samuel. They've brought it to us, and it'll kill us all!"

THE TOLLSTONES WERE gone within an hour. The servants, except for young Dobbs, took their own holiday as soon as master and mistress were out of sight.

Soon thereafter, Blackwood and Alice met in the Tollstones' office with a small group of people that Mr. Crade had assembled. These included an apothecary named Overton from nearby Heyshaw, the local squire, and one of the parish overseers.

Mr. Crade had already prepared the way. Rumors had spread of a serious illness at the school, he'd told the group. Complaints had been made of inadequate care. These rumors and complaints had reached the ears of certain prominent persons who owned property in the West Riding. At the behest of one of these individuals, Mrs. Smithers and Mr. Rookwood and the two girls had been employed to look into the matter. They had practiced a small deception in order to allow the group to inspect the premises without interference or concealment.

Nobody asked who Mrs. Smithers and Mr. Rookwood were, and so Mr. Crade did not tell them. If his little group were suspicious, they gave no sign. Mr. Crade had chosen them because he believed they would be more sympathetic than others. To many other locals, this was a school for wayward girls. If they were treated harshly, it was as they deserved.

Even so, in spite of sympathy and a wish to do good, the group expressed doubts that an inspection, regardless of what it revealed, would accomplish much. Still, they were willing to do what they were asked to do.

Alice and Blackwood had come prepared for skepticism. Moreover, they had one piece of good luck: One schoolmistress had remained. Miss Nalder was new to the staff. She was not happy with the school, and had recently applied for a position elsewhere. Her strict conscience, however, would not allow her to abandon her young charges.

She offered an eyewitness account of the way the school was run.

Blackwood and the others got to see for themselves. He thought he'd been prepared. He wasn't oblivious to London's impoverished masses. He knew that women and girls suffered most. He'd read Mrs. Wollstonecraft's book.

All the same, he found it . . . difficult to accept.

He knew the previous Duke of Ripley had not been right in the head. Even so, it was hard to believe he'd sent his daughter to this place.

Several of the girls were truly ill. None could be called healthy. Miss Nalder reported a system of insufficient food, clothing, and instruction, and more than sufficient work and hard discipline.

As the group were leaving the dormitory, he drew Alice aside.

"I ought not to be surprised," he said softly. "I've learnt enough from you. I've read the stories. Nevertheless . . ." He shook his head. "I remember what you said about going to the Marshalsea. You said you'd found it salutary to see for yourself. I find this salutary, you may be sure."

She smiled up at him. "It will be even more salutary if we can put our hands on something truly useful." Her gaze turned inward. "You noticed her jewels."

"I noticed they were unusually well-dressed for schoolmaster and schoolmistress. A Bond Street tailor made his coat, I'll wager anything."

"He didn't inherit wealth," she said. "The fees are moderate."

"Sufficient to clothe and feed these girls a good deal better," he said. "In which case one draws the logical conclusion. Well, then, let's see what we can find. They were in rather a hurry. Did they take time to collect their records, I wonder?"

They did not, it turned out. While the others talked to Miss

Nalder, he and Alice searched. They found two sets of records. He found the false ones in Tollstone's study. She found the alternate set of books in Mrs. Tollstone's sitting room.

At the end of the day, after leaving Miss Nalder, Hannah and Polly, and two women from the next village, to look after the schoolchildren, Alice and Blackwood met with the others in the dining parlor of the nearby King's Arms.

They presented the two sets of financial records, which showed that the Tollstones kept for themselves all but a fraction of the money intended for the children's upkeep.

"This does explain how they could afford fine clothes and furnishings and their holiday house at Margate," Alice said.

"This is shameful," Mr. Overton said. "The children are ill all too often, and I'm rarely summoned. I hear of it, but I cannot go where I'm not asked."

Blackwood turned to the lawyer.

"Glaring discrepancies, beyond question," Mr. Crade said.

"I am not a lawyer," Blackwood said, "but I daresay that *fraud* is not too strong a word."

Mr. Crade nodded.

There was the crux of it, Blackwood thought. Property was sacred, above all things, including children's lives.

One couldn't change this thinking. It was too deeply ingrained.

That meant one must find a way to use it.

"We *might* expect to prevail in a criminal trial," Blackwood said. "We ought to find any number of parents and guardians who'll be outraged about the misuse of their money. On the other hand, they might strongly object to being associated with the poor treatment of their children. They might worry that their neighbors will say, 'Why didn't you look into the place more closely?' They won't like seeing their names in the newspapers in a sordid case like this."

"If you imply that the matter were best not made public," the squire said, "I agree."

"Certain questions may prove awkward for us to answer," Mr. Crade said.

Awkward for a number of people, including the parish overseer. But also for persons like the Blackwoods and their group who'd pried where some would say they had no business to do so.

"We can't let the school continue as it was," Alice said. "We've observed the conditions. We've heard Miss Nalder's account of her experience. We have Mr. Overton's report."

A debate ensued.

In the end, thanks to Blackwood's subtle prodding and Mr. Crade's equally subtle guidance, the group agreed to keep the school open, with Miss Nalder appointed headmistress. The parish would provide funds, temporarily, to address the worst of the conditions. Mrs. Smithers and Mr. Rookwood would apply to their employer to supplement these funds.

In the meantime, Mr. Crade would arrange for the appropriate officials to contact Mr. Tollstone at his seaside refuge and inform him of the evidence against him. They would invite him to make financial restitution, rather than take his chances with criminal proceedings and disagreeable publicity. As part of this restitution, he would turn over the Tollstone Academy to the Heyshaw School ladies, and cease all opposition to their efforts. The present school would be extensively cleaned and refurbished, to begin a new life in keeping with Minerva Society principles.

The matter being settled to everybody's satisfaction, the group dispersed.

When he returned from seeing them off, Blackwood found Alice at the window of the dining parlor.

"Dragons dead enough for you?" he said.

She turned to him. Her eyes shimmered. "Thank you," she said.

"I ought to thank you," he said. "This was a lesson to me. I haven't quite taken it in, but at least now I understand—not merely in my mind, but in my heart—why the work is so important to you. Why you persist, even when your spouse whines about your not attending to his every whim."

"You were not unreasonable," she said. "It's a long journey, simply to try to right one wrong. And I have been away . . . excessively."

"Your brother, Ashmont, and I have traveled to Yorkshire often enough, most usually for a rest cure at Castle Ancaster," he said. "This was more productive. I'm especially glad I had the opportunity to observe your performance as the Widow Smithers."

"You made a fine Mr. Rookwood," she said. "And the girls did beautifully." She smiled. "Little urchins. But good girls, all the same. Both products of the Minerva Society. That's what can happen when we find promising children and are able to help them along. Who knows? After this experience, and meeting Miss Nalder, Polly or Hannah might decide it's a fine thing to be a schoolmistress, and teach other children."

"That would be a fine thing, indeed."

"All the same, I'm not sure I could have done so much without your talent for machination."

"All those pranks. Excellent practice."

"I'm glad I chose you," she said.

"I'm glad you did."

What a waste his life had been before. How empty it would have been without her. Marriage wasn't easy, but it had made his existence infinitely richer. *She* had made his existence infinitely richer.

She came to him and set her forehead against his chest. "Affinity."

He brought his arms about her. "Yes."

ON THE FOLLOWING day, Alice and Blackwood set out for London.

They hadn't traveled two miles when she asked to stop the carriage.

"I want to see it," she said. "I want to see it differently."

And so they stepped out into the road and walked to a wall and looked out over the moors. The heather was in bloom, swathes of glorious purple stretching over the harshly beautiful landscape under a cloudy sky.

"I loved these moors," she said. "When I was very little, my nursemaid would take me for walks. She'd grown up here. Then my father sent me to the school. I was a duke's daughter. It made no difference. I was treated the same as the others. The Tollstones knew my father didn't care."

"Ripley says he had a maggot in the brain," Blackwood said. "He says your father wasn't always that way."

"The man with the maggot is the only father I remember. I can never repay Uncle Charles and Aunt Julia for rescuing me. The Minerva Society isn't the only reason I put up with the royals. I do it for Aunt Julia, too. And everything you said was true—about the children and being a knight and fighting back." She looked up at him. "I never told anybody except Cassandra how I truly felt. But I've told you. And you listened. It took a while, but you listened."

"Yes, it took a while," he said.

He'd taken the trouble to try to understand. And he did understand.

She ought to have realized he would. Perhaps she had. Perhaps in her heart she'd always known she could trust him, absolutely.

She drank in the air, the never-forgotten smell of the heath.

"I didn't know I was shackled to that school, in my head," she said. "Now I'm not."

"In that case," he said, "may we now live happily ever after?"

Chapter 29

*P*arliament rose on the day Alice and Blackwood frightened the Tollstones out of their school. Since then, the majority of the upper orders had left London, some for their places in the country, some for the seaside, and some for the Continent.

The Blackwoods planned to leave, too, and the house was in the throes of packing and reorganizing. To escape the turmoil and keep out from underfoot, Alice and Blackwood were about to set out for Regent Street, where a curiosity was being exhibited at the Cosmorama rooms. "Napoleon Breathing," a life-size figure of the late emperor, was reputed to be exact in every detail, with remarkably lifelike features. Apparently its chest rose and fell in an exact representation of breathing. The numerous newspaper articles had made Blackwood curious about what it was made of and how the illusion of breathing was done.

They had stepped out of the house and were about to climb into the cabriolet when the groom Pratt ran into the forecourt.

"They've taken him!" he cried. He stopped short when he saw the duke and duchess standing, staring at him.

He dragged off his hat and bowed. "If it please Your Grace." He was gasping.

"What's happened?" Blackwood said. "Who's been taken?"

"Jones, Your Grace. The new boy."

IT HAD HAPPENED very quickly. Pratt and Jonesy had been returning from their weekly errands for the head groom. They'd paused at Hatchett's White Horse Cellar to buy muffins from the muffin man there, Jonesy being partial to the delicacy and owning a prodigious appetite.

An altercation of some sort broke out, as often happened at that busy place, resulting in a lot of shouting and pushing. In the tumult, a large man, who appeared to be a coachman, had grabbed Jonesy and dragged him away.

The boy hadn't gone willingly, Pratt told them. He'd shouted and struggled, but suddenly stopped. Amid the general chaos, it was hard to see what happened next. Then Pratt saw the boy flung into the back of an old coach. It looked like a hackney coach but bore no identifying number.

Pratt had started to chase after the vehicle when a stagecoach arrived, adding to the general confusion. With everybody pushing and shoving and arguing, all busy with their own concerns, nobody paid Pratt the slightest heed. By the time he was able to break through the crowd, the vehicle was long out of sight.

"I found a constable," he said. "I told him what happened, but it was too late by then. They was long gone."

He was distraught. Jonesy had become a favorite in the stables. He worked hard and he didn't complain, but above all, he had a way with the horses.

"It was like they was brothers and sisters, Your Grace," Pratt said. "Him and the creatures. He learnt their ways so quick. I don't know what the world's comin' to, Your Grace, I don't. What'd anybody want with him?"

A good question.

After Alice and Blackwood had collected as much information as they could from the groom, they sent him back to the stables.

Alice stood in the forecourt, looking about her. "I had resolved to be philosophical if he ran away," she said. "But he
didn't run away."

"Apparently not." Blackwood, too, looked about him, but
he was thinking, not seeing. "Needle in a haystack comes to
mind," he said.

"Yes."

"I'd better apply to Bow Street for a principal officer," he said.
"Nobody is more skilled at finding people."

They returned to the house, and to his study. He wrote a short
letter to the chief magistrate at Bow Street and was about to ring
for a servant when Dawson appeared, bearing a folded piece of
paper on a tray.

"This just arrived, Your Grace," he said. "In view of today's
events, I took the liberty of detaining the ticket porter."

Alice rose from the chair where she'd been sitting, staring at
her shoes—obviously as much at a loss as Blackwood was—and
moved to the desk where he stood.

The folded paper was cheap and none too clean.

He unfolded it. Written in pencil, in coarse capitals, was the
message:

EFF YOU WANT THE BOY BACK, SEND YOUR LADY WITH 500
POWNS SEELT UP SAFE INSIDE OF A TRAVELL BAG TO SAINT
BOTOLF CHURCHYD BY THE BULL AND MOUF AT 6 OCLOCK
TOMORROR. NO PLEECE AND NOBODY ELLS ONLY HER LESS
YOU WANT HIM IN PEECES.

He passed it to Alice, who read it once, twice, then looked up
at him with a puzzled expression.

"Five hundred pounds?" she said.

"Leave it to you to notice that first. You don't turn a hair at
the prospect of going, alone, to a churchyard in Aldersgate to
meet somebody who threatens dismemberment. No, you take
note of numbers."

"It doesn't ring true," she said. "Somebody who can't spell, writes in pencil on cheap paper, demands such a sum?"

"That isn't the only false note," he said. "I can't be sure of Maggie Proudie's territory, but I should have guessed it encompassed that part of London. She and I had a bargain."

"More than a year has passed since we collected him from her," Alice said.

"She let me know when Jonesy was taken up, only a few months ago." He shook his head. "Either somebody has dared to be a renegade and risk her displeasure, or this is not what it purports to be."

He met Alice's gaze.

"We'd better talk to the messenger," she said.

THE TICKET PORTER, John Ridding, awaited them in the same room where Alice had awaited Blackwood as a laundress.

Ridding offered little enlightenment. His stand was near Hatchett's. A coachman had given him the message to carry here. The coachman said that a passenger had asked him to send it, the passenger needing to be elsewhere urgently. No answer was wanted. The coachman had paid Ridding sixpence, though he'd had to travel so short a distance—not even a quarter mile.

No, Ridding didn't know who the coachman was but was sure he wasn't one of the regular drivers. Still, they were always coming and going, changing routes. It might have been one of the night coachmen.

Blackwood paid the ticket porter a crown to make up for any revenue lost while he was delayed at Blackwood House, and let him go.

"It isn't difficult to dress like a coachman," he told Alice. "Noblemen have done it." He smiled at her. "You could do it."

"I suppose I could, but that won't help us find Jonesy." She moved across the room to look at a picture. It was the one she'd been studying on the morning more than a year ago when she'd arrived to demand his help. It was a print of one of Henry Alken's steeplechase paintings.

Life with Alice was rather like a steeplechase, Blackwood thought. An adventure, certainly.

Apparently, a never-ending one.

"A man pretending to be a coachman at a coaching inn," she said, turning away from the picture. "A coach pretending to be a hackney coach—old and nondescript. Nothing elaborate here in the way of arrangements. Except the ransom note. Five hundred pounds, Giles. For a stable boy. Would Maggie expect that much?"

"Maybe fifty, if she was in a humorous mood. But that's the sort of sum one might expect for, say, government secrets. Or a duchess."

Alice shook her head. "I find it difficult to believe she's behind this."

"As do I. Maggie is no fool, and kidnapping Jonesy would be dangerously foolish, considering our bargain."

"Would she be willing to help us, do you think?"

Yes, this was Alice, he thought. She didn't pause for a moment at the prospect of employing a gang leader whom hardened criminals feared.

"For a price, certainly," he said.

"Then the question is how to find her."

"She seemed to think I could." Blackwood still had in his hand the ransom note, as well as the letter he'd written to Sir Frederick Roe at Bow Street. He looked from one to the other. "Maggie or Bow Street. I can't do both."

"Certainly not," Alice said. "Bow Street would like to get their hands on somebody like her. Not that I blame them. But she did alert you when Jonesy was captured. We can't betray her."

"One or the other," Blackwood said. "We risk failure either way. Which one, then?"

"The note warned us against police," she said.

"The principal officers are quite good with disguise," he said.

"Yet some miscreants can detect them from a furlong away. Keeffe would tell you so."

He glanced down again at the ransom note. "If this didn't smell of trickery . . . But never mind. I'm going to put my money on Maggie. She believed I could find her. I'd rather she didn't discover she'd overestimated my intelligence." He considered. "I might as well start at the Cock in Fleet Street. She did not seem to be a stranger there. Will you accompany me?"

She shook her head. "If I go to a tavern, I'll need a disguise. That would take time I can spend more productively. Not to mention that she likes you better. I'm going to see Keeffe."

BLACKWOOD TOLD HIMSELF not to have high hopes of locating Maggie in time. Her lair would be a closely guarded secret, which nobody but persons tired of life would reveal. Still, one must begin somewhere. Having decided to begin with Maggie, he could only follow where his intellect and instincts led.

The Cock was busy at this time of day. He loitered outside for a time, examining his surroundings, especially the other loiterers, including some unpromising young specimens. He didn't see the youth who'd found him at the Haymarket last month. After a few minutes, he went inside.

He wasn't hungry, but he ordered a meal and a tankard of porter. He found a newspaper and read it. And waited. And waited.

The waiter came to ask if there was anything else. Blackwood ordered more porter and said, "I was expecting to meet somebody here." He took out his pocket watch and shook his head. "Women have a curious sense of time."

A humorous conversation ensued. Coins changed hands, and Blackwood said, "I breakfasted with the lady here a good while ago. Last year. I wonder if she forgot our appointment today. Or perhaps she mistook the place."

The waiter regarded the coins in his hand. "Last year, Your

Grace? In the forenoon, was it? Not very busy then, I'll warrant. May I ask some of the others if they recollect?"

To assist the others' memories, Blackwood added more coins and a description of the dilatory female.

Time passed. In the Cock's dim light, Blackwood read the shipping news and the sporting news. He sent for another paper. He perused the positions wanted and the list of books published this day. He read the accounts of the wrecks of the *Amphitrite* and the *Talbot Ostend Steamer*. He read on. He came to the last page and was perusing the latest report from Bow Street when he heard a familiar voice.

"Missed me, did'yer?"

Maggie Proudie slid into the seat opposite.

"THAT WAS QUICK," Blackwood said.

Maggie shrugged. "One of these coves tole one of my lads who was outside. They said you was waitin' for me."

"I guessed one of your lads might be in the vicinity."

She nodded. "Then, when I was comin' here—you know, not wantin' to miss our randy-voose—I heard some things. I heard somebody nabbed a boy, the one you took last year. I tole you he was more trouble than he was worth."

Blackwood passed the ransom note across to her. "Somebody thinks he's worth a great deal."

She read the note and laughed. "If all his teeth was gold, he wouldn't fetch fifty pounds. Unless he's your squeaker. But he ain't, is he?"

"Most certainly I never fathered him—or anybody else, to my knowledge."

She returned her attention to the note. "I'll tell you somethin'. Mebbe I'm wrong, but it looks to me like somebody tried to make this look like the note I wrote for you that time. The one for the gentry cove in Golden Square." She pointed. "See? That's how I made my letters, to scare 'im. I don't write like that usually. I know readin' and writin'. My pa taught me, 'n I can do it proper. Another thing: I spell better 'n this. Not like you, mebbe, but better 'n some. I know how to spell what's on an inn sign. That's one o' the ways I learnt."

Blackwood sat back. "That's interesting. The coincidence. The same boy. Copying your writing."

"Ain't it?"

"Let me buy you dinner," he said.

"I'll let you," she said. "But first let me talk to some of my lads."

WORD TRAVELED MORE quickly through London's underworld than even among the upper orders. By the end of her dinner, Maggie had received several verbal messages, and Blackwood had sent two written ones to Alice, reporting on progress.

The second was short:

> *We're about to set out. I'm to keep in the background, and let the mistress of crime manage matters. We must act quickly, though. The kidnappers have Jonesy in an unpleasant neighborhood well away from the rendezvous point. They won't expect us.*
>
> *I'm sorry to leave you out of this part of the excitement, but I do it in hopes that you will be well-compensated by tomorrow, if not sooner.*
>
> *I remain*
Your humble and obedient husband,
B

ALICE, MEANWHILE, WAS not idle. She'd received Blackwood's first message shortly after she returned from visiting Keeffe. By then, she'd put together a few clues and developed a theory.

She sent a message to Lord Consett.

Locating him wasn't difficult. Like so many other gentlemen, his lordship was a creature of habit. His servants had suggested to the footman Thomas three places where he was likely to be found. Thomas found him at the second.

By late afternoon, Consett and Alice sat in Blackwood's barouche under the trees in Berkeley Square, across from Gunter's Tea Shop. They were enjoying ices. That was to say, Alice was enjoying hers. Consett regarded his as though it bore a skull and crossbones.

"But I can't say," he said. "Gave my word, you know."

"And a gentleman doesn't break his word," she said. "It simply isn't done."

"I'm so glad you understand, Duchess."

She leant toward him. "Here is what I also understand. If you do not tell me where Lord Worbury is hiding, I shall break all your teeth. That way, you'll be able to say 'I can't say' in perfect truth."

He covered his mouth.

"You must have heard about my encounter with the miscreant in Kensington last year," she said. "I am not afraid to bruise my knuckles. And do not think of trying to run away, because Thomas is on watch to make sure you don't get in an accident." She frowned. "Or maybe to cause one. I forget."

Consett looked from her to the burly Thomas.

"Or maybe I'll simply tell your mother about a few of your and Lord Worbury's not very gentlemanly activities."

His face went white.

She waited.

"Ch-chelsea," he said.

She smiled. "Well done. That's a start. Where in Chelsea, precisely?"

LIKE SO MANY malefactors, the kidnappers, Bill Ford and Abner Grigg, made up in brawn, brutality, and bluster what they lacked in brains.

When Maggie Proudie turned up unexpectedly in their hiding place, the bluster crumbled. Two of her assistants—men, not boys—relieved the kidnappers of their various weapons, and nobody argued about it.

At present the two who'd taken the weapons lounged by the door. A third leant back near a window, to discourage flight via that route. Other gang members waited on the stairs and on the street below.

I envy her power, Alice had told Blackwood. Until this moment, he hadn't truly understood.

He wished Alice could see that power in action: the effect of one not especially large or threatening-looking woman on this pair of brutes.

"But this kid ain't the same 'un, Missus Maggie," Bill was saying, trying to make light of matters. One didn't contradict Maggie Proudie without long and careful thought, not to mention cartloads of tact.

Bill's body, however, had got all the power, leaving his brain nothing to work with. "That 'un you didn't want bothered, why, he was a street brat. This 'un—only look at 'im."

True, Jonesy wasn't at his best, having been manhandled into a coach and bumped along numerous side streets and alleyways to elude pursuit, then tossed onto a pile of second- or possibly fifth-hand clothes. On the other hand, one could hardly mistake the quality of his attire. A neat cap. Sturdy boots. Nothing torn or patched.

Unlike the grooms, Blackwood's stable boys didn't wear livery. All the same, their attire declared them gainfully employed by a prominent personage.

Jonesy remained mute, obviously waiting to see which way the wind blew.

Blackwood, who was dressed as a hackney coachman, had him by the hand. Nonetheless, a child as quick-witted as this one wouldn't necessarily feel safe while Maggie was nearby with her minions.

The boy's hand was cold in Blackwood's, and he trembled a little.

A child. He was only a child, after all.

"I'm lookin' at *you*," Maggie said.

She slapped Bill in the head.

The *whack* must have been audible at the bottom of the three flights of stairs they'd climbed to find their quarry. Jonesy winced at the sound. As did Abner. Bill staggered and clutched his head.

With his ears ringing, Bill wouldn't be useful for a bit, and so Maggie turned to Abner. "Who tole you to steal the boy?"

Abner looked at Bill. Maggie raised her hand to assist the cogitation process.

The men began to talk.

Blackwood House

HOURS PASSED. MIDNIGHT passed.

Finally, shortly after two o'clock in the morning, Alice heard the rattle of wheels in the forecourt. She hurried down the stairs to the entrance, arriving in time to see Blackwood disembark from a hackney cab and Jonesy hop out after him.

Alice raced out into the forecourt.

While Blackwood paid the driver, she crouched in front of the boy.

"You're unhurt?" she said, taking off his cap and smoothing his hair.

He pulled away from her ministrations and looked down at himself, as though not certain he was all there. "I ain't hurt. Only I orter 'of seen 'em comin', Yer Highness. Wasn't watchin' proper."

"Probably on account of the large muffin in your mouth at the time," Blackwood said.

Jonesy looked up at him. It was a long way up. "Vey knocked it outer my mouf!"

The hackney rattled away, out of the court and into Piccadilly.

"Let's be thankful they didn't break your teeth in the process,"

Blackwood said. "You were so quiet back there, I did wonder if they'd cut off your tongue."

Jonesy shook his head. "Vey tole me to stopper my jaw. Vey said it was a job, and don't make it hard. Vey said they'd let me go tomorrow, arter vey got the money. I din't believe 'em. But vey wasn't so bad as some."

Alice looked up at Blackwood. It was hard to read his face in the dark.

"I were more scairt of Maggie," the child said.

"So were they," Blackwood said. "I'm sorry you weren't by to see it, Duchess."

"As am I, but I had my own business to attend to," she said. "We can talk about it later. Let's see to Jonesy first. He's had a long, trying day—and he was cheated of his muffin. Nobody in the household has wanted to sleep. They're all worried about him. I daresay Cook will find something for him to eat."

THE SUN WAS sending up its first exploratory rays by the time Alice and Blackwood got to bed. After time spent in Bill and Abner's lair, Blackwood had badly needed a bath. He'd come to his wife's bed mainly to make sure she was asleep, and not fretting about anybody or anything.

He found her sitting up, book in her lap. She set the book aside.

"Are you not tired?" he said. "This has been a long day, wearing on the nerves, I should think."

"My nerves are made of iron," she said. "I am tired, but I can't bear to keep my triumph to myself."

She told him about her conversation with Consett.

Blackwood laughed. "You threatened him with his mother. Oh, Alice, that is . . ."

"Brilliant," she said.

"Wicked, I was about to say."

"Not that I actually knew anything to accuse him of," she said. "But the threats of violence weakened his resolve. He was primed by the time I administered the coup de grâce. Still, I do wish I could have slapped him in the head the way you said Maggie did Bill. Consett needs to be slapped. Repeatedly. With a cricket bat."

"It won't help," Blackwood said. "One can only hope he finds less villainous friends in future."

"I did let him know it was unwise to continue Worbury's acquaintance," she said.

"Ah, yes. Worbury. One last matter to clear up. But we'll talk of that tomorrow."

"It is tomorrow."

"Later today, then."

"Yes, but let me say one more thing. You rescued Jonesy. You found Maggie, and you found the kidnappers, and you got that child away safe. In a matter of hours. I can't imagine another nobleman doing what you've done this night. I'm glad I chose you." She ran her hand down his chest.

"Am I a victim of wishful thinking, or are you feeling amorous, Duchess?"

"I feel particularly fond of you at the moment." She slid her hand down farther.

"Do you know, I'm growing fonder and fonder of you at present." He drew her into his arms. "There must be a way to express my feelings. Let me think."

"Thinking doesn't come into it," she said.

Chapter 30

Evening of Friday 6 September 1833

The sun had set and the moon hadn't yet risen when Lord Worbury entered the coffee room of the Fox and Hare.

He arrived early in order to make sure he wouldn't encounter any of his acquaintance, good or bad. Even though this coaching inn was not the sort that catered to persons of quality, a little extra caution did no harm.

He'd been extremely careful about the location. In a coaching inn, a travel bag would be a common sight. The neighborhood ought to be reasonably safe yet well away from the major, bustling hostelries.

He needed to get in and out quickly and easily.

The run-down Fox and Hare suited well enough. Stagecoaches and farm wagons formed its primary clientele. Its accommodations were primitive.

Still, he surveyed his surroundings several times, to be sure all was as it ought to be.

His confederates didn't worry him. Bill and Abner had done the odd bit of work for him from time to time. Nothing too complicated or risky. Sadly, certain persons to whom his lordship owed money fell into the too-risky category.

Making off with a child, though, was child's play, ha-ha, they'd told him. They did not care about whys and wherefores.

They did not ask annoying questions. What they asked was simple: their fee and the child's whereabouts. Worbury promised them fifty pounds—twenty-five apiece. He'd paid ten in advance. Practical matters settled, the pair needed no further details.

Earlier in the day they'd sent a message via ticket porter to the place where he received mail and messages under an assumed name. He'd written the message as well as the ransom note when they took the assignment, because they were illiterate. Two words sufficed: *Got him.* Bill had turned it this way and that and squinted at it before declaring that it would do.

Now, seeing no signs of unwanted visitors, Worbury claimed a box compartment at one of the windows looking out into the stable yard, and ordered coffee.

He looked at his watch. Thanks to the dip in his finances, it wasn't the fine quality of the one he'd lost last year at the time of the ghastly experience with the so-called Georgie Foster. As to that . . .

It couldn't be helped. Worbury would rather have arranged for the Blackwoods to receive the filthy brat's mangled body, but one couldn't have everything, and he was in dire need of money.

Even they wouldn't pay five hundred pounds for a corpse.

His coffee arrived, and a moment later, a plain-looking woman and her family came through the door. A widow, no doubt. Widows were one of his specialties. Not this one. Judging by her and her offspring's threadbare attire, he'd find no profit there.

Two more people entered. Coachmen. Hat brims pulled low. Blue glasses, as some wore against the glare of the sun, though there wasn't much sun in the coffee room. Speckled neckerchiefs up to their chins. Shabby coats.

No, this inn did not attract premier travelers or drivers.

He heard nearby church bells strike seven.

A while later, two large figures darkened the door. One carried a carpetbag. They looked about the coffee room.

They were not Bill and Abner.

Worbury took out his watch and frowned at it. A quarter past seven. They ought to have had more than sufficient time to get here from St. Botolph's.

"They're not coming."

He looked up.

One of the coachmen stood looking down at him.

He took off his blue glasses. He was a she. A she to whom he was related.

Worbury's gaze shot from the Duchess of Blackwood to the man who carried a carpetbag.

"Not him," said Her Grace. "Mr. Ford and Mr. Grigg are engaged elsewhere. They send their regrets. They've sent the bag as well, because you'll need it."

WORBURY LEAPT UP, fist drawn back to knock her out of the way.

Blackwood—the other coachman—set his hand on his shoulder and pushed him back down onto the seat.

"I wouldn't try that if I were you," the duke said. "She hits back. Hard."

Sweat broke out on Worbury's forehead. "I don't know what this is about. I was here peaceably enjoying a cup of coffee."

"Of course you were." Alice slid onto the seat opposite. "And we'd like to keep the peace. For instance, we're strongly opposed to kidnapping and holding children for ransom. And do you know, Mr. Ford and Mr. Grigg are strongly opposed to fraud and double-dealing. They were shocked to learn that the ransom they were to collect was five hundred pounds, not one hundred."

Worbury stiffened.

"Foolish fellows," Blackwood said. "Half for you and half for them, you told them. They trusted you."

"They're not happy now," Alice said. "It took our combined efforts, along with the kind offices of an acquaintance, to prevent their coming here to cut your throat."

"Clean off your head." Blackwood made a slashing gesture across his neck. "That was the idea."

"Naturally, we discouraged them," Alice said. "So untidy. I've heard that a garotte is more efficient."

Worbury looked wildly about him.

"Were you thinking of calling for help?" Alice said. "Please do. I'm curious what you'll say."

"I don't want to cause you any more embarrassment than you've caused yourself," Worbury said. "I've done nothing. I don't know what sort of scoundrels you've been talking to, but this is all nonsense. I don't know anything about any kidnapping or five hundred pounds or one hundred pounds, and I don't know these men you're talking about, whoever they are."

Blackwood shoved Worbury aside and sat down next to him, blocking escape.

"Very well," he said. "You know nothing about it, and what can we prove, after all?"

Alice took out a piece of paper and looked at it. "Not very much, it seems. Outstanding debts to . . ." She pushed the paper toward Worbury. "Have I got the figures right?" She shrugged. "Maybe it doesn't matter. They've found out where in Chelsea you've been holed up. I can't promise that they'll be waiting for you, but it does seem likely."

Worbury stared at the paper, his face going white.

"Don't forget the other thing, my dear," Blackwood said.

"Oh, yes. As of now, you've acquired a shadow or two." She glanced over at the widow—more usually known as Maggie Proudie—who nodded. "Or five. A dozen? Enough, at any rate. They've all had a good look at you. Henceforth, no matter where you go in London, they'll be there. Somewhere. Your creditors will pay handsomely for the information."

Blackwood signaled, and the man with the carpetbag approached the table. He set the bag down at the duke's feet and withdrew to a table near Maggie's.

"The bag does not contain five hundred pounds," Alice said. "It contains what Mr. Ford and Mr. Grigg claim was your share of the alleged ransom for the alleged kidnapping of our stable boy. Fifty pounds. For travel expenses."

"But I . . ." Worbury trailed off, his panicked gaze going here, there, and finding escape nowhere.

"A hackney awaits outside to take you to the Tower Stairs," Alice went on. "There you'll find a pair of travel companions waiting for you with tickets for the next steam packet to Calais. You won't be lonely. Your new friends will see you onto the packet and across the Channel to your destination." She beamed at him. "There. A trip abroad. For health reasons. Won't that be pleasant?"

A HACKNEY COACH took Alice and Blackwood back to Blackwood House.

"And to think I once believed marriage a dull business, the sort of thing a man did not contemplate until he was tired of life," he said.

"It will seem dull after this," she said.

"That I very much doubt." He studied her for a moment, then turned his attention to the coach's dark interior. Probably best not to see it in daylight. He looked down at himself. "I truly hope these garments do not house vermin."

"I recommend a hot bath," she said.

"You'd better examine me for unwanted creatures first."

"It will be my pleasure. But you will need to remove all of your clothing."

"Must I?"

"You don't want me to miss anything."

"I have a feeling you won't. You will not spare my blushes."

"Probably not. But of course you will need to serve me in the same way. I shall be obliged to remove every stitch. I shall be hot with shame."

"Because you are so shy and modest and delicate. So decorous and circumspect. What else is it that draws me to you? Your quiet demeanor and dignified reserve—except when you are threatening to break teeth or knocking a fellow on his arse."

"I didn't knock Bray on his arse. He lost his balance."

He leant back against the seat. "That was fun, wasn't it?"

"Tonight, you mean?"

"Yes, that was fun, too. Being with you is fun. Being married to you is even more fun. I ought to have done it years ago."

"Years ago I wouldn't have you."

"But you had me eventually."

"I was between a rock and a hard place." She shrugged. "I've tried to make the best of it."

"I believe you've made the best of me," he said. "I do love you, Alice."

He heard her breath catch, and it dawned on him then that he'd never said the words aloud. Thought them countless times. *Idiot.*

She turned toward him. "Do you, indeed? Or has the recent excitement addled your brain?"

"I suspect I've loved you from the moment I saw you climbing out of the window at Camberley Place."

"I haven't loved you nearly as long," she said.

It was his turn to catch his breath.

She continued: "Only from the time you didn't interrupt when Cassandra and I pummeled Worbury."

"I remember you smiled at me. Was that love?"

"Very possibly. Who can tell, at the age of twelve? Then, when I was seventeen—"

"I'm sorry about that," he said. "I was a stupid boy. Very stupid."

"No, you were a gentleman," she said.

"Worse and worse."

"You might have done what you liked with me. I didn't realize then. Girls are kept in ignorance."

"I was clumsy and unkind all the same."

"You did me a kindness. You were nineteen. And I went away

to have a life more interesting and independent than most girls are allowed."

"And to become the woman you are," he said. "Very well, then. It was not well done of me, but it might have been worse."

"Never mind the past," she said. "We've accomplished great things this day and night. Let us celebrate."

And they did. After scrupulous physical examinations and a shared bath, they celebrated in the time-honored custom of loving couples everywhere.

Then, about the time dawn broke, Blackwood awoke, and knew what he had to do.

Chapter 31

Friday 13 September 1833

Hundreds of lights shone in the vast garden of Blackwood House. They glittered in the large stand of trees that screened it from the neighboring garden, which in turn formed a further barrier between these properties and Berkeley Square. They sparkled from poles and ropes erected for the purpose, and they shimmered on stands under the large canopy where Weippert's band played from a fanciful orchestra stand.

What it seemed to be was a miniature version of Vauxhall, which was the effect Lady Charles had created years ago at Camberley Place on one memorable night.

Ripley was there with his duchess. Ashmont was there was his duchess. Lady Charles was there and Lord Frederick. Doveridge was there and Lynforde, both still wifeless. Blackwood's sisters had come, along with the nieces and nephews deemed mature enough for the gathering. Lady Kempton was there, along with others of the Blackwoods' family and friends.

London was quieter and the weather somewhat cooler than would be perfect, but Blackwood decided that this sort of thing couldn't wait until late summer of next year. And so his household had had to pause their packing and prepare instead for a party.

Alice had been kept out of it.

"You've more than enough to do with your orphans and strays," Blackwood had told her. "Leave this to me and Ripley. We've years of experience with parties, and probably can manage one that isn't too indecent, if your aunts will lend a hand."

And so all she had to do was dress for the occasion and look after the guests. She wore a dramatic black dress embroidered with rose China asters. A black blond lace scarf circled her neck. A thin chain dotted with diamonds trailed across her forehead and round her coiffure. The latter was the usual fashionable insanity of braids and loops that appeared to shoot from her head like fireworks, with interwoven diamonds adding to the effect.

But all the fireworks were Alice, as far as Blackwood was concerned.

She was the fireworks of his life.

He told her so, and she laughed, and guests turned their way and smiled.

He even danced with his own wife, more than once.

And when the party was at its height, he drew her away, deep into the lamplit trees, where he'd had an arbor built, like the one they'd passed through on that night so long ago. Near it was the tall shrubbery, concealing them from the others.

And he said, "Alice," and he set her hand on his arm, the way she'd done that time. Then he pushed down her long glove and bent his head to kiss the inside of her elbow.

She said, "Oh. Giles. Oh."

Then she was in his arms. And this time it was one long, clinging kiss. This time he didn't break away. This time he let himself fall and fall and fall into the sparkling sea that was this love of his, this strange, wild girl.

He pushed her up against the arbor and let his hands rove over her. He kissed her neck and her ears and her jaw. He made kisses over the smooth skin at the edge of her bodice. Her hands weren't idle meanwhile. She let them rove over him, as though she were only now discovering him, as though they weren't an old married couple of a year and more.

And at last, when they were hot and panting, he said, "Now we must stop."

"Why?"

"Guests."

"How inconvenient."

"I'll make it up to you later."

She drew in one breath and let it out. Then another and another.

And she said, "You've made it up very well so far."

"I wanted you to know what I would have done if I hadn't been a damned gentleman," he said.

"Thank you," she said. "I always wondered."

At last they drew away from each other. It was only then she realized what he'd done.

She looked back toward the house, all the glittering lights in the trees, the music.

"You recreated it," she said. "Not only our first kiss, but the party. The magic."

"But this time with a happier ending," he said.

It wasn't exactly the end.

But this time they did live happily ever after.

Author's Note

NEWS AND GOSSIP. In the fine tradition of publishers of my time period, for whom copyright, basically, did not exist, I have stolen liberally from periodicals of the time. Adapting their verbiage for my fictional *Foxe's Morning Spectacle* is a way of creating for readers the feeling of being there. These samples of the prose of the early nineteenth century ought to make clear why I do not attempt elsewhere to write exactly in the style of the era.

MONEY. Until 1971, English money wasn't based on a decimal system. It went like this:

Twelve pence in a shilling (*bob*, in slang).

Twenty shillings in a pound or sovereign (a *glistener*).

Twenty-one shillings in a guinea.

There were numerous smaller and larger units of these denominations, such as:

Ten shillings in a half sovereign.

Five shillings in a crown.

For more, please see Wikipedia's article on "Coins of the Pound Sterling," under "Pre-Decimal Coinage."

As to value then compared to value today, this is a tricky

subject, as you'll discover if you search online. Multiplying by seventy to one hundred will give you a *very* rough sense.

LOCATION, LOCATION. Most of the sites in the book did exist and some still do. Here's a sampling:

The Arch at the Green Park is better known to us as the Wellington Arch. It's had some adventures. It started with no figure at the top. Some years later, an equestrian statue of Wellington crowned it. Then that came off, and the bronze sculpture of today replaced it. The arch itself was moved in 1882–1883.

Kensington Gravel Pits is now Notting Hill Gate.

St. George's Hospital is now the Lansdowne Hotel.

The Cock in Fleet Street has been rebuilt a few times, and is now known as Ye Olde Cock Tavern.

Porto Bello Lane is now Portobello Road, and yes, Kensington at one time was rural, and parts of what's now Notting Hill were "developing into a slum whose notoriety was probably unsurpassed throughout London. In the same year that the dignified buildings of Onslow Square were begun, the average age at death was just over eleven and a half years for the people of the potteries and piggeries," according to Annabel Walker and Peter Jackson's *Kensington & Chelsea*.

The place I called the Lovedon Arms did exist under another name. The trouble is, it had several names, and sources don't agree. For instance, some authors call it the White Horse, and others say it's the White Hart. Some maps label it the White Horse, others the Holland Arms. An 1825 document has this name, listing Mrs. Noke as proprietor, as does a document of 1838. You get the picture. And so I gave up trying to find historically correct nomenclature and instead called it the Lovedon Arms, after the hero of my story "Lord Lovedon's Duel," upon whom I had bestowed Holland House (which I renamed Castle de Grey).

The Colosseum deserves a blog post, or possibly several. For all the wonderful details of its creation and contents, I recommend Richard D. Altick's *The Shows of London*.

"Napoleon Breathing" was an actual exhibition at the Cosmorama rooms on Regent Street. Descriptions appear in several newspapers of 1833.

DRESS. My ladies wear fashions appearing in ladies' magazines of the time and fashion prints in museum collections.

THE RIOT ACT is usually understood as a figure of speech. However, it was an actual Act of Parliament. In cases where a large gathering threatened to turn into a disturbance of the peace, an authority figure would read the following: "Our sovereign lord the King chargeth and commandeth all persons, being assembled, immediately to disperse themselves, and peaceably to depart to their habitations, or to their lawful business, upon the pains contained in the act made in the first year of King George, for preventing tumults and riotous assemblies. God save the King."

SPECIAL LICENSE. There were strict rules about when and where weddings took place. However, for the upper orders, as always, there was an exception. "By special license or dispensation from the Archbishop of Canterbury, Marriages, especially of persons of quality, are frequently in their own houses, out of canonical hours, in the evening, and often solemnized by others in other churches than where one of the parties lives, and out of time of divine service, &c." —*Law Dictionary* (1810 and later editions)

BOUDICCA VS. BOADICEA. *Boadicea* is the name commonly used throughout the nineteenth and much of the twentieth century. "Boudicca, or Buduica (we do not know exactly how to spell the name, but neither, presumably, did she) . . . For Roman writers, she was a figure simultaneously of horror and fascination. A warrior queen, intersex, barbarian Cleopatra: 'very tall in stature, with a manly physique, piercing eyes and harsh voice, and a mass of red hair falling to her hips,' as she was described centuries later by someone who could not possibly have known what she looked like." —Mary Beard, *SPQR* (2015)

FIGARO IN LONDON was a satirical magazine, the precursor to *Punch*.

MRS. TROLLOPE'S BOOK ABOUT THE AMERICANS refers to Frances Milton Trollope's *Domestic Manners of the Americans*, published in March 1832. The Americans were not amused. It's still in print as well as available online, and it is still very readable.

MARY WOLLSTONECRAFT. While not precisely a feminist in today's sense of the word, she was certainly one for her own time. *A Vindication of the Rights of Woman* is still in print and available online as well.

These and other historical references in the book will be described and explained in more detail on my website blog, with pictures. Subscribing to the blog will not only bring story background and other interesting historical material to your inbox, but will keep you up-to-date with book deals, book progress, and other matters. Illustrations for my books appear on my Pinterest page, too. If your question or concern isn't answered in these places, you're welcome to email me via the Contact Loretta page at my website, LorettaChase.com. Though I do try, I'm not always able to answer everybody.

THE OTHER DIFFICULT DUKES. In case you were wondering about Blackwood's two friends and the cryptic references to the ladies in their lives:

The Duke of Ripley's story is *A Duke in Shining Armor*.

The Duke of Ashmont's story is *Ten Things I Hate About the Duke*.